SKULL RACK

Ron Braithwaite

AUGUSTA

Skull Rack
By Ron Braithwaite
A Harbor House Book/2007

Copyright 2007 by Ron Braithwaite

For information address:
HARBOR HOUSE
111 TENTH STREET
AUGUSTA, GA 30901

Jacket and book design by Nathan Elliott
Mexican Ornament Font by Klaus Johansen
ISBN: 978-1-891799-77-8

Library of Congress Cataloging-in-Publication Data is available on the
Library of Congress Web site.
Braithwaite, Ron, 1943-
Skull rack / by Ron Braithwaite.
p. cm.
ISBN 978-1-891799-77-8
1. Mexico--History--Conquest, 1519-1540--Fiction. 2. Inquisitor General
(Spain)--Fiction. 3. Mendoza, Antonio de, 1492?-1552--Fiction. 4. Cortés,
Hernán, 1485-1547--Fiction. 5. Historians--Fiction. I. Title.
PS3602.R34446S57 2007
813'.6--dc22

Printed in the United States of America
10 9 8 7 6 5 4 3 2 1

That man is the product of his failures and successes

Comes as no real mystery.

That nation is a victim of its founder's excesses

Is simply a fact of history.

—de la Peña

Chapter 1

Burgos, Castilla-León
January 14, 1581 3:05 A.M.

"You have no authority over me!" The prisoner was a tall man tending to fat. "Sit down, Padre. Considering your record of service I quite understand your displeasure but—how shall I put it—certain of your writings have come to our attention." The words were spoken by an ancient man, clad in the vestments of a Bishop of the Dominican Order.

"I am no heretic!"

"We haven't said that you are."

The small room was illuminated by the flickering light of two candles as well as by a small fire blazing in the hearth. The two men were separated by a large oaken table worn smooth with age. The old man was seated but the younger man was standing with both fists clenched.

"I insist that you inform me of the charges brought against me! Not only am I a Jesuit, but I am an Old Christian who supports Mother Church with all his heart and soul." The younger man's voice dropped to a threatening tone. "I am not asking—I demand!"

The younger priest, who was clad in a silken nightgown, was handsome to the point of effeminacy. His face was unlined and his eyes were large, luminous and dark. His hair—though unkempt—was long and lustrous black. If it had not been for the gray at his temples the priest would have appeared years younger than his actual age of forty-eight. Under ordinary circumstances his countenance would have been beatific. Tonight, however, was anything but ordinary.

"You demand?" mocked the old man. "I'm afraid that I cannot release you and, as you should know better than anyone, I'm certainly not obliged to inform you of the accusations."

The right side of the ancient Bishop's face was disfigured by three parallel scars that extended from his receding hairline to his jaw. In the flickering light, his face was Satanic. The younger priest seemed to deflate. He looked around then seated himself carefully. The chair creaked under the strain.

"Someone has borne false witness against me. Who is it?"

"False witness? We have several witnesses but we won't share their names with you—there could be retaliation and we wouldn't want that, would we?" The old man flexed his fingers, blue veins bulging under his transparent skin. "These gentlemen have borne valuable testimony in many previous cases and will, no doubt, prove themselves valuable in the future."

"*Estoes injusto*, a mistake..."

"*Claro, que es injusto*," oozed the old man. "I won't even attempt to deny it. Your arrest was not, however, a mistake. It was simply—well—simply an unfortunate necessity. Let's say that there are certain doctrinal considerations."

"How is this possible? I don't understand." The younger priest was on verge of collapse. "I have served Mother Church faithfully for thirty-two years—since Anno Domini 1547—and have done all that was in my power to rid España of the infection of Lutheranism. I have, with every fiber of my strength," he said, as he clinched his fist as if he were crushing an orange, "relentlessly exposed the followers of the Torah and Mohammad. I have lived my life for Mother Church. How now could *Santo Oficio* turn on me?"

The ancient Bishop looked his victim in the eye. "You speak as if the Inquisition were your personal property and as if your interests were the interests of *Santa Iglesia*. Has it occurred to you that you might be suffering from the sin of self-pride?"

Stunned, the younger priest remained silent.

"Although I'm not required to do so I believe that certain courtesies should be extended to a fellow cleric, even one who has erred. I shall explain." The old man's face was skeletal in the flickering light. "Your crime is not one of unbelief. Quite the contrary, you have drawn our attention precisely because of your piety."

The younger man's cheek twitched.

"I see you don't understand." The ancient Bishop explained, "The heresies that started in Germany and are spreading like a plague over Europe are the product of excessive belief, not disbelief. Men, like you, whose belief is intense and inflexible are the problem, a problem that could have been rooted out early had the Church recognized that excessive piety was a greater danger than was," the Bishop's smile was sardonic as he commented, "a certain—perfume—of hypocrisy. Surely you're starting to understand.

"But I harbor no thoughts of..."

"Neither did Luther nor his ilk—initially. They harbored no thoughts of heresy." The old man chuckled, mirthlessly. "They were more holy than is the Pope." The old man looked the soft priest right in the face. "They were much as you are now.

The Church has reigned for fifteen hundred years precisely because of its ability to bend and adapt, even when those adaptations included certain necessary compromises. You are incapable of compromise and are therefore dangerous. You must be excised from the body of our Holy Mother Church—your fate will be an example to others. If good men such as yourself can perish in the flames, then who is safe?"—The old man's voice dropped an octave.— "I see you are starting to understand—both Church and State are protected by a shield of fear."

"I have been condemned? Without so much as a hearing? You have no proof!" The priest had undergone a complete transformation. His skin was now pale and his voice cracked.

The older man stood up, his hands clasped as if in prayer—his voice was soft but sinister. "I'm afraid you are mistaken. You have already had your hearing."

"A hearing before my arrest?" The younger priest felt as if his head were going to burst. "I have never heard of such a perversion..."

"Don't tempt my patience, Padre. You're an Inquisitor yourself and I know full well that you have presided in trials in which your victims were condemned without the technicality of their physical presence,"—the old man continued— "and as for proof, it is abundant—you have condemned yourself by your own writings."

The younger man's voice trembled. "Everything I have ever said or written has been in the service of God and Church."

"So much the worse. Your errors are so fundamental that you, who have consigned them to paper, have failed to recognize their perversity." The old man's gaze was steady. "You see I have come into possession of all of your religious treatises and have examined them closely. Your doctrinal errors are subtle, almost undetectable. Their subtlety makes them all the more dangerous."

"You can't be serious?"

The old man was silent for seconds but then went on. "Oh, but I am quite serious. On first analysis, the Council itself failed to detect the poisonous nature of your tracts. It was therefore necessary for me to help them identify your—perverse—logic. Your condemnation was a matter of course."

"You...?"

"I considered, of course, the nicety of extracting your confession under torture and, make no mistake about it, you would have confessed. Such a confession would have been superfluous, however. Besides there is always the possibility that you might implicate others."

"But I have done nothing. There is no conspiracy."

"Exactly, but there are always others to implicate, are there not?" The old man shook his head. "You, of all people, know how it works. When the ropes tighten even the most innocent man will sell out his wife, parents and children—there are always others to implicate. Let us say that in your case, however, only you..."

"My writings are blameless!" The younger priest was feeling a resurgence of indignation.

The old priest was completely silent for seconds. He then leaned forward and spoke very slowly and distinctly, "*Lo entiendo.*"

For more seconds the younger man sat in silence, trying to digest the Bishop's words. "You know it? Is this just some kind of joke? You will, of course, release me immediately."

"I'm truly sorry." The old man's face cracked into something like a grin. "I cannot do so for the Holy Office has condemned you to die at the stake during the great Auto de Fé in Sevilla."

"But the Council will..."

"No, it will not," the Bishop said bluntly. "The Council won't listen to you but, if it should listen it won't believe you; and even if it believes you it will not care. You have been caught like a fly in a web and your fate is certain. I have my motives and the members of the *Suprema* have their own. You have grown, shall we say, conspicuously wealthy during your tenure with the Holy Office. Your lands, possessions and money are forfeit. You have profited from the destruction of your wealthy victims and now the Council will profit from your downfall."

"But why have you done this to me?" Tears welled in the younger man's eyes. "You don't even know me."

"Oh, but I do know you. Are you not the Padre Enrique Mendoza who wrote *Las Historias Glorias* of our miraculous conquests in the New World?"

"I am the same man."

"I've read them in detail and have noted your pious interpretation of these events, that God guided the enterprise and even the Holy Saints participated in the battles."

"Yes, that's true."

"Your volumes are lengthy, well documented and scholarly. The labor of a lifetime, am I right?"

"They are the most important things I've ever done."

"That being the case, I have a few things to tell you, for it is a sin for a man to die in error and it is wrong to send a man to his death without his having an opportunity to recant. Your work of a lifetime is a fabric of falsehoods and your life," the old man's voice fell to a whisper as he said, "has been wasted."

The scarred Bishop stood up stiffly, and started to pace back and forth. "I'm a very old man now—dry and withered—but in my youth I was as strong and tough as Cordovan leather. I was the genuine article, a Conquistador, a soldier of Hernán Cortés and later, one of Pizarro's men. I have done things that no man should ever do and I have seen things few men have seen and no man will ever see again. I have seen the *Lago de Mexico* with her glistening white cities and the great city, *Tenochtitlan*; the mightiest of them all, shining like a jewel in the lake's waters. I have seen the great Moctecuzoma borne on a litter and covered in green feathers and gold. I have personally known Cortés—he with his smooth tongue and honeyed lies." The old Bishop pointed a bony finger at the younger priest. "I am the last man alive who knew Hernán Cortés."

"*No es possible!*" contradicted the younger man.

The old man ignored him and went on. "I was there during *La Noche Triste*, when hundreds of our soldiers were captured and later I trembled with dread as these same men were dragged up the steps of the *Templo Mayor* where, screaming, they were sacrificed to the Devil. *Vidi infera.* They had their hearts cut out, one by one.

We few soldiers conquered an empire of millions. We did it

in the names of España, Catholicism and gold—especially gold. We did the absolutely impossible. We met, defeated and slaughtered armies of tens of thousands. We demolished *Tenochtitlan* foot by foot, destroyed her temples and filled in her canals with rubble. You have written that we did this in the service of God—I disagree—I tell you that we did it because we were in the service of the Devil...*El Diablo y Hernán Cortés.*"

"You speak sacrilege!" the soft priest hissed. "It is you, not I, that merit the stake."

The old man cocked his head. "An unfortunate attitude, considering your situation but, then again, you might just be correct. By the way,"—the old man paused a moment for full effect— "did you know that I myself am a New Christian, a *converso*, a *marrano*—a Jew? No? How could one such as I achieve the status of Inquisitor-General of the *Suprema* if my blood were impure? But then again wasn't the humble Tomás de Torquemada, confessor to Queen Isabella and founder of the Second Inquisition, part Jew?" Seeing surprise on his victim's face, the old man cackled, "Oh, I see that you didn't know. More to the point, though, is the fact that I am, in my own way, a victim of the Inquisition, a victim of prigs such as you. My family was torn apart and destroyed by *Santo Oficio*. Yes, some of our ancestors were Jews but we were also hidalgos, sincere Catholics, loyal to Church and Castile. My father was a Christian knight who fought at Granada in the final battles against the Moors. He even agreed with the Church and Crown's aim of *limpieza de sangre*, the purification of Spanish blood of all traces of Jewish and Moorish influence. Can you wonder then when he assumed that we were safe when the Inquisition arrived in our town of San Miguel? Unfortunately, my father hadn't been observant enough. Many of the best families in Castile were *conversos* and my father didn't recognize that *limpieza* would extend to all New Christians and that the Holy Office was searching for any evidence of secret Jewish practices, even in places where they never existed. He didn't recognize that accusations of *marranismo* were leveled primarily at those New Christians with wealth, lands and money and my father underestimated the Holy Office's greed."

The ancient man coughed and spat on the floor before going on. "Years later I learned the identity of the man who had accused my father. He was a local man, a greedy merchant, tempted by promises of wealth. Before he died he told me many things, although he didn't tell me what his accusations were. He claimed he—forgot. Then again, it could have been almost anything or nothing at all. An accusation that a converso ate meat on Friday, or never ate pork at all was enough to condemn him as a Judaizer. If he speculated on the nature of purgatory, or prayed facing a wall or was seen to nod his head while praying, he was a Jew. My father, older sister and brother were tortured. Somehow my father and sister survived the tightening ropes of the *potro* without confessing to any crimes—my brother, Juan, was subjected to the *toca* but the torturer was un-skilled and poured too much water down his throat." The Bishop paused to let his words sink in. "He choked and died."

At the Auto de Fé, that carnival of faith and ignorance, both my father and sister were forced to wear the peaked hats and sanbenitos that were later hung in the cathedral as eternal memorials to our family's shame. My sister was imprisoned in a windowless cell. She survived for two years only to later die of neglect and despair. My fa-ther and my long dead mother were condemned to the flames. My mother had been dead for seven years but they exhumed her bones and burned them next to my father. Just before the end, the priest asked my father whether he would recant and kiss the cross. My father told him that he would gladly kiss the cross of our Blessed Savior but, on his eternal soul, he had nothing to recant. My father therefore went to the stake without the mercy of strangulation or even that of dry, fast burning wood. Instead the executioners piled green wood around him and my father slowly roasted to death."

The old man stopped his narration. "I hope you are enjoying my story. As a scholar and an expert on the Conquest I believe that you deserve to hear the whole thing—don't you agree? I'm not much of a storyteller, but I'm sure you can make some intelligent observations."

The younger priest only stared at the table. "Why should I waste my last hours listening to your lies?"

The ancient Bishop, who had been pacing, slowly turned to the younger man. "Yes, your fate has been sealed but—the fate of your works is not yet settled. As they stand now, I will have every volume in all of Spain located and they will be used to heat your funeral pyre."

The younger man sprang to his feet, on the verge of launching himself over the table. "*No puedes!* You absolutely cannot!!"

Despite his frailty, the old man didn't flinch. "*Bien. Bien.* You value your work as much, and possibly more than your life. Perhaps, you and I can discuss an—arrangement. Listen to my proposition, if you will."

The younger man sat back heavily, his eyes flaming.

"Your books on the Conquest are riddled with falsehoods which I find offensive. The fundamentals, I must admit, are not entirely incorrect. Your errors, though serious, are largely peripheral and the result of excessive—how to put it—Jesuit fervor."

The younger priest, now looking confused, was silent.

"Your writing style is strong and, the fact is, I myself have wanted to produce an accurate journal of the Conquest. I am now close to ninety years old and will not see many more winters—I will never accomplish this task on my own." The old man paced back-and-forth twice before speaking again. "I propose that the two of us—collaborate. I will narrate my experiences to you and you will take notes and make the necessary changes. In the end, your works will be much improved and I will have the satisfaction of knowing that the truth has been told."

"But my life?"

The old man's eyes were blue ice. "Your stake has already been hewn from wet pine but—on the other hand—I want my story told. Your cooperation will..."

"But the book will no longer be mine—it will be yours."

"The more is the pity."

"And the *Suprema?*"

For the first time the old man spoke harshly, like the grate of an axe striking bone. "*Yo soy la Suprema.*"

Chapter 2

"You have accepted my offer?" Pale morning light filtered through the barred window. The Bishop, buried in his white robes, was cadaverous.

The younger man, now garbed as a Jesuit priest, was disheveled. His eyes were lifeless and his face was puffy. His voice, however, was defiant. "If I cooperate with you I will do so in peril of my eternal soul. It's better that my books burn."

"Spoken like a true zealot." The Bishop had anticipated the refusal. "But your life?"

Mendoza's body sagged but he immediately recovered. "*Nullum aeternum est.*" At least I will die a Jesuit, a credit to my order.

"Really a terrible shame, Padre," the elderly Bishop said. "I was rather looking forward to our literary collaboration, but—given your refusal—*Guardias! Guardias!*" Two shabbily uniformed men burst into the room. "Pablo, Alejandro, please be good enough to escort Padre Mendoza back to his cell. He's to be permitted neither visitors nor communication with the outside world until he is relaxed at the Auto de Fé. Dismissed!" The guards, one in the front and one to the rear, started to lead Mendoza out of the room.

"Oh, by the way." The Bishop held up a restraining hand. "Is it possible that your works—in their current form, of course—are more important to you than is the truth?"

Mendoza's pent-up fear was transmuted into towering rage. He spun on his heels to face the old man. "*Son la verdad!*"

"Certainly, but your sources were archival and, even then, second or third hand accounts, were they not?"

"I researched them carefully—checking and double-checking them for inconsistencies." Mendoza, forgetting his danger, was transformed into the pedant that he was.

The old man's eyes gleamed, visualizing events of long ago. "Still unlike your dusty references, I am precisely a first hand account. I am in the unique position of helping you to correct errors in your original editions. For you, I present the rare opportunity of your being able to compare your present record with my memory. Our collaboration needn't entail the destruction of your life's work. Instead you must think of it as a new and improved second edition—it will still be your work. "

"My work? With you dictating and my taking notes?" Mendoza looked like he'd tasted a lemon. "I'd be nothing but your clerk."

"Better a live clerk than a dead Jesuit."

Mendoza grimaced.

"Relax, Padre, I will be an active participant in our project but the end result will, in all truly important aspects, be your own."

"Forgive me for my continuing skepticism, your Grace, but if you'd simply wanted to help me improve my works, you would have made your proposal openly. You wouldn't have gone through this charade."

The old man carefully placed his fingers together, forming a cage. "Your arrest is no charade, Padre. Whether or not you are precisely guilty of all charges is, perhaps, irrelevant—the flames will blister your skin and boil your blood in either event. Remember—I know who you are. You are, in my considered opinion, little more than a stiff-necked *sectario*. You would have never cooperated voluntarily. Even now, faced with the probability of extinction, you are unbowed. On the other hand, I have respect for your intellect. It follows that our collaboration must go far beyond a mere scribbling of notes. Memory is a fragile thing and your records will help to fill in my lapses—no, let me rephrase that—let us say, instead, that my eyewitness will help you —perfect—your original works."

Mendoza's eyes flickered as the old Bishop continued, "I'll admit that a certain emptiness has crept into my soul over the years. You, on the other hand, are a true believer. We are an unlikely pair of collaborators but, an open discussion of our interpretation of events and, indeed, of our differences, may very well produce a work—our work—that will be remembered for generations to come."

"Why should I trust you?"

The old man stood up wearily, his shadow on the wall more substantial than was the man himself. "A true believer lives by faith, does he not? You will know the truth of it as we proceed with our work."

Mendoza said nothing but the Bishop gestured to the guards. "Pablo, Alejandro. Wait outside while the Padre and I continue our discussion." The guards strode out closing the door behind them.

"As perhaps you are beginning to see," the ancient man went on, "our cooperation has mutual benefits but, before we begin, I must tell you that there are stipulations."

"Stipulations?"

"You will remain a—guest—in our facility until our labor is complete. You will have no contact with anyone save myself and your guards."

"But surely..." The Bishop stopped the priest with a wave of his hand.

"We will work any time day or night, at my discretion. Unfortunately, I have certain responsibilities as," —the old man almost laughed— "Inquisitor-General. Our work schedule will be necessarily irregular."

"How will you justify all of the time you will be spending with me?" Mendoza seemed to relax. "After all, having been through it before, I have a good idea as to how much time a revision will entail. Even if all goes smoothly, we could be talking about months, even years."

"I don't think it will take quite that long because the structure of your present edition will be unchanged. We will only add and subtract a few facts and make a few mutual observations. As far as the time spent with you, that is my own concern. Suffice it to say that I find it necessary to interrogate you closely both for the sake of Holy Mother Church and the salvation of your immortal soul."

The younger priest leaned forward. "My property?"

The old man smiled his twisted smile. "I have taken steps to insure that all of your property will be held intact by the Holy Office. After completion of our work, you will be"—the old man's hesitation was imperceptible—"exonerated, and your property will be returned, intact. You have my word on it."

"Your word?"

"My word as a Bishop of the Holy Catholic Church and successor to the Twelve Apostles. Now I must tell you a few things for your own safety. You and I will talk of many things. I wish for you to confide in me and I, in turn, will confide in you, absolutely. I will tell you things that you may be tempted to use against me—don't even begin to consider it. During your confinement you'll have contact with no human beings other than for myself and your guards—make no mistake, the guards are totally loyal to me. Alejandro, for example, has lost everything he has ever had to *Santo Oficio*. A word or gesture from me and you'll be found hanging from a rafter of your cell in the morning—as a suicide you'll not even merit last rites or a grave in sanctified ground."

"Even if we finish our work, you can't afford to let me live."

"No. That's not true." The ancient priest spoke very gently, as if to a child. "We will always know where you are. We know you have a sister, brothers and elderly parents. We know you have loved ones. You will say nothing. Shall we begin?"

The younger man's body sagged. "Where are my writing materials?"

"In the box next to the fire."

Near the hearth was a large box of dark wood closed with a hinged lid. Mendoza opened the box and inspected its contents.

The Bishop continued, "I've done what I could to achieve authenticity. As you can see I've managed to acquire several Mexican codices painted on the original amatl paper. Accompanying them you will see the Spanish translations prepared by native Padres. The ink is purple and permanent and is leached from a tree that grows in the swamps of Nueva España. It's the same tree for which *Provincia del Campeche* is named.

I've even given you writing quills, las plumas, prepared from the wing feathers of Mexican domestic fowl. You will, of course, recognize that of the *guajolote*, the fowl that we now call el pavo or turkey. You may not be quite as familiar with the black quills. They've been taken from the wings of the Mexican duck, *el pato real*.

You'll also see you've been provided with copies of your own works and we can quickly obtain any other necessary documents. As we go on we will compare my testimony with what you've already written and make the required changes. I must warn you, however, that your present text is so pious as to be superstitious—the end product will be far more secular."

"Let's get on with it then. Maybe I can use your knowledge."

"Good, at your core you are a realist. We'll start where we left off. My early statements do not apply directly to the Conquest but will help to explain who I am and how I survived the judgment." Irreverently, the ancient man crossed himself backwards and said, "Of *La Inquisición Sagrada*. I'll tell you how I learned the arts of war and how I exacted my revenge on those swine who so wronged my family."

Chapter 3

"First, it amuses me to inform you that I, a high prelate of the True Faith, the Bishop who holds your fate in the palm of his hand, do not believe in your Christian God. Neither do I believe in the divinity of Jesus nor that of the Blessed Virgin. Saints? Primitive household lares, no more, no less. No, I don't believe in God but I do believe in Satan and I believe in *Santa España* and the power of Holy Mother Church. Life has made me what I am. In some ways I envy you. Your faith, misguided though it may be, has filled your life and you know that you will be in the presence of God. I, on the other hand, am empty and hopeless—I cling to what little time I have left."

Mendoza interrupted, "How is it possible to believe in Satan without a belief in God?"

The old man licked his scarred lips. "It's because long experience has taught me that evil is the force that shapes men. Indeed, I have seen *El Enemigo Malo* in the land of Spain and I've felt his protective hand spread out over the Holy Tribunal. I've seen his shadow in Cuba where Indios are enslaved and worked to death on our encomiendas. I've seen his images on the temples of Mexico, sneering, as captives by the hundreds, had their quivering lives sliced out of their chests. I've seen him seed Mexico and Perú with deadly disease while, in his service, Españoles robbed, raped and killed, claiming that these things were in the service of God. I have seen his shape in the treachery of man—who, indeed—save it be a Basque, Frenchman or a Moor—is more treacherous than is a Castilian?

That said, let me tell you how I came to be—the creature—you see before you now. I was merely a child when my father died so I escaped direct punishment. Still, just as in all such cases, my family's fortune was forfeit and all that was left for me were dishonor, humiliation and, a thirst for revenge. Even by this early age my transformation had begun."

The old man focused on the younger man. "Even the Holy Office makes its mistakes. One of her officers dragged me to the cell where my father was kept—this was not out of kindness but to serve as a warning that I must never challenge *Santo Oficio*. Wearing shackles that were too big for my wrists my warder pushed me down the dreary passageways until I was halted in front of a grated door. I was shoved into my father's cell. I can still feel the cold and I can still smell the mold and the urine. My father, who I could see but poorly in the light of the guard's torch, was a skeleton clad in filth-caked rags. The cell door slammed shut and the light disappeared. My father clutched me to his bony chest. I can still smell him. It was as if he were already dead. He didn't speak for a long time and, when he did, it was a hoarse whisper."

"Speak softly, my son."

"Yes, father, I understand."

"Listen to me carefully for there is little time."

"I will, father."

"Your brother is dead, your sister is imprisoned and I have been condemned to the stake."

I had no words.

"Because you are a child, Rodrigo, you will be permitted to live."

"But..."

"Everything is forfeit—even our good name." I must have tensed. "That's right, Rodrigo, no one can take our honor—but you'll have to fight to keep it—you must pick up my sword."

"I can't..."

"Rodrigo, my son, I spent my life fighting for Castile—*Castilla y la Cruz Sagrada*. I've been bloodied and driven back but I was never beaten and I was never defenseless—even now, although these dogs don't recognize it, I am not defenseless—I still have you. Kneel down, Rodrigo."

In the blackness of the cell, I knelt down in front of my father—I could feel the force of his presence. He placed his hands on my head.

"I give you a great charge, Rodrigo—your life is no longer your own—it belongs to your forefathers. Do you swear it?"

"I..."

"*Swear it!*"

"I do."

"You are the spear that I cast into my enemies. You are dedicated to honor and revenge. *Swear it!*"

"I swear it, father."

"You will have no mercy—no pity. *Nunca! Swear it!*"

"I swear it."

"Rodrigo, I dedicate you to great things but, in so doing, I condemn you to hardship and loneliness. Your time will come—remember your family's honor and make yourself iron."

"I will, father."

"So, Rodrigo, it is done. May the God of Abraham have mercy on both of us."

My father wept—I thought that his tears were for himself and the fate of our family. As a man, however, I came to understand that he wept for the sin of what he had done to me, for he knew what I must become.

My warder pushed me into the street with no more than the clothes on my back and a crust of black bread in my hand. "Have you ever been hungry, Padre?"

"I fast for the souls of our dead."

"*No, Padre. Hambriento!* So hungry that your ribs stick out and your only thoughts are of food. So hungry that you would be willing to steal, even kill, for a meal. Hunger so terrible that you can't sleep because of the cramps in your gut."

"No, Excelencia, never that hungry."

"Too bad, Padre—you might have been more sympathetic for those innocents that you condemned to starvation."

"Never have..."

"*Silencio!*" The old man commanded. "You see, Padre, even those who might be moved by kindness to feed and shelter a child orphaned by *la Inquisicion* are frightened to do so.

I was more lucky than most. Relatives had the courage to sneak me the occasional tidbit. It wasn't much but it saved me from death by starvation or exposure. I survived as well as I could, sleeping in fields and haylofts and begging for food and pennies. As I grew older and stronger, I was able to do odd jobs and actually started to make my own way in life. By the time I was fifteen I could do a man's work. I was given a dilapidated hut by an hacendado, Don Pedro Ortega, and I tilled his fields and protected his flocks from the wolves that were numerous in those days.

I was and am grateful to Don Pedro, for the work he gave me restored some of my dignity. Nevertheless, even though I had learned to read and write before my father's death, I was no better off than the most humble campesino. Neither would I have much opportunity to better myself for, as you are aware, the disgrace of condemnation is inherited by the children, the grandchildren, and down through the generations—never are the heirs of this singular honor permitted to hold even the lowest of public offices, nor may they be lawyers, physicians, bankers, merchants or even shopkeepers." The old man cackled like a bird. "Especially, they are denied entrance to the Holy Orders."

Mendoza slammed his fist on the table, "For the purpose of

our dialogue I must therefore ask the obvious. You are not only a respected *Episcopus Dominicorum* but you are also Inquisitor-General of the entire Spanish kingdom—yet, you are the spawn of condemned Judaizers. You are a foul unbeliever, an atheist. How in God's Holy Name, is this possible?"

The old man leaned forward slightly. "A fair question, Padre Mendoza. Did I not tell you that The Church is—flexible? With the right connections and enough money, Satan himself could become an Archbishop, Cardinal or even the Pope—he probably already has. My reasons for seeking my vocation are my own but—wealth, safety, and position were all considerations. Also, I recognized that *Santo Oficio* was an unalterable fact of life. I decided to befriend it, corrupt it, and subvert it—as much as was humanly possible. I've been able to save some of the innocent and even a few of the guilty. I've even been able to punish a few of the more enthusiastic Inquisitors." The Bishop pointed an index finger at Mendoza. "*Oculum pro oculo, et dentum pro dente*—an eye for an eye, a tooth for a tooth."

Mendoza shuddered, "How can you tell me such things? No matter how terrible your threats are, you can never be certain that I'll remain silent."

"The lies of a desperate felon that will, if you do not show the proper enthusiasm for our mutual project," the old man snapped his bony fingers and said, "still turn into smoke. My name is now Obispo Luís Márquez de Montesiños, quite an impressive appellation, don't you think? A few silver coins, a corrupt notario, an altered document and I was a different person, an Old Christian without the taint of Jewish blood. I was born, however, Rodrigo de la Peña de Márquez. Don Rodrigo de la Peña, if you will, because as I told you, for generations my family had been hidalgos, warriors of the Holy Cross.

I, the young Rodrigo, had become nothing higher than a common peasant who had lost his title along with his inheritance. On the other hand, even though I was only ten years old when my father died, I'd seen enough to know that I was destined for better things than life behind an ox and endless furrows in the dirt. I fashioned myself a rough sword of wood, a pike, and a leather shield. Of course, all boys make these things and play at war, and we boys on Don Pedro's farms were no different. I, on the other hand, had a plan.

In our spare time, we boys would practice our martial skills. We warriors numbered only four or five but still we divided up as opposing armies of Moors versus Christians, drew our battle line, and fought until it grew dark. We used our pikes like spears and at other times like clubs to crack our opponents' heads."

"Obispo," Mendoza interrupted, "I assume that, as a descendant of nobles, you soundly trounced these campesinos?"

"Your assumption, Padre, is incorrect—if anything, I got the worst of it. Many a time, I was so bruised that I could barely work the next day. Then again, I'm not tall and my arms aren't long and a long arm can sometimes make the difference in a fight. These early experiences, however, may have saved my life because I learned to compensate for my weaknesses and, just as important, it taught me that enthusiasm and bravado are no substitutes for quick reflexes and cold calculation. Yes, there are times when a desperate situation requires desperate courage but it requires combat experience and wisdom to distinguish this situation from the more common one of dogged combat with its ever present fear. Fear, if properly appreciated will save your life. Blind terror, on the other hand, is the destroyer of both armies and men. On the sad night of La Noche Triste, however, our army, was seized by bone-numbing fear and the result was death and defeat."

Chapter 4

"I wander from our subject. I believe I was telling you about my childish dreams of future glory—I wasn't more than fourteen or fifteen years of age when I met a man who was to change my life. He was, as seemed to me then, a very old man of 60 years. He had long white hair, penetrating black eyes, and a hooked nose. His skin was dark for, you see, he was a Mudejar, born in the land of the Berbers.

I never learned his real name but his Christian name was Ignacio Tamayo. He worked as a goatherd on another farm and was so poor that he had but two suits of clothes—one for work and another, slightly less used, for the religious holidays. His home was a humble dugout covered by sod but, nevertheless, he was a man of education and kept many books in three wooden boxes. Poor though he was, he had respect, and I always called him *El Señor Tamayo*. For some reason he took a liking to me and, at the end of the day, he told me stories from his youth. As we all know, appearances can be deceiving and many a proud man has fallen to a low state—this was the case with Tamayo."

"I was a great knight of the Nasarids." Tamayo looked around as if suspicious of eavesdroppers. "I fought many battles against the Infidel and once, before the cliffs of Ronda, I fought a great duel with the Christian champion, El Azote, known as the 'Scourge of the Moors'."

"What happened?"

"I slew him but, in an act of chivalry, I returned his harness and armor to his retainers. The only thing I kept was his horse."

"Then why are you living like...?" I didn't finish, embarrassed by my own question.

He frowned, "If you learn nothing from me, learn this. Be careful of what you say and do not make the wrong enemies. When our Sultan, Baobdil, said he would surrender Granada, I called him a coward to his face. He didn't have the courage to face me in a contest of honor but he had the power to keep me from retreating to Africa. In revenge, I converted to the religion of Jesus."

Tamayo leaned forward and spoke to me with passion, "It is a foul sacrilege to claim that a man can be fathered by Allah but know that Jesus is our prophet, too."

"But the Moors believe in Mohammad."

"Yes, my son, he is the greatest prophet, *may he be blessed by God*." He looked at me intently. "Are you not a marrano?"

"*Sí, El Señor*."

"Then we are both New Christians and you would not betray a friend?"

"Of course not, señor."

"Then I will tell you the secret of Taqiy'ya. By law, it is permissible, nay desirable, to lie to one's enemies. For a Muslim to convert to the Catholic enemy is simply to practice Taqiy'ya."

"But..."

Senor Tamayo's eyes were spellbinding. "Let me swear to you, now. There is but one God and Mohammad is his prophet. I obey all of the commandments and, in the privacy of my home or in the fields, I pray five times a day. I study the Holy Qu'ran for it is the very word of God as recited by the Archangel Gabriel to Mohammad, may he receive Allah's mercy."

"Our priest says that the Bible..."

Tamayo shook his head. "The Christians pretend to honor their Book but they have gone far astray. They say they believe in the one God of Moses and Ibrihim, but they also worship before graven idols of Jesus, Mary, the Spirit and those infidels they call Saints. I tell you that Christians are no better than the unclean savages from the depths of Africa. Allah, the compassionate and merciful, punishes all unbelievers. They cannot escape his wrath and, for them, there will be no Paradise. They will suffer eternal torment—boiling water will be poured down their throats. I don't enjoy telling you these things, Rodrigo, but if you continue to practice superstition and idolatry, this will also be your fate."

"Boiling water?"

"So it has been written," Tamayo said, "but Allah is compassionate and merciful and, even though you are a marrano, I will teach you Islam's pillars of faith."

I hesitated but, as a boy, I was not only eager for knowledge but was eager to learn things forbidden by *Santo Oficio*. "I would like to learn from you, Senor Tamayo."

I studied hard and I learned to read the Qu'ran in Arabic and together with Señor Tamayo, I studied the *Sunnah* and *Tadith*. He taught me *Al-shari'ah*, the laws of righteousness. Then, from the depths of his hovel, Señor Tamayo produced books from ancient times for, as a Muslim, he honored all writings of literature, war and science.

Señor Tamayo also told me stories that ignited my imagination. He told of knights, angels, jihn, and sea-travelers to far lands with strange people and monsters. He also showed me things that I didn't know. He showed me how to make a bow for, as you know, the Moors are experts with this weapon. He took the horns of a great wild goat and split them lengthwise. He did the same with the springy wood of a tree that grows close to water. He fashioned both the horn and wood to be the same size and glued them together with a paste made from the hooves of an ox. For added strength he bound them all with the sinews of a stag that had the misfortune of becoming tangled in a fence. I watched very carefully as he connected both limbs to a handle of wood.

"Now we must wait, my son, for it is best that the bow be seasoned."

While we waited, Señor Tamayo showed me how to make arrows of wood from a certain tree with very straight twigs. He showed me how to gauge the proper length and he showed me how to straighten them further. He cut and filed arrowheads from a broken harrow left in the field.

"I want you to know as many things as possible, Rodrigo, for knowledge may save your life. Know that an arrowhead may be filed into many shapes, depending on their purpose. If the intention is to kill an animal or an unarmored man, the arrowhead must have broad and sharpened wings."

He cut and filed points shaped like a bird in flight. "Behold," Señor Tamayo tested the edge. "It cuts like a knife and makes a broad wound. Death is swift."

Tamayo continued his work. "If you must battle armored men and their armored chargers, the arrowhead must be small and dart-like, then the armor will be pierced and your enemy disabled." He cut several of this shape as well.

"The arrows must be fletched for no matter how straight they are shaped, they will never fly properly. It is best to use the flight feathers of a falcon for they are the swiftest fliers."

Finally the arrows and bow were ready. Tamayo, with the little money he had, purchased a strong cord from a shopkeeper and, with it, he strung the bow. I was delighted and Señor Tamayo let me try it first.

He smiled when I couldn't bend the bow and then took it from me, nocked an arrow and, pulling on the string with four fingers, flexed the bow to its limit. He sighted the arrow and let fly, striking a bushel of packed hay twenty paces away. The arrow penetrated up to its feathers. Señor Tamayo spoke to me as he wiggled the arrow free.

"Do not be discouraged, Rodrigo. Pray to Allah, use your back and protect your bow-fingers with leather. You are growing older and stronger and, with practice, you will surpass me."

I worked on it and finally pulled it back with difficulty but, with concentration, the task became easier. Señor Tamayo taught me how to shoot and, with time, my accuracy improved.

●●●

"Rodrigo," Señor Tamayo said, "you now have a real weapon but, in that wars are never common enough, you must now gain experience by hunting. This I am too old to train you in. You must learn for yourself."

I taught myself to hunt. I learned to follow an animal's spoor and to approach without being seen or heard. I learned that, in order to get a hit and a kill, it was best to get very close. I also learned that at this close range the act of drawing a bow is easily detected by most animals. I therefore learned to watch the wind and to make myself nearly invisible by painting my face with mud. When everything went very well, my arrow struck a deer or a shoat. Then the hunt really began for, the animal would seldom fall on the spot. Usually it bolts and runs deep into dense brush.

It takes a sharp eye to detect the occasional droplet of blood or, when there was no blood, to distinguish the track of a wounded animal from the more numerous tracks of others that are unhurt. When there is no blood and the ground is hard with no visible trail, I had to think like a beast, asking myself what course I might take if I were struck in the chest or liver. With practice, it can be done, and I have found boars, which are beasts that do not bleed well, half a league from the place they were first struck. To find one's prey under these conditions is more satisfying than making an accurate shot.

As I told you Señor Tamayo was very poor and otherwise had no meat. The flesh of young animals was also best because Señor Tamayo's few teeth were worn to the gums. When I brought him meat—even the unclean meat of a pig—he was grateful and always said the same thing.

"Ay, Rodrigo, the Holy Church is wrong. You are not a marrano Jew. You are a killer."

Burgos, Castilla-León

Mendoza put up his hand. "I must stop you here, Episcopus Márquez—or do you prefer 'Montesiños'?"

The ancient cleric held up his right hand from which a great ring sparkled. "Given the privacy of our circumstances, I prefer that you use my given name of de la Peña."

"Certainly, Episcopus de la Peña." Mendoza shook his head in bewilderment. "I am trying to follow your story but I am bewildered. Are you a Christian, Jew, Morisco, or atheist?"

The Bishop pretended deep concentration. "I am all of them and I am none of them. Does that answer your question?"

"But you studied the lies of Mohammad."

"I studied the words recited to the Prophet, true, but I remain unconvinced."

"Still, even to listen to the words of Moorish heretics is to wallow in sin."

"*Ridículo, Padre. El saber no ocupa lugar*—knowledge takes up no space in one's mind. It can only be harmful when used for evil."

Mendoza was determined to win a point. "Doesn't your experience with beasts prove God's presence?"

"How so?"

"God gave man dominion over all beasts," Mendoza explained, "their fear of human-kind confirms the truth of it."

The old man scratched his temple. "Perhaps, you're correct. Even a bear or a boar flees at the sight of a man."

Mendoza smiled.

The old man continued, "They even fear our smell. I'm told that even huge beasts in Africa are terrorized by the scent of a human."

"This is absolute proof of Heavenly Power, Excelencia."

The Bishop shook his head. "Since the age of Adam, men have hunted all beasts, from the most timid to the most savage. Those that were foolish enough to confront man long since learned a hard lesson—even the largest and most fearsome of animals now keep their distance."

Chapter 5

Other than my friendship with Ignacio Tamayo my prospects were grim. My work in the fields barely provided me with rough food and clothing and I knew that if I were ever to escape this kind of life I must be able to accumulate at least a small pile of money. I was able to turn my protection of the flocks into extra profit. In winter, when the harvest was done and it was too early for plowing, I spent more time with the flocks of sheep. In the warm months of the year sheep dogs provide adequate protection from wolves. This is because wild prey, especially the young of deer and boars, are abundant and it is easier for a wolf to face a fawn or a shoat than to face an angry hound. All this changes in winter—meat become scarce and the wolves become desperate. At these times, wolves grow bold enough to attack flocks of sheep, even those defended by dogs. Indeed, they will even attack the dogs themselves and more than once I found the tattered remnants of a dog's hide with its chewed bones scattered over the bloody earth.

The best protection for sheep during this time of year is a shepherd because a wolf is usually deterred by the presence of a man—not always though. Truly starved wolves will attack sheep even as the dogs bark and the shepherd screams his curses. In these cases, if the shepherd is resolute and shows no fear, he can still drive these beasts back into the forest. He must be courageous, though, and woe betide the man who runs from a pack of these starved beasts.

Watching sheep is not an occupation to appeal to an active mind so, to pass the time and make money, I experimented with different designs of traps and snares. I perfected my techniques and became proficient at snaring hares and rabbits and would even capture the occasional fox or lynx. When I found signs that wolves were stalking my sheep I used traps of stronger design.

I remember the first time I snared a wolf. I used a strong hempen cord but, when I checked it the next morning, I found the ground torn up, the cord chewed through and no sign of the wolf. I purchased lengths of wire and improved my design.

Finally, I actually captured a wolf. He was a grizzled old beast, thin from the winter, but with a magnificent coat shining with gray and black and umber. He had been snared during the night and, as is common with large animals in snares, had strangled himself during his struggles. I carefully removed his beautiful skin saving his urine and the stink around his bunghole because the scent of a wolf is the best way to trap another wolf. I stretched and dried the hide and, along with my other skins, was able to sell it for a good profit.

"Bunghole?" Mendoza blurted out, "If you must bore me with this nonsense about wolves, perhaps you can enlighten me as to why such a disgusting measure is necessary."

"The wolf is but a dog, Padre. Like any other dog he can't help but stick his nose in places it doesn't belong, especially the bunghole of another wolf. Contrary to your expectation, the smell of malodorous things drives an otherwise intelligent wolf into an ecstasy of stupidity. The result is a skin pulled tight on a drying rack."

●●●

I redoubled my efforts and became an expert at wolves. In addition to snares, I found that I could capture them by driving nails pointing to the center of a circular trap. If the trap was cunningly placed and scent was used, the wolf would sometimes, incautiously, place his foot directly through the trap and then be unable to extract it. If captured in this fashion, the wolf would be quite alive on my arrival and greet me with growls, bared teeth, and glowing yellow eyes. Nevertheless, a trapped wolf is not brave and will always cower. Unlike a free wolf, he will never attempt to attack but only to escape.

I quickly learned that I need take no particular precautions with these animals and could finish them with a well-directed blow from a club. One day, however, this practice very nearly cost me my life. When checking a trap, I discovered that I had captured an animal quite unlike any that I had seen before. It was a cat, a very large spotted cat—its presence an impossibility—a fully-grown leopard. He was crouched flat to the ground and a low almost inaudible growl issued from the trapped beast's throat as his long tail twitched back-and-forth. His green eyes were evil incarnate. They followed my every move.

I'd never heard of a leopard in España although I had heard that the Romans had imported these animals for their games. Perhaps a few had escaped and their descendants had managed to hold on over the years. Either that, or there may have been an ancient but natural population of these animals so rare that they were virtually never seen. No matter, I now had one in my trap and knew he was considerably more valuable alive than as a dried skin.

I would have returned to Don Pedro's farm for help, but realizing that the cat had already almost torn his foot through the trap,

I decided that I would have to manage the task on my own. To defend my actions, I must say that it was not as if I were totally inexperienced. I had once trapped a large boar in a pen and was able to entangle him with loops of rope. I finally managed to tie his legs together and wrap a cord around his snapping jaws. Using a reluctant ox, I dragged the enraged boar all the way back home.

The other peasants were overjoyed—we placed the animal in a stout cage, fattened him with scraps from the kitchen, and the boar became the centerpiece of a great fiesta during the religious holidays.

I decided to use the same technique on my leopard. Fetching a rawhide rope from my pack I fashioned a noose and, not knowing whether or not trapped leopards behaved like wolves and without getting too close, I threw the looped end towards my leopard. It was a good throw and the loop settled around the surprised animal's neck. It spat a warning, its eyes flashed fire, it jerked forward and its trapped foot tore free—it was on me like a bolt of lightening! My whole world became a mixture of spotted hide, slashing claws and rending teeth.

I didn't feel a thing, only shock and a feeling of unreality as if I were watching the whole drama from a very long way away. I watched as the leopard bit my shoulder, tore at my head with his claws, and ripped at my belly with his hind feet. Somehow I managed to hold onto the rope. With a jolt I snapped back into reality, and found myself on the leopard's back, my knees pinning the leopard's chest, its claws and teeth striking into nothing but the earth and thin air. The leopard bucked and twisted but I held on—tightening, always tightening my hold on the noose. The cat went berserk but almost as quickly as it had started, the leopard weakened and went limp.

I remember holding my death grip on the noose, fearing that the sleeping cat might reawaken, until I too weakened and collapsed. The other farm boys found me there, lying half-conscious beside my leopard. I remember staring at the beast, disappointed that my blood was marring his perfect, spotted coat. Although I didn't know it then, José Madresa, who was my best friend, later skinned the cat and carefully salted and dried the hide. He returned it to me when it became clear that I'd live. I still bear the scars from that fight.

Burgos, Castilla-León

"Look, Padre Mendoza. You can barely see where the leopard clawed my scalp because the wounds are no longer so obvious due to my gray hair...*Santiago*! It's almost white, now. When I was younger, and my hair was almost black, there was a broad slash of white hair, from my brow to my nape, where three of the leopard's claws cut my scalp to the bone. You have no trouble seeing the scars on my face but they are nothing. They may have marred my good looks but I was far too pretty for my own good anyway. Besides, as I subsequently discovered, certain kinds of women are aroused by a man who shows the proof of his battles on his hide." The old man licked his scarred lips. "Do you know much about women, Padre?"

"I honor my vows, Excelencia."

"That's not what I'm talking about, Padre. Do you know much about female nature?"

"I've been called on to counsel women."

"Then we're getting somewhere, Padre." The ancient priest leaned forward confidentially, "Men would be repelled by a clawed woman so why is it that some women are not repelled by a clawed man?"

"It is because," Mendoza reasoned without conviction, and said, "men are more rugged looking than women."

The Bishop beamed. "Is that why men of all ages prefer young women?"

"Indeed, Your Grace."

"Smooth skinned, fewer wrinkles?"

"*Exactamente, Obispo.*"

"Also, Padre," the old man continued, "are not young women more—*malleable*—than older women?"

"Certainly, the combination of beauty and agreeableness makes younger women attractive."

"Nothing more, Padre?"

Mendoza shrugged his shoulders.

The Bishop's eyes glittered. "There's more to it than beauty. Life scars on our souls just as surely as it wrinkles our skin. These features, in a man, are not necessarily unattractive to a woman—they may even be desirable. Men-blind fools that they are–dislike these traits in a woman. They want a girl who seems innocent, untarnished by life's cares."

"Did you recognize these things when you were young, Obispo?"

"Not at all, Padre. As a youth, I was sensitive about my disfigurement so as soon as my face would support a few hairs, I grew a beard. The scarred marks on my chin and jaw produced white hair just as did the scars on my head."

"But you're clean-shaven now," Mendoza, despite the conditions of his confinement, had a carefully pruned upturned beard and a long pointed mustache stiffened by beeswax.

"Physical vanity is of no importance to a man as old as I am. To be certain, I always detested the necessity of tending my facial hair."

"But it's the mark of a man."

"True enough," the old Bishop stared at the younger man's face as if seeing it for the first time and said, "but the grooming and primping that come with a beard and mustache, is the mark of a woman."

Chapter 6

"Don Pedro's wife, Doña Catarina and her servants treated my wounds. Mortification set in and for two weeks I wandered in and out of consciousness and death stood very close. I was young, though, and once the crisis had passed I healed quickly and, within the month, was able to do light work and within two months I was back to my usual routine. I gave the leopard skin to Don Pedro and his wife. They tried to pay me but I told them that I owed them far more than a spotted skin. You see, although I was poor, I still had my honor. Later they returned the skin to me, all soft and beautifully tanned. They returned it to me along with ten silver pieces. I tried to return the money but they wouldn't accept it. Did I not tell you that Don Pedro was not only a gentleman but a man who showed true hidalgia, something we seldom see in these decadent times? I really think Don Pedro respected me for what I am, and maybe he sensed that I was meant for better things than a goat pasture in Extremadura. I kept the skin for years. I took it to Italy and even carried it to Mexico and used it to pillow my head when I tried to sleep. I even had a chance to compare it to the skins of the tigres mexicanos I recovered from the bodies of Tenochca warriors. Interestingly, the skin of my leopard was very similar, indeed, to the skin of these tigers. I spoke to some Mexica who actually hunted these cats. They told me that with the use of small dogs trained to follow their scent, they hunted them in the forest and in the mountains. Sometimes the tiger would try to hide in a tree but usually it made a fight on the ground. The hunters approach with their spears at the ready and the cornered beast, just like my leopard, would charge, skewering himself on the spears. Sometimes, however, it would break through the spears, killing dogs and men. Rarely, and to my mind even more horribly, the impaled cat forced himself up and along the spear until he reached his tormentor.

In *Tenochtitlan* I actually saw several of these beasts alive. Next to the palace of Moctecuzoma was a great menagerie where there were animals from all over Mexico. There were human oddities, as well, including dwarfs and other freaks of nature and horrible things of graven stone, dedicated to Satan."

Mendoza looked doubtful. "I knew, of course, about the menagerie of animals but freaks...?"

"Indeed, Padre," the old Bishop confirmed, "they were better than anything we see here in Spain. I saw brothers covered with fur, a man with a tail as long as your arm, a girl with two heads, people with crab's claws and a woman with six breasts. One man had huge bumps on his body like a cocodrilo. Amazing, I tell you. The place was so large that hundreds of keepers labored constantly to provide for the unfortunate inmates. The stink was so bad as to make one retch, especially in that the Mexica fed the meat-eaters on human flesh from their numerous sacrifices. During feeding times, the cacophony of howls, roars, and birdcalls was so overpowering as to leave one senseless. Still, if one could somehow disregard these inconveniences it was a very interesting place, indeed. There were green and red parrots and finches in every color of the rainbow. There were two kinds of birds the Mexica regarded as sacred. The one is the size of a crow and, in the language of the Mexica, is known as Quetzal. It is green and red with long emerald tail feathers, feathers that were used on Moctecuzoma's litter and robes. The other seemed too tiny to even be a bird. Like the Quetzal it is green in color for, to the Azteca, green is a holy color. The creature is the size of a thimble and it sips the nectar from flowers. It performs this feat by beating its fragile wings so rapidly that it can hover while taking its meal..."

"Yes, I've heard of these, Excelencia," Mendoza interrupted, "It is el picaflor—the hummingbird."

"In their language, Padre, it is *Huitzilin*, and, despite its size and daintiness, it is the incarnation of that most dread of Mexican gods, Huitzilopotchli, the one to whom thousands were slaughtered every year. I also remember that there were many kinds of deer, rabbits, pigeons and quail and a huge creature that seemed to be both ox and a sheep. It had sharp horns and was dark brown in color—the front half of its body was covered by thick wool. By its size and obvious strength it would seem to have been well suited as a draft animal. The naturales must have been too stupid to consider this possibility for, in all of Mexico, only human beings did hauling and carrying."

The old man continued his lecture: "There were also animals that I had seen on our march. One, known as coyotl, looked much like a large jackal and squealed like a pack of pigs. There were also several kinds of foxes, small cats and an animal like a badger only more ferocious. There was another animal that they kept in a pool of water. It was like a great fat rat but with a flat tail. There were osos, smaller than the bears in our carnivals, with ink-black fur and pointed faces. There were lizards and snakes of many kinds. Some of the lizards were huge, longer than a man, with wattles under their throats. There were serpents longer than four men laid end-to-end and thicker than a fat man at his waist. I was told that these snakes would wait in ambush, seize men and women, crush them in their coils and swallow them whole—but this was superstitious nonsense. More likely they are eaters of babies and children."

The Bishop paused to give Mendoza time to catch up his dictations. "An even more interesting serpent was one of the viper tribe that we sometimes encountered on the march. It can grow as long as a man and, amazingly, had castañuelas on its tail to warn people of its presence. One of our soldiers, on the way to *Cempoalla*, not recognizing this warning, was stung on the foot by one of these vipers. His leg turned black and swelled to twice its normal size.

He vomited, pissed black blood and—two days later—he died. Most interesting to me—given my painful experience—were the big cats. One was a león of sorts—the same as those in Africa but not so big and without a mane. The first time I saw these leónes in the menagerie they paid no attention to me. They were tearing apart the torso of a freshly slain victim. Then there were the Mexican tigers—I wondered how these ferocious beasts had been taken alive. One of them especially held my attention. He was powerfully built, almost as big as a real lion or a tiger from the Orient, and stockier and more robust than a leopard. His head was broad and his legs were short and powerful with huge paws. I stared at him and, unafraid, he stared right back at me with unblinking green eyes."

He continued: "Now let me tell you something else interesting about this menagerie. During the destruction of *Tenochtitlan* much of it burned and the starving Tenochca devoured the surviving animals. The tigres mexicanos were an exception. Either because of fear or because of heathen beliefs, these cats were left untouched. They even grew fat because their keepers gorged them on the innumerable dead. Cortés, finding these cats alive, ordered their handlers to put them into portable cages and sent to Villa Rica along with other plunder from ruined *Tenochtitlan*."

He said, "Three ships at Villa Rica were filled with treasure never reported to the army. Some was intended for the King but most was for Cortés, either for bribes to officials who might favor his cause or directly into the coffers of Cortés, himself. On the voyage over, a French pirate captured two of these treasure ships—I can't remember the pirate's name. It's rather amusing when you think about it. Much of the treasure of New Spain, from the sack of an Empire and the impoverishment of our soldiers, taken by a Frenchman who, no doubt, wore women's undergarments and diddled his crew. I'm off my track. The third ship—the uncaptured ship—contained the tigers. One of the animals—the one I saw—escaped and attacked the crew. The cat killed two sailors and mauled a third before leaping into the sea. It was fortunate for the rest of the crew that the animal took his own life—if he had not the beast would have eaten every person on board. That would have been a fine sight. A treasure ship manned by the partially eaten dead and prowled by one very fat Mexican tiger. It would have gone down in the history of navigation."

Burgos, Castilla-León

"I hope you are getting this all down because you seemed to have missed the part about the menagerie in your *Historias*."

"My sources concentrated..." Mendoza said.

"Of course, of course. Your sources concentrated on the roll of our Holy Legions, not on the accomplishments of the heathen. But it's interesting, don't you think?"

Mendoza considered this before replying, "It's, perhaps, of some academic interest, but of no importance when measured against the scope of the Conquista."

"This barbaric zoo, Padre, has considerable significance, even for one as disinterested in natural history as you appear to be. It has an enormous importance as to future exploration—there are even theological implications."

Mendoza shook his head. "I don't follow you."

"Let me help you then. How many times did God create man and woman."

"Once, of course."

The Bishop nodded in agreement. "Then how is it that human beings were found in the Indies and Nueva España?"

"As you know, Obispo, this question has been answered, not only by our biblical experts, but by the Holy Father himself. The Indios are cursed descendants of the Lost Tribes of Israel. They got to the New World by boat."

"Are not all animals descendants of those on Noah's Ark and did not the Ark make landfall somewhere on Ararat?"

"Yes, that is what the Holy Scriptures teach us."

"Then how did animals reach Nueva España?"

Mendoza was on shaky ground and he knew it. "Perhaps they were brought there by the ancestors of the Indios."

"By boat?" The Bishop was sarcastic.

"Why not? After all, didn't Noah accomplish a similar task?"

"Is it not strange that the Bible didn't mention such an amazing voyage?" Mendoza was silent.

"Now let me tell you what I think." The Bishop stood up from his chair and started to pace. "Most of the animals in the Mexican menagerie were similar to those beasts that we are familiar with in Europe and Asia. The odds are excellent that those creatures that do not have wings must have walked to the New World. Magellan, in circumnavigating the world, has taught us that the continents are not connected in the south. Therefore, these animals must have reached their present location in Nueva España from the north. It logically follows that the continents of Asia, Europe, and America must be connected in the north."

"Such speculations, Your Grace, I must say in all candor, are heretical."

"I'm glad you think so, Padre."

Chapter 7

"I have digressed but I will continue. It was June of 1511 and I was but nineteen, maybe twenty years old, when I heard that Spanish forces under Cardona, the Viceroy of Naples, were fighting the French in Italy. Taking the small amount of money I had saved, I gave my farewells to my friends as well as Señor Ignacio Tamayo.

Tamayo placed his hand on my shoulder. "I'm proud of you, my son, for war is the finest occupation for a man. Good luck to you, and may Allah grant you many victories—and—give you the satisfaction of revenge."

I also went to my patrón, Don Pedro, and received a different response. He asked me where I was going and what I expected to do. I told him that, if they would have me, I intended to join our Spanish armies in their noble enterprise, although I hardly knew what that could be.

Don Pedro asked me to enter his hacienda, which, as you know, is a privilege not usually accorded to a peasant. I remember him on that day, for it was the last time I saw him. He was tall and lean although stooped with age. He moved stiffly for his chest and back bore the scars from a Moorish lance. I remember Don Pedro looking at me with his sad brown eyes.

"*Sabe loque hace?* Are you sure you know what you are doing? To volunteer to be a soldier is only to volunteer for death and disease in a foreign land. Honor and glory are rare and filth and hunger are certain. Stay here where, if you keep away from wild beasts," Don

Pedro smiled and said, "you will be safe."

I told Don Pedro that I was determined. He shrugged as if to indicate that he always knew this was to be my path—to be certain, it was the same path that Don Pedro had chosen for himself. Two small windows dimly lighted the room in which we were standing. In the poor light I admired the trophies of Don Pedro's victories. There were shields, lances, armor, and Moorish helmets. There was a torn coat of mail still dark with ancient blood. There were curved scimitars and a knife with a wavy blade. There was even a saddle fashioned in the Moorish style.

On the other side of the room were those things that Don Pedro revered even more. There was a worn oaken bench for prayer and above it a wooden crucifix. The cross was nearly as large as the one upon which Christ actually suffered. On it was the Man-God Himself, carved out of solid oak. The wooden body writhed in eternal torment under a sign that proclaimed him "Iesvs Nazarenvs Rex Ivdeorvm." Bright red paint dripped endlessly from every suffering wound.

The body of Christ sanctified those earthly things that Don Pedro had used during the *Reconquista*, during the final battles against the Moors. Leaning in one corner was a great war spear tipped with sharpened steel. On the same side hung an old-fashioned helmet with a dented rim. There was also a breastplate of steel that covered both the chest and the back and there were greaves and a gorget of blackened leather. On the other side hung a target of old leather and bronze, a coat of chain mail and a small knife. Above Christ's head, in a special place of honor, hung a sword encased in a cracked wooden sheath. The sword's location was such that, as it appeared to me then, God the Father himself might unsheathe it and take revenge for the murder of his Only Son.

"Your father and I were comrades during the Wars. If he were still alive he would give you his weapons and wish you success. He isn't alive and I'm growing old."

He turned and lifted each piece from the wall.

"You'll need this helmet, breastplate, gorget and greaves. Put the knife in your boot or, if you are wearing sandals, tie it to your leg under your pantalones. I'd give you my chain mail but it is too heavy for a foot soldier. Neither will I give you my lance. A weapon such as this is for a man on horseback. I can't afford to give you a horse. Even if I could, I wouldn't give it to you because you have not been trained in mounted combat. Also, a horse is for titled nobility—a position that you, through no fault of your own, no longer possess.

Now I will give you some advice." Don Pedro went on. "It's natural that you should have feelings of hatred, but you must give up all thoughts of vengeance. *El Santo Oficio* is too powerful and those who are foolish enough to stand in its path are ground into the dirt.

Also, you must keep in mind that you're still little more than a boy. I've seen you play-fighting with the other boys and I'm sure that you think that you are prepared for battle. You are not. The first time you meet an experienced foe he will kill you as easily as you squash a beetle under your foot. I've heard that our captains in Italy actually train their new men for combat—don't depend on it, though. Make friends with one or two real veterans and ask them to train you to the point that you are almost a veteran yourself before you meet the enemy the first time—then you might have some small chance." Don Pedro's eyes glistened. "To improve your chances I'll give you one other thing."

He called for a servant who carried a ladder into the room. The servant leaned the ladder against the wall, climbed up and removed the sword. He gave it to Don Pedro who then hefted the sword as if testing its weight.

"It's not much to look at, is it?" Don Pedro said.

The sheath was fashioned of dark cracked wood sealed with dull varnish. The place it would attach to the belt was a simple iron ring. The projecting hilt was wrapped in old dark leather and the hand guard was nothing more than a short metal post.

I was in no position to be particular. "I'm sure it is good enough."

"Good enough?" In one smooth motion, Don Pedro slid the sword from its sheath. He looked at the blade for a moment and then, using his free hand, grasped the blade close to its tip. He flexed the blade far past the point that most blades would bend or break. He released his hold and the blade snapped back into position. Otherwise the sword was unremarkable. The blade was straight and overly long and a little wide. There was not a hint of tarnish and I could see no chips or dents. It seemed to have never been used.

"This weapon has been in my family for generations. I hoped to pass it on to my son...but that was not to be. He died before his second birthday."

"A family heirloom, I can't take it, Don Pedro."

"You'll insult me if you don't—I don't know why—but I know that you are the one who should have it. You must protect it well and, if you do, it will protect you. This is not just any weapon. It has a history or, should I say, a superstition. It was the story told to me by my father and, in time, it is the story that you'll tell to your son. *Sientese.*"

Don Pedro took his seat in a straight-backed chair and I seated myself on a stool covered with leather. Don Pedro held the sword across his lap as he continued to speak.

"Spain has seen more grief than most lands—foreigners have occupied us and used us as their battlefield—Celts, Carthaginians, Romans, Visigoths, Vandals and, the very worst, the Moors. Less well known is that we were invaded by northern pirates. Such was their evil that they remained heathen long after the time that all of Europe accepted the Light of Our Blessed Savior.

These pirates hauled one hundred long ships onto our beaches. They ravaged the towns and the countryside, burning, looting, and raping. With a hatred of all things Holy, they demolished cathedrals and monasteries and they put the priests to the sword. Along with their loot they seized all those that they met, especially the Brides of Christ. They loaded the weeping women onto their ships and carried them off for their pleasure.

One of our knights resisted them with his mace and laid many low to the ground. Finally, however, he was overwhelmed and forced to his knees. The knight was taken to their godless leader who, exhausted with murder, was taking his rest on the sand. There is no mercy in such men—there is only torture and death.

● ● ●

"Because of you, Christian, eight of the Raven Banner no longer are. How must I deal with you?"

"Give me a weapon," the Christian said, "and I will show how I will deal with you."

The pagan only laughed, "Well spoken, black-hair. I will give you a weapon for we have cast the runes to decide on your fate. They tell us that you are one who has been chosen by the great god, Thor. Like you, He slays his foes with a hammer." The pagan took the sword that was strapped to his back and gave it to the Christian.

"With this sword I pay for the things that we have taken. I pay for your fields, your crops and your ruined towns. I pay for your slaughtered people. I pay for the slaves we have harvested from your land. I pay for the use of your women. This sword is payment enough for it was forged in the flames of Hell. It was forged by the One-Eyed God, who, for the sake of wisdom, hanged himself from the tree—the same as your Christ. Still the weapon was unfinished and white-hot when Valkyries carried it to the Hall of the Slain. There its blade was quenched in the blood of all the men who have ever died in battle. For this reason, it has a thirst. See that it drinks."

● ● ●

Don Pedro smiled. "I don't believe the tale, of course, but the weapon is very old, possibly Roman or Vandal, and is truly well-made." Don Pedro carefully tested the blade with his thumb. "Despite the fact that its seen many battles, there's no hint of damage. It has never been sharpened—its edge is always keen. The balance is perfect and, although it has no magic and must be used with skill, those of us who have used it have sensed its thirst. The weapon is called *El Bebidor del Sangre*—Blood Drinker. Keep it with you at all times."

"*Muchas gracias, Don Pedro.*"

"I'll also tell you what I think." Don Pedro leaned forward. "I'm not certain about the sword but those *paganos* left us with a gift, indeed."

I thought that Don Pedro would present me with something more. "You've been good enough to me, already."

His smile was troubled. "No, it's nothing I can give you for it is something you already have."

"But..."

"Before we had it we had nothing—our enemies used us like women and pushed us into the Pyrenees. With it, year after year, century after century, we drove the invaders out of our lands. Nevertheless, it's a dangerous thing and, now that the Moors are gone, Castilla is too small to contain it."

"I don't..."

He stroked the blade of the sword. "That's because it's a thing of the soul although some show it in the tint of their eyes." He reached forward and brushed my hair from my face. "It is the mark of the beast." He slid the sword back into its sheath and handed it to me, "The sword belongs to you."

With this Don Pedro gave me the weapon and walked out of the room.

Burgos, Castilla-León

Without looking up, Mendoza asked a question. "And did you honor your patrón by taking good care of his sword?"

The Bishop stood up stiffly and pulled his robe aside, revealing a sword hanging from his hip. He slowly unsheathed the weapon and held it up so the flames from the hearth reflected in its blade.

Mendoza was now watching very closely. "You kept it all these years?"

"All these years... I was a warrior...now I am feeble and old. Long ago I should have fulfilled my part of the bargain and given it to a stronger man. Too late—too late—it has become part of my body—part of my soul."

The Bishop moved suddenly, unexpectedly. The blade slashed into the wood of the table a fraction from Mendoza's right hand—Mendoza fell from his chair.

With difficulty, the old man prized the blade out of the wood. Again he held it to the light—flames danced along the blade.

"Behold, Padre Mendoza! The sword has been in a hundred, maybe a thousand fights and has clashed with Indio stone and French, German, and Spanish steel. Still the blade is perfect—no nicks or defects. Not once has it touched a sharpening stone but its edge is still keen. All that it has required is that I wipe off the blood."

Recovering from his fright Mendoza spoke rapidly. "It certainly is rather remarkable, Your Grace. Very well made."

The old man twisted the sword in the flickering light. "I wonder how old it is? I wonder how many battles its seen, how many men it's slain? Still it's entirely perfect."

The Bishop laid the sword on the table. "Pick it up, Padre. Test its balance—feel its..."

Mendoza carefully picked the sword up by its leather-wrapped pommel. Momentarily he considered—running the Bishop through. He dropped the weapon as if it had burned his skin.

The old man's face cracked into a grin. "You felt it, Padre." It was a statement not a question.

"The thing is accursed!"

The Bishop slipped the blade back in its sheath. "Accursed, indeed. I'll tell you what I think. I think it was forged in the flames of Hell—I think it is as old as time—I think Satan himself will use it in the last battle. I will also tell you what I know. Only the chosen can feel its power."

Mendoza blanched, "Chosen, Your Grace?" .

"Yes, Padre." The old man nodded at Mendoza. "As it has been written, "Many are called but very few are chosen.""

●●●

At that time in my life I never speculated on such things. I was simply pleased that my patrón, Don Pedro, had equipped me so handsomely. True, the chest armor was big for me and the iron helmet was a little small. Still they would have to do. Too cumbersome to carry, I'd have to wear them with my shield strapped to my back. It took me almost two very hot and sweaty weeks to walk to Valencia, sleeping in barns and open fields. I must have presented a rare sight to the village children. They flocked after me with a thousand questions. Sometimes ruffians, to impress the girls, would shout insults and throw stones at me. I noticed, however, that they never approached me too closely. What a difference a little armor makes. Late one afternoon, though, in the hills outside Méligua I had an altogether different experience.

Two men, dressed in rags and brandishing knives, launched themselves at me from ambush. One was in too much of a hurry, tripped on his feet and went sprawling in the dirt. The second reached me before I could act. The blade of his knife clanged against my helmet. Somehow I got my foot in his stomach, kicked as hard as I could, launching him several feet into space. Recovering, I fumbled for my sword and had just freed it from its sheath when the first man slashed at my face. Suddenly, the tramp's eyes bulged. He dropped his knife, reached down with both hands and clutched at my sword. The blade had penetrated his abdomen. I jerked it out.

The second tramp turned to flee. With both hands I chopped

down with all of my strength. The tip of the blade cut the man's back, along his spine, from his neck to his hip. He went down in a heap, screaming like a woman.

Stunned, I could only stare at my work. One man was staggering, hunched up, bright blood pouring over his hands from his ruined belly. The other man was writhing on the blood-soaked ground.

The fury of the moment having passed my first instinct was to run or get help. Then again, tramps though these men may appear to be and bandits they certainly were, they might also have friends and relatives in the closest village.

My first blows had been in self-protection but my next blows were calculated and deliberate. I made a mess of the man on the ground and had to stab him a dozen times before he strangled on his own blood. Determined to make a better job of it with my second man, I swung a powerful blow meant to decapitate him. My blow missed slightly and the blade sliced halfway through his skull. He dropped, dragging my sword and me along with him. To free my weapon, I put my foot on his head and pulled with all of my might.

Sick at what I had done, I dragged the bodies off of the road and concealed them with loose earth, a few rocks and bushes. I kicked dirt over the blood, wiped the blood from my hands and weapon and continued on my way. I walked a very long time before stopping.

Now I was a veteran of sorts. I had killed men who were trying to kill me and I had prevailed. Still I knew nothing more about real warfare than I had learned while play fighting with my friends. But I had learned a few lessons. Instinct and fast reflexes can be lifesaving. I also learned some things about killing. The thrust of a sword, even to a vital area such as the chest, is not instantly lethal, and a man, even thus wounded, might prove himself dangerous in the moments before death. Also, in battle, where other enemies are present, it is a mistake to strike an enemy in the head and become temporarily disarmed.

I felt no sense of triumph, only disgust and an overwhelming guilt. Examining myself, however, I realized that I was not in the least bit sorry that I had killed these vagabundos. My shame was very little more than my religious training and the fear of discovery.

I knew that my act of self-defense could be interpreted as murder. Still, I told myself, I was volunteering for war and, I already knew, that war was merely another name for sanctioned murder. War was legal killing, killing often rewarded by rank and prestige—I found this thought comforting. Killing without guilt. There was a freedom and moral clarity to it. Nevertheless, I moved as quickly as possible and was relieved to find that my guilt subsided with distance.

Italia

"You're a likely looking lad. You've even got your own armor. It even looks like you've been in a few scrapes already." The recruiting officer was a brutal looking man. He was seated at the table of a cheap cantina, a flagon of wine in front of him. A fat girl, wearing a dirty black dress, was seated uncomfortably on his lap. She was kissing the ugly officer's neck as he massaged one of her breasts. The man, never stopping his work on the girl, stared at the scars on my face.

I wasn't about to disillusion the officer about my combat experience. "Sí, señor. I'm just what you're looking for. I was told that those who enlist are to receive ten pesos."

The cantina was dank and smelled of cheap wine and unwashed bodies. The floor was of packed dirt.

"Oh you'll be paid right enough. In Italy you'll probably even get rich." The girl winced as the officer gave her an especially hard squeeze. "I guarantee it. I'd be over there right now raking in the money if this pig of a Frenchman hadn't messed up my arm." He indicated his right arm by pointing with his chin but, judging by the vigor that he was squeezing the girl's breast, there appeared to be little wrong with it.

"Yes, a kid like you, even if your looks have been spoiled by a few scars, will be a welcome addition to our forces. Some of our older veterans will really appreciate your—assistance," The ugly officer's smile was crooked.

"Thank you, señor."

Never once stopping on the girl, he pulled a dirty paper out of his pocket with his left hand, and handed it to me. On it was a list of names and marks. "Paco!" He nodded toward the barkeep. "Give the boy something to write with. That's right. Just put your mark right down there, below the others. *Madre de Dios!*" The brutal man breathed in mock respect. "I see you know how to write your name—they'll probably make you generalissimo." He stuffed the paper back in his pocket. "You are now a recruit, subject to military discipline. Before the sun rises Monday morning you are to show up at the docks and report to the master of the caravel, *Señora Margreta*. He'll pay your enlistment money. You are then to embark for Napoles."

I could hardly believe my good fortune. "*Muchas gracias, señor.*"

"Now get your ass out of here, I'm sick of looking at you," with this the ugly officer stood up, slinging the fat girl under his injured right arm in an act of amazing strength. The girl squealed in mock alarm as the two disappeared into a room in the back.

●●●

I found a cheap inn, hard by the docks, and shared an ill-smelling room with six or seven other men. Worried that I might not report to my ship on time, I spent a restless night and awoke to the sounds of snores and dogs barking. I didn't know what time it was but, unwilling to take any chances, I quietly rolled up my bedding, carried it outside, and completed my wardrobe so as not to disturb the other sleepers.

The day before, I had located the *Señora Margreta*. She was docked between two larger merchant vessels—her appearance was not reassuring. She was scarcely forty cubits long and, at one time, had been painted like a French harlot. That was a long time ago, though, and her garish paint had largely peeled off revealing rotting cracked timbers. Her deck was filthy and piled with uncoiled rope. Barnacles thickly fouled her hull.

Now, however, I dismissed the ships failings as I stepped out onto the dock. I had arrived at least two hours early so, dropping my bedroll on the dock, I sat on the dock next to the ship, alone with my thoughts. The night was dark and silent and the dock moved slightly with the gentle roll of the tide. The smell would, over the years, become as familiar to me as the smell of my own body. The smell of a harbor is difficult to describe, but is the same all over the world. It is the combination of many odors, most of which taken separately would be foul. Salt water, rotten kelp, dead fish, garbage, the filth of sea birds. Somehow, however, the combination is memorable, striking a chord deep inside. A hand grasped my shoulder and shook me hard.

"*Quien eres?*" a rough voice asked.

Rousing myself as quickly as possible I tried to respond appropriately, "*Rodrigo de la Peña y usted?*"

"*Yo soy el Capitán Pablo Gomez, comandante de esta caravela. Tú eras uno de los mozos?*"

"*Sí, señor.*"

My teeth were chattering. The cold is always worse just before dawn.

"De la Peña. Damn fancy name for a snot-faced recruit. Get on board. One of the crewmen will show you to your berth. You are the first to arrive but there will be twenty-two of you, so I hope you are not offended if your quarters not are up to your usual standards."

"Am I to receive my money, now?" I said as I hurriedly gathered up my things from the dock. As I stepped out onto the gangplank, I was shocked to receive a sharp boot in my backside—I almost toppled into the water. Gomez cackled behind me. "There is your payment, *cabrón estúpido*."

●●●

Only nineteen men of the scheduled twenty-two actually reported to the ship. The other three had apparently reconsidered military service. Even so, we were packed into the stinking hold so tightly that we could hardly breathe. We were men turned into cargo and not very valuable cargo at that.

"Once we are underway," announced a dark-skinned sailor with a Moorish accent, "I'll let you know when you can come up to the deck—even then, only two at a time will be permitted out. Any more, and you can expect punishment." Gomez was obviously taking no chances. I heard the slide of a great bolt and knew that we were locked in.

Shortly, however, we could hear shouts, the sound of running feet on the deck overhead, the movement of heavy equipment, the splashing of oars and then, the snap of sails. We could feel by the roll of the ship that the ship had cast off from its mooring.

Too late now. The roll of the ship increased to sickening proportions and, from what little I knew of the sea, I realized that we had passed out of the bay and into the open ocean. Most of the recruits were vomiting and the foul air became even more foul. I didn't feel too good, myself. Hours passed before we heard the bolt sliding again.

"Out now, two at a time, for fifteen minutes." The hatch was left open and we tasted the fresh sea air. By the time it was my turn, the sun was already low on the horizon.

"Up front, over the side." Clinging to the rolling ship I managed to discharge my reluctant bowels. I was then herded back into our prison.

During the days of our stinking, puking, louse infested passage I got to know some of the other recruits. Most were young men such as myself. They were poor and filled with visions of glory and wealth. Some, like myself, wanted to do what we could do to further the Holy Cause of España, even as our forefathers had done during the Reconquista. Everyone was disillusioned. Well, almost everyone. One recruit was an old veteran, Felipe Sandoval, who had previously fought in Italy under Capitán Grande, Gonzalo Fernandez de Córdoba. He was maybe fifty years old with almost white hair.

Sandoval was philosophical. "Don't complain. Our present sufferings are as nothing. When I was fighting under our Capitán Grande we often went days without food. We fought in the mud and the heat and the cold and died by the hundreds. By the Great Whore's Son, we went months without pay."

I was more shocked by his words than I was by our voyage. "Then why have you re-enlisted?"

"It is because, even though we sometimes starved, we also sometimes ate. Even though we went without pay, we were eventually paid. Even though we died—well, we all die, don't we?" He looked up at me almost as if he recognized me from long ago. "After leaving the service of El Capitán Grande I returned to my home in Navarra. I had a little money and I had a large dream. I bought a few acres of land and got me a wife and we had four children. I killed myself with work but the ground was hard and stony. There were two dry seasons back-to-back and I couldn't grow enough to feed my family. The winter came and took my wife as surely as a thief steals your purse. The children...." The old man stared into the nothingness of the hold. He didn't continue.

Chapter 8

We landed in Naples and, half-dead, we were welcomed by a thick-armed officer of uncertain rank, wearing chest armor and a casque helmet. His teeth were rotten stumps. We recruits gathered around him.

"Is it actually you, Pedro?" The officer slapped my white-haired shipmate on the back. "After all these years I can hardly believe it. I thought you would be fat in Navarra. Never mind, I'll talk to you later. Why don't you wait for me at the end of the dock but, right now," —pointing to us recruits— I need to have a little talk with these turds."

Our white-haired comrade moved away, a faint smile on his lips, while the rest of us quaked with fear.

The officer put his hands on his hips as his lips curled in a snarl. "You are the most miserable looking specimens I've ever seen. Just look at you." Some of us looked around. From what I could see, the officer was an accurate observer. "You are a disgrace to *Santa España* and are not fit to carry water to real soldiers. Nevertheless, the army needs cannon fodder and you cabrónes will have to do. Personally, I doubt that you'll even slow down the enemy. The French will slaughter you like so many sheep."

The officer looked at us with undisguised contempt. "You mozos are the lowest of the low—what's this?" The man was looking at my small pile of possessions. "One of you characters actually owns armor. I am so-o-o impressed." I don't think he was really impressed. "You mozos should feel honored. You've got a real soldier in your midst. Step forward, soldado!"

I didn't move.

"Step forward or I'll cut off your shrunken balls!"

I took one hesitant step forward.

"*Madre de Dios!* You're a dangerous looking character!" He was really starting to enjoy himself, "Been in a few knife fights have you?" Indicating the scars on my face. "You were probably fighting with some fucking Morisco over who would get first turn sticking it into some fucking burro. We can hardly wait to see what kind of warrior you are, mozo. Pick up your weapon."

The officer indicated my sword in its scabbard. I picked it up. "*No, no, no, mozo!* You can't kill a man with a sheathed weapon. Take it out." I slid the sword out of its scabbard and carefully placed the sheath on the dock.

"That's it. I see you keep it nice and shiny. I'll wager it belonged to your papá. Kill me!"

I froze, hardly believing what I was hearing.

"*Mata me!*"

I spoke for the first time. "No, señor. I have nothing against you."

The officer leered grotesquely. "Oh, is that so." He stepped forward and slapped me as hard as he could across my face. The blow stung my face but not nearly as much as it hurt my pride.

"Kill me!"

"No, señor," I snapped back. "You aren't armed."

"*Mata me, cabrón!*" Do as you're ordered!" He slapped me again, even harder.

Alive with rage, I fought to control myself.

The man was no longer smiling. His face was tight and his eyes shined with something I didn't understand. He stepped forward to slap me again.

Something inside of me exploded. Bebidor struck into thin air as something hard hit my sword arm, almost tearing the weapon out of my grasp. At the same time, an armored boot took me full in the crotch. As I was going down, a fist crashed into my face. I hit the ground, tucked my sword under me and rolled at the same time. Another kick glanced off my back. Somehow I came to my knees and, two-handed, I struck at a booted pair of legs that danced away just out of reach. Another kick was directed at my arm. It missed but then I missed with a backhanded stroke. I staggered to my feet, the taste of blood metallic in my mouth. The officer was crouched feet away looking at me with a lop-sided grin.

"*Mata me, mozo,*" he whispered.

I almost struck again but waited until the pain in my crotch subsided. Holding the hilt of my sword with two hands, I took one painful step forward. Laughing, my opponent backed up the same distance. My mind was clearing and suddenly everything came into focus. Behind the officer, the magnificent blue bay of Naples stretched away to the south. Beyond, a cone-shaped mountain thrust up, a smudge of smoke curling from its apex.

My weapon warmed in my hand. I took another cautious step forward and made a half-swing with my sword. The officer leapt back deftly, looking for his opening. I feinted, shifting my body as if I intended a powerful stroke. He almost committed but held back at the last possible moment.

It hit me like a hammer. My enemy's only advantage was my rage and reluctance to kill. His only tactic was for me to over-commit to a sword stroke, and then hit me hard.

I smiled a bloodstained smile at the man. "Only obeying orders—*Vaya con Dios, Jefe.*"

Something passed over the man's face. I made another stroke but was careful not to over-commit. He did the only thing he could as I came forward relentlessly. He stepped back again and then again. Fear oozed from his skin—it excited me. I jumped forward, sword cocked back for the kill. Magically, the officer vanished—from below—a great splash. I leaned over the side of the wharf and saw the man struggling below in the filthy water, weighed down by his armor. Choking and gagging, he had just enough strength to flounder to the nearest piling. He clung to it more tightly than a woman clings to her lover.

"*Mata me, Jefe!*" I ordered, "*Mata me, mozo. Mata me!*"

● ● ●

I don't know what I expected, but I certainly didn't expect to see our army camped like a bunch of so many gypsies. The army was sprawled over many acres and was made up of adobe hovels, multi-colored tents, wooden barracks, broken-down carts, scurrying chickens, skinny dogs, huge heaps of refuse and clouds of flies. The smell was overpowering and was a mixture of horse and cow dung, rotting garbage, cooked food, and human waste. A pall of smoke rose over the camp from the numerous cook-fires. Everywhere there was mud.

"I wish to welcome you to our little community." The speaker was a tall handsome man dressed in the crimson brocade of an aristocrat. "I'm Capitán de los Reyes and I'm here to tell you a little about us and even more about what we expect out of you before you are separated and sent to your respective companies."

The Captain was speaking to a gathering of one hundred or so recruits. We were lined up on a sodden plain broken by an occasional tuft of grass. The sky behind the Capitán was a tumble of huge gray clouds.

"From this moment on you are no longer Castellanos, Andaluzes, Aragoneses, Catalanes o Vascos. Now each and every one of you is Español."

A murmur of disquiet rippled through our ranks.

"*Silencio, desgraciados!* You are now under the command of Capitán-General Pedro de Navarro. We are Spanish mercenaries. We fight for money and we fight on behalf of the highest bidder." The Captain let his words set in for a moment. "We fight with and against the Italians, the Swiss, the Germans, and the Pope."

There was a stunned silence. One of our recruits, a gangly pimple-faced youth in dirty blue clothing, stepped forward. "We are Catholic! We will never oppose the Holy Father!"

The Captain gave the recruit a long stare then answered in a patronizing tone.

"You, and all of these others," indicating us recruits with a wave of his hand as he continued, "will do exactly as you are ordered. Captain-General Navarro determines whom we will fight. The French sodomites are always our enemies. In the past, when the Pope has unwisely allied himself with the French, we have attacked his forces with every ounce of our power."—He paused to add emphasis to his statements— "We are Españoles and as infantry, we are the best in the world. Yes, the Alemanes, Suizos, and some of the Italianos are good but we are the very best and we command the best prices. We give our employers their full money's worth."

The religious recruit who had apparently appointed himself as our spokesman, interrupted, "*Pero Capitán—los Francés...*"

The Captain's face flushed with anger. "Step back into line, recruit, and do not speak or ask questions unless you are ordered to do so!"

Chastened, the recruit stepped back and stood rigidly at attention.

The Captain went on, "Despite your comrade's impertinence, I'll answer the question. Yes, the stinking French are good enough but that is unimportant. It's enough to know that whoever our enemies happen to be, you must defeat them. We do not break in battle and, if we must, we die. We may retreat but we never run. Presently you are just recruits and you will be trained before you are committed to battle. You will be trained in all of the weapons of war but, as Españoles, you will be primarily espadas—swordsmen. We meet the enemy's infantry and defeat him in fixed combat. Our army is heroic but, I want you to remember this carefully, no individual is a hero. Our tactics are mass tactics. An individual fighter is worse than useless and is a threat to the entire unit. You will fight in accordance to this principle. You will obey your officers to the letter and in all things. Disobedience will be punished mercilessly. Do you understand?"

I did, indeed.

"I mentioned the Swiss, Germans, and Italians. They are fellow professionals and must be respected as such. Depending on the party we contract with, you may be required to kill them or to support them—it's all the same."

We recruits, who had expected a holy war fought with devotion, were confused.

"Another thing, so that there are no misunderstandings," the Captain went on, "desertion, looting, and cowardice in the face of the enemy are all punishable by hanging. Anyone who commits rape will be publicly castrated and disemboweled."

Later, I saw men hanged for cowardice, desertion, and even for sleeping while on duty. I even saw two well-deserving rapists executed slowly for crimes against Italian women in friendly villages. Following the successful assault on a walled city, however, discipline evaporates and then—God help the innocent inhabitants. Nothing, not even summary executions, could prevent some soldiers from committing the most unspeakable crimes.

"Pay is based on rank and will be paid out on a monthly basis." The Captain went on, "Money for uniforms, food, and basic supplies will be deducted from your salaries. Armor and weapons are the property of the army and will be issued to you without charge. You must keep this equipment meticulously clean and functional. Any loss or damage, including that which may occur in battle, will be deducted from your pay. All captured items, including the weapons of dead or captured enemy, are the property of the army. The army will ransom enemy prisoners taken, if of any value, as hostages. An appropriate share of the ransom monies will be meted out to the unit responsible for the capture."

●●●

We were quickly divided up and I, along with three others, were assigned to a company commanded by our Jefe—Antonio Rangel. The encampment was indistinctly separated from adjacent ones and was made up of an assortment of huts, tents, and ramshackle wooden buildings. Nothing looked military. Men dressed in miscellaneous garb were engaged in various tasks. Some were sitting in front of their tents, working on their clothing and equipment. Still others sat around cook-fires, talking. Women moved through the camp, carrying clothes to be washed or helping to cook food. One decrepit old hag was driving a flock of geese through the camp. A man, sitting at a campfire, stood up and pointed at one of the fowl.

The old woman, with a speed and agility that I wouldn't have credited her with, seized a protesting bird by its neck. As the man paid her, she passed the goose over to him. The man grasped the bird by its head and, using only his wrist, swung it around like some animated windmill. The goose, its neck neatly broken, flapped wildly. The soldier walked to his nearby cook-fire and tossed the convulsing bird to his comrades. They plucked the bird, its feathers scattering in the light breeze.

Our guide, who was so young that his chin sprouted only several carefully tended hairs, informed us, "This is your new home, muchachos," indicating a tent that would scarcely accommodate four sleeping bodies. "Make a few friends and maybe they'll let you move into their larger tents. Breakfast is a half hour after sunrise; later there will be drill and weapons practice. Hasta luego."

I dropped my roll of possessions as several men from the camp joined us recruits.

●●●

"*Mucho gusto, amigo, mi nombre es Raphael Flores, y tú?*" Pleasantly surprised by my reception, I shook the hand of Raphael Flores. He was a well-developed man of medium height, probably in his mid-thirties.

"*Yo soy Rodrigo de la Peña, mucho gusto.*"

Flores had a narrow, but handsome face and, unlike most of the soldiers, he was clean-shaven. His complexion was olive and his hair was black and carefully oiled. His dress consisted of tight black pantalones and a blue-striped camisa with puffy sleeves. Considering the camp conditions, he was immaculate.

"You're one of our new recruits—we're glad to see you. We had a fight with the Milanese last month and lost a couple of men. Just last week, another one of the boys got the bloody flux and died, so you gentlemen will just about make up the difference. Don't worry about your accommodations. There's plenty of room in some of the other tents but we've found that, rather than put the new men into tents with men that they might not get along with, its better to bunk them together until they make their own friends."

"Thank you for the information." I had expected our reception to be less friendly, so I was feeling some relief. "As you can see, there's not enough room for the four of us and our gear."

"Yes, I can see that. Where did you come from, Rodrigo?"

We spent the rest of the afternoon in conversation. Raphael invited me to sit with him and some others around a small fire. A middle-aged woman served us a meal of tough beef, cabbage and warm beer. Raphael gave me his undivided attention and told me a lot about himself and the company. Although still only one of the common soldiers, he was a veteran with nine years of service and had fought in many battles throughout Italy. He warned me of people and situations to be cautious of and, without my asking, offered to give me special weapons training.

"I can't thank you enough, Raphael." I really meant it. "The faster I can get trained, the better."

"Don't worry about it, Rodrigo. You'll be held back in the rear ranks until you have a little experience. You'll get a taste of battle without risking yourself or anybody else." Raphael giggled happily, "I intend to look after you, compañero."

We talked a little more and then, getting a little sleepy, I wandered back to the tent. The other three were already there and were whispering in the dark. "Here's Rodrigo." It was the religious recruit who had questioned the Captain. "Let's see what he thinks."

"Qué?" I replied, not knowing what it was all about.

"Juan and I are getting out of here," spoke the whisperer. "Carlos says he's staying. How about you?"

I didn't know what to say. "You locos must be out of your minds. We just got here today."

"One day's more than enough," the whisperer replied. "This is not what I bargained for. We plan to get out of here while we still have a chance."

"Where will you go? Remember, there's a lot of water between Italy and Spain. Besides, deserters are hanged."

"We aren't deserting because, as far as I'm concerned, we aren't really in the army yet. We'll find some way to get home."

I still couldn't believe it. "The army will consider it desertion. If you two fools do go, do it while Carlos and I are asleep."

●●●

In the morning, Carlos and I were the only residents of our tent. We dressed quickly so as to make it to the morning meal.

One of the soldiers stared at us. "Where's the other new men?"

Carlos, who was a big man with the open honest face of a

peasant, pretended to look around for our tent-mates and replied, "Somewhere around here…"

The soldier shrugged and dropped the subject, as he ladled porridge into his bowl. The desertion of the missing men wasn't detected until the morning roll call.

"What do you know of this, de la Peña?" asked our Jefe.

"Both men were complaining last night, but I never thought they'd desert."

He knew I was lying. "Well then, Señor de la Peña, you will have the privilege of witnessing military justice." He tapped his thigh with his officer's baton. "If those two cabrónes won't serve as soldiers they'll serve as examples."

●●●

The next week was spent in combat training, with Raphael giving me individual instruction. We spent most of our time practicing with sword and shield although Raphael also taught me some of the finer points in using mace, battle-hammer, axe, and even the pike.

"As espadas, we all carry swords," Raphael said, "but most of us also carry either an axe or a hammer. The hammer is better at penetrating armor but the axe is more versatile. You'll train in both because, depending on your assignment, you may be required one or the other. The lanza, mosquete and ballesta—lance, musket and crossbow—are only for men specially trained in their use. You'll be a common sword-swinger but its good to know something about all weapons. If one of our pikemen goes down it is sometimes lifesaving to pick up his fallen weapon."

Raphael and I practiced for hours, as I improved my physical condition and tried to perfect my skills.

"You're lucky, Rodrigo," Raphael said. " Right now the army is out of work, so we have plenty of time to train. When I entered the army I was thrown into the fight almost immediately. I didn't have a special friend and, before I learned what to do, I was nearly killed. Lucky for you that you have me."

"How much time before you think we'll see battle again?" From the things I had been told, I was hoping that it would be a very long time.

Raphael, sensing my discomfort, laughed, "Who knows? Knowing these stupid Italians, we'll be back in business soon enough.

Don't worry, though, you are the fastest learner I've ever seen—I tremble for the enemy."

Maybe, Raphael trembled for the enemy, but he certainly didn't tremble for himself. He was as quick as a weasel and as sly as a fox. He could always counter my clumsy moves and he killed me time and again. Slowly, painfully I improved but I was no match for Raphael's experience.

●●●

As a member of the unit, I also practiced arms drill. I learned to march smoothly and obey all of the various commands. Oftentimes, we would divide up into opposing forces and clash in mock combat. We were trained to fight as mixed units of spearmen and swordsmen. The pikes, which were nine cubits in length, were supposed to discourage horsemen and to hold the enemy infantry at a distance. The swordsmen were to take care of any enemy who managed to penetrate the hedgerow of pikes. *Hombres de ballestas y mosqueteros* were sometimes incorporated into the line of swordsmen but, most commonly, because their aim was often obstructed by friendly infantry, they operated on the flanks.

Less frequently, we had the opportunity to practice with our potential allies and enemies, Swiss and Landsknechte pikemen—the advantages were mutual professionalism. We learned how to operate with and oppose a skilled force of massed pikemen. They, in their turn, honed their skills with and against Spanish infantry. We learned to obey orders shouted in German just as the Germans had to learn orders in Spanish."

Burgos, Castilla-León

"I must stop you here, Excelencia." Mendoza was puzzled, "What you say is, to my nonmilitary ear, strange. These Germans and Swiss with whom you were practicing, were men who you might be required to kill or might be required to kill you. Were not things a little—strained?"

"Not at all, Padre." The old man tilted his head to one side. "We were as friendly with the Swiss and Germans as we were with one another, maybe even more so. After all, war as we practiced it in Italy, was just a business. Certainly this is how the Swiss and Landsknechte regarded it. Depending on their contracts, German companies often fought against German companies and the Swiss against the Swiss. It was all very professional with no personal animosity. It was, after all, just killing."

"Cavalry," —spoke our Captain one day— "as long as we are arrayed in battle formation, cavalry will avoid us. On the march, cavalry will keep its distance. The light cavalry always hangs on the distant flank, looking for their opportunity. Their only chance comes should we be routed and flee disorganized from the field. We are Españoles and won't be routed but, if any of you is ever tempted to run, let me tell you what the enemy will do to you. He will ride you down and skewer you through the back—just as you deserve.

Heavy cavalry is another thing, altogether. Both the horse and rider are heavily armored, almost impregnable, but they are slow. They are at no advantage against well-formed infantry. They do constitute a real danger, however, should they catch us, extended, on the march, for, at such times, the arquebusiers don't have the fuses lit on their muskets. To prevent this disaster we always move with skirmishers to the front, so that we have plenty of forewarning. In the event, however, that we're surprised, avoid panic and form up as quickly as possible so that our musketeers will have time to prepare their weapons. We'll now practice an attack by heavy cavalry."

We practiced and we practiced again and again, as Spanish and German heavy cavalry ambushed our strung-out marching force. The practice was terrifying enough—monstrous, armored horsemen would suddenly be on us, thundering through our line and yelling like locos. Men scattered but quickly formed up defensively, providing a satisfying conclusion to our exercise. I knew that the real thing could be far different, however.

Chapter 9

Two weeks after my arrival at the camp, we were ordered to attend an execution in the morning. Both of my comrades had been captured only a league from our encampment. Farmers who resented their fields being raided by night had reported them. Our entire company had to attend the execution and we were ordered to form a hollow square around a rickety gallows that looked as if it had been used many times before. The two men, their hands tied behind them, each with a guard on either side, were marched silently to the scaffold. The timbers creaked under their weight as they mounted the steps. Their clothes were filthy and their faces were bruised and swollen. Without wasting time, Capitán Rangel quickly read out their names, their offences, and the sentence, then stepped away and stood facing the gallows. A noose was hanging from an overhead beam three hand's breadth's above the top of each victim's head. The hangman placed a stool between the two men and then stepped up and adjusted the nooses. Tearfully, my comrades alternated between pleading for their lives and chanting *Pater nosters* and *Ave Marias* as the guards bound their legs tightly. The guards then lifted both men off the deck as the hangman cinched a noose around each neck. The men were let down gently until they were hanging by their necks, their feet almost touching the platform. Their faces turned purple, their eyes bulged, and their mouths worked in silent screams as their tongues swelled in their mouths and blood streamed from their nostrils. Their bodies flopped on the ends of their ropes like two horrible fish hauled up from the depths. Both voided visibly and audibly. Their bodies writhed for a full fifteen minutes until they were forever still.

● ● ●

"They looked like a couple of nice boys," Raphael said later. "I feel a little guilty. Maybe if I had taken them aside, when they arrived, like I did you...well, you know what I mean."

"Yes, I suppose I do." Somehow Raphael didn't look like the guilty type.

"I'll tell you what," Raphael said breezily, "it's high time that we get out of camp and go into town. I'm sick of the food around here, anyway. I know some cheap places where we can get some real food. Then, we can hit the cantinas and drink until we can't stand up."

I wasn't really in the mood for an excursion. "I'm pretty new around here. I doubt they'll give me leave time—especially," I explained indicating the hanging corpses, "after what happened to my tent-mates."

"Hey, you're my compadre." Raphael slapped me on the back. "I've got connections and know how to pull all the right strings. Your leave is as good as signed already."

"Maybe we can meet some girls?" I suggested.

Raphael frowned. "We don't need any women. They're just whores, anyway."

● ● ●

Two days later, Raphael approached me again. "I just wanted you to know that I'm working on our leaves. You know—I was thinking—it's just Basilio and me living in our big hut. We've been talking it over, and we'd like you to move in with us."

Even though the hut was better than my tent, I was coming to realize that a little of Raphael went a very long way—Basilio, I actively disliked—there was something about his eyes...

"I don't know. Carlos and I have plenty of room now and I don't want to leave him alone—*muchas gracias, como quiera.*"

Raphael tried to persuade me. "Look here, Rodrigo, Carlos can take care of himself—think how nice it's going to be with the three of us—I'll help you move your things." He started to move toward my tent, watching if I was following. I wasn't.

"No. I'm staying with Carlos. I really don't want to move."

Raphael spun around on his heels, his eyes flashing. "What's going on between you and Carlos?"

"What?" —I didn't understand, but I was wary— "I simply don't want to move."

The fire in Raphael's eyes subsided as he gained control of himself. "Well, if I can't talk you into it, we can still be friends, can't we?"

● ● ●

I didn't see Raphael for some time but, unfortunately, as it turned out, he returned. He strode up to my tent, where I was stitching a tear in my camisa. "I need to talk to you!"

I didn't look up. "Talk."

"In private."

"Where, then?"

"Follow me," he insisted.

Dropping my work, I followed Raphael to a scrub-covered hillock, some distance outside of camp. As we walked Raphael chattered amiably, "As soon as I saw you, I knew that I liked you. I've never seen anybody quite like you. Your scars don't repel me, at all, especially the way that they fade into the white slash of your hair. That, along with the blue of your eyes and your tanned face, makes you the most striking looking fellow I've ever seen." Raphael placed his arm around my shoulder in a comradely fashion. "You're just lucky that Gustavo didn't get to you first–he's such a pig." He led me into a shallow arroyo surrounded by thick brush, then stopped. "This is the place I was looking for–plenty of privacy here."

"What's going on, anyway?"

"Nothing at all. I just wanted to let you know how fond I am of you. That's all." Raphael looked me up and down. "We are going to be such close friends." He stepped closer, putting one hand on my shoulder, drawing me close. His other hand clutched at my groin. Disgusted, I thrust him away.

He stood there, smiling. "I can see that you are a little confused–funny–Basilio wasn't reluctant at all." From nowhere he produced a whip-like cord, two-thirds the length of a man. His wrist moved slightly and I felt a shocking blow across my left cheek. Immediately there came blinding blows to my head, neck and chest. I turned to run but was brought down by a series of powerful blows to my legs.

"I know this may be unpleasant," Raphael said, "but it's only for your own good. Later, after we have become even better friends, you are going to thank me. They always do." The whip flickered over my body, again and again, ripping my clothing and my skin.

Failing to escape, I begged for mercy.

"Keep your voice down," Raphael ordered. "We don't need company."

I pleaded for him to stop.

"Not quite yet," Raphael replied, sweetly. "You need to learn obedience first." Raphael handled the whip like an artist.

My flesh twitched with each blow. "Anything–anything you want."

Raphael aimed several better directed strokes. "Yes, I think you will. I want you to take off your boots and your stockings," Raphael's voice was husky and he said, "and then your pantolones. Now!"

Shaking with pain, I took off one boot while, simultaneously, Raphael dropped his own trousers to his ankles–his excitement was grossly obvious. I slid my hand down my leg and started to pull off the other boot. My right hand closed around the hilt of the hidden dagger. In one motion, I threw my boot at Raphael and launched myself in his direction. Raphael, cat-like, jumped back, avoiding my thrust by a fraction but tripped on his fallen trousers and fell backward, directly into a thorn bush. He tried to escape, but the thorns held him in a vice-like grip. His efforts only succeeded in entangling him further. I watched his struggles for a moment and then reversed the dagger so that the sharpened edge of the blade was up.

"God, no!" he screamed. "Don't do it!" He let out a terrified screech as I struck him low in the stomach, slashing up at the same time. His bowels flopped out into the dirt and his penis, like a dying weed, wilted, and shriveled.

Filled with hatred, I recited Raphael's words back to him. "I think I'll put my boots back on, if you don't mind—I wouldn't want to get any thorns in my feet." Raphael clutched helplessly at his intestines as his life's blood ran down his bare legs.

"Later, you'll thank me for this." I said observing the tears in my shirt. "It's a dirty shame about my shirt, though."

"Help me," Raphael whimpered, "Help me."

"Maybe if you pull your boots off." I wiped the blood off my knife in the dirt. "No, I can see that won't be enough. Don't worry, though, I think that help is on its way." I could hear the sound of feet and brush breaking. "Over here!" I cried, "Over here!"

Burgos, Castilla-León

"Really, Obispo de la Peña, I think you could have saved me from this disgusting episode. I can understand your anger but, once Raphael was tangled in the brush, you had all of the advantage. You committed murder."

The Bishop held Mendoza's gaze and shrugged. "Technically, you're right, of course but, then again, some people need killing. Let's call it justifiable murder and leave it at that. Besides, if I had let Raphael live, he would have lied about what really happened, and I would have been twice his victim. As it was, I still had some difficulty talking my way out of it, but when I showed the evidence of Raphael's beating on my skin, my Captain believed me—I suspect he already knew a lot about Raphael, anyway. As a matter of fact, the whole incident rather increased my standing amongst the other soldiers. On the other hand, it's strange how an image will stick in your mind. I can still remember Raphael impaled on that thorn tree and—except for his dangling guts—thinking how much he looked like the tortured Christ on the Cross." The old man lifted his eyes skyward and quipped in Latin, "As they say, "*per aspera ad astra*—through the thorns to the stars."

I went to Raphael's hut to have a talk with Basilio. I could see that he had been weeping.

"I thought it best that I have a little discussion with you, Basilio, considering how close you and Raphael were."

Basilio's eyes said it all.

I squatted down in front of him and started to doodle in the earth with my knife. "I'm concerned about you, Basilio. It occurs to me that your living in this great big hut all by yourself is going to be hard on you. On the other hand, Carlos and I are living in a tent that is too small for two people." I made a few scratches in the soil to give my words time to sink in. "I propose that we trade residences." I looked up from my work in the dirt and looked Basilio directly in the eyes. "As a matter of fact—I insist on it. You have one hour to get your things out."

"*Pinche cabrón.*"

I brushed his comment aside with a wave of my hand. "No thanks are necessary, Basilio." I started working on the dirt, again. "By the way, I just wanted you to know. If I should happen to have an accident, Carlos has promised to kill you.

Burgos, Castilla-León

"That will be enough for our first day, Padre Mendoza."

Mendoza looked unhappy. "Will I be given decent quarters or will you force me to stay in that cubicle where I spent my last night? It was so small that I couldn't lie out straight and I was tormented by the sounds of scurrying rodents. The odor was appalling."

"You were, however, given the opportunity to bathe and put on your vestments..."

"Yes, but another night like the last and I fear I must die."

"A comfortable apartment has been prepared for you," said the old man.

"A cell."

"Yes, Padre, but such a lovely cell."

Chapter 10

Burgos, Castilla-León
January 16, 1581 8 A.M.

"I trust you're refreshed, Padre?"

"As refreshed as anyone in a dungeon can be."

Two days had passed since their last meeting and, Padre Mendoza, clad in spotless vestments, did indeed look refreshed. The old Bishop sat bareheaded facing the younger priest. His white robes and the silver crucifix only served to make him look more deathlike.

"You're unhappy with your accommodations? I'm distressed. I've gone to great expense to make things comfortable for you. After all, you must admit that the rooms are large and airy."

"They are cold and dank. I'm starting to develop the grippe." Mendoza forced a cough.

"Terrible, Padre. I'll see what I can do but I've already given you the best that I have. Your cell is the same one that the infamous caliph, Abu bin-Medina, was housed prior to his immolation."

"I'm honored."

"I'll see what more I can do." The old man rubbed his forehead. "I sincerely thought you would be pleased to have your own desk, bed and chest of clothes. Have we not brought your cats to you?"

"Yes, Obispo, but I fear for their health, too."

The old man clucked in a parody of sympathy.

"The stone floor is, no doubt, cold. I'll have carpets brought in. After all, I wouldn't want anything to happen to your cats."

"I'm so grateful, Excelencia."

"I'm sure you're hungry, Padre." The old man turned his attention to a pewter cauldron to one side of the table. He lifted the lid and ladled its contents into a brightly painted bowl. "Would you, perhaps, enjoy some caldo?"

"What kind?"

"*Estómago con maíz.*"

"Tripe? Are you determined to kill me?"

The Bishop, without looking up, chuckled. "Now, we wouldn't want that, would we. I recommend that you try some of the stew. I became accustomed to it during my time with the Indios."

The smell from the bowl was rich but Mendoza was suspicious. "How is it prepared?"

"I was fortunate to acquire a Mexican housekeeper from *la Provincia de Oaxaca*. She, of course, knows all of the ingredients but I think I can get close. First it is necessary to cut cubes from the stomach of la vacca."

"But the Mexicans had no cattle."

"True. They used deer—ciervos—but cattle are an adequate substitute. Then it is necessary to add chopped chiles, ajos y cebollas las dos blanco y verde."

"They didn't have onions or garlic, either."

"True, we have made some modifications but I think the changes are for the better. Then you must add the kernels of maíze swollen in lime water."

"Hominy."

"That's correct. I also like to add beef shanks and pig's feet. After all these things have been added, cover with water, cook for three or four hours and season with salt." The Bishop sipped the liquid from his spoon and closed his eyes. "The result... *es muy sabroso.*"

"I would prefer roast mutton with truffles."

The old man ignored him. "My housekeeper only prepares Mexican dishes because my appetite is no longer stimulated by plain fare. I'm afraid you must eat this or nothing at all."

Mendoza's hunger overruled his good sense. "I'll try it."

"Help yourself, Padre."

Mendoza ladled the stew into a bowl and then used a silver spoon to sample the liquid. He cautiously sipped at it.

"It's rather piquant."

"That's the point, Padre."

Mendoza tasted several spoonfuls and tried pieces of meat and white tripe. "It is quite delicious when you get over the idea of the thing."

"Indeed, Padre, ...like life."

Word filtered through the army that Viceroy Cardona had made an agreement with Venecia and the Papal States against Francia and the Imperial Forces. Within days, we were ordered to march north. The rumors were that we could expect a fight when we got to our destination. The march, though long and dusty over mountainous roads, was leisurely for the army could move no faster than its supply wagons. Also, our commanders seemed to be anxious to not overtax either themselves or our soldiers with forced marches. Oftentimes we camped for days before moving on again. At the same time our speed made it possible for the multitudes of camp followers to keep up with our pace. Some of these were merchants who helped supply the army. Most, however, were women and children. Some of the women were the wives of the soldiers and helped by foraging and doing much of our cooking. Still other women were prostitutes, many of whom had traveled great distances to partake of the bonanza that was an army on the move. They plied their trade openly, setting up tents and luring men with seductive looks and lascivious gestures. Our priests preached against the use of these painted harlots but some of these holy men were their best customers.

Many of the women, however, were pitiful creatures, the flotsam of war. These were the wives and lovers of soldiers who had perished. Mixed with these were women from the towns and farms devastated by war. These women had one thing in common—desperation, for they had no one to protect or feed them. These women, though numerous, would have been even more so, if it were not for the fact that their ranks were continuously thinned by famine and disease. They survived as well as they could by cooking and mending and making themselves useful. Many tried to survive honorably, but most, by dint of their great poverty, were ultimately reduced to the status of common whores. At any one time, our camp was visited by several of these women. They were usually dressed in rags and would try to earn a few coins by cleaning our equipment, cooking and cleaning and washing our clothes. They would try to befriend us and, if they were able to find a little extra food, they would share it with us, in hopes that we would return the same favor when they were hungry.

Most of these women were cautious around the rough soldiers but, if approached with any degree of respect and a little food or money, were willing to share their affections. This was not true of all of them, though. I remember one girl in particular. She was little more than a child and her ragged dress hung in tatters to her ankles. She was pretty in her own way, waifishly thin with large eyes set in a round little face. She had beautiful black hair, brushed smooth and hanging to her waist. She was more shy than the others and the soldiers' efforts at familiarity were always gently rebuffed. While she was working around the camp I noticed that she would look up at me but glanced away if I tried to look back. Ashamed, I thought that she might be staring at me because of my scars. Even so, I tried to build up enough courage to speak some common pleasantry to her and even practiced my words so that they would come out right. My courage failed me, though, and I continued to admire her longingly from a distance.

Burgos, Castilla-León

Mendoza came to attention, indignation written on his face.

"I hope my story isn't distressing you, Padre? I wouldn't want to offend you, would I? I realize, though, how much the normal attraction of a man for a woman must disgust you. It must disgust you almost as much as your misuse of small boys disgusts me."

"Who has told you these lies?" Mendoza dropped his plume and started to stand.

"Sit down immediately!" The Bishop raised his voice. "I know all about you—everyone knows—it's common knowledge. Until now, there have been only whispers because you have been protected by the Church and the Holy Office."

Mendoza knew of the rumors that floated around him. "Lies, only lies, repeated by my enemies! Did not Jesus say, 'Suffer little children, come unto me.' I've only obeyed this admonition. I desire only to love and protect children. Can I help it if my actions have been misinterpreted?"

"Lies? Of course they must be lies. Holy Mother Church would never condone such abject perversity, would it? Would it?" The old man stopped and breathed deeply a few times. His voice dropped an octave. "Now let us continue."

My fear increased as we marched north. Some of the older soldiers seemed to take pleasure in frightening Carlos and me with tales of previous battles. They gleefully told us of the remorseless advance of the Swiss and Landsknechte pikemen, of the skill of the French swordsmen, and the horror of the enemy cannonade. Worst of all, it seemed to me, were their stories about the terror of an attack by heavy cavalry, armored automatons bereft of mercy. My fear was heightened by rumors of enemy scouting parties. They were reportedly light cavalry that disappeared like the mist when countered by our skirmishers.

●●●

The day finally came when we were ordered to form up in preparation for a battle. We marched in column through a forest and then entered a fertile plain. Through the heat waves we could see a walled town in the distance. Although I couldn't see much from my position in the rear ranks, there were whisperings that a mixed force of Italian mercenaries and Frenchmen were marshaled against us, not too far away.

There were shouted orders and, just like in training, our column moved to the left and right and became a line, four men deep. I was two men back from the front line but, through the space between the soldiers to my front, I could see the enemy's line but four hundred paces away. There were fluttering flags, bristling pikes and soldiers in gaily-colored uniforms all drawn up for battle exactly as we were. With relief, I heard that our line over-lapped them on both flanks—we outnumbered them by more than two to one.

For several minutes all was still and then, with a roll of drums, we drew our weapons and advanced in cadence. We reduced the distance to the enemy line by half when, suddenly, there were tremendous explosions from the direction of the enemy line. Cannon balls whistled overhead and one skipped along the ground and plowed into our line. I couldn't see exactly what had happened but judging by the screams, we had taken our first casualties.

"*Adelante! Paso redoblado!*" The order rang out and we picked up our pace to a jog. There were more detonations to our front as the enemy musketeers opened fire. The man in front of me collapsed. I nearly tripped but was able to leap over his body. Then, the front line collided with the enemy like a hammer on an anvil. Shields, swords and pikes clanged together as musketeers and crossbowmen fired their weapons between the gaps in our ranks. I was almost deafened when an arquebus went off in my ear. Then, almost before it began, it was over. The enemy's front collapsed and enemy soldiers were fleeing across the field faster than we could follow. From our right flank, light cavalry appeared, pursuing the routed enemy. French cavalry countered them briefly but they, in their turn, were defeated and fled. After that, all I could see was dust in the distance, as the enemy fled and the light horse pursued.

We were ordered to continue our advance. Our lines parted, so as to avoid stepping on the few dead and wounded. Our advance continued to within three hundred paces of the town. We were ordered to halt. Our commander shouted our demands in Italian. After a time, a voice replied from the enemy wall. I didn't know what had been said but, even though I didn't have much of a view, I could see that a table and several chairs were being set up between the wall and our army. Captains from both sides seated themselves and engaged in animated conversation. This went on for fifteen minutes or so—longer than the time taken for the entire battle. Then I saw that the officers were signing papers.

The enemy Captains reentered the town and, minutes later, the gates opened and the entire enemy force marched out in column and marched away to the north, its banners fluttering proudly. A garrisoning force was then split off from our army, and ordered into the town. I, along with the rest of the army, was ordered to return to our encampment. I must admit to some bewilderment for, as I realized, I had become a veteran without doing a thing. As a matter of fact, I hadn't even seen very much. The casualties on both sides had been trivial. I was almost disappointed. Almost.

●●●

Back at the bivouac, I looked for Carlos, wanting to find out what he had seen of the battle. I couldn't find him so I eased the tension by discussing the events with the more experienced soldiers.

I told them that I hadn't expected the fight to go so easily. They surprised me by telling me that most of their battles were similar. Sometimes the opposing armies wouldn't even fight. Negotiations led to the bloodless retreat of one side or the other. It was not unheard of for regiments or even entire armies to—when offered enough money—to switch sides. On only rare occasions would there be an all-out, killing battle. Remembering what these same soldiers had told me before the battle, I realized that they had played me for a fool.

We lined up for afternoon roll call—five men were absent. Two men were known wounded, another one killed, all by the same cannon ball. A crossbow bolt had hit another man. The fifth was Carlos. Several men said they'd seen him go down, but didn't know if he was dead or wounded. Shocked, I asked the lieutenant for permission to retrace our route to see if I could find him.

Permission was granted. I was given the password and told to be watchful of enemy horsemen. I retraced our march as quickly as possible, because it was late and the shadows were lengthening. I reached the plain just before sunset. The sky was on fire, lending a ruddy hue to the battlefield. I looked for Carlos among the scattered debris. It took me awhile but I found him partially hidden by a small bush. He was on his side, his knees slightly drawn up. His eyes were half open and there was a trace of blood was on his lips. I called out and he did not stir. I touched his hand but it was already cold.

As gently as possible, I moved his body to look for his wound. I found it quickly enough. There was a bloody round hole in his armor. The hole was in his back and the metal of the armor had been punched inward. From the position of his body, however, I could tell that he had died facing the enemy. I pondered on the mystery but the answer came to me soon enough—Basilio was an arquebusier and served in the same part of the line that Carlos had served. My hatred overwhelmed my sorrow.

To lighten the body, I removed and hid his armor and weapons. Carlos wasn't a small man so it was with great difficulty that I partially dragged and carried his body back to our bivouac point. Three times I had to call out the password as nervous guards challenged me in the dark.

"*Quien vive?*"

"Rodrigo de la Peña. Yo soy de la compañia de Jefe Rangel."
"Contraseña?"
"San Telmo."
"Pase, soldado."

• • •

On my return I was hailed by one of our veterans, Paco Migues. He was a man in his thirties and had pale red hair and amber eyes. He was short but with a powerful physique—a born soldier.

"Are you hit?" Migues was seated next to a fire and could see that I was covered with blood.

Exhausted and panting, I waited a moment to reply. "No, but Carlos here has been killed."

"Too bad." Migues and a couple of others got up to look at the body. "Where did he get it?"

I rolled the corpse over and pointed to the wound in the middle of its back.

"Get a torch," Migues ordered. "I want to get a look at this."

A torch was produced and, in the flickering light, Migues probed the wound with his index finger. "A musket ball broke his backbone. He'd have gone down as if pole-axed."

"He was my friend," I said.

"El mucho al hoyo le vivo al bollo," he said. "Get over it."

"He went down facing the enemy," I said, bitterly.

Migues digested this information and shrugged his shoulders, "Accidents happen..."

"Carlos was murdered."

Chapter 11

"De la Peña says you shot Carlos in the back."

After the night's previous questioning, I had dug a cold grave for my friend. Now it was morning and Rangel had ordered the company together.

"He's a liar and a coward," Basilio spat.

Our Captain regarded Basilio with contempt. "You were posted to the rear, close to and behind Carlos."

Rangel knew of the bad blood that existed between Basilio and the two of us—he was as suspicious as I was.

"I never had a chance to fire my weapon."

"I find that interesting, Señor Valle, in that you were supposed to be shooting at the enemy."

"Check my weapon, then," Basilio snarled, "you'll find it's clean."

"I have no doubt that it is, *desgraciado*." Rangel looked around, "Did anyone see Basilio fire his musket?"

No one replied.

"You're lucky, Señor Valle—nobody actually saw you shoot Carlos." Rangel's sunburned face was a mixture of disbelief and disgust. "Therefore, I am unable to file charges against you. On the other hand, you have presented me with a problem. Sooner or later, you will kill Señor de la Peña or de la Peña will kill you. I will then be forced to punish the killer and my company will have lost two men. I could transfer one of you to another company but that won't solve the problem. Sooner or later, there will be murder." Rangel paced back and forth, giving himself time to think.

He stopped in front of me and looked me directly in the face. "Dueling is against army regulations—technically speaking, of course."

The Captain, without dismissing the company, did an about-face and deliberately walked away.

I owed Carlos a death. I didn't stop to think as I stepped out of line and faced my enemy. "*Basilio, tú eres pinche puto cobarde. You will give me satisfaction.*"

I don't know what reaction I expected but, considering the fact that Basilio had shot my friend in the back, I probably expected a display of public cowardice. I was surprised by Basilio's defiance.

"Rodrigo has insulted me and placed his challenge. I accept and, as the challenged party, I have the right to my choice of weapons—I choose mosquetes at ten paces. I also get to choose the place and time. The place is just outside of camp." He pointed to the east, "The time is as soon as the weapons are loaded."

Basilio was an expert arquebusier. I had only loaded and fired this weapon twice during training. Also, he was giving me no time for even rudimentary practice.

"I agree."

●●●

Paco Migues assigned himself the role of duel-master and also appointed two seconds. Because of my inexperience, Migues gave me the more useful of the two. His name was Pedro Garza, the much-wounded veteran of many battles. He was the leader of the mosqueteros and despised Basilio Valle.

I was given first choice of, what to me, appeared to be two identical weapons.

"Take that one, the one on the left," Garza ordered.

Garza shouted a request to Migues. "We'd like to test fire the weapon."

"No one is to touch the muskets except for the combatants," Migues said.

"Request denied."

Garza shrugged and turned back to me. Both Basilio and I were presented with a bag containing coarse black powder. Using a short copper tube, Basilio confidently ladled powder down the muzzle of his weapon. Garza gave me a similar tube.

"Make sure you fill it and don't lose any on the ground," he said.

My right hand trembled as I scooped up the powder. I had to steady my wrist with my left hand but I lost no powder as I poured it down the barrel. Basilio was amused.

"Tap the butt of the musket on the ground, four or five times," Garza instructed. "A little harder—that's right. We want to make sure that the powder makes it all the way to the back of the chamber."

I banged the butt of the weapon on the ground. Basilio rolled his eyes. I noticed that he didn't duplicate my action. Instead, he placed a lead ball in his mouth and spit it down the muzzle. He then tapped the butt of the gun against the ground. He didn't bother with a ramrod.

Garza was more cautious. He opened a leather pouch that hung at his side. "Here's the ball and the patch. It's already been greased." He then showed me how I must wrap the ball in the patch of greased cloth and seat it in the muzzle with the palm of my hand. When covered by the patch the fit was so tight that the ball merely rested on the muzzle.

"That's right," he told me. "Now, use this to push it down a little." He handed me a T-shaped piece of wood. One side of the 'T' fit my palm. The opposite end fit the muzzle. I pushed the ball down as far as I could—a finger's length.

"Push it down the rest of the way with the ramrod," Garza said. "Make sure the ball is all the way down and in contact with the powder. If you leave a space the gun can explode."

It was a very tight fit and it was with effort that I pushed the ball down until it would go no farther.

Basilio had already finished his preparations. "Hurry up with it! I don't want to wait all day to kill you, de la Peña."

Garza produced a needle from the pouch. "We don't know when the musket was cleaned. Push this through the touchhole into the chamber. Work it around to clean out any burnt powder that might have been left behind from its last firing."

I did as I was instructed and pushed the needle through the fire-hole and worked it around vigorously.

"This is powder that I've ground especially fine so that it goes off quickly," Garza opened a small pouch that contained dust-like black powder and said, "fill the touchhole with it."

I filled it to overflowing.

"You're ready now. Point straight. You've got just as good a chance as he has."

I knew that Garza was lying.

Migues lit the fuses of both weapons. The fuses smoked and glowed with evil light.

The distance was already marked off. Basilio and I were to be separated by ten short paces—I could smell my own sweat. As the other soldiers stood in the background, Migues announced the rules.

"You will stand facing one another. When I drop my sword, you may raise your muskets and fire. I will personally kill the man who raises his weapon before the drop. If the first man misses, he must stand the fire of his opponent. If he flees, I'll kill him. If both miss, or both weapons misfire, the process will be repeated until one man is dead or so wounded that he can't continue."

Migues drew his sword as we two combatants took our positions. My body trembled as I looked Basilio in the eye—he was grinning.

"This is in repayment for Raphael, cabrón."

Migues lifted his sword tip up and slashed it down.

Basilio was fast and snapped his weapon to his hip before I could think to move.

His primer ignited with a flash and a puff of smoke. I waited for death....nothing...nothing...nothing...misfire!

Basilio's smile turned into a grimace as I lifted the heavy weapon to my shoulder and carefully sighted along its barrel. Basilio, knowing what the penalty for running would be, tried to stand resolutely.

Time stood still. I pulled the lever toward the stock, the serpentine with its smoking fuse touched the powder. The primer flashed, Basilio flinched—and—nothing happened.

Basilio started to smile.

"Whap!" I was pushed back as my musket discharged. Everything was obscured by smoke. As it cleared, I could see the result of my shot. Basilio lay on his back, a hole where his nose had been. The back of his head was missing as blood seeped into the underlying soil. Pieces of skull and gray-pink brain were scattered for five paces behind the body.

Pedro Garza spoke to me, pointing with his chin toward the newly deceased Basilio. "This is what comes from taking shortcuts."

Burgos, Castilla-León

"So you had your revenge," Mendoza commented, "But perhaps if you hadn't dealt so harshly with Basilio, neither Carlos nor Basilio need have died."

The Bishop thought about it a few seconds before responding. "I'm afraid you're wrong. In some twisted way, Basilio was as attached to Raphael as a dutiful wife is to her husband." —Mendoza blinked, which brought a smile to the old man's lips— "I trust you're not offended, Padre?

After Raphael's death, my only chance of surviving Basilio's anger was to frighten him into inaction. I erred in that I never considered the possibility that he would shoot one of us in the back. If I had, I would have cut his throat that first night." The old man continued as if speaking to himself. "My survival was not due to any skill on my part. I survived the duel by luck and luck, alone. First,

Basilio's weapon misfired and second...I aimed for the middle of the puto's stomach. Even at ten paces, the arquebus is not accurate. My ball through his face was simply...an act of God," he said as the ancient Bishop's face shone with a malevolent light.

Afterwards, our Jefe gave me a reprimand in front of the company. "You have demonstrated your courage, de la Peña but, thus far, you have proved yourself to be more dangerous to our company than you are to the enemy. You are innocent of any crime but you've managed to deprive us of the use of soldiers valuable to the army. In the future to you must fight for three men. Do you understand?"

Chapter 12

I missed the comradeship of my friend, Carlos, but the activity of the camp, along with routine drills helped to divert my mind. One evening, while I was concentrating on polishing some rust off my armor, I was surprised by the sound of a voice in my ear.

"I would gladly do that for you, señor." The Spanish was awkward but the voice was soft and musical. It was the girl that I had so long admired but had been afraid to speak to.

"It isn't necessary," I stammered. "I'm almost finished—maybe some other time." A shadow passed over her lovely face.

Thinking fast, I continued, "On the other hand, my boots are muddy and perhaps..."

"I would be happy to, señor!" She waited expectantly as I removed my worn boots. She took them both and, as I polished my armor, she squatted down beside me and scraped the dried mud off with a stick. She glanced up at my face. "You've been wounded in battle?"

"Mis cicatrices?" I pointed to my scars. "No, they are from an accident at home."

"And your home, señor? Do you have a large family? Do you have a sweetheart? Have you been in the army long?"

"No, I'm an orphan and I've never had a sweetheart. I've been in the army for less than a year. You?"

"I'm an orphan, too, Sir. My parents died of the plague when I was little."

"I'm sorry about your parents but I can see they trained you well. You're very polite but I'm not much older than you are, so you don't need to call me 'Sir'. My name is Rodrigo—Rodrigo de la Peña. What's your name and why are you here with the army?"

"My name is Angela." Her dark eyes clouded over. "I had a sweetheart. Perhaps you knew him. He was a soldier here—his name was Francisco Malvina. We met in my hometown of Padua and I went away with him. We were to marry as soon as he could get enough money. Later we were to go to his home in Andalucia, where I could meet his family and we would live on their farm."

"Where is he now?"

"He was captured by the French." She averted her gaze. "They hanged him along with the others." She crossed herself and was silent for a long time before she went on. "I would be glad to help you again. I won't ask for anything but sometimes I get a little hungry..."

Any of the other soldiers would have been glad to share his bowl with Angela but I'm sure I was the first one that she ever approached. Perhaps she was desperate and thought that I, despite or possibly because of my scarred face, would do her a kindness. My heart melted.

"Sometimes even we soldiers don't have enough to eat but that which I have I'll gladly share with you."

"Oh, thank you, señor! I'm ever so grateful. I'll be here in the morning. I will find some oil and do a proper job on your boots. I'll do your belt and your straps, too!"

That night we sat by the fire, a little distance from the other soldiers. Some smiled as I shared my soup and stewed mutton with her. She tried to pretend that she wasn't famished but her body trembled as she stared at the food. I could sense her struggle as she forced herself to eat slowly. I saw to it that she ate almost all of my food. My body went to bed empty that night, but my soul was full.

●●●

Angela was there bright and early in the morning. She had indeed managed to find some oil and worked on my boots until the leather was soft and supple. Then, without a word, she worked on my other leather things until they were in a similar condition—I saw to it that she had enough to eat. Every day she came looking for me and busied herself doing whatever she could to help me. Sometime her help would extend to all of the soldiers in my mess and she became our regular cook. When the other soldiers weren't near, we loved to talk. We told each other our stories although, I never told her what had actually happened to my family. I told her that they had died of the plague, just like her family.

Mendoza interrupted. "Why would you be unwilling to tell the girl the fate of your family?"

"It's because the Holy Office is almost as respected and as powerful in Italy as it is here in Spain. Angela was a lovely person but she was unsophisticated. I was afraid that she might feel that any condemnation leveled by the Church, must be justified. Besides, I barely knew the girl. I reckoned that there would be plenty of opportunity to tell her the truth should our friendship ripen."

Chapter 13

Again, the army was on the move. The French, under Gaston de Foix—along with Imperial forces—were laying siege to the Papal city of Ravenna. Our companies marched northeast, along the right bank of the Rio Ronco. We halted one league short of Ravenna and, along with other Spanish and Papal troops, established a fortified camp, complete with entrenchments and bastions. Pope Leo's force of thousands of Italian troops made up our left wing. They filled in the gap between the river and our entrenchments. Pescara's light horse was bivouacked on our right.

I'd never before seen so many soldiers gathered together in one place. I was told that our entire force totaled at least fourteen thousand infanterías and caballeros along with an impressive number of artillery pieces. Clearly, our Commandante Cardona was not only expecting a battle, he was expecting a big battle. Having never before seen such an array of power, I knew we should easily prevail. Nevertheless, I was also relieved when our Captain announced, in the event of fight, we'd be held back with other reserve companies.

●●●

Word filtered through the ranks that a large force of the enemy had crossed the Ronco and that we should expect a fight—I remember that it was Easter day, 1512. There had been several indecisive cavalry skirmishes when we started to receive the occasional cannon round from the direction of the enemy lines. Our artillery, emplaced to our front, took up the challenge. Over the hours, the tempo of shelling increased but the damage to our side was minimal because we soldados had been ordered to lay down behind our parapets. Most cannonballs passed harmlessly overhead. Also, spring rains had softened the ground and, those cannonballs that struck nearby, buried themselves on impact. Nevertheless, the whine of cannon balls whistling through the air and pounding into the soil was terrible indeed.

Then, everything changed for the worse. On our right, there were the explosions of nearby cannons. Their balls came in low, through our unprotected side and plowed into our packed ranks. Some of the soldiers stood up to flee but our officers shouted for us to hold our position. We did. I flattened myself as much as I could and grasped the soil with my fingers. Twice, I was bounced into the air by the strike of a nearby round but, on returning to Mother Earth, I clutched her with even more love than I had previously. I don't know how long this went on—a lifetime.

Through the din of the cannonade, and to the left and to our front, I heard screams, shouts and cheers from thousands of voices. Later, I learned that our Italians had been unable to stand the fire and had been driven into the plain to their front in a disorganized mob. Imperial Landsknechte and the French gendarmes slaughtered them. Although we didn't know it yet, we Españoles had been outflanked to our left and our right. Now, to add to our misery, musket balls and iron crossbow bolts ripped into us.

"Prepare!" The order echoed up and down our lines. I got to my knees in readiness for the attack, as did my comrades to my left and my right. Something clanged into the armor of the man on my left. From nowhere the fletched end of a crossbow bolt was protruding from his chest. The soldier, who was merely a boy, turned to me with a piteous look as bright blood bubbled from his lips.

"*Listos!*" All of us tensed for the assault.

"*Adelante!*" The ranks to my front, rose out of the ground and started to clamber over the parapets and bulwarks to their front. My company rose as one and drove forward.

"*Paso redoblado! Muy pronto!*" We picked up our pace and, despite withering fire, we made our way over and through the obstructions. We entered a plain, hazy with sulfurous gun smoke. Although we hadn't seen a single enemy, we charged forward, drawing our swords. At first, all I could see was the backs of our advancing men but then, to my left and front, I could see a forest of pikes, some vertical and others oblique. Landsknechte were driving the routed Italians like stampeding cattle.

Our front ranks collided with French infantry but instantly overran them, opening a hole in the French ranks that my company penetrated. We hit the Landsknechte formation in the flank before their rear ranks could lower their pikes. The Germans regarded armor as cowardly—we shattered their force and killed them like dogs. I personally killed two before they knew I was on them. After all these years, I still remember that one of them wore a black top hat and another a blue coat with silver buttons.

Our company had been in the reserve but now, almost accidentally, we were the leading edge of battle. Any knots of enemy resistance, we overcame. Terrified Frenchmen and Germans fled the battlefield in total rout—or—so I thought.

"*Retirarse!*" It must be a mistake. We must advance, not retreat.

"*Retirarse! Retirarse!*" Our Jefe had taken up the order and, with his blood-smeared sword, was motioning us back toward our trenches. Confused, we reversed our direction. It was only then that I saw disaster looming. French heavy cavalry had broken into our rear. Some of these were riding our men down with their lances and others were slashing with their swords and axes. Avoiding these horsemen as well as we could, we ran back to our entrenchments even faster than we'd advanced.

After this it became a slogging infantry battle, French infantry against our infanterias and German pikemen against our lanzas. Slowly, slowly we were forced back by the enemy's superior numbers.

"*Corre!* The enemy has flanked us! *Corren por sus vidas!*"

But I couldn't run, as ordered. I was engaged with two French swordsmen and, without exposing my back, I couldn't retire. Realizing that I was abandoned, I thrust at one grim-faced Frenchman who was missing most of his teeth. Bebidor and I became one creature.

The point of my blade missed gap-tooth's shield and caught him under the arm. He fell back mortally wounded. Realizing that I would soon be surrounded I backed up as quickly as I could, while countering the strokes of my second opponent. I let my shield fall a little low but, when he slashed at my head, he over-committed and exposed himself. Bebidor sliced through the sinews of his forearm—his sword fell from his grip. I turned and ran, expecting a blade between my shoulders. I stumbled over the broken ground and tripped over mutilated bodies but I ran as I'd never run before in my life.

I don't know how far I ran but I didn't slow down until I knew that I had far outdistanced the enemy. I caught up with two hundred or more of our infantry who, along with ten or so musketeers, had formed a line to slow down the enemy's advance and to protect the retreat of our forces. Gasping and exhausted, I joined our line and faced the direction from which the enemy must approach.

My blood turned to ice as I saw horsemen appear to the front of us. Up to that point in my life, it was the most terrible sight I had seen. There were fifty French gendarmes, mounted on powerful warhorses. The horses had been matched for size and color and each was as black as the pit. The knights were clad, head to foot, in burnished and blackened armor. The feathered plumes in their helmets were black as was the armor on their horses. Each knight carried a thick wooden lance. The iron tips of most of these lances dripped with blood and their armor glowed red in the setting sun. To me, they were the triumphant forces of Hell at the last battle of Armegeddon.

The knights wheeled their mounts and came at us at a gallop. Their lances, which had been held high, were lowered to take us at chest level. The mosquetes exploded just as the enemy struck our line. I jumped aside as a lance grazed my helmet, almost knocking me down. The horsemen drove completely through our line either killing my comrades on the spot or scattering them like so many partridges. The horsemen rode on in grim pursuit—once more I was alone.

One huge knight, however, reared his horse and came back at me at a gallop, leaning out over his horse and aiming along his lance—I didn't have time to pray. I dodged as his lance caught the edge of my shield. The shield was wrenched out of my grip and, spinning, flew out of my reach. The horseman, frustrated, wheeled his horse again and tried to ride me down. Dodging, I made a two-handed swing with Bebidor but, striking only armor, it sprang from my hands. Skillfully, the knight wheeled his horse once again—I lifted the axe from my belt.

He charged down on me. The lance tip scarcely a hand's breadth away, I stepped to the inside, swinging up with my axe. The horse struck me hard and rode right over me. The horse stumbled and almost went down but kept on its feet. I was knocked onto my back. I couldn't catch my breath, and I felt as if something inside me had broken. No matter, my doom was upon me.

Laughing, the knight reared his charger again and started to trot forward, the tip of his lance pointed directly at me. From high on the horse's neck, bright blood squirted, painting a red swath on the earth. The horseman, with his eyes fixed on me through his visor, didn't know that his horse had been wounded. Wildly cursing, he spurred the dying animal. The horse slowed to a stop, stood there for seconds and then—collapsed. The knight tried to jump free. He almost made it but, weighed down by his armor, he couldn't move fast enough. The dead horse rolled, trapping the knight's left leg under its body.

I staggered to my feet. The knight, struggling to free his leg, managed to draw his sword.

After having been terrorized by this man, I wasn't feeling merciful. On the other hand, a high-ranking hostage was safe passage to my lines.

Not knowing the French word for "Yield," I called out, "*Rendirse, señor!*"

"*Au Diable!*" The nobleman screamed his refusal. I raised my axe. It was no more difficult than killing a chicken.

Somehow, I limped back to the lines of our defeated army. It wasn't until much later that I learned that the French commander, Gaston de Foix, while pursuing our retreating forces on his black charger, had been killed—I've always wondered.

Burgos, Castilla-León

"You did say that you wanted a productive dialogue, Obispo."

"That's true, Padre Mendoza. I invite your comments."

"You've just recounted another example of your unnecessary lethality. The battle was lost and your opponent was trapped and helpless. His death only added to the sum tragedy of the carnage. Not only that but, in indulging your anger, you exposed yourself to the danger of the imminent return of his comrades. Why didn't you simply—run away?"

The Bishop took a very deep breath. "It is because, despite the verdict against my family, I am an hidalgo. This mounted knight, in his arrogance and despite his advantage, never afforded me the courtesy due to my rank—he never gave me the opportunity to yield."

"But he couldn't have known that, could he? To him you were just another soldier—another peasant."

"That's quite correct, Padre."

That night, as I limped into our hastily fortified encampment, I heard a woman's voice. She was questioning other stragglers as they filtered back into our lines.

"Have you seen him? Have you seen Rodrigo de la Peña? You can't miss him. He has a shock of white hair and white in his beard. Have you seen him?"

"*Si, señorita,*" a soldier answered. Even though the voice was weary, I could tell it was Migues, "The last time I saw him, he was surrounded by the French. After that..."

In the light of the half-moon, I could see the shimmering outline of a woman as insubstantial as a ghost. She was wringing her hands and looking up the road from which the last remnants of our defeated army were shuffling along. As I limped closer, I could see that she was weeping. She didn't recognize me.

"Have you seen Rodrigo de la Peña? You can't..."

"I'm here, Angela."

There was a moment of silence as she tried to make out my features in the dark. "Rodrigo?" she queried in disbelief, "*Rodrigo de la Peña?*"

"Yes, Angela. It's me."

She could see me better as I approached within a few feet. "Ay, *Gracias a Dios!*" She dropped to her knees in prayer while crossing herself. "Thank you, Lord, for your mercy."

"It's going to be all right, Angela." I paused for breath. "Do you think you could find me some water?"

"I'll get you some right away but let's first get you back into camp." For the first time she noticed my filth and the way I was carrying my body. "Oh, Rodrigo! You're wounded. What must I do to help you? I'll do anything, anything at all!" Her voice, which had been full of relief, switched to something like panic.

Waiting for me in the dark, as the carts of dead and wounded had rumbled through, Angela had known more terror than anything I felt on the battlefield.

"Don't worry," I said as soothingly as I could. "I'm not wounded. I'm only tired and a little bruised. I need a good night's rest ... If you'd like to help me, let me lean on you a little, because my leg is a little sore." I put my arm around her shoulders and she used all of her strength to support me until we found where the pitiful remnants of my company were encamped.

I let myself slide to the ground.

"Don't go anywhere—I'll get some water." Angela disappeared into the dark. I looked around me and could see that there was the occasional tent but most of the men were either sitting or lying on the bare ground without any shelter. Some were silent, others moaned from their wounds.

From nowhere, Angela reappeared carrying a skin full of water. It was filthy, but I drank until I choked.

"Drink more slowly, Rodrigo." Her voice was gentle. "I can get more." She helped me out of my armor and started to undo the loops of my blouse. "You're soaked. I have an extra blanket to wrap you in while I'm washing your clothes."

I stopped her. I doubted that Angela had an extra blanket.

"Why do I need your blanket, Angela? What's happened to our tents and bedding?"

Angela hesitated, perhaps fearing my reaction. "Gone. While we were moving camps, cavalry raided our supply train. What they didn't steal, they burned. They say that generals Pescara and Navarro have been captured."

I digested this unpleasant information. "I'm going to be fine, Angela." I looked at the figures in the darkness. "Some of these others are in worse condition than I am. If you want to help, see what you can do for them—don't worry—I'll be perfectly all right. If you want to help, get some water for the other wounded. I'm not going to move. I promise...I only need a little...sleep..."

● ● ●

When I awoke next morning, I was covered in Angela's blanket. Two women were slicing at the nearby carcass mule, the belly of which was starting to bloat. Two other women, one of whom was a care-worn Angela, were grilling its steaks over the coals of a small fire. Our friar, Padre Seca, was working his way through the wounded men, in some cases giving comfort and, in others, last rites.

I was stiff and when I tried to raise myself, I found that I could barely move. I limped a short distance away and emptied my bladder. I was shocked to see that my water was bright red and even more shocked when the stream stopped abruptly as a excruciating pain mounted in my groin—I nearly collapsed. Suddenly, the pain disappeared as a large clot discharged itself and my bloody stream went to completion. Shaken, I stumbled back to my place on the ground.

"What's wrong, Rodrigo?" Angela's eyes were wide. "You're as white as a sheet and— just look—you're covered with sweat."

"Nothing's wrong. I just stood up a little too quickly. I'd better lie down, again."

"Yes, lie down." She still looked concerned. "I've brought you some meat. It's a little tough. I've cut it up for you. I'll even feed it to you."

"Eat it yourself. I'm not very hungry—maybe later."

● ● ●

During the next days I spent most of my time resting, while Angela tended to me as well as she could. I was still a mass of aches but my bloody water gradually turned pink and finally returned to its normal color.

"You're a sight, Rodrigo," Angela said with some humor. "You look like one solid bruise. Something big must have hit you. What was it, anyway?"

"Just a horse. If I had known how short of food the camp would be, I would have dragged it back here by his tail."

Burgos, Castilla-León

Mendoza stopped writing, a distressed look on his face. His stomach was gurgling.

"Yes, Padre."

"I don't wish to interrupt your narration, Your Grace, but if I could be provided with a chamber pot..."

The old man shrugged, "Of course, you should have mentioned it earlier. Look under the table."

Mendoza eyed the pot with distaste. It was filthy. "Perhaps a clean pot?"

"You are soft, Padre. When we were in Nueva España I squatted under the nearest cactus and wiped my ass with tree bark."

Mendoza's guts gurgled loudly again. "Excelencia, I don't wish to be importune but a little privacy..."

"Certainly, Padre. You may turn your back."

"But, your Grace..."

"Rápido, Padre! I can't wait all day."

Picking up the pot, Mendoza turned his back, adjusted his clothing and squatted down. Amused, the old man observed that Mendoza was having difficulty.

"I'm a very busy man, Padre Mendoza. Please hurry things up."

Mendoza strained without results.

"Please, Padre," the old man said, "the moments of my life are slipping away."

There was an explosive sound and a fearful odor. Unconsciously the Bishop crossed himself. "My God, Padre, the fires of Hell burn within you."

The odor grew stronger.

"Must I call a sepulturero, Padre? Surely your guts are long dead."

Incensed, Mendoza glanced over his shoulder with a menacing look. "I need something to clean myself with."

"Absolutely, Padre, as soon as you return to your cell. In the meantime put your pot near the door. I'll have the guards remove it as quickly as possible and bury its contents far from human habitation."

Mumbling to himself, Mendoza returned to his chair and seated himself very carefully. He dipped his plume in the ink and continued to take notes.

Chapter 14

After our defeat at Ravenna, the enemy probed our defenses. Our fortifications not only held but we were strengthened by reinforcements and improved supply lines.

Nevertheless, we were forced to countermarch back to Napoles. Certainly, we consoled ourselves, we would have prevailed if our Papal allies had not cut and run. That was thin gruel, for we Spaniards had lost hundreds killed and more than a thousand wounded. Even Generalissimo Navarro had been wounded and taken captive by the enemy. My company, alone, lost half its strength. Thirty of our men, including our brave Jefe, had been slain. Sixty or seventy others were wounded or captured. Unfortunately we weren't given much time to regroup. We received a new Captain by the name of Valdés.

We were heartened by the news that the Emperor Maximillian, whose Landsknechte pikemen had devastated us at Ravenna, had switched sides to ally with our forces. While I was trying to recover my strength, the combined allies pushed the French from their recent conquest of Ravenna. They then—with Germanic efficiency—systematically drove them from Verona, Bergamo, Brescia, and Padua.

●●●

During my convalescence, with nothing much to do, I entertained myself by writing poetry. I sometimes wrote poems about home and noble figures from the Spanish past. Mostly, however, I wrote sentimental doggerel about Angela. She, of course, had never learned her letters but I enjoyed watching her face as I read my poor lines to her.

The woman who launched a thousand ships
Fairer art thou, my poor heart drips
Soft is your skin and ruby your lips
Form of a Goddess, the curve of your hips
Nectar of wonder, enchanted, I sip.

Virtuous lady of the firelight
Voice sweet music in the night
Tresses raven, eyes so bright
My soul exalts at the ethereal sight
Purity and sanctity, all in white
I am thy servant, thy humble knight.

Angela's smile was sweet but tinged with...sadness? "That's so...sweet, Rodrigo. I just wish I could be all of those wonderful things to you, but I'm not and I'm so very weak. I am just a poor woman of."—she gave me a look that I'd never seen before— "flesh and blood.

She changed the subject. "I almost wish that you'd received a wound that would have kept you from battle."

I envisioned myself crippled, living in gutters. "Unfortunately, I'm not wealthy, Angela, and such a wound, if it didn't kill me outright, would probably kill me through starvation. I'll not beg."

"I'd take care of you." I looked at how small she was and knew she would have a hard time taking care of herself, let alone two people. "Please, Rodrigo, you don't have to be a soldier." —She hesitated, considering if she should continue—"I can help you. We can... You can do something else."

I could see the turmoil in her eyes, so I answered as gently as I could "You are my closest friend, Angela, but I'm a soldier. It's all I want to be."

Angela took several deep breaths. "Then you must promise me not to be brave. Do your duty but please...please, for my sake... if not for your own, try to stay out of the thick of the fighting."

●●●

Staying away from the fighting was proving difficult. Perfidious Venecia had switched allegiance and signed a treaty with the French. Viceroy Cardona had decided to punish the Venetians.

Commanded by Pescara, who had been ransomed from the French, we marched forward, encountering a mixed force of mercenaries at Vicenza. I was among the first to clash shields with the enemy.

Our numbers were nearly equal. In both opposing forces, pikemen were massed in the center with swordsmen and arquebusiers to the flanks. It was as much a pushing match as it was a pike and sword fight. Our line struggled against their line, pushing to achieve a break. My opponent was no older than I and was even less experienced. His swordsmanship was both desperate and clumsy. I found an opening and wounded him in the thigh. He staggered backward as I pushed forward to meet the enemy's second rank. The next enemy soldier slashed wildly but my single thrust avoided his sword and shield and caught him in the neck just above his armor. The wounded man clawed his way behind the enemy's third-rank. I looked around and realized I was at the leading edge of a wedge into the enemy's line of battle. Screaming, I battered my third rank opponent, at which point he turned and ran, taking members of the fourth and fifth rank with him. Suddenly I broke completely through the enemy force, followed by a dozen or more of my comrades.

We fell on the enemy from behind. Realizing that they had been flanked, the enemy, caught between our men to the front as well as our men to the rear, started to give way. At first their line gave only a little but then, just like a few stones rolling down hill starting a landslide, their entire force started to move as panic set in. What had been a dangerous fighting force turned into a mass of terrified individuals, throwing down their weapons so that they could run all the faster.

We gathered prisoners, as the cavalry rode down the panic-stricken refugees, lancing them wholesale. We camped in the field, tended the wounded, and buried our dead. The next morning we were on the march again, headed for Venecia. The next days were not noble. Aristocratic prisoners were feted and ransomed but commoners were beaten and hanged. Our big guns shelled Venice itself, as our skirmishers, meeting no opposition, torched the towns around the lagoon.

●●●

Following this action, some of our previous paymasters, satisfied with the results of their investment, stopped their delivery of monies to our Spanish commanders. Refusing to fight further, we withdrew from the lagoons around Venice, settled into our camps and tried to make the best out of a bad situation. With no money to pay for provisions, many of us were forced to forage. Even so, many of us went hungry. I did my best to provide for both Angela and myself. Angela also proved herself useful. Occasionally, she arrived with a hare or a partridge she had snared or mushrooms she had gathered in the fields. Sometimes she even came up with a chicken that she had stolen from some hapless farmer. Usually there was not enough to share with the others, so Angela and I often built a small fire for the two of us.

Despite all the time we spent together, Angela was a private person and kept some distance between us. I knew, from the things she told me, that she still loved her dead soldier. I might have wished it were otherwise but, or so I thought, that was simply the way things were and the way things must continue to be.

One evening the two of us had just finished our spare meal of salt pork and greens. Angela was pensive and said very little during our meal. She stared at the flames that flickered blue and yellow in the dying fire. She spoke without looking up.

"I have something for you." She was concentrating on the fire. "I could have brought it here but I wanted to keep it as a surprise. I have it in my tent." She glanced up at me as if gauging my reaction. "I would like to give it to you there."

Several times in the past Angela had hinted that I might visit her home. I knew, however, that she did this out of simple courtesy so I, reciprocating her consideration, had always deferred. She always came to my campsite, never me to hers. I did know where she lived, of course, for all of the women lived in an area set aside for the various camp followers.

This time, however, her request was more than a hint. This embarrassed me because I had nothing to give her in return. "I don't know what to say, Angela. Whatever it is I'm bound to like it."

●●●

The camp followers, because of the services they provided and because they required military protection, had their settlement bordering on the army's camp. They were ramshackle dwellings with tents large and small. Despite the fact that night had already fallen, washed clothes still hung from ropes and the branches of trees. Ragged children ran, screaming and laughing, through the dust. Angela showed me her tent that she had stitched together from tattered pieces of tenting that she had scavenged after our defeat at Ravenna. The fabric was old and faded but the stitching was perfect and tight. In a few places where the material had worn through, she had meticulously over-sewn with patches of various colors. It was clear that Angela carefully husbanded the little that she had.

She invited me inside, where it was impossible to stand upright. She knelt down and lit a stubby candle. She had a pallet on the ground for a bed with a ground cover and an old quilt. Her possessions were few and pitiful. There was a crucifix and a painted figure of Our Lady. There was a broken mirror, an old hairbrush and a comb with broken teeth. Her few clothes were neatly stacked in a wooden box in the corner.

"I'm glad you came," she smiled. "Why don't you sit down?" I sat crosslegged on the ground "I've wanted to take you here for a long time but I was waiting until we knew each other better. I've wanted to be able to talk to you without whispering."

She sat on her pallet and looked at me with her gentle eyes. I was ashamed at the transformation my body was undergoing.

"Yes, this is very nice."

She took my hand in both of her own and held it for a while, saying nothing. "You've been so good to me. Nobody, not even my Francisco, was as kind to me as you have been."

She bent over and brushed my cheek with her lips. I was too stunned to react as she edged closer to me and kissed me on the lips.

"I've made this present for you." She produced a small package, covered with brightly covered paper and bound with a green ribbon. I had no idea where she could have found the wrapping materials in our impoverished camp. She must have gone to a great deal of effort.

"Thank you so much, Angela." I carefully undid the ribbon and removed the paper, without making any tears. Inside was a small, roughly made wooden box. I lifted the lid. Lying on a bed of faded red velvet was a small crucifix. It had been carved intact from a solid block of rose wood. The cross was perfect and had taken many hours to fashion.

Angela looked beseechingly into my eyes. "After I carved it, I took it to the priest who blessed it for me. I want you to promise to wear it for me. It will protect you from harm."

I had to wait a moment before I could talk. "This is the most wonderful gift"—my voice caught in my throat—"that I could ever receive. I will wear it, wherever I go, the rest of my life." I shook my head. "I'll never be able to give you anything nearly so...."

"You already have, Rodrigo." Her voice was filled with something that I'd never heard before. "Oh, but you already have. It's one of the things that I love about you. You've been so... decent... to me and you don't even know what you've done." She said.

"After Francisco died, I thought that the sun would never shine again. For a long time the world was a place of shadows, and I didn't care if I survived. I wasn't interested in anything or anybody but, the first time I saw you—I don't know why—I was... moved. Then, on that terrible night after the battle was over, I waited for you in the dark but," her voice fell to a whisper, "I thought you would never return."

"Life is so very short, my love," she continued, "and I owe you so very much. You've fed me and cared for me and have asked for nothing. I have very little, Rodrigo, and I will never be able to repay you. Even so, I want you to know that everything I have is yours."

Now here I must mention that I had little experience with women. Certainly, there had been a few girls at home. It had all been great fun, exchanging a few kisses and sometimes a caress. It had never gone farther than that and I had no understanding of women.

"You've given me your friendship," I responded nobly. "I have no right to ask for more." As I told you, I knew nothing of women.

Her eyes filled with tears. She put her hands on my shoulders and kissed me again. Her arms encircled my neck as she pressed her body close against me. Her lips were warm and yielding and the pure taste of her was sweet. We pulled apart gently but, moved by forces beyond my control, I took her again and kissed her half-open mouth. My hand reached for her breast but she held me by the wrist. Ashamed of my weakness, I pulled my hand away.

"Oh, dear God." She released my wrist and kissed me again while I felt her softness through the thin fabric of her dress. Both of us fell back on her pallet, kissing tenderly while pressing our bodies closer together. I kissed her throat and her shoulder. Moving slowly, and fearing that she would stop me, I loosened the top loop of her dress. She made no move to stop my hand and seemed to relax as my kisses moved down to cover her newly exposed skin. Her breasts were large and perfect and filled my hands to overflowing as her nipples became rigid. My excitement became unbearable.

While fondling her gently I kissed her lips and explored her mouth with my tongue. She took my head in both hands and forced it down to her breasts. She moaned as I suckled her. I pushed up her dress and caressed her with my fingertips. Lovingly, desperately, she was kissing me again while undoing my shirt, pulling at my pantalones and feeling the hardness between my thighs. Trembling with desire, we undressed one another.

Her skin was as smooth as velvet. She licked her lips with the tip of her tongue as I, with awe, explored the secrets of her body. Inexperienced, I hardly knew what I was doing but she adjusted her hips as throbbing, I forced myself into her. There was resistance at first, but then she admitted me—a little at first and then more—the feeling indescribable—fully. Her body was all moisture and warmth, as we gently pumped against each other, silent except for our breathing and the pounding of our hearts. I wanted it to go on forever but I couldn't....

"More time, Rodrigo," —she breathed— "please...please... please... more...more...."

I forced myself to think of other things—anything—and my urgency subsided. Suddenly Angela gasped and her hips flexed hard against me. She held her breath so long that I thought she would never catch it again. Then she sighed and her body relaxed. A few more thrusts and I felt myself overwhelmed as my body released its seed in pulsing spurts.

Burgos, Castilla-León

The old man had been observing the Padre's reaction from the corner of his eye. Mendoza's discomfort was increasing, which was a very good thing. To be certain, the Bishop enjoyed inflicting pain on the Padre more than he enjoyed the retelling of passions long dead. In an attempt to increase Mendoza's misery, he prolonged the story and added an insult.

"I'll explain something to you, Mendoza, because someone with your—proclivities—will otherwise never understand. Men and women in many ways are quite different but in other ways they are very much the same—lovemaking, for instance. Many people believe men, because they seem more lusty than women, are therefore more lustful than women. Nothing could be further from the truth. A woman's desire is every bit as powerful as that of a man, maybe more so. The difference is how the two sexes go about achieving their very similar goals. A man pursues a woman thinking that his main purpose is to get between the woman's legs. His feelings for the woman seem to him, rather secondary—or so he thinks. A woman, on the other hand, wants security and protection and will give herself to the man that she thinks will best provide it. The better she feels about her protector, the stronger will her lust be. The man pursues, the woman pursued but, in the end, they achieve exactly the same thing."

Mendoza made no reply. He clinched his jaw and stared down at the paper he had been writing on. The old man's face creased into a sickly smile as he went on.

"My encounter with Angela is a case in point. You might think that Angela was delivering her body as my reward for my kindness—she was, indeed, but it goes more deeply than that. My protection, to her was love in the ultimate sense of the word and she gave me her soul in return. Her love ignited her body and her lust for me was every bit as great as my lust for her. There is nothing impure or cynical about it. It is simply the way it must be."

After Angela and I had finished we lay there quietly, looking into each other's eyes and softly stroking each other's bodies. "I've loved you for a long time, Rodrigo and I've been dreaming that we could be together like this. It was more wonderful than I could have imagined and I'm so very happy." She touched my face with the tips of her fingers. "My tent is small, I know, but I want you to come here and live with me." Her eyes glowed with an intensity I'd never seen before. "I need you here beside me."

I thought about it for a moment but, considering what we had just experienced, there was no decision to make.

"I'll move in as soon as I can. I have equipment, so we'll need something bigger."

I remember that her beautiful face broke out into a radiant smile. She held me closely and covered me with kisses as I felt myself stiffen again. She was wanton and the need of our bodies was overpowering. We made love again and then again.

●●●

The next months were, by far, the happiest in my life and, I'd like to think, the happiest in hers. We were poor in material things but we laughed and we planned for the future. I was able to purchase a larger tent that we erected closer to my camp. I was able to buy her some nicer clothes and even an ornament or two. But happiness is a fleeting thing and The Evil One—*El Enemigo Malo*—rules our lives.

Mendoza had enough, "I must stop you, again, your Grace—you're right about my lack of understanding about certain things because I, unlike you, have enforced a strict celibacy on myself."

The old priest raised his eyebrows, "Oh?"

Mendoza, intent on delivering his own insult, pretended not to notice. "On the other hand, it seems to me that, even given your inexperience with women, you would have previously divined this Angela's carnal interest in you and availed yourself of her services."

For a moment it seemed that the ancient priest might explode. Padre Mendoza drew back, realizing that he had gone too far. The old man, however, replied in an even voice.

"I may have loved her and desired her but she was—can you possibly understand it—perfect—and, if she hadn't approached me herself, I would have never touched her. Nunca. You forget that I am *Don Rodrigo de la Peña*." The Bishop's voice dropped to a sinister hiss. "*Comprende, Padre?*"

Chapter 15

The detestable French, that most miserable of races, had retreated to their own country after their numerous defeats. Now, under their new king, Francis I, they penetrated the Alps and fell on the land like a pack of wolves. Soon the enemy was loose in northern Italia and was attempting to join forces with the Venetians. The Pope, with his Italian mercenaries and the Emperor, with his huge numbers of Swiss pikemen, were massing their forces in Milano to repel the invading French with their Venetian allies.

Now, all over Italy, money poured like water. All of the interested nations were trying to buy additional mercenaries or, if that failed, to bribe the mercenary forces to stay out of the fight. The French got the better of it. They managed to hire not only thousands of Germans but they successfully bribed half of the Swiss pikemen to retreat to the mountains before the first cannon was fired. The Imperial forces were stripped to the bone.

The Spaniards, for the most part, elected to stay out of the fight. Our commanders, including Pescara, were tempted by gold. We allied ourselves with the Emperor and, after our months of inaction and poverty, we marched north. Only the necessary merchants were permitted to accompany the army. All others had to stay behind, protected by a detachment of guards.

Angela held me tightly, almost as if she could keep me from going. "Promise me again, Rodrigo," she begged, "that you'll think about me and stay away from danger."

"I promise, Angela." If it were possible, I had every intention of avoiding danger. "Besides, I'm wearing your crucifix. God will protect me." I had doubts about God's protection but it was enough that Angela truly believed.

The mention of the crucifix made her relax a little. The priest's blessing was powerful magic, indeed. "Just promise to be careful, anyway."

●●●

The Swiss and Papal forces were occupying Milano. Our few companies of Spaniards camped outside the city walls. We had settled in when we heard rumors that our allied force was going to make the first move. We were to attack the French who were entrenched nearby, just outside of the small town of Marignano. One blighted morning in September of 1515 our army marched forth but without its usual fanfare. We hoped to catch the enemy by surprise.

Our force was made up of Swiss pikemen, interspersed with arquebusiers, halberdiers, and swordsmen. These men marched in perfect cadence in regiments, twenty-five men deep. Their pikes were ten cubits long, which meant that only the first four or five rows of pikemen were in any position to damage the enemy. The following ranks were to add weight and muscle to the charge and to replace those who fell in the front ranks.

Reinforcing the Swiss were Italians from the Papal States and other Italian mercenaries hired by the Pope. Some Neopolitan companies had joined forces with our Spanish companies and were primarily arquebusiers mixed with swordsmen. We Españoles, of course, were primarily espadas, although, learning from our experience at Ravenna we had increased our number of mosqueteros and had entire companies of well-trained lanzas—pikemen.

It seemed to me that we should have made our attack during the night for our advancing army produced clouds of dust that must have been visible for miles. Amazingly, we achieved complete surprise. Our Swiss hit the enemy like a great hammer. First, the French light cavalry were driven in and then the phalanx struck the Landsknechte a devastating blow. The German front ranks were almost completely wiped out but then—the disciplined troops that they were—they stepped over their dead, reformed their front and stopped the Swiss cold. The two opposing armies fought as if the fate of the world hinged on the results of their efforts. We Spaniards marched to the right flank and engaged with French infantry who were trying to flank and disrupt the Swiss. We, in our turn, were trying to do the same against the Germans.

I can still remember it—two massive armies almost hidden by gun smoke and rising clouds of dust. Pikes projected, bristling, above the haze. We held the French at bay with our shields, even as arquebusiers and crossbowmen fired their weapons into the faces of the French infantry and into the packed ranks of the German pikemen.

The Swiss put their backs into it and pushed the Germans steadily back. French heavy guns retaliated, cutting bloody swaths through the Swiss ranks. The Swiss, to their credit, never wavered. Seeing the damage the cannons were inflicting, our officers ordered an attack on the guns. We let out a blood-curdling screech and smashed the French to our front. The enemy artillerymen, seeing our advance, tried to limber up their cannons and pull them out of danger.

"*Maten los caballos!*" I screamed.

There was the explosion of muskets and two horses dropped in their traces, immobilizing one gun. I grabbed a fallen pike, parried with a sword-wielding artilleryman and pinned the pleading man to the ground. Then, running and with all of my strength, I attacked another team of horses.

I thrust the spear deeply into the guts of a bay colored horse. The animal screeched, lashed out with his hooves, tipping the caisson over. Desperate to protect the cannon, a crimson-clad German broke ranks and came at me with lowered pike.

I thrust my lance at him but, with a skillful twitch of his pike, my weapon flew from my hands. I dropped to the ground, drew my sword and rolled under the tip of his pike. Using Bebidor like an axe, I hacked at the shaft of my enemy's pike breaking off its metal point. The disarmed soldier sullenly retreated to the protection of his phalanx. I let him go.

I looked around and saw that we were in possession of a dozen or more enemy cannon. We soldados were inexperienced but knew the basic principle—the range was very short. Powder, tamp it down, roll down the ball, point it at the enemy phalanx, match—*fuego!* The damage to the enemy was sickening. Heads, limbs and torsos went flying but the Germans, just like the Swiss, never faltered. They even managed to force back our troops—screaming cursing men went down in heaps.

One of our crews must have used too much powder for, with a massive explosion, their gun exploded, pieces of jagged metal whirling in every direction. All four men in the makeshift crew were instantly converted to bleeding projectiles. The explosion toppled a nearby cannon, killing two of its crew. Something hit me hard in the head, knocking me to my knees. I was covered with blood and thought I was dead. I felt my face and my scalp but there was no wound. My helmet, which had been torn from my head, was dented but not penetrated. Through the buzzing in my ears I heard a bugle signaling retreat. At the same time, I heard shouted orders.

"If you can't drag 'em away, spike 'em."

I looked up and could see that our forward ranks were about to be overwhelmed by a force of French heavy cavalry and infantry.

With courage borne of desperation, our men tried to drag the newly captured guns back to our lines. There wasn't enough time so we rendered them useless by driving copper nails that had been issued to all of the soldados, into the touchholes and breaking them off.

The enemy engulfed us but, in the dust and disorganization of combat, the French didn't recognize me as one of their enemies. I was carried backward by the enemy surge until I reached the front lines where, reversing myself, I again became one of their Spanish foes.

I can't remember how I survived. All I remember was the mindless emotion of combat, with its shouts and screams, clashing of weapons, the roll of drums and the shrill of the bugles sounding advance and retreat. Most of what I remember, though, was the heat, exhaustion and unbelievable thirst. The sun went down as we, like slavering beasts, continued to fight under the silvery light of the moon. Fitfully, the fighting sputtered out as it grew too dark for men to identify friend from foe. Those of us still alive slept where we fought too utterly weary to fear the morning's light. I slumped to the earth with two dead men as my companions.

●●●

I awoke to the sounds of fifes and the roll of drums. The sky, to the east, was just starting to brighten, but the surviving Swiss were already drawn up into their phalanx as their great trumpets toned martial airs. Across the way, toward the town of Marignano, the French played competing tunes. As quickly as my body would allow, I roused myself and joined with other Españoles, none of whom were from my original company. Just as on the previous day, we attacked.

This time there was no surprise. In perfect cadence, the Swiss and Germans advanced towards one another with vertical pikes. When their front ranks were only one hundred paces from each other, with beautiful precision, the foremost pikes were lowered to the horizontal even as the ranks behind brought their pikes to forty-five degrees—it was like the shuffling of a huge deck of cards. I was, and still am, awed by the Swiss and German courage for there is almost nothing to protect the front ranks from the sharpened steel.

At the time, though, I didn't stop to consider the courage of the German-speaking pikemen. Crossbow bolts whirred through the air and cannon balls tore huge gaps in our ranks. Nevertheless, with momentum on our side, we very nearly broke the enemy line. To our front, I could actually feel the French line starting to unravel. Some enemy soldiers threw down their weapons and ran for the rear, even as their own musketeers and crossbowmen screamed insults and shot them in their backs.

Then, in the sun's early light, it was over. Thousands upon thousands of fresh Venetian troops poured onto the field and stiffened the faltering French and Germans. Slowly, inexorably, our lines were forced back as our officers gave orders for the rear ranks to retreat under the cover of the front ranks. We were not routed and we did not run but we were defeated. We had left thousands of Swiss, Italian and Spanish soldiers bloating under the sun and it had all been for nothing.

Burgos, Castilla-León

"Padre Mendoza? I have a question for you, one I've pondered for years."

"Then, I certainly hope I can provide the answer."

"When two sides go to war, there is usually a loser and usually a winner."

"A fairly basic observation, Your Grace."

"For the side that loses, all of its sacrifices in blood and wealth, are for exactly nothing."

"Yes, Your Grace, that is almost always the case."

"Not only that, Padre, but many of the sacrifices of the winning side are also tragic."

"How so?"

"Just ask the father, mother or wife of a soldier fallen in battle, whether the fruits of victory were worth the life of their dear one. If they answer truthfully the answer will be 'no'. Another way of putting this is that everyone, who is crippled or killed in battle, has lost his personal battle."

"That may be true, Excelencia, but the interests of the State supercede the interests of the individual."

"Let me, in principle, accept your assertion, Padre. The fact is, however, that once the State submits itself to battle, it may very well be defeated in which case, as we have already established, its own interests and sacrifices are for nothing. In totality then, when you factor in both the risk of defeat and the reality of the death and injury—even to its victorious participants—it is difficult to justify war except under the most extraordinary circumstances."

"I can't disagree, Your Grace, although we might disagree on how extraordinary those circumstances must be."

"I haven't yet made my case, Padre—I'm only preparing the ground." The ancient priest absentmindedly scratched his chin. "Have you ever noticed how people flock to an execution?"

"Certainly, Your Grace." Suspecting a snare, Mendoza was cautious as he said, "Honest people want to see justice done."

"Then why is it that people will also flock to the scene of an accident?"

"It's because they want to help or because ...of... curiosity."

"Curiosity, indeed. Why is it, then, that people love stories of passion and war and violence? They certainly don't wish violence or harm on themselves."

"Excelencia," Mendoza pounded the table and said, "I know where you're going and couldn't disagree with you more. These things are interesting, exciting—nothing more."

"Nothing more," the old man repeated bitterly, "but why do you think that these things are so....exciting?"

Mendoza looked puzzled. "I don't understand your question."

"I'll put it another way, then. Why isn't the simple story of a life on a farm or a lovely spring day, as interesting as a story of conflict and strife?"

Mendoza rolled his eyes. "It's obvious. It's the activity, the movement. It's...it's...."

"Padre Mendoza, I hope you don't feel that I am questioning your intellect," the old man lied, "but, I have asked these same questions of others and the answers are always the same."

Mendoza started to protest but the Bishop waved him down.

"We are all infected with the sin of Cain. As terrible as scenes of death and carnage may be, we are drawn to them as a moth is drawn to flame. In some deep, black recess of our souls, we lust for it. The Romans were enthralled by mass homicide in the arena. The barbarians of Africa and the Indies howl with glee as they flay their helpless victims alive. The Mexicans butchered their own people by the thousands to satiate their false Gods. A child's eyes glow when he hears a blood-soaked nursery tale or a story of *El Cid*. You, Padre Mendoza, have prayed to God and felt your soul uplifted as you hardened your heart and incinerated..."

"You would equate the work of the Holy Office with the tortures of heathen barbarians?"

"I would indeed," the old man said. "I'm not establishing myself as a paragon, however, for in my travels, I have done as bad and worse. I see it on myself for I have reveled in destruction. I may not believe in a loving God but I do believe in my own iniquity and I search for answers. I must come to the conclusion that there's something infernal deep inside all of us that secretly loves these forbidden things. This terrible something explains why we do violence to one another and, at the same time, explains our fascination for blood and destruction."

"What you have said is illogical, Obispo de la Peña. In the one breath you suggest that these things are terrible and with the next breath you say that we love it."

"Yes. Both are unfortunately true but my real question is 'Why?'"

Mendoza decided to end the interrogation. "I don't agree with your premise."

"Then I must answer my own question." The old man's voice dropped. "What if our human design is flawed?"

"That's impossible. We are made in the image of God. We are therefore perfect."

"Come now, Padre Mendoza. *Santo Oficio* punishes people based on their imperfections, does it not?"

"We are potentially perfect."

"Closer, Mendoza, closer. What if built into our perfect design is a deliberate flaw, a perfect flaw—a flaw so profound that there can never be peace in the world."

"God would never condemn us in this way."

"You make my point, Padre." The old man shrugged his shoulders.

Chapter 16

We were ordered to protect the rear as the Swiss and Papal Italians retreated to Milano. As we formed our battle line, disorganized bands of heavy and light cavalry tried to break through to our rear. Knowing the danger of these horsemen, I picked up the musket and tool bag of an Italian who was missing both of his shoes and the side of his head. Ignoring the hiss of musket balls, I went through the ritual of loading.

Clouds of dust from the direction of enemy lines grew larger. The forms of lancers and cavalrymen emerged. Feeling naked, I stood the attack of a lance-bearing knight. His visor was open and, for a moment, I could see his eyes.

He leaned way out over his saddle and sighted along the top of his lance. At the same time I sighted along the barrel of my musket and, for a moment in time, we were locked together in eternity. The spell was shattered by an explosion, recoil and gout of dirty smoke. The knight's right leg windmilled with the strike of the ball, knocking him side-ways from his saddle.

I leaped forward and seized the lance from the wounded man's hand. I butted it down and prepared for the second wave—it was soon in coming. A light cavalryman, his helmet and breastplate sparkling in the sun, bore down on me with his iron-tipped spear. His aim was poor and his spear splintered in the dirt. His horse drove itself onto my lance. The animal reared up, toppled backward, taking my lance and his rider with him. The cavalryman tried to scramble free but his dying mount's hooves broke him.

Determined to take a noble prisoner, I tried to force my first victim to his feet, but my ball had smashed his armor and his leg was mangled. I positioned myself under the moaning man's arm as we hobbled, three-legged, back toward Milano. We'd gone scarcely one hundred paces when I realized I was doing all of the work by myself. I released my newly won captive and he collapsed to the earth—dead.

●●●

Later, agreements were signed with the French king, so we were permitted to return to our old encampment. The return was hard, encumbered as we were with wounded men, and with a shortage of food and draft animals. Water was too scarce for washing and all of us were crawling with vermin. Many of the wounded died on the route. Worse, healthy troops started to fall ill and die. It was on the sixth day of our return march when I started to feel unwell. It was nothing particular, just a sickly feeling in the pit of my stomach. Soon, I developed a headache that, building quickly, became so severe that I felt it would split my head. I tried to march on but couldn't. First, I was on fire and then I turned to ice—my clothing was sopping with sweat. Along with other sick soldiers, I was forced to rest in the shade of a tree as the rest of our troops disappeared down the road. I was beyond caring whether or not I was abandoned. All I could manage was to crawl to a muddy puddle at the side of the road.

I had a companion. A half-naked soldier lay there on his belly. His only clothes were blue-and-green pantalones and, like me, he had come for a drink. His face was submerged in the water and his hands clutched the soil as tenderly as if it were the breasts of a lover.

Disinterestedly, I examined myself. I was burning with fever and a purple rash covered my skin—I was racked by spasms of coughing. It was mild at first but then became constant and exhausting. Somewhere between life and death, I lay there for days.

●●●

"Can you talk to me, Rodrigo? Do you know who I am?" Angela was wiping my face with a moist cloth.

"Yes," I rasped, "I know who you are."

"You have been very sick but you're getting better."

Though it hurt to move my head, I could see the canopy of a large tree past Angela's worried face. I was still in the same place where I had left our march.

"How long have I been here?"

"I think three days. When you didn't return I asked the other soldiers. They told me you had become sick and had to drop out of the march—I found you the day before yesterday. You were completely out of your mind but you're getting better, now."

Trying to sit up, I could see that she'd built a small fire. The embers were glowing but I couldn't tell what time of day it was. The man still lay with his face in the puddle. The body had swollen to the point that his trousers, which had been loose, were now stretched and impossibly tight—the exposed skin was a moving mass of shiny green flies. The miasma of putrefaction was stifling.

"I'm famished," I said. "Did you bring food?"

Chapter 17

After the Battle of Marignano, treaties were signed and, except for a few nearly bloodless assaults on minor Italian cities, things were quiet as Angela and I adapted to a peacetime routine.

"Why is it, Angela, that you spend so much time away in the afternoons?"

Angela didn't know what to say. "I go to the priest."

"To the priest? But why daily?"

"I go to the Confessional."

I knew that Angela was far more devout than I was and I admired her for it. Daily confession, though, sounded like overdoing a good thing especially in that I hadn't confessed once since my arrival in Italy.

"Why would a woman as blameless as yourself need to confess at all, let alone daily?"

Angela looked both confused and embarrassed. With her eyes downcast, she whispered, "I confess for the sin of our love making."

"Every time?"

"Yes."

I took some seconds to gather my thoughts. At night when I touched her, there was never any reluctance—she was always warm and passionate.

"Look, Angela. I desire you but I love you, also. If I'm causing you pain, I'll move somewhere else."

Her answer was instantaneous. "No! I'll kill myself, first."

"I don't understand."

"I love to go to Confession. The priest is a good man and he understands. He always gives me ten Pater Nosters and Ave Marias and you and I are saved from these things that we do. Besides... there is something else..."

Still pondering her logic, I asked, "What is it?"

"I was afraid to tell you." She looked down at her feet. "I was afraid that you'd be angry with me. I was afraid that you would send me away."

"Ridiculous. Even if you were excommunicated," She looked up at me sharply. "I'd stay with you. What is it?"

She took a deep breath. "I'm carrying your child. I've known about it but I have been afraid to say anything."

She looked as if she would cry.

I was overwhelmed. I threw my arms around her and held her as tightly as I dared. "Send you away? Madness. This is wonderful."

Admittedly, I was lying but I told her what she wanted to hear.

"Oh, Rodrigo!" Her voice was full of relief. "I'm so ashamed. I thought you'd send me away." She thought for a few moments before she went on. "I'm just a simple woman and I thought I had no right to bear your child. I don't deserve this wonderful thing."

"It's I who am undeserving."

She looked up at me with a radiant smile. "We'll name the child after you."

"But she might be a girl."

"No. He will be a boy. I learned of a witch-woman who follows the Germans." Angela unconsciously crossed herself. "She told me that she has cast the runes for me and the child will be a boy."

I flinched remembering the runes of Don Pedro's story. I didn't know what they were but, despite the legend, I doubted they had more power than my crucifix. I kept my doubts to myself. "If this is the case, I would like to name our boy in honor of my own father."

●●●

Our next months were spent as pleasantly as camp life would allow. Angela didn't know one day of sickness—she simply glowed with happiness.

"Tell me more about your father, Rodrigo. He must have been a very good man to have had a son as wonderful as you are."

"His name was Don Jorge de la Peña. He gave his name to my

older brother which is why I am Rodrigo, which is the name of my father's grandfather."

"*Jorge*," she whispered to herself. "Our son will be a great man, an hidalgo of merit, just like his father and his grandfather."

I had been giving my predicament great thought and had come to a decision. "Yes, he can be, Angela, but not unless you are my legal wife."

Angela was struck dumb. "Your wife, señor? Please don't tease me. I've dreamed of it but I know it can never happen."

"It will happen, Angela. I've been thinking about it for a long time—I'll make arrangements with the priest."

She blinked rapidly. "I'm just a poor woman who follows the army."

"We will marry, Angela, but first there is something which I must tell you. Before, I didn't see any need to tell you but now that you're going to be my wife and will bear my child, it's only right that you should know all of the truth."

"You're not of noble birth? It doesn't matter."

"No, that's not it," I spoke very softly. "I told you that my family died of the plague—that wasn't true."

Her face dropped. "Why wouldn't you tell me the truth? Are your parents not dead and you've been disowned?"

"No, Angela. Nothing like that. They are, I'm afraid...quite dead." I watched her closely. "My family was condemned by the Holy Tribunal."

She looked up at me with a blank look on her face. "The Holy Tribunal. I don't understand."

"*Santo Oficio.* The Church. *La Inquisición.*" My voice filled with hatred.

"*La Iglesia Madre?*" Her eyes widened in shock. "But...what could they have done?"

"Nothing, nothing at all. We had the bad luck to be born conversos, Christians with Jewish blood."

"Jews?"

"You must understand. It was a false accusation. We are Christians but we were condemned for the unpardonable accident of our ancestry."

A flurry of emotions passed over her lovely face. "*Judios*," Angela said the word as if she could taste it. "I have never known a

Jew...before." She gave me a piercing look, "before."

"I'm not a Jew, Angela. I'm as Christian as yourself."

"You never go to mass. I have to make excuses."

"These things don't make a person a Jew."

She held her swollen belly protectively. "The priest has taught us how the filthy Jews sacrifice Christian babies."

I reached out to her but she pulled back as if struck by a snake.

"Angela. Be reasonable. I'm the same man you loved but minutes ago. Nothing has changed. I love you—you're going to be my wife."

She looked at me as if I had just crawled from some hole in the earth. "You lied to me. You tricked me and you had your filthy way with me!" She started to sob uncontrollably. "What am I to do? Oh, Dear God, what am I going to do?"

Burgos Castilla-León

Mendoza pulled on his beard. "So your effort to protect yourself with a lie ultimately failed. Even so, you personally were not under the judgment of *Santo Oficio*, so the reaction of this young woman would appear to have been excessive and ill-considered especially when small details such as the fact that she had been living with you in sin and was pregnant with your bastard child are taken into account."

"Ah, Mendoza, you prove yourself to be the fool I know you to be. Your ignorance is understandable, though. You, as well as most of the human race, live in a fog of misunderstanding."

"How so, Your Grace?"

"I spoke to you before of the differences and similarities between men and women. I've learned, through painful experience, that some of these differences are, indeed, profound. Despite this, neither men nor women usually understand the significance of these differences and are therefore continually frustrated by one another."

"How does this apply to your...ah...misunderstanding with your mistress?"

"Angela's anger was due more to the lie than to my revelation—women are far less tolerant of a lie than are men."

"Come now, Your Grace, a lie is a lie. A small lie is a small lie and a great lie is a great lie. Men tolerate or condemn them exactly the same as do women."

"No, Mendoza. Many a man has fallen afoul of this buried trap. In this regards men and women are not the same—women especially detest a lie. Not only that, but they're not as capable of judging the degree of an untruth as is a man."

"I've never heard such preposterous nonsense."

"Men, as they deal with one another, crawl along a sticky web of lies, great and small. We smile at the man whom we hate. We negotiate with the man we mistrust and we swear fealty to the man who we know doesn't deserve more than the thrust of a sword. We do these things, Mendoza, because we, as men, are the ones whom the responsibilities of leadership fall. We do it because to do otherwise would involve us in an eternal round of violence. We do it to avoid bloodshed and to maintain the peace. "

"It's no different with a wo...."

"Oh, but it is. Women speak more honestly with one another. They confide things with another woman that a man would never confide in another man. Because they speak the truth, their friendship with other females is stronger than is the friendship between a man and a man. Conversely, because they speak the truth, they are also more likely to become bitter enemies. As unpleasant and venomous as this can be, women are more at liberty to engage in the unvarnished truth because they never need face one another over the point of a sword or the barrel of a musket."

"An interesting theory..."

"Perhaps God left men and women incomplete. Either that, or he has a truly celestial sense of humor. The problem is that most of us fools try to deal with women in the same way we deal with men, and the result is"—the old man burst out into squeaky laughter—"confusion."

Chapter 18

That night Angela wouldn't let me into her tent so I sat by the fire listening to the conversation of the other soldiers.

"I tell you, Paco. I've seen enough of fucking Italy. I've got my eyes set on bigger things."

Migues was used to this kind of big talk. "Like what?"

"Like the Indies, hombre, the Indies. I'm told that all you have to do is to scrape away the gravel and you can pick up gold by the cart load."

"Is that right? I think I'll book passage on the next caravel." Migues didn't plan passage farther than his hut.

"Yes, that is right. Besides there is land there, rich land for the taking and they're giving away *encomiendas de los Indios* to work the land. All I'll have to do is to lie back and be waited on hand-and-foot. No more following orders. Once I get there, those brown-skinned cabrónes will be following my orders."

The speaker was Jose Maldinado, a one-time carpenter from Badajoz. He was a big friendly man who had been in the army seven years and I knew that he had his discharge papers.

Migues' voice dropped, "*Las propiedades?*"

"*Si, absolutamente. Tierra y esperanza y muchas, muchas mujeres.* They say those Indio women can't control themselves—they do it for nothing." Maldinado laughed while clutching his crotch. "I can hardly wait to get my hands on those little lambs. When they feel my prod they'll turn into good Christians right enough."

Maldinado was as bald as a turtle. He was one of the few men whose looks were improved by a steel helmet.

"Who's giving away all this rich land, anyway?" Migues knew as well as anyone that, as a common soldier, he would always be land-less. Land was for the aristocrats.

"The Council of the Indies. *Hombre!* They're crying for men like us. Men who have been around and know how to use a sword," Maldinado clutched his crotch again. "All that land is wasted on those heathens, anyway. It's there for the taking, if you've got the balls."

Migues' hand went to the pommel of his weapon.

"No, Paco. I didn't mean it like that. I just meant that it's time to pull out of Italia. By the Whore's Son, I'd like you to come with me."

Migues relaxed. "I'll sleep on it."

●●●

Close to the fire, I slept on it as well. Of course, I had heard of the Indies—soldiers talked of it all the time. I knew that the rumors of limitless wealth were probably exaggerated but still, as they say, where there is smoke, there is fire. It stood to reason that in these newly discovered lands there would be property aplenty for those who arrived first. *Las encomiendas de los Indios esclavos*—I liked the sound of it. A plantation of Indio slaves was appropriate for an hidalgo, even one who had lost his title.

I had considered all of this many times but had rejected it because of Angela. To my way of thinking, the Indies were the place for a single man willing to take chances, not for a man with a wife and a child. The hard ground under me reminded me that things had now changed.

● ● ●

"Rodrigo?" A small hand touched my shoulder. "Are you awake?"

"*Sí.*" I hadn't been sleeping.

"Rodrigo, I need to talk to you." I said nothing "I'm just a poor stupid girl." Her voice was tremulous, fearful. "I am sorry for the awful things I said. It wasn't me. It was *El Diablo.* Please... I want you to come back and be with me. You are my very life and I can't live without you."

I was silent.

"Please, Rodrigo. I'm on my knees. By the Blessed Virgin and all the Saints in Heaven, I didn't mean the things I said."

"Go back to bed, Angela. I'll talk to you in the morning."

"Oh Dear God, take away my tongue. I swear I didn't mean it." Her fear had turned into panic. "I love you more than life itself. I'll spend the rest of my life trying to make up for my sinfulness. I'll do everything for you."

"Go back to bed, Angela."

She started to sob. "Please, forgive me, Rodrigo. Please."

"I forgive you, Angela," I said without feeling; "Now, go back to bed."

To forgive Angela was easy. To forget the words that had been spoken was more difficult.

Burgos, Castilla-León

"Excelencia?" Mendoza had once again put on his self-righteous face.

"You have a question, Padre?"

"It is true that we may not be able to forget a slight but, to fully forgive a trespasser, it is necessary for us to put the memory of a wrong behind us. We must subordinate the memory of a wrong to the act of forgiveness, itself. *Errare humanum est sed venia divina est.* Only in this way can we truly forgive or may we receive the full benefit of our forgiveness."

"Your point is well taken, Padre. Unfortunately for me and now, for you, I do have difficulty putting certain things behind me. They sit on my breast like a great leaden weight and the weight only grows heavier with the years. I truly forgave Angela. I understood her reaction to my untruth and to the abruptness of my revelations—it is probably what I expected. Maybe...just maybe...it's what I wanted. In any event, once the words were said, my feelings for her disappeared like smoke into a gray winter's sky. Once it was gone there was no way to recapture it."

"But did you even make the effort to recapture it, Your Grace?"

The ancient man blinked hard and stared at a spot on the wall. His hollow face was lifeless. He continued in a voice scarcely above a whisper, "Oh yes, I tried but...it is like trying to grasp water. The harder we try, the faster it trickles away...the effort itself hastens its loss."

The rays of the rising sun, falling on my face, awakened me. There was a chill breeze blowing in from the north but, otherwise, it was a morning like many others. Stiff, from my night on the ground, I stretched the aches from my body.

"De la Peña?" My questioner was a short black-haired soldier by the name of Alejandro Ortejeña. He was as ugly as a goat and he wore an old gray poncho against the morning's cold. "It looks like your woman threw you out and high time if you ask me—maybe she needs the company of a *real* man."

It was too early to rise to his insult. "*Posible, Señor Ortejeña,* but somehow I doubt you measure up."

Ortejeña laughed. "You're probably right. It's so cold this morning I couldn't find it to take a pee. *Madre de Dios!* I'm not sure if it froze off or just shrunk up."

I knew what he meant.

"Alejandro?" I decided to change this fascinating topic. "Migues and Maldinado were talking last night about the Indies. Have you ever given any thought to going over there?"

"*Hombre!* They tell me it's always warm there and, when it gets cold like this, I think about it all of the time, especially when I have to pull down my pants and take a dump. But, then again," Ortejeña made a broad gesture and said, "how could I leave this paradise. I've got me that hut over there and I just love the food and the elegant company—besides there's the money. I send everything I make back to Castilla for the benefit of my sainted mother—I couldn't give up my steady income." I knew, for a fact, that Ortegeña spent everything he had on cards, drink and whores. He went on, "You're not thinking about it, are you?"

"They say it's the land of opportunity."

"The opportunity to get eaten up by cannibals."

I knew that Ortejeña was as brave a man as existed among the mercenary soldiers. Still, the thought of being digested by heathens didn't appeal to him.

"Just look at the bright side of it, Alejandro—you'd probably give them the bleeding flux."

Ortejeña grinned from ear to ear—it only made him uglier. "Or constipation, which leads me to a question for our priest."

"And what might that be?"

"What happens on Resurrection Day if you have turned into cannibal dung?" I started to laugh until I saw that the man was serious.

●●●

"Rodrigo? Can we talk now? You said we could talk this morning." Angela had come up silently and had been listening to my conversation with Ortejeña. She looked as if she had no sleep and her face was streaked with tears. I led her back to our hut.

"You aren't leaving, are you? You aren't going off to the Indies?" Her voice was a sob.

I waited until she had some control of herself. "I'm sorry," I said quietly, "I'll leave you with most of my money."

"No. I don't believe you, Rodrigo. You're just trying to make me pay for what I said yesterday—you're just trying to scare me."

"I don't want to frighten you, Angela, but I'm leaving. I forgive you for what you said but I don't feel the same..."

"No, Rodrigo, please. I'm going to have your baby."

"Aren't you afraid that I will sacrifice it on a Hebrew Altar?"

"Please, Rodrigo. Don't be so cruel. If you leave I'll have nothing. I'm begging you!"

"I'm sorry, Angela. I don't want you to suffer but my feelings have changed. I wish I could do more but I can't any longer. All I have is a little money for you and the child. Other than for my armor and clothes, everything is yours."

"Rodrigo." Angela was struggling to control herself. "I know that you're tired of Italy. I've known it for a long time, maybe longer than you—let me come with you. I won't ask for much. We don't have to marry. I'll take care of you. If you want other women, I won't complain. Just let me come with you."

I shook my head, collected my gear and left her weeping. It's the last time I ever saw her.

Chapter 19

Burgos, Castilla-León
January 21, 1581, 7:15 A.M.

"Five days have passed since I requested your presence, Padre. I can't say that I'm pleased."

Mendoza held out his hands in supplication. "Please, Excelencia, you know I have been ill. Even now my sufferings are so great that I can barely sit in this chair."

The corners of the old Bishop's mouth were grim but his eyes twinkled. "Can you describe your malady?"

"Everything I eat passes through me like fire." Mendoza glanced to his left and right as his voice dropped to a whisper. "My bottom...my bottom feels like a piece of raw meat."

"Hmm. Perhaps it is something that you ate. Our chef tells me that you prefer rich sauces. I'm of a mind to provide you with simpler fare."

"Please, Obispo, that can't be the cause. I'm still eating my regular diet but my condition is improving."

"Then it's a mystery, Padre. By the way, my cook has prepared some breakfast. I'm sure you'll enjoy it as much as I do. We're having huevos and chopped jamon seasoned with garlic butter and smothered in red and green chiles."

"Maybe...maybe... you could leave off the chiles, Excelencia."

"*No creo, Padre.*" The old man's face broke into an outright grin. "Not a chance."

Although the Indies were my destination, I made a point of returning to my hometown of San Miguel in Extremadura. I had no intention of renewing old acquaintances—it was better that I not be seen. In some strange way, the evil that I had done to Angela increased my hatred of those who had destroyed my family—not that it really mattered—I had long since sworn to avenge my family and now my time had come.

Before I left my home, years earlier, I learned the name of the cabrón who betrayed my father. His name was Jaime Sánchez, a dealer in wool and hides. Sánchez, the fool, had been most incautious. It seems that he was proud of his crime against my family and boasted of it to anyone who would listen. He had been of modest means but the Holy Office had seen to it that he was well rewarded for his lies. He now enriched himself from the fruits of my father's fields and lorded it over better men than himself.

Like Odysseus of old, returning from the ruins of Holy Ilios, I disguised myself as a beggar clothed in greasy rags. Unrecognized, I followed Sánchez's movements for over two weeks. I could have slain him many times but I enjoyed the hunt as I have enjoyed few things in my life. I stayed my hand.

I remember Sánchez well. He was a dark-skinned zoquete with thick lips and a foul odor. He was exceptionally tall and rolling with fat. Nevertheless, he took great care of his appearance. His hair and beard were always groomed and his mustache was carefully waxed. He was coarse and ignorant and could neither read nor write but, to my disgust, he affected the dress and manners of an aristocrat. He was especially fond of purple velvet cloaks and, although he knew nothing of the art of combat, he wore a great Moorish saber. In his stylish cap were the white plumes of cranes. When dealing with lesser mortals, he would never look directly at them. Such was his height, he would only look over them. Twice, it amused me to beg alms from my victim. The first time, he thrust me away and the second time he struck me across the face with his cane.

Finally, after learning his habits, I tired of my game. It was dusk when I waylaid him on a lonely stretch of road as he was returning home from his stolen fields. He was completely surprised when, despite his weight, I tumbled him from his horse—he hit the ground like a great sack of manure. I had my knife at his throat before he could think to move. I disarmed him and marched him a long way into the underbrush. I didn't want the two of us to be disturbed.

Sánchez was suitably terrified but, when I told him who I really was, he almost collapsed.

"Don't you recognize me, Don Jaime?" Sánchez affected the title of an hidalgo. It amused me to use the title he had arrogated to himself.

"Sí, señor. You are the one who I so wrongly failed to give alms. If I hadn't been distracted I would have been more generous. Here, I have money—gold—in my purse. Take it all. Take my cloak. It is worth one hundred pesos. I give you my horse..."

As I had hoped, he lunged at me. I jumped back, tangled his legs and, as he toppled like a great tree, I kicked him as hard as I could in the face. I heard bones break.

"*Por favor, señor,*" Sánchez blubbered through the blood bubbling from his broken nose and shattered teeth. He crawled to his knees and wept for mercy, if not for him at least his wife and children. He offered me wealth and money. I laughed.

"Señor Don Jaime. I am Rodrigo, the son of Don Jorge de la Peña. *Ahora me conoce?* I have returned from the Wars and I have returned for your worthless life."

Sánchez blanched white and even the flow of blood from his face slowed.

"*No fue mi culpa. La Inquisición...*The Holy Office discovered that I, myself, am a converso. They threatened my family. What could I do? They wanted names and proof. I told them what I knew—nothing more—you would have done the same. *Por favor, señor.* I suffer unbearably for the things that I told them, but what could I do? Someone else would have betrayed your father, anyway. All I did was to protect my own family."

I hesitated as if considering the worthiness of what he had told me. "Perhaps I have misjudged you, Don Jaime. Of course, a man must protect his family." Sánchez' relief was almost pitiful. "Can you recall the things that you told the Holy Office?"

"*No sé, senor.* It has been a very long time and I no longer remember."

"Sí, Don Jaime, it has been a very long time. Do you also forget how you came in possession of Don Jorge's property?"

Sánchez' eyes widened.

"No matter, Don Jaime. You are an unimportant commodity. What is important is that I learn the names of those who pressured you to bear false witness against my family."

"It has been a long time, señor."

I fingered the blade of my knife. "*La muerte es para siempre, mi amigo.*"

He stammered in terror. "If ...If I tell you their names, will you promise to never reveal that I was the one who talked."

I chuckled, "It occurs to me that you are in a poor position to negotiate. But, just as I said, you're nothing. Those who forced you to testify are those who are guilty."

"Then I'll tell you because you are a man of honor." He hesitated, knowing the consequences of his confession. "I was interrogated by Bernál de la Garza and Federico Delujo. Padre Mata was there, too. Later, I gave my testimony to the Holy Tribunal."

My stomach churned. Padre Mata was the village priest of San Miguel.

"Who was on the Tribunal?"

"I do not remember, señor. I was frightened."

"That is unfortunate, Don Jaime. I was really enjoying our discussion." I stared at Sánchez's fat throat.

"Oh yes. I'm starting to remember now. Padre Renato Medina, and Padre Roberto Ajuntas and Padre Benito de Luna. God help me, I don't remember the others."

"Who was the presiding officer?"

"*El Arzobispo de León de Salamanca.*"

I spent the rest of the night with my newfound friend. He was reluctant to tell me what he knew about the fate of my family but

I was most persuasive—I took my time. Once he started talking he told me much more than I ever wanted to hear. I left him face down in the dirt.

Burgos, Castilla-León

Mendoza had a stricken look, "You promised Sánchez his life if he told you the truth—you broke your word and murdered him, anyway."

"I never break my word and I never promised him his life. Quite the contrary, I informed him that I had come to take it."

"But you implied...."

"I implied nothing, Padre. He heard what he wanted to hear. Such is the power of fear."

"You have never actually promised me that I..."

"That is exactly correct, Padre. Shall we go on."

Sixteen years had passed since the condemnation of my family. It took me weeks to locate all of the men Sánchez had identified. Unfortunately, Ajuntos was safe in France and two others were already dead. Padre Mata had died in respected old age and Bernál de la Garza had died fighting against the Moors of Oran.

So as not to reveal my hand, I took no action against the living until I knew the exact location of them all. I moved first against the lesser men, lest the purpose and direction of my attack become obvious. Federico Delujo was easy. He was a local man, one of the *Santo Hermandad* who, profiting from his association with members of *Santo Oficio*, had become the wealthiest man in Extremadura. Even though the corpse of Jaime Sánchez had been found days earlier, the fool never drew the obvious conclusion. He took no precautions and, after questioning him painfully, I delivered his soul to *El Diablo*.

The priests were more difficult. Although they had retired from service on the Holy Tribunal, they recognized the danger posed by all those that they had wronged—their cloisters were almost impregnable and they were protected by guards. Still, I planned my attacks carefully, penetrated their defenses and slaughtered both de Luna and Medina in their own feather beds. The only sound was the hiss of air from their severed windpipes.

Archbishop de León was rumored to be ill. He had not been seen for months. As a humble supplicant, I entered the grounds of his cloister and hid in the stable until vespers. I found an open window and pulled myself up and through it. The halls were dank and lit only by the light of an occasional candle. The distant chants of monks echoed monotonously from the walls. I waited a long time—until all was silent. I stole along the corridors to the place I knew that the sick priest was being nursed.

The room was closed off from the hall by a heavy door studded with iron nails. From behind the door, I could hear a scrapping sound—the door wasn't locked. Knife in hand, I turned the latch and pushed the door open with my shoulder.

The odor of corruption was a physical blow. Inside, how shall I describe it, was the *thing* that had been Archbishop Amparo de León. He stood facing away from me. His wasted body was naked and the floor was smeared with his filth. Hearing the creak of the door, he slowly turned to face me. His face was immobile and devoid of human expression and his eyes were the half-open eyes of the dead. He moved forward, his feet slapping against the foul floor.

Stunned, I forgot all thoughts of revenge—Satan had exacted it long before. Amparo de León was a victim of the French Disease—the gift from a whore. Along with his reason, the disease had destroyed his very being. Now, soulless, his body continued to live. I left the same way as I entered.

Burgos, Castilla-León

"So the sight of this pitiful creature softened your heart?" Mendoza said.

"No, Padre, that's not it at all. Time and circumstances exact their revenge on all of us. I threw a stone into a very large pond—ripples spread out from a small center, growing constantly wider. There was no end to it. Punishment of the guilty is no solution for, you see, we are all punished whether we are guilty or not."

"Very cynical, Your Grace. Why then do you continue to exact your rev..."

"No, Padre," the old man said. "It's not revenge. It is not even justice." The Bishop leaned forward, the candlelight illuminating his scars. "I'm but a small stick thrust into the gears of a pitiless machine. There are men who are the willing slaves of this machine but the machine itself is the enemy. Revenge against an institution, is pointless—I can only hope to impede its function."

Chapter 20

On Don Jaime's highbred gray, I rode to the port city of Palos. Just outside of that town I managed to sell the animal. I didn't get the full value but, then again, the buyer wasn't particular about ownership papers.

Not wanting to spend too much time waiting, I was obliged to obtain passage on the first outbound caravel, *María Esquina*, captained by a rogue named Sancho Jiménez, and crewed by men who appeared to be escapees from the lowest prison. I slept poorly on our voyage and then only with Bebidor in my hand.

The ship proved herself to be a whore of the worst sort. Her hull was waterlogged and riddled with, la broma, the shipworm. She rode low in the water and wallowed in the swells like a pig. Once, during only a moderate wind, her rotten mainsail tore completely in two. All of the passengers and half of the crew spent much of the time vomiting over the side—this was as much from fear as from seasickness. We barely made Teneriffe in Las Islas Canarias. I deserted the ship with no intention of boarding her again. Later, I learned she disappeared with all hands somewhere between Las Canarias and the Indies.

Waiting for another ship, I had an opportunity to observe the islanders. Some, of course, were Españoles who had arrived following our conquest some years earlier. There were still many of the original inhabitants, however. They were primitive half-clothed people who lived from the sea or by herding flocks of goats and sheep over the rocky mountains that covered the island. Most interesting and, despite the fact that Africa is the nearest landmass, is the fact that the islanders are not Negroes. The islanders are a polyglot of different races. True, a few have Negroid features, but many look

Moorish and still others are fair with light hair—I even saw a woman with blue eyes. Some of the Spaniards told me that these people were descendants of the ancient Antlantians described by Plato. Such may be the case but, from what I could see, they must have lost all traces of that great civilization because these people are filthy and live like animals.

●●●

I didn't have to wait long to continue my voyage although, more careful this time, I rejected several ships that appeared less than seaworthy. I was finally able to obtain passage on a decent looking ship that was refitting following her passage from Spain. She was the *Santa Isabella* and her crew looked reasonably competent. Her Captain was a strange and taciturn man who, during our voyage, presented himself dressed and rouged as a woman. Other than for our Captain's peculiarities, our crossing to the Indies would have been uneventful had we not lost our way and become becalmed for a week. By the time we made landfall we were nearly out of water and, that which we had, had become foul and contaminated with salt. Nevertheless, we were fortunate in that, during our passage, we lost only two men, a crewman and a passenger.

The Captain's navigation was less than perfect but we made landfall, and I remember the exact date, on September 14, 1517. We coasted to the east, looking for Santo Domingo. Instead, the first town we encountered was the town of Santiago de Cuba. Our Captain had not only missed the town of Santo Domingo, he had missed the island of Española altogether—it is only due to fortune that we encountered land at all. Not trusting our Captain further, I disembarked along with most of the other passengers. As far as I was concerned, Cuba was as good as Española and, in that Cuba had been more recently settled, possibly better.

Burgos, Castilla-León

"Excelencia, might I ask a technical question?"

"Certainly, Padre."

"Thus far, your narrative has been entirely of events prior to Cortés' invasion of Mexico. Am I to assume that this is only background information that won't be included in the final edition?"

"Your assumption is incorrect, Padre. It all goes in."

"Into my *Historias Glorias?*"

"Correct."

"Then, might I ask, now that we now seem to embark on the actual Conquest, how will your statements be used?"

Unconsciously, the Bishop bared his worn teeth. "My witness will replace those parts of your document that are incorrect. In those cases where your information is factual, my evidence will be used for detail."

Mendoza leaned forward, the muscles of his face taut. "No publisher will touch the book. He would be burned for heresy."

"You're quite right, Padre. I've arranged to have it published in Alemania."

Mendoza was stunned, "Germany—Lutherans—*Heretics?*"

"Correct again, Padre. They'll be delighted to read of the killing of a few Inquisitors."

Mendoza sat back, fuming, "You'll never get away with it—copies are bound to get into the hands of *Santo Oficio*."

"I'm an old man, Padre. After my death..."

Mendoza jumped to his feet. "After your death! What about me—I'm still young—I'll be recognized as your collaborator."

"A terrible shame, Padre."

La Isla
de Cuba

Cuba is a land of contrasts. On the one hand, it is beautiful with verdant forests and gleaming white beaches—on the other, it is hot and constantly wet. Mosquitoes and biting flies are so abundant as to make life a torment. In those days the town of Santiago was not much to look at. A few stone buildings were in the process of construction but most of the others were of dried mud or rough lumber and the streets were always muddy from the frequent rains. I have even seen ox carts get bogged in the middle of town. Here I saw the first Indios I had ever seen—I wasn't impressed. They were naked and some were darker than Moors. Their hair was long and tangled and many had sores on their legs and arms and some of them had the wounds from whips on their backs. All of them, without exception, had dejected, hopeless countenances. Some were listless and ill, sitting in the mud, barely moving out of the way when a horseman or cart rumbled through.

To my great disappointment many of the Castilians were in scarcely better condition. Although some were well dressed and moved purposefully, others were emaciated and dressed in rags. Some of these men hobbled painfully, crippled by diseases they had acquired from the native women. Others showed the yellowish complexions that I recognized as the hallmark of recurrent fever. To be certain, these fevers were not uncommon in Spain and Italy but in Cuba and the Indies no one escaped their effects.

I recognized that success in this land was by no means assured and I had better move decisively. I, along with some of my fellow passengers, attempted to locate the Governor, Diego Velásquez, or the Governor's agent. It seems the Governor was indisposed and that his agent was on an important errand. This situation persisted for a week. Finally the Governor's agent, I think his name was Hernández, appeared in his office. Happily, he had land available for the lot of us. Less happily, except for one fortunate who happened to be a cousin of the Governor, there were no extra Indios to work the land—they had all been parceled out as encomiendas to the earlier settlers. It was obvious to all that land without Indio servants was worthless so my situation was now worse than ever.

●●●

I learned that the Governor was putting a force together to chastise a tribe of rebellious Indios located in the interior of the island. I was also told that any captured indígenos would be awarded to soldiers who volunteered for this expedition. We were able to muster eight horsemen and thirty-two of infantry, ten of whom were armed with ballestas—crossbows. We also had six Indios whom we would use as guides and scouts. I soon realized that fighting in this country would be nothing like fighting in Italy. The forest was hot, dripping and all but impenetrable. It wasn't possible to see further than the man in front of you. It was a land perfectly suited for ambush.

Sweating under our armor we moved forward cautiously. For two days we saw nothing but stinking, rotting forest complete with leg tripping vines, stinging nettles and the drone of biting insects. On the afternoon of the third day, in an area where the forest opened up slightly, the stillness was pierced by an ululating scream and the forest came alive with naked howling savages. Arrows sang through the air and thudded into the ground and nearby trees. The soldier in front of me collapsed with a fletched shaft protruding from his neck. A stone-tipped spear glanced off my breastplate. I was on the spearman like a cat on a rat. Bebidor flashed and a head rolled in the dust. I made a nice backhand stroke and surprised a naked man armed with nothing but a bow. He lifted his weapon to protect himself but it snapped as Bebidor sliced through his face from his chin to his forehead. Choking, the Indio recoiled, clutching his face, blood spurting in pulses.

Through the screams of the Indios, I heard the shouts of our Captain ordering us to regroup. We Spaniards formed a back-to-back circle while our horsemen attacked knots of the enemy with their lanzas. Although we had already lost five or six of our men, the tide of battle started to turn. Crossbow bolts thunked into the savages as we swordsmen repulsed every assault. The Indios broke and the horsemen rode them down. They speared them through their backs, as we swordsmen attacked. We chased them back to their village that was made up of simple huts covered by grass and palm. Still their warriors turned to fight us in a last ditch effort to let their women escape—they couldn't hold us for a minute—we killed a few and forced the others to surrender.

It was quite a sight. Slack-breasted women squatted in the dirt, moaning and pouring dirt on their heads. The very small children stared at us with their large black eyes while older children scurried around squealing like terrified piglets. We rounded them all up including the lightly wounded warriors. We forced those who were uninjured to minister to those who were hurt and then we tied them all together for the long march back to Santiago. We killed the severely wounded, torched the village and left the very old to their fates.

All in all, it was a rewarding excursion. We lost seven Españoles killed but, of these, three were Basques and don't really count. Most of the rest of us had wounds but most of these wounds were minor. We had reacted sharply and effectively and had killed twenty-six of the enemy outright. We had also taken more than two hundred captives. True, when the division of spoils occurred, we soldiers would get only a few savages apiece and some of these were children. Still it was a start toward making our fortunes.

It turns out I was overly optimistic. The fat Governor Velásquez, who had not even attended the expedition, claimed the Crown's share plus his own share of the Indios—others he divided among his favorites. After this apportionment there were less than two savages per soldier. Of these the caballeros got three apiece because they had supplied their own horses at their own expense. Other than a cut across my nose, I received exactly nothing. It would only be a matter of time before I became one of those sickly Castilians I had seen loitering in town. My feelings for Governor Velásquez can hardly be described.

Burgos, Castilla-León

The old man leaned forward in explanation. "Of course, I shouldn't have been all that surprised and—as a Castilian—know full well that those in authority always take advantage of those with less authority. It is a fact of life and, as such, is not so much as a venial sin. Velásquez simply acted in accordance with this time-honored principle. It's merely a reflex. A man always takes care of himself, his friends and his relatives before he considers strangers. *Proxiumus sum egomet mihi.*" The old man shrugged and said, "To do otherwise would be the real sin, would it not? But I've always been a slow learner. When Cortés offered us riches we believed him. We were vulnerable because we were greedy and greed made us blind. We wanted to believe him. If we suffered, bled and died for Cortés and received little in exchange, we have only ourselves to blame."

The younger priest, with a contemptuous snort, stopped writing. "Excelencia, you're quite a hypocrite. You despise *Santo Oficio* because of its perceived excesses and persecute those of us who have served her in all sincerity. You, on the other hand, in the enslavement of free men and women, are by far the worse criminal."

"You may be right, Mendoza, but, considering our relative situations, my hypocrisy is totally irrelevant. We Soldiers of Christ," the emaciated old man lectured, "simply never considered that our acts, or those later in Mexico or Perú, might be anything other than righteous. I did nothing the others weren't doing and, without the labor of Indio slaves, I would have been unable to survive. Besides, as we all thought then, the Indios were infidels and, for their salvation, mind you, it was better that these people be slaves and Catholic than free and heathen.

Looking back through the prism of years, especially because I no longer believe in salvation, I must wonder. Now let me ask you a question. Under our enlightened administration, the Indies are now almost empty of their original inhabitants and Negroes are being imported to replace them. We even see some here in España. Is the situation so different?"

"Of course it is," Mendoza snorted. "The Indios are free men but blacks, as we have been taught from the Testaments, are accursed and destined to be the servant of servants."

The old man smiled. "I'm sure you're quite right—as a matter of fact, I am convinced of it.

Chapter 21

With no other prospects and with the small amount of money I still had, I purchased supplies including a spade, machete, axe and hoe along with some seed. I placed all of my possessions in a well-worn handcart. I remember that its solid wooden wheel was slightly lopsided which gave the cart a jerky motion as I pushed it along. I left Santiago, alternately pulling and pushing my cart while walking the seven leagues to the property I had been allocated close to the coast. I couldn't be sure of the exact location of my land because

I had no money left to pay a surveyor, so I could only estimate its boundaries based on a description and a crude map.

The property was land only in the technical sense. Mostly it was impassable swamp, penetrated by watery channels and choked with mangrove thickets. My exploration quickly taught me that even those areas that appeared relatively dry were oftentimes covered by the incoming tide—I also learned to be wary. Twice, huge scaly monsters—*los cocodrilos*—launched themselves at me from their hiding places in the dense scrub. I had always heard that these creatures were sluggish but nothing could be further from the truth. They can run with a terrifying speed and I was only able to save myself from their jaws by wounding their armored heads with my espada, Bebidor.

I finally found an elevated island in the swamp that even had a little dry land that never flooded. Here, I cleared a patch of land as well as I could, and made a shelter of mangrove and cane. Having seen the Indio villages, I thatched my hut with the razor-sharp grass that grew luxuriantly in the swamp's mud. Every afternoon, the sky clouded over and rain came down in sheets. I discovered that my roof leaked from multiple places and, it wasn't until I had added many layers of grass, that my abode became reasonably dry. Even so, my small hacienda was almost unlivable—mosquitoes buzzed in ravenous clouds. They were able to penetrate my hut and made my first nights unbearable. I chinked my hut with mud and was finally able to keep most of my tormentors outside. In front of my hut I always kept a small fire burning. By sitting in its smoke I was able to cook and do other tasks while avoiding some of my bloodthirsty neighbors.

I survived as best I could by reaping the harvest of the swamp. Herons, egrets and other water birds were present in great numbers and gathering eggs and capturing the young was no problem during their breeding season. Also, the waters were alive with fish that I caught with hook and line or by using a harpoon that I had fashioned with my knife. Large water rats, which the Indios called hutias, climbed in the mangrove trees and swam in the channels. I was able to snare many of these for they were, despite their appearance, quite delicious. In the meantime, I cleared and worked the land for my garden and planted my seeds for the native crops. These plants grew readily in the fertile soil but protecting them from the hungry denizens of the forest proved difficult especially during those times when I was down with recurrent fever which was, unfortunately, often.

I was surviving but barely, thinking how much better off I'd been in Italy or even as a peasant in Extremadura. I learned, however, that there was a market in the skins of cocodrilos. To catch them I sharpened, at either end, hardwood sticks of one finger length. To the middle of these now sharpened sticks I would attach a stout line, almost a rope, and then I would pierce the body of a snared hutia, lengthwise, with my sharpened stick. The opposite end of my line I would secure to the trunk of a large mangrove. From an overhanging limb I would hang my hutia bait a forearms length from the surface of the water. I would then check my bait the next morning, for cocodrilos hunt mostly by night. If I had luck, the bait would be gone, my line would be stretched tight and an unhappy cocodrilo would be sulking at the other end. If I played the beast carefully, I could work him into the shallows and kill the beast with a blow to the head. Then it was only a matter of beaching the carcass and removing his belly skin. You see, only the skin of the belly is valuable for it is free of the armored plate of the back and sides. Even so, the skinning was always difficult for the skin of these beasts, unlike the skin of a deer, wolf, or even a sheep, is attached firmly to the underlying meat and can never be freed with the fist but only by cutting it away with a knife.

I dried and smoked the skins in a cabaña that I made for this purpose and when I had enough to justify the journey, I traveled to Santiago de Cuba to make my sale. In this way I was able to make a little money and was even able to purchase medicines, a few extra tools and foodstuffs, and even some clothes to replace those that I had worn out. My situation was anything but promising but I was young and optimistic.

Chapter 22

One day, while on one of my trips to Santiago I was approached by one of the men, Juan Pedro de Alva, who had accompanied me on my voyage from the Islas Canarias and had been a fellow soldier on our ill-fated expedition against the Indios. De Alva, who was a man of my age, was the fourth son of a petty Aragonese aristocrat. As a fourth son, he had not received an inheritance and was, like me, struggling to make his fortune in the Indies. I can remember my shock when I saw him—he had undergone a complete transformation. He had been a fine looking man, tall with broad shoulders, high cheekbones, and compelling black eyes, but now he was shrunken and emaciated. His dark hair and beard were dull and lank. His skin, as well as the whites of his eyes, had the yellowish cast of a sufferer of chronic disease. His cheeks were hollow and his clothing was dirty and ragged. Nevertheless, he approached me enthusiastically.

"Have you heard the good news, Rodrigo?"

"What news?"

"The Governor is outfitting a fleet to explore the lands to the west of Cuba." De Alva could barely contain his excitement.

I shrugged my shoulders. "So what? It's just another way to get killed while helping the old ladrón get richer than he already is."

"No. This is going to be different. Did you know that Francisco Hernández de Córdoba sailed off and discovered the island of Yucatán and did you know that this land is populated by Indios that wear cotton clothes and live in stone houses?"

"Yes. I heard."

"Then did you hear that these Indios are covered in gold and jewels?"

"Not exactly—I heard that they had a few small trinkets that had a little gold in them. I also heard that the Indios killed over sixty of Hernández's men and the rest of them barely made it back alive."

De Alva's face fell. "I'm sure you're wrong, Rodrigo, for why else did Don Diego go to the expense of raising another expedition with two hundred and forty men, commanded by Juan de Grijalva. They're not back yet but the *San Sebastian*, under Pedro de Alvarado, returned with reports that the land is not an island but a continent." De Alva's eyes lit up again. "Alvarado's men say that while they were sailing along the coast, they could see towns with silver houses. They also said that, in the interior, there are great cities with plazas paved in solid gold."

De Alva's kind of talk was as common as dirt in Cuba—somewhere, everywhere, nowhere—there was gold beyond imagination. It was always on the next hill, or in the next valley, or maybe on a nearby island. Somehow most gold-seekers simply withered away and died. The few who got wealthy in the islands did it with agriculture or by selling goods to the dreamers.

"We'll talk about it again, Juan, when the rest of Grijalva's people get back. I think it would be wise to talk to them before jumping off into *esta tierra del oro*."

De Alva shook his head vigorously. "That'll be too late. The Governor may be a pig, but he's no fool. He has talked to those who have already returned and is so convinced that he's requested and, by distributing money to a few of its members, has received permission from the Council of the Indies to outfit still another fleet and head back to *Yucatán* as soon as possible. Some are saying that he's supposed to await the Prueba Real but, the Governor is so excited by the discoveries, he plans to send out the fleet as soon as it's ready, even if Royal permission doesn't come through."

"So excited? Or is he just trying to keep the whole thing to himself?"

"Well some people say, that Velásquez is moving fast because he fears the King might give the *Carta Real* for exploration to Diego Colón, the Great Admiral's son."

"Now that sounds more like the Governor Velásquez that I've come to love—a little bribery, and he isn't going to be troubled by a small technicality like the Royal Permission." I stroked my beard. "Given the Governor's enthusiasm for this expedition, I'm sure that this glorious enterprise is going to be honored with his personal corpulent leadership."

For the first time de Alva looked a little uncertain. "Not exactly. I'm sure that the Governor has pressing concerns here in Cuba. He's looking for a Captain-General."

I patted de Alva on the back. "Well, he need look no further although it will take me a few days to put all of my numerous and important affairs in order—after that, I'll be willing to take on this hazardous post. Hmm—I'll have to give it some thought—it may be difficult to keep my ships afloat after I've loaded them with all that gold."

De Alva was not amused. "You might not be exactly what Velásquez has in mind but, make no mistake about it, he's in deadly earnest. He's already gathered six brigantines and, when Grijalva gets back, his caravels will be added to the fleet. The way I understand it, practically every free man on the island is joining up—I've decided to go myself."

"I'll pray the rosary for you, Juan. By the way, how do you think the Governor is going to find this Captain-General? At one time or other, he has managed to cheat every man on the island—how can he trust anyone?"

"I'm not sure he can but, the way I hear it, he has his eye on Hernán Cortés. Have you heard of him?"

I searched my memory. "A little. Isn't he the alcalde of some pueblito a few leagues from here. What do you know about him? Is he experienced enough for the job?"

"Maybe. I've checked around and heard a few things. He's about thirty-six years of age and originally came from Medellín in Extremadura. Everyone who knows him says that he is a fine fellow—he's been in the islands for years and used to be the Governor's secretary and is also the Godfather to Cortés' only child."

"*Ah ha!*"

De Alva went on seriously, "But it's not what you think—there is no love lost between Cortés and Velásquez. Twice, the Governor had Cortés arrested and imprisoned and, at one point, even condemned him to hang. In both cases Cortés escaped and holed up in a church."

"And this is the man that Velásquez plans to make his Captain-General? This is the most hare-brained adventure I ever heard of."

De Alva went on, "The story gets even more interesting—one account has it that the first arrest was because Cortés was plotting a rebellion against the Governor. Another has it that all the trouble was over a woman."

"Look, Juan, I don't believe for a moment that a man as greedy as the Governor would be stupid enough to appoint a man who had already been in rebellion against him—let's hear your story about the woman."

After living for months without company, I was hungry for gossip.

"Well, the way I heard it, at least, Cortés, who's a well known lady's man, was caught in *flagrante delicto* with one of the few Castilian ladies on the island, Doña Catalina Suárez. When her relatives insisted that Cortés do the honorable thing—he refused—possibly because La Señora is reported to be quite ugly. The family appealed to Governor Velásquez and Velásquez backed the family up and ordered the marriage—Cortés continued to refuse. Velásquez ordered Cortés arrested and jailed. Cortés only yielded when faced with the threat of the hangman's noose. Cortés and Catalina were wed with the Governor as the bride's sponsor. Later the Governor became the Godfather to the couple's daughter."

I laughed until I cried. "Thank you, Juan—that's the funniest story I've heard in a long time." I sobered up. "Has it occurred to you that this Hernán Cortés just might be the slave of his overworked penis? He sounds like just the right kind of man to lead a bunch of idiotas into a new continent loaded with blood-thirsty savages."

De Alva pursed his lips and went on almost as if speaking to himself. "Well, it's true that he has left a string of half-breed children between here and Santo Domingo. I was even told that he left España because of some woman trouble."

"It sounds like this Cortés is one Hell of a man," I said, "but still, there are the arrests and the threatened execution. These are reasons enough to prevent the Governor from appointing Cortés as Captain-General."

"I'm sure you're right," De Alva said. "The way I hear it, though, is that Cortés has made a compact with two of the Governor's confidants—Andrés de Duero and Amador de Lares—as to a mutual division of any gold, jewels or other wealth that Cortés might come by. These gentlemen apparently prevailed on the Governor's better judgment, citing the Governor's Godfather status to the Cortés' child. Besides, what else can the Governor do because, as you said, every man on the island, including the two of us, hates the miserable cabrón."

Chapter 23

Although Velásquez never profited by it and as no one, including himself, could have ever predicted, Cortés was surely the best, or perhaps the luckiest man that could have been picked for an adventure the likes of which no one could have ever imagined. He was mild mannered and unassuming and, despite aristocratic blood, preferred the plain name of Cortés. Many people assume, because of his fame and accomplishments that he was a big man, even a giant—they would be wrong. He was short, perhaps a palm's breadth shorter than me, and I am not tall. His hair and beard were a red-brown color that bleached in the sun and he was so fair skinned that he was constantly sunburned. On the other hand he was well built and hardy. He was well trained in the use of all weapons and the match for any man in a desperate fight. Still, he would not have cut a very impressive figure if it were not for the fact that, when he was able, he always dressed well. Perhaps this was out of vanity but I believe it was calculated to impress the simple soldiers that he was a man of importance and command.

For more than two years I had occasion to observe this man of contradictions. He was perhaps the most courageous and the most intelligent man I have ever encountered. He understood men like a beekeeper understands his bees. The beekeeper needs courage to do his work and, if he is stung, he must not react. He must handle his hive gently. He soothes it and calms the angry bees. If he must, he replaces the old queen with one that is new, and crushes the old queen under his thumb. The bees work hard, give all that they can in hopes that they can put away enough for the winter but, in the end, the beekeeper steals their honey for himself.

Cortés was like that. He was able to draw out the best that a man had inside of him and he was able to exploit a man's every foible and weakness. He radiated complete sincerity and was therefore totally convincing. He made the soldiers believe that he loved them and was ready to sacrifice and die for them. In return men, even men who had reason to mistrust him, believed him and were misled. At the same time Cortés was one of the most single-minded man who has ever existed. No one, whether Indio or Castilian, was safe from his greed and those of us who listened to his lies came to regret it. I came to hate the man but still I respect him for the purity of his ambition and I am proud that I can say that, in serving under him, I became a part of history.

If Cortés had a weakness, and he had very few, it was that of seeming over-righteousness. He acted as if he actually *believed* that he was the tool by which God would Christianize all of the heathen lands. This much is understandable and is quite in keeping with our Castilian crusading spirit. What is not understandable, however, was his willingness to risk our entire undertaking for the short-term satisfaction of smashing idols and forcing the Indios to worship the Blessed Virgin and the Trinity. As a matter of fact, Padre Olmedo, who was our actual representative of God, had to dissuade him from many of his more rash actions.

Later, during our expedition, I saw things, truly strange things, that made me wonder about the essential nature of Cortés. He was not only courageous; he was much too courageous. He was not only ingenious; he was brilliant. He was not only pious; he was fanatical. Not only was he duplicitous; he was the father of all lies. Not only was he greedy, ambitious and treacherous but, in him, these sins became virtues. He was the reincarnation of Agamemnon, Achilles and Odysseus, all in the same man and entirely in a more effective form. Most importantly, he never hesitated, not once. It was if he knew, absolutely knew, that he would not fail...*could not fail.* It was as if...."

Burgos, Castilla-León

Mendoza stopped writing and looked up sharply. "Come now, your Grace. After all, you are the one who is an unbeliever. Yet you describe the man in terms that are well nigh supernatural. Your fanciful description of Cortés hardly accords with any of the reports that I've ever read. Cortés, although the instrument of God, was merely a man. He may indeed have had his faults but God would never have used a man as flawed as you describe."

The old Bishop held Mendoza's eyes without blinking and then turned away, looking at a small brown bird flitting in the branches of a naked tree just outside of the room's only window.

"You're right, Padre. A loving God would never have used such a man so there must be some other explanation. You know, of course, that one of the many reasons for the unlikely success of our expedition was that the Mexica confused Cortés with one of their own gods."

"Of course. The facts are well documented in my own works but you are not, I should hope, implying that there was more to

Cortés than the confusion of ignorant savages."

The Bishop laughed a mirthless laugh. "I imply nothing. I was only saying that Cortés was not only our Captain, a leader par excellence, who, time after time, gambled against the impossible and came out the winner. He was lucky, beyond comprehension. He was a gambler against odds and his luck far surpassed any logical expectation. Most people, including you Padre, who know the basic facts, recognize this and assume that it was not luck, but the intervention of the Holy Spirit—what an incredible joke. I was there and saw the brutality, the disease, the fornication and the slaughter. It is blasphemy to give God credit for these atrocities. El Diablo, on the other hand, gave his blessing to all of our undertakings and strengthened our hands."

Mendoza tapped on the table. "I disagree. The collapse of evil oftentimes necessitates a little pain, as they say, to make an omelet et cetera. For the sake of Israel, God ordered the destruction of Jericho and all of its inhabitants. For the same reason God also ordered Saul to slaughter the Amalekites, utterly. The destruction of the Mexican Empire was no different. The Empire collapsed in blood and flame but our victory ended, for all time, the cruelty of the Aztec sacrificial altar and brought to the Mexicans the sublime light of our Catholic religion. When you look at it from this point of view Hernán Cortés deserves canonization."

The Bishop positively grinned. "Santo Hernán Cortés, I like the ring of it. The Caudillo would have laughed but he would have liked it, too." The old man leaned forward. "Thief, liar, hypocrite, fornicator, murderer, I think Cortés would make a very appropriate saint."

The old man stood up from his worn wooden chair, his robes hanging loosely around his skeletal frame. He slowly paced back and forth speaking slowly, as if no one else were within hearing.

"Is it possible that there is such a thing as an unloving God, one who is indifferent to human suffering? One that never loses because, either way things turn out, he always wins. Could it be that the Cortés was nothing less than the familiar to such a God—a soldier of Satan—miliz satani. Could he have been the saint of such a God?"

"The Devil exists, your Grace, but is not a God."

The old man paced back-and-forth twice before uttering a word.

"Padre Mendoza, in your studied opinion what are the dominant forces on earth, joy and happiness or pain and sorrow?"

"We strive for happiness."

The old man stopped pacing and turned to face the younger man. "You have side-stepped my question. What are the dominant forces?"

"All life ends in death."

"Yes," said the old man as she paced, "and between birth and death there is work, love, ambition and joy mixed with pain, grief and fear of the grave. If you place both issues on the scales, the forces of sorrow are the heaviest."

Mendoza reluctantly agreed, "Perhaps."

"Perhaps, indeed," the old priest repeated to himself. "The forces of pain are the strongest." The trap slammed shut. "Evil rules our lives."

"No!" Mendoza started to stand up.

"Oh yes, Padre." The Bishop motioned for Mendoza to sit down again. "Despite what you might think, I take no pleasure in my conclusion. If evil rules then Satan is stronger than God." The old man licked his thin lips. "On the other hand, we have been taught that, in the great war in Heaven, God prevailed and Lucifer was cast out."

Mendoza felt the trap loosen. "That is correct, which means that God is far stronger. He only permits the Devil to exist to further His Eternal Plan."

"Padre Mendoza?" The ancient priest's face looked like one of the long dead. "Is not Satan the Prince of Liars? Would he not teach us a lie? What if, in fact... Satan prevailed?"

While in Santiago de Cuba, sometime early in November of 1518, I was struck by another bout of fever and was forced to rest in an abandoned hut until I could move around again. I can remember that I had nowhere to lie but the damp earth. I also remember that my attack was severe and that my suffering body alternated between hellish fevers and teeth-chattering chills. I must have been unconscious because, when I started to improve, my goods were gone and sandals had been stolen—my pockets were turned inside out. The few pieces of silver that I had from the sale of my skins had disappeared.

I was in this miserable situation when Hernán Cortés, himself, arrived in town. From my bed on the dirt, I heard a roll of drums, and a fanfare of trumpets as a crier shouted:

"In the name of His Majesty, His Viceroy Diego Velásquez, and the Capitán-Generalísimo Cortés, all who wish to conquer and settle newly discovered lands and receive a share of gold, silver and other riches, and an encomienda of Indios once the new lands are pacified are invited to join."

Semi-delirious, I lurched down the street to where a man was sitting at a desk located under a spreading tree. On each side of the desk there were red and white banners on which these words were emblazoned:

"Let us follow the sign of the Holy Cross in the true faith, for under this sign we shall conquer."

More curious yet as to who in the benighted realm of Santiago de Cuba would be flying flags honoring the vision of Constantine the Great, I decided to take a closer look. The fever must have affected my mind for I was one of the first to enlist. Cortés, who I had never seen previously, was handsomely attired wearing a velvet cloak trimmed with loops of gold, a medallion and a gold chain, and a plume of feathers. He had short auburn hair and a pleasant countenance. His beard nearly covered a hairline scar that extended from his lip to his chin. Later, I was to learn, the scar came from a knife fight over a woman in Santo Domingo.

Even though I must have looked a very sorry specimen, Cortés stood up, took my hand in both of his and looked me in the eyes. "Your hometown, my boy?"

"San Miguel de Extremadura, Señor."

Cortés smiled warmly. "I am from Medellín, not too far from San Miguel. We're neighbors. Perhaps I know your family?"

I hesitated and gave him my full name. A cloud passed over his face but then he smiled again. "No, I've never heard of your family, Don Rodrigo, but a fellow Extremeño is always welcome."

I wondered how he knew I was Don Rodrigo?

"Do you have combat experience?" He was looking at the scars on my face.

"Sí, senor, six years in the Italian campaigns."

Cortés now really looked interested. "With what kinds of weapons are you experienced.

"*Yo tengo experiencia con la espada, hacha, lanza y martillo de batalla.*"

Cortés replied quickly, "As far as we know the savages have no metal plate so we won't need axes or battle hammers. Do you have experience with the crossbow or musket?"

"I also have," remembering my duel with Basilio said, "some experience with the musket but—except for a few practice shots—none with the crossbow."

"Good. Very good. Do you have your own armor and weapons?"

"I have my own armor and my sword." Fortunately, I had left my equipment back at my ranchito—otherwise I would have nothing.

"Good. We will also provide you with quilted cotton protection. The Indios use it themselves as practically their only armor—we'll use it under our regular armor. It may be hot but it helps to prevent our armor from chafing the skin. Besides it's an extra layer of protection and protects those parts of the arms and legs not covered by steel armor. Can you handle a horse?"

"Sí, senor, I can handle a horse and, when I was a boy, I even trained a few. But I wouldn't want to mislead you, I'm no caballero."

Cortés fingered the scar on his lip. "*No es importa.* The enemy we encounter will not be able to distinguish a skilled horseman from a man who can barely sit upright on a horse. Nevertheless, I will use you as a foot soldier because that is your experience. We are taking horses, however, and should the need arise I will expect you to fight mounted." Cortés paused for a moment. " Many of our volunteers will have never been in a fight before. I'm depending on you to protect these men until they are adequately trained."

"Yes, Sir."

"Sign your name here." He indicated a paper with a growing list, most of which were not signatures but only marks. Without looking down at my signature, Cortés went on. "You can write which, in addition to your other talents, will prove useful—I respect those with education. As you may know I myself studied law at Salamanca. And you?"

I hesitated, remembering the nights I had poured over books that I had borrowed from Señor Tamayo and Don García. " My formal education is... limited. I can read, though, and have done what I could to learn Latin and study the classics."

At this point I noticed something interesting. Cortés' vernacular speech, now became more formal—he pronounced his words with an elegant lisp. Cortés, as did many successful leaders, attracted support by addressing men in the accents that they themselves used. In Cortés' case, vulgar speech was but an act for his vulgar soldiers.

Cortés went on, "Are you familiar with Ovid and Thucydides?"

"I am more familiar with the *Histories* by Livy and, of course, the stories of Homer and the *Aeneid* of Virgil."

"Yes, Homer." Cortés tapped his fingers. "*The Iliad* is wonderful but I only wish he hadn't ended the it with funeral games of Hector. His *Odyssey* is a bit too female for my tastes. What do you think of Tacitus?"

I had a complete feeling of unreality. Not only was I suffering the after-effects of the fever but I was standing under the hot Cuban sun discussing ancient literature.

"His description of the ancient Teutones was excellent and his lines on the Roman conquest of Britannia were poetic, even haunting."

Cortés beamed with genuine pleasure. "You mean, of course, where he writes, 'They made a wasteland and they called it peace'."

"Exactly."

Cortes' eyes twinkled. "Perhaps Tacitus was overly judgmental. Pax Romana, no matter what its costs, had many benefits." Cortés went on without pausing, "Do you know any languages? Do you speak Basque or Catalan?"

"No, but, in the army, I was often bivouacked with Italian and Landsknechte troops so I am fluent in the Neopolitan dialect and can even get by in German and Puertugese."

"*Haben sie feinde soldaten getöten?*"

I was surprised Cortés spoke German and even more surprised

at his question.

I struggled for the words— "*Jah, 'Ich war in schlacte nach Ravenna und Marignano'* or is it '*der Ravenna und Marignano*'?"

"I really don't know." Cortés laughed at himself. "I don't speak much German, either. We have already enlisted some Italians and even one German—you can help them feel at home. I think that you will prove useful, indeed, to our *Santa Compania*. Do well, Rodrigo, and I will reward you with rank. After you pick up your things and return here to our gathering armada, I ask that you help our Escribano, Señor Diego de Godoy, to record the various contributions of our investors and soldiers."

With this he dismissed me with a nod and turned to the next man in line who, as I noticed, he greeted just as warmly as he had greeted me.

Chapter 24

I returned to my home as quickly as my unshod feet would permit me. My mind was clearing now and I was starting to have serious reservations about my decision. On the other hand, I now had no choice for I had given my word and had signed my name. I collected my weapons and the few clothes and other personal items I had. Over time I had acquired two yellow dogs and a small herd of eight skinny pigs that were so tame that they would follow me like pets. I loaded my goods, including eight sacks of dried fish, on my cart and, trailed by my dogs and my pigs, I reversed directions and returned to Santiago. I gave my dogs to a shopkeeper who, in exchange, gave me thin cakes of cassava bread. I then donated my dried fish, cassava bread and pigs to the expedition so that I would have some small investment in the enterprise beyond that of my naked life.

It was not difficult to locate the Escribano. He was sitting under the shade of a half-collapsed shed near the harbor. His desk was a rough plank held up by two wooden sawhorses and, in front of him, several men stood in line. The one closest to him was displaying his gold neck chain even as Godoy scribbled notes with a black plume. Nearby was a small corral in which several pigs were huddled in stunned disbelief at what they were seeing. A butcher and two Indios were butchering a pig. The carcass was tied by the hind feet and was suspended from a pulley tied to a branch of a tree. The Indios controlled one end of the rope as the butcher guided the animal into a barrel of boiling water in preparation for scraping. I tapped the butcher on the shoulder and pointed to my own small herd of pigs—he nodded his understanding. The Indios, with my assistance, herded the pigs into the corral. My pet pigs began squealing when they smelled the blood.

I introduced myself to the Escribano. "Are you Señor Godoy?"

"Wait your turn in line, mozo."

"Certainly." I measured him. He was well dressed with a blue sweat-soaked blouse and pantalones of the same material but darker. His head was large and covered by stringy black hair that hung to his shoulders. His face was pasty and his nose was large and lumpy. The overall impression was one of softness.

It was finally my turn. "Señor Cortés said I was to help you."

He sputtered, "Then, why have you just been standing there?"

He stood up and gave me his chair. Expecting some instruction, I sat down. Godoy promptly walked away. I was on my own. I studied Godoy's list so that I might duplicate his work. It wasn't complicated and, being the sole proprietor of the list, I could see how easy it would be for me to fatten my own account. I was making an honest report until I was distracted by an especially loud squeal—the Indios had seized my favorite sow and were dragging her to the gallows. With a quick stroke the butcher sliced her throat—a jet of blood squirted covered his apron. I decided to give myself credit for three extra pigs.

As the men arrived I checked off their names from Cortés' original list. Under each name I noted those items donated to the expedition versus those items that were the man's personal property.

"What's this?" Juan de Alva stood before me. If anything he looked sicklier than before. "I knew you'd join up but I never thought you would already be one of the Jefes."

"I'm not. I'm just doing a job. What do you have to declare?"

"This is it. My helmet, sword and a shirt of mail."

"And your buckler?"

He shrugged. "Stolen. I hope that Cortés will give me another one on credit."

"I wouldn't worry if I were you. Most of the men don't have any more than you and some have less. I hear we're buying weapons from Grijalva's people and are having smiths make others. Do you have anything else?"

"I have a knife and the shirt on my back."

"Duly recorded." I nodded. "*Adelante!*"

I continued my work until dark and started again next morning.

●●●

"*Rodrigo, mi compadre!*"

I remembered seeing the man but I couldn't recall his name. It must have showed on my face.

"You didn't forget me, did you? I'm your old amigo from Italy."

"*Hijo!* How could I forget! You were the one who gave me the idea of coming to this bug-infested place." I laughed. "If you weren't so well-dressed I'd knock you down."

José Maldinado was, in fact, well dressed and, despite the heat, was wearing a gold-colored cloak. He had grown a great gut since I last saw him.

"It looks like you've done right well by yourself," I observed.

"Good enough but I'm going to do better. That's why I am signing up with Cortés."

I looked at his stomach. "I don't know if he's going to be able to feed your great belly. We are going heavy on frijoles, cassava and salt pork."

"That's good by me—I need to trim down a little. If this thing gets any bigger," he patted his swollen stomach, "I won't be able to find my worm, anymore."

On the ground behind him a team of Indios were piling bundles of goods.

I shook my head. "What do you have to report?"

"Ten sacks of salt, fifteen loads of dried fish, and five loads of bacon and salt pork. I am also giving four pairs of huaraches, five swords, three breastplates, six spears, two crossbows, one mail shirt and four shields and bucklers." I dropped my mouth in astonishment. When I last saw him in Italy he had almost nothing.

"Is that everything?"

"*Es todo.*"

"And what are you claiming for yourself?"

"Four crates of clothes, a sword, breastplate, helmet, shirt of mail, greaves, knife and an axe. You'd better put down this neck chain, too. I wouldn't want anyone to claim that it belonged to him." Its links were solid gold and it weighed in at the equivalent of two hundred pesos de oro.

I scratched my head. "You've grown rich my friend."

"This is nothing. I've got me this nice encomienda in Española with plenty of fruit trees and cattle. My women will take care of it when I'm gone."

I cleared my throat. "You've already got what you need. Why chance it?"

Maldinado laughed from deep down. "We are going to have one Hell of a lot of fun, hombre. That's why I'm going."

"Fun?"

"A lot more fun than Italy. Migues is coming, too."

"Migues?" Now this was a surprise. Migues was one of the best but I never pictured him in the Indies.

"Did he get rich, too?"

"He did good but that is not what's important. With us old-timers from the Wars, we'll cut through those Indios like a hot knife through soft butter. I feel sorry for the poor ignorantes. It's going to be fun I tell you—more fun than anybody can imagine."

●●●

Paco Migues arrived shortly thereafter. Unlike Maldinado he was lean and fit. His skin was baked red by the tropical sun and his nose was peeling. He was dressed in a tan suit of rough homespun cotton with a broad belt of black leather. His face was shaded by a straw hat and his red hair had bleached almost white.

"Hola, Paco!" I welcomed him.

"Rodrigo!" he roared right back. "I'd heard you were around but I didn't know that you were running things." I shook his hand and found that it was as hard and rough as my own.

"I wish I were but I'm just one of the esclavos. Where have you been, hombre?"

"In Espanola with José. He has a couple of well-placed relatives in the Council of the Indies and they gave him a good encomienda in the mountains. José has been damned good to me and gave me a piece of his farm. How about you?"

I cleared my throat. "I've done well enough. I have this rancho down on the coast just a few leagues from here—one of these days it's going to be worth a fortune."

Migues eyed my rags. "I'm glad to hear it."

I decided to tend to business. "What do you have to report?"

"Thirty-three salted chickens, four bags of dried frijoles and six bags of dried maíz."

"And your personal belongings?"

"One helmet, shield, gorget, greaves, sword, a spear and a change of clothes."

I jotted it down. "Done."

"What can I do to help? I don't like standing around."

"I'd get down to the ships and give the sailors a hand packing things in. That way you'll get a better idea as to which ship is carrying what cargo. Let me know what you find out."

Migues laughed, pulled himself straight and snapped his heals. "*Absolutamente, El Señor.* Your wish is my command."

Chapter 25

Three hundred and fifty of us soldiers gathered in Santiago de Cuba in preparation for the embarkation. Wealthy or poor, we were all adventurers and gamblers. To be certain every man who had left España for the Indies had done so in order to make his fortune. Some of our volunteers, like Maldinado, had already achieved this lofty goal yet they gambled everything they had, including their very lives, in order to participate in yet another adventure. Some of the wealthier men, hopeful of getting a bigger share of the profits, even outfitted the poorer soldiers.

Others, however, such as Diego de Ordaz, who was steward to the Governor, were not especially eager to go. They were to spy on the expedition.

Whisperings were heard that friends of the Governor were trying to convince Don Diego to withdraw command from Cortés and replace him with another. Cortés heard of this and hurriedly loaded the vessels with supplies and arms of all kind including guns, powder, crossbows and other weapons. We even raided the butchery and made off with of most of the town's supply of meat. We embarked and were hoisting up our anchors when Don Diego rushed to the shore shouting something unintelligible. Cortés didn't listen and the fleet set sail.

●●●

We were still undersupplied so we made for the south to Puerto de Trinidad, which we reached in a few days. Here, Cortés again set up his banner and recruited as many men as he could. We recruited Pedro de Alvarado, who was the first of Grijalva's Captains who had returned to Cuba. His ship had returned with fifteen thousand pesos of gold treasure that the Indios from the coast of the new land had exchanged for glass beads. Pedro's four brothers also joined up. In addition we were also able to recruit two Captains from Grijalva's three ships that returned to Cuba after Alvarado.

One of these Captains was Alonso de Ávila, a man in his middle thirties. His abrasiveness was matched only by his courage. The other Captain was Franciso de Montejo. Montejo was the same age as Ávila but, unlike him, had an easygoing manner. Montejo, as I can recall him, was a man of medium height with light hair and eyes. His head was rather large and his nose good and straight. He had a ready smile and he had the build of a warrior. Unfortunately, he was an unswerving partisan of the Governor.

Another Captain—Cristóbal de Olid—arrived late to our gathering expedition. When the last three ships of Grijalva's fleet did not appear, the Governor sent Olid on a search mission. Grijalva had already departed the shores of Yucatán so Olid never found him and returned just in time to join Cortés' fleet. This was his misfortune because, years later, Cortés had him hanged for rebellion. All of this was in the future, however, and, at the time at which I am speaking, Cristóbal seemed to be very much in control of things. He was a big man with broad shoulders and short brown hair. His lower lip had a strange way of crinkling when he smiled which wasn't often. He had a way of muscling around smaller men that, as you might imagine, I didn't appreciate.

We also recruited other notables such as Juan de Escalante, Andrés de Tapia, Javier de la Concha, and Gonzalo Mejia. Gonzalo de Sandoval and many others came from the town of Santispíritus, fifty-four miles away. Some of these men owned farms in the area and were able to supply indispensable items such as cassava bread, dried beans and salt pork.

● ● ●

While in Trinidad, I was approached by the town's alcalde, Francisco Verdugo. He mistook me for a Governor's man.

"Señor de la Peña...that is your name isn't it?"

I didn't know how Verdugo recognized me. "Yes, it is."

"I'm told that you helped Don Diego on one of his forays against the indígenos. Am I right?"

I nodded.

"*Muy bien*. Don Diego has ordered me to arrest Hernán Cortés. The man has stolen some money. I want you to assist me."

"And if I assist you?"

"Of course, of course, my boy," he said with a wink. "Don Diego's friends will be amply rewarded—we wouldn't want it any other way. Don't worry, the expedition will go ahead as planned only under the capable leadership of Señor Vasco Porcallo."

I knew of this Porcallo. He was a famous boracho—a drunkard—who entertained himself by cutting off the testicles of his Indios.

"I'll be delighted to help you, Señor Verdugo."

I helped Verdugo straight away by informing Cortés of the Governor's intent. Cortés was in the cabin of his flagship, writing at his desk.

"Caudillo, I don't wish to disturb you but I have urgent information."

Cortés looked up. "Yes. Go on."

"I have just learned that the Governor plans to place you under arrest and to give your command to Porcallo. Give me the word, and I'll gather others of your friends—we'll fight!"

Cortés regarded me calmly through his cat-like golden eyes. "Porcallo? Thank you for the information, Don Rodrigo, but I believe that a matter such as this is best handled diplomatically," He pondered the issue. "Rather than calling together our friends, I would instead like you to ask those members of our expedition who most publicly favor Governor Velásquez to report to me here on my flagship as soon as they are able."

"Caudillo?"

"Just do it, please." He started writing again.

●●●

I located a half a dozen of Don Diego's friends. It wasn't difficult. They were loudly proclaiming their dissatisfaction with Cortés to anybody who would listen. They were taken aback when I told them that Cortés had requested their presence.

"*De la Peña, mi compadre*" —Montejo greeted me— "Cortés doesn't have the stomach for an adventure of this magnitude whereas Porcallo has. Keep it in mind that I've already been over there and, as an eyewitness. I can tell you that not only our fortunes but our lives are at stake. Don't you think it is best that we place our money on the fastest horse?"

I tried to be as agreeable. "I'm sure Porcallo's the best choice. Still, what do you have to lose by talking to Cortés?"

"*Mi cabeza?*" Montejo laughed while rocking his head side to side as if it were lose on his shoulders. "You're right, though, and besides, he may have something amusing to say."

I was not present at the meeting but I heard bits and pieces later. Cortés petted them and smoothed their feathers. "Yes, Gentlemen, I can reassure you that I am devoted to the Governor. After all, not only is he the godfather to my only child but he has honored me by giving me this post."

Diego de Ordaz responded, "Perhaps, Caudillo, but the word is out that Don Diego wishes to replace you."

"That's because he is corrupted by disloyal people who wish to cheat him. My responsibility is to see to it that he is adequately served and gets everything he is due. For that matter, gentlemen, I fully intend that each and every one of you also get your due. I can guarantee you, that under my leadership all of you will become rich beyond all possible imagination. Think of it! " Cortés slammed his fist onto his desk. "I am not like those debiluchos, Hernández and Grijalva and, as long as I have a breath in my body, I will not back off until we have squeezed every last ounce of gold from the new land."

Francisco de Montejo cut in, "Hernández de Córdoba might not have backed off, either, if he hadn't the misfortune of getting himself killed." Reportedly, everyone laughed.

Cortés repeated himself to make sure that everyone got the point. "I am going to make all of you rich!"

The Caudillo's powerful logic carried the day and no move was made against Cortés. He then called me into his office.

"Don Rodrigo, I'm a little tired and I would like you to help me write a letter to Governor Velásquez. Would you mind taking my dictation?"

"*Cómo no, señor?*" Cortés offered me a straight-backed chair and a sheet of fine writing paper. Cortés dictated slowly, giving me time to keep up with his words.

My Dearest Don Diego,
    I trust that you and your family are well. I write this letter to inform you that preparations for our voyage are going smoothly and that we are in the process of securing more food and adequate armament. I must tell you how saddened I was to learn that you are dissatisfied with my performance as Captain-General of your armada. I was so distressed that, at first, I seriously considered resigning my commission but have now determined to perform my duties so responsibly as to cause you to completely renew your faith in me. I will always be your man no matter what adversity we may face.
    With Greatest Respect,
    Hernán Cortés, Capitán-General

Cortés reviewed the letter quickly and then signed it with a flourish. "What do you think of my letter to the Governor, Don Rodrigo?"

It will probably just confuse him." Cortés folded the letter, dripped molten wax onto it and impressed his seal ring into it.

"Do you really think so?" Cortés smiled. "You may return to your regular duties. By the way, would you check with the progress of the blacksmiths' work? They are manufacturing armor and extra helmets."

Not only did I check on the blacksmiths, but I was able to convince two of them to join our grand enterprise—it wasn't difficult to do.

Chapter 26

Once our preparations were complete in Trinidad our small armada sailed for San Cristóbal de Habana on the Cuban north coast. A disgusted Caudillo arrived five days late. His flagship, the *Santa Maria de la Concepcion*, struck on a sandbar. The ship couldn't be floated again until most of its cargo was off-loaded to a nearby beach.

In Habana we commandeered a ship belonging to Juan Sedeño. Sedeño, not realizing that he was fated to bleed to death on a wind-swept hill in *Tlaxcala*, made a virtue of necessity. He joined our adventure and volunteered the ship's cargo of cassava bread, bacon and salt chicken.

● ● ●

"Don Rodrigo," a careworn Cortés later ordered me to his cabin. "I have a favor to ask you. It seems that our expedition is to be honored with the presence of the niece of the Great Admiral, himself. She's a spy for her overly ambitious cousin, Diego Colón. I have reason to believe that the Colón family has designs on our endeavors."

Diego Colón was the son of Cristóbal Colón and had inherited the title of Admiral from his father. Until recently he had been the true governor of all of the Indies, with Diego Velásquez only a lieutenant governor. I wasn't aware, however, of intrigues involving the Colón family.

"Why don't you order her to remain behind?"

"Easier said, than done," Cortés said. "She is a major investor in our expedition and owns one of our larger ships. I have warned her of the hardships but she won't listen. La Señora insists that she has the right to attend personally to her investment."

"Shall I toss her into the sea?" I was making a joke but, from his response, I could see that Cortés took me seriously.

"No. That won't be necessary—at least not yet. I'm afraid

that the Lady and I have gotten off on the wrong foot but, unless I'm seriously mistaken," Cortés smiled conspiratorially, "she and I will soon be on the best of terms. I would like you to go to her cabin and invite her to a private dinner tonight, in my cabin."

"At what time?"

"I have many things to do so make the invitation for 10 pm sharp. I would appreciate it if you would escort her to my cabin."

"Her name, Caudillo?"

"Like her uncle she is Genoese, but she is the widow of a Catalan nobleman. Her name is Dona Francesca de la Barca. Her ship is the nao, *Santo Domingo*."

"I will go immediately, Sir."

● ● ●

As instructed, and with her Captain's permission, I boarded the *Santo Domingo*. I stated my business and was escorted to the lady's stateroom. The room was small, austere and crammed almost full by wooden boxes and chests. A single small porthole broke the darkness. The light from this window illuminated the woman with whom I had come to speak. While seated in a straight-backed chair she was using a wooden crate as a desk. I could see that she was checking off columns of listed supplies. She rose to greet me.

The woman was taller than I and she was, perhaps, a year or two older. She stood very straight and proud. Her dark blue eyes were large and luminous and her gaze was confident. "And what is your business, here?"

Her Castilian was perfect and pronounced with an elegant lisp with but the faintest touch of Italy. Despite the heat, her scent was summer roses.

I was overwhelmed by her presence. I stammered, "Compliments of the Caudillo, Señora. He begs the pleasure of your company for dinner tonight at 10 pm. He asks that I escort you to his table at that time."

I stood at attention and resisted the temptation to examine her closely. Even so, I was awestruck. Her hair was midnight pulled back in a bun. Her cheekbones were high and her mouth was a little large with perfect white teeth. Her nose was aquiline and her skin was smooth and fair.

Her eyes expressed amusement, almost as if she could sense my discomfort, "You may tell El Señor that I am indisposed this evening."

Now, the term, *El Señor* is the same term used for Our Savior or for a great lord. She spoke the words, however, as if they were a slur.

Taken aback, I didn't know what to say. She was clothed in a dark green gown that hung gracefully to her ankles and was drawn up tight at her narrow waist. Her bosom was perfect and her bodice was cut low. What exposure there was, was tantalizingly hidden by a veil of dark lace that formed a delicate collar at the base of her throat. I was facing the most beautiful woman I had ever seen... and...she knew it.

"You may leave."

Without another word, I turned to leave but—she stopped me. "Wait one moment, if you will. What is your name, soldado? I always like to know who I have been talking to."

"Rodrigo de la Peña, My Lady."

"Well, Señor de la Peña, it is very nice to make your acquaintance." She took a step toward me, looking straight into my eyes. She reached up and lightly touched the scars of my face with her fingertips. "I trust you have killed the one who has so disfigured you."

Her touch was ice.

"As a matter of fact," remembering my death-struggle with the leopard, "I did."

"Good." She ran the tip of her tongue over her upper lip. "Dismissed."

Chapter 27

In Habana, we soldiers disembarked and made ourselves busy checking and cleaning our armor and weapons. We also offloaded our artillery, consisting of ten brass guns and some falconets. We cleaned and tested the weapons. Powder was loaded in quantity and both stone and iron balls were obtained, the former having the advantage of shattering on impact and the latter the advantage of range. We also busied ourselves making padded cotton armor from the cotton that was abundant in the area. I could see that such armor would be of little avail against a well-directed spear or sword thrust but that it could prove lifesaving against a glancing blow or if struck by a light, stone-tipped arrow.

"Why all the horseflesh, Maximo?" I asked an old man grooming a sway-backed horse that, with fifteen others, was being readied for embarkation. "The way I see it, they're a lot of trouble for exactly no reason. Just look at these sorry beasts! There's not one decent caballo in the lot. Those that don't die on the voyage will probably have to be cut up for camp meat."

I was used to the high-strung chargers of our Italian campaigns. These horses looked as if they would collapse under the weight of an armored man.

"The Caudillo's orders, Rodrigo. It seems he believes in horses no matter what the quality. By the Blessed Whore's breath, I understand that he's bought every last nag in all of Cuba, which isn't saying much." Maximo García was all sinew with a shock of white hair. His skin was almost as black as the horse he was grooming. He continued his explanation: "Some of our officers have fought savages in Española as well as Cuba and some of the other islands. They say that horses scare the shit right out of them. If that's the truth, then I'm all for horses."

I was in a complaining mood and García made as good of a target as any. "I'm told that our four bigger ships are going to hold two or three apiece and that each of our little brigantines is also expected to carry a horse. If one of those things gets loose he'll capsize the boat. I'm not going to particularly care shit about Indios if we get capsized and drown on the way over."

García poked me in the ribs with his elbow. "Don't you worry, muchacho. These nags will be lashed down so tight that they won't be able to fart."

I changed the subject. "Did you see the size of some of the dogs that we're putting on the ships?" A frisson ran up my spine. "If we run out of horses, we could saddle up the dogs and ride them into battle. I've seen them used in Italy. I don't trust them. They're no good whatsoever on a well formed up battle line and they're entirely too vicious to use on a routed enemy. Half of the time, they'll turn on our own troops."

"They're mastiffs, not just perros and the boss does like them.

You'll just have to get used to it."

García was right about the horses. To protect the horses and ships, each horse was hobbled by all four feet and a halter was attached to two upright beams that prevented the animal from throwing his head around wildly. Straps around his chest and girth were attached to four straps connected to overhead beams. In this way the horses, despite the length and difficulty of our voyage, were immobilized but not injured. With our horses, weapons and supplies secured we made ready to sail for the distant new lands. In the meantime, Governor Velásquez' messengers arrived from Santiago de Cuba demanding that the expedition should be halted at all costs. Cortés laughed and we set sail on February 10, 1519.

YUCATÁN

Chapter 28

Burgos, Castilla-León
January 21, 1581 2:46 A.M.

Padre Enrique Mendoza stood in front of the sitting Bishop. Both men were wearing nightgowns but a multi-patterned quilt warmed the Bishop. The old man's face was a mask but his eyes shined with amusement. Mendoza's face was a combination of anger and relief.

"Your Grace, I must protest. I was sleeping soundly when your hooligans brutalized me."

Minutes earlier, guards had dragged the heavily snoring Padre from his feather bed. They had given him no time to clothe himself or even to put on shoes. In his confusion Mendoza had assumed that the old Bishop had ordered his immediate execution. Now, in the presence of the Bishop, in the same room in which they worked on the manuscript and in front of a crackling fire, Mendoza's worst fears subsided.

"I'm sorry you are inconvenienced, Padre, but I couldn't sleep."

For a moment Mendoza was struck dumb.

The old man continued, "Rather than toss in my bed I decided to get a little work done."

Mendoza, considering his limited options, swallowed his bile. "Very considerate of you, Excelencia."

"I thought you'd see it my way. *Homero!...*" The Bishop ordered one of the guards. "Would you be good enough to fetch the Padre his slippers and his cloak. Put a little more wood on the fire, tambien. The room is still cold."

Homero cast a baleful eye towards the priest, blaming him for the inconvenience. Mendoza shuddered.

"Now where did we leave off, Padre?"

On leaving Habana, we had a total of five hundred and ten troops of whom thirty were ballestas and twelve mosqueteros. There were also seventy-five or so sailors, including some foreigners. We also had two men of God—Juan Díaz from Sevilla and the far more intelligent Barolomé de Olmedo, a Mercedian friar from a town of the same name. We also had the self-proclaimed physician, Pedro López. Also present were two or three hundred Cubano Indios, some of them women, as well as a handful of black slaves. We also had a few women who called themselves Conquistadoras—but were, in fact, common whores—*soldaderas*. These women included the two sisters of Diego de Ordaz, three or four maids, and two other women who went as housekeepers. The Ordaz sisters were tougher and more ugly than most of the soldiers. Several of the other women, given the scarcity of Castilian women, were reasonably attractive. María de Estrada was one of these and another, Louisa Alvárez, was, in fact, truly beautiful though not as beautiful as was Dona Francesca de la Barca.

Our eleven ships consisted of four caravels and seven smaller, open brigantines. All of the ships were ordered to assemble at Cabo San Antonio and then sail together to the island of Cozumel, discovered earlier by Grijalva. Ten ships assembled at Labo San Antonio but the ship commanded by Pedro de Alvarado was nowhere to be found. Our fleet waited for a time but then proceeded westerly.

Forty-six of us soldiers and a seasick horse were crowded into the leaky brigantine commanded by Francisco de Morla. Except for the crowding, the filth and the baling of seawater, at first the journey went smoothly—then the weather turned foul with high winds and building seas. There was a loud snap, the rudder tore off, and our little ship tipped over taking water over her starboard side. She then righted herself but, despite the fact that the sails were yarded in, she careened over the sea like a drunken thing, taking on more water and in imminent danger of capsizing. We all—at that time I was still a believer—went to our knees praying for deliverance. Our prayers were answered, by whom I can't be certain, and the wind abated. When the seas calmed enough another ship was able to come alongside and gave us the extra rudder that they had stored for just such an emergency.

● ● ●

"We'll need a couple of men to go into the water to help attach the rudder." De Morla shouted. "Do I have any volunteers?" Nobody stepped forward. "Come now, one silver piece for each volunteer. Do I have any takers?" Nobody moved. "I'd do it myself but

I never learned how to swim. Are any of you swimmers?" One hand went up. I raised my hand, too. "That's more like it, men. Each of you gets a silver piece when the job's complete."

"Capitán de Morla," I said. "For the last two days we have been entertaining ourselves by dropping garbage off to the tiburones that have been trailing our boat. Those things might make things uncomfortable."

"Nonsense. Those fish are just scavengers, nothing more. Just to make you feel better about it, though, I'll order two musketeers to stand on the stern. If you are really worried, I'll even tell them to keep the fuses burning. Any overly inquisitive tiburon will be blown straight to Hell."

● ● ●

For a day and a half, in the rough seas, we struggled to attach the rudder. The two of us spent many hours in the water, lashing on ropes and trying to set wooden pins, all the while terrified of the unknown depths. On the second day, when our work was almost complete, I saw a fast moving shadow. I pulled myself hard against the ship. The tiburon grazed me, abrading my back with his rough skin. Frustrated, the monster doubled back, and found my friend, the sailor—I think his name was Pico—clinging to a rope and making the last repairs. The muskets exploded up above and Pico screamed once, just as the fish hit him. The water turning red around him, Pico tried to climb the rope. He cleared the surface, but the flesh of his right thigh was shredded and blood spurted in fountains. Poor Pico almost reached safety but his strength failed him. He flopped back into the water.

Unthinking, I swam to the man's side and tried to keep his head above the water. Suddenly, his body was jerked out of my grasp as the monster seized Pico again. The fish grabbed his shoulder, spun itself around wildly and tore Pico apart. Another tiburon darted in and now it was my turn to climb the rope. Lucky for me, the tiburone's attention was entirely on Pico, and I made it back into the ship with nothing worse than a few scrapes. Hours later, quaking with fear, I was obliged to reenter the water to complete the last repairs. Fortunately, the tiburones did not return.

● ● ●

The other ships of the fleet had been able to offer little help but they had sailed around waiting for us to complete our repairs.

The rudder in place, the ships proceeded to Cozumel, where we found that Pedro de Alvarado's ship had arrived two days earlier. It seems that the first thing that Alvarado and his men had done on touching ground was to loot the local village and frighten all the natives into hiding. Cortés was outraged on all accounts, especially at Alvarado's insubordination. Cortés reprimanded Alvarado in front of the assembled soldiers.

Despite his humiliation it was difficult not to be impressed by Pedro de Alvarado as he stood there on the beach. He was bareheaded and clad in black zapatos, blue pantalones, and crimson camisa with puff sleeves overlaid by mirrorlike armadura de pecho. He looked like exactly what he was—a Conquistador.

The man, himself, was tall, straight and clean-limbed with broad shoulders. His long hair and beard were pale gold, almost white, and glowed in the sun. His eyes were a clear and innocent blue and when he smiled, which he did often, the world smiled with him. His beauty was the sea and the sky. Women loved him and, perhaps not so remarkably, so did most men. That Cortés should have a weakness for Alvarado was inevitable. They were both stained by the same evil and both worshiped at the feet of the same terrible gods. Cortés always permitted him more freedom and responsibility than he should have had, to the near ruination of the Conquest. To look at him then, though, no one would have known it. Pedro stood erectly, the gentle sea breeze ruffling his fine hair. He took his punishment like a man.

"Capitán Alvarado, your ship left Cabo San Antonio against orders. Do you have any explanation?" The Caudillo's face betrayed no emotion but the muscles of his neck and jaw twitched.

"My pilot, Camacho, decided that, given the condition of the sea, it would be best that we make the crossing immediately."

Alvarado's innocent blue eyes met and held Cortés' golden ones.

Cortés turned to two flanking soldiers. "Arrest Camacho and slap him in irons. I want him to be an example to the others." He turned back to Alvarado. "Why did you rob these Indios?" Cortés pointed in the direction of the deserted village. "You know how important it is to establish friendly relations with these people."

"It wasn't me, Sir," Alvarado replied. "The men—well, I don't want to speak harshly of them—but the men got a little out of control. It won't happen again, Caudillo. You have my word of honor."

"To make amends, Captain Alvarado," Cortés said, "I want you to collect all of the loot that your rascals have squirreled away. I also want a tabulation of everything that was destroyed or eaten. Judging by that pile of feathers, your men must have feasted like pigs the last couple of days. Those items that are recovered will be returned. Those items which are beyond recovery, like those fowls, will be paid for in trade goods, the expense of which will be deducted from your personal share of the profits in this expedition."

"*Sí, Caudillo, no hay problema.*" Alvarado was the picture of damaged but dignified pride.

"Oh, there's just one more thing, Captain."

"*Sí, Caudillo.*"

"It seems that several of the local maidens were... dishonored. This is highly unfortunate and will not ingratiate us with the locals although I imagine that a few beads can mollify their complaints. A bigger problem, however, is that one of the women, the cacique's daughter as it turns out, now insists on accompanying us on our journey. You wouldn't know anything about this would you?"

Chapter 29

Now, Cortés performed one of those deeds that was bound to offend the Indios more profoundly than the theft of fowls and the defilement of a few maidens. Nearby was a mosque of Indio design. It a pyramid of sorts with steps and a temple at the top, filled with graven devils. This temple, like all others that I subsequently visited, smelled like a burial crypt and was caked with old and fresh blood. On the day of which I speak, one of their priests, clad in filthy black robes, climbed to the top of this building. He set fire to incense called copal and, from a cotton bag, he produced living birds. They were fat quail— codornices—with black and white faces. He removed them one at a time, pulling the head off of each. The headless bodies fluttered maniacally, sprinkling blood on an altar of stone. He sacrificed twelve quails, all the while delivering a sermon of wickedness to the Indios below.

With Cortés was an Indio given the Christian name of Melchior. Hernández de Córdoba captured him during the first expedition to *Yucatán*. He now served as our interpreter.

"Tell them, Melchior," Cortés ordered, "that their gods are an abomination that we will not tolerate."

Melchior interpreted but the Maya, for these are the Indios of *Yucatán*, showed no comprehension.

"*Martínez, Ortega, de la Peña!*" Cortés shouted. "I want the three of you to climb to the top of that pyramid, pry up those monstrosities, push them over and let them tumble all the way to the bottom."

"Caudillo," Ortega protested, "I'm no coward but if we do as you order we will all be killed."

"No, you won't be so much as scratched. You're doing God's work and He will protect you. I will help you." Cortés started his march up the templo without looking behind to see if we were following. We were.

The climb was steep and the steps were short, barely the length of a Castilian boot, and covered with old and stinking blood. Subsequently, we learned that these features were common to all of the Indio mosques—the steepness was a ceremonial necessity. It was important that a victim who was slain on the summit would tumble all the way to the foot of the structure without the embarrassment of having the corpse hang up somewhere on the steps.

At the top of the mosque, I pushed the stinking priest roughly aside. Along with the others, we succeeded in sending the stone idols crashing down the steep steps all the way to the bottom. At the same time, I grabbed the hilt of Bebidor fully expecting instant retaliation. Instead these savages looked on with dumb amazement, no doubt shocked that we hadn't been struck dead. Finding lime in the village, we whitewashed the temple and set up a new altar on which we erected a cross and an image of Our Lady. One of our friars, Juan Díaz, then said mass and Cortés gave a sermon about God and other holy matters. He ordered the heathens to protect the altar and worship at it. Days later, we were pleased to find that the Indios were carefully attending to their new altar. They were burning copal in front of it and the newly whitewashed surface was flecked with droplets of fresh blood.

"Padre Olmedo?" I asked our Mercedian friar, who was a narrow, beetling man dressed in a brown frock. He was staring in puzzlement at the blood-spattered altar.

"Yes, my son."

"If these Maya worship Our Lady exactly as if she were one of their idols, what good are we doing by smashing their idols?"

Olmedo shook his head. "Probably none, my son. When the time is right these devils will fall of their own weight, but that time is not now."

• • •

In Cozumel we received reports of Castilian captives on the Yucatán mainland. Cortés sent out couriers with beads and other objects, as ransom. Eventually, our efforts produced, or so we thought, an Indio. He was dressed as a Maya and his skin was just as dark. His name was Jerónimo de Aguilar, a native of Palos. Later on I got to speak privately to this Aguilar. Of course, I was interested in how he had come to be the first Castilian on these shores.

"Señor de la Peña." Aguilar's Spanish was halting from years of disuse. "Eight years ago some of us were sailing from Darien to Santo Domingo. The ship foundered on the rocks of Alacránes. Fifteen of us—thirteen men and two women—set out in the ship's boat and tried to make it to Jamaica but, because we had only one pair of oars and no sail, reverse currents drove us to this accursed land."

"Where are the other survivors?"

Aguilar looked at his feet. "We all were captured by the Maya. Five were sacrificed and their bodies were eaten at a great fiesta in our honor.

"Eaten?" I couldn't believe what I was hearing.

"That's right, señor, it is their custom. The rest of us were put in pens to fatten, but we were able to break free and were taken captive by another chieftain, a cacique by the name of Xamanzana. He kept us as slaves. All the men except for me and Gonzalo Guerrero died and the women were worked to death grinding maíz."

"But how did you survive?"

Aguilar turned his eyes to the Heavens and crossed himself. "By the Grace of God, before I ever came to Darien I proclaimed my vocation. Therefore, even when in the hands of the savages, I honored Our Lord and abstained from women. My captor suspected I was playing false and, one night, sent me a beautiful young woman to rob me of my chastity. Even Christ in the Wilderness never faced such a terrible temptation—I resisted. The cacique knew me to be a holy man and made me a papa and leader."

I was amazed. "But where is Guerrero?"

"He wouldn't leave." Aguilar had a haunted look in his eyes. "He told me that he was satisfied with his life in Yucatán. He was a poor man in España but here he's respected and has become a great cacique and a leader in war. He also has a wife and three children."

"Even so, I should think he would come to see his old countrymen."

"He doesn't want to see you—he's been tattooed and had his nose, lip and ears pierced like a savage. It was also he who ordered the attack on de Córdoba's people."

Chapter 30

Our expedition worked its way north along the coast. We intended to disembark and chastise the Maya of Champoton because it was they who had inflicted the great defeat on the earlier Hernandez de Córdoba expedition, two years earlier, with fifty-six Spaniards killed. The winds and tides were unfavorable so we were forced to bypass Champoton and sailed further up the coast to the mouth of the Rio Grijalva, known to the Maya as the Tabasco. The Grijalva expedition had landed in this area without incident so it was to our very unpleasant surprise that the riverbanks and mangrove swamps were crawling with warriors painted black-and-white for war. Many more had gathered in the town of Ponchonton about a half league from the river.

I found out later that the reason for this welcome is that the great chieftain of Tabasco was the brother of the leader of the Champoton Maya. The Champoton leader accused his brother of cowardice for his lack of aggression toward the Grijalva expedition. The Tabasco cacique, stung by this rebuke, intended to regain his honor by destroying our army.

For the moment, however, we weren't privy to this information and thought that peace might be obtained through negotiations. It was now that Aguilar's knowledge of the Maya tongue proved invaluable. Cortés, through Aguilar, spoke to some Indios that had rowed close to our ships in canoes.

"We come here in peace and to teach you things by which you will gain your Salvation."

A short squat Indio with a bone protruding from his lower lip replied from a canoe occupied by ten others, "Come ashore, demons. Come ashore if you dare!"

"All we want is to trade for a little food and water."

"For your blood and flesh we will trade our spears and arrows!"

With this the nearby Indios started to howl while pounding on drums.

"Then," Cortés spoke through Aguilar, "we find you in contempt of your rightful ruler, King Carlos of Spain. We bear no responsibility for what will now happen."

The Maya may have understood some of this because they showered our vessels with arrows and stones. We returned fire with crossbows and muskets. The closest canoe took the full brunt of the fire—it was cut to pieces. The others paddled quickly to the surrounding mangroves.

Cortés then dispatched a boat and messenger from his flagship instructing the Captains to assemble in his vessel for a council of war. At the same time he dispatched Cubano Indios to determine the best routes to the enemy's town.

Later, that night, de Morla gave us soldiers our orders. "Before first light, you men will go ashore close to a road our spies have found. Sixty-five soldiers from other ships will join you. At the same time the Caudillo, with the main force, will travel farther upstream and land on the far side of the town. We are not to move until the first musket shot. Then we will push inland and we must permit nothing to slow us down until we have joined with the main force. All of you mosqueteros and crossbowmen must be careful of your targets because, at some point, our main force is going to be in front of us."

One nervous soldier, who couldn't have been more than seventeen years of age, spoke up.

"How many muskets and crossbows will we have with us?"

"Ten crossbows and four muskets."

"A little thin, Francisco," observed an older man.

"Thin or not," de Morla said, "you all have your orders."

●●●

Our forces reached the riverbank unopposed and hid in the tangle of dark mangroves. Swarms of blood-sucking insects descended on us but we bore their assault in total silence—we waited for the signal to attack. An hour passed and it was growing light when, farther down the river, there came the din of drums, blowing conches, trumpets, screams and gunshots. Guided by one of our scouts we pushed inland to strike a broad well-trodden sendero.

There were the sounds of a great battle in the direction of the main force but we encountered no opposition. It looked like the Maya were tricked and the way was open to Ponchonton—we were mistaken. The forest, which had been quiet, erupted with screaming, whistling savages. I didn't have much opportunity for observation because of the pure shock of the onslaught. One painted devil, looking huge in his feathered headdress, swung a wooden sword studded with tiburon teeth. The blow would have taken my head off if I hadn't deflected it with my shield. Bebidor moved of its own volition and disemboweled him.

Our force formed up tight and, despite multiple attacks, we advanced down the path towards the town. We waded through a swamp and twice we had to stop and tear down wooden barricades while fending off barrages of missiles and stones. The assaults intensified at the obstacles. Like some kind of great bird, one feather-clad warrior launched himself at me from the top of one barricade. I jerked to one side as his spear thrust into thin air. The warrior hit the ground with a bone-breaking crunch and a yelp of pain. I didn't stop and, along with my comrades, scrambled over the barricade directly into the face of another attack.

It was our organization against their numbers. Despite their incredible bravery the Indios were basically a rabble trying to engage us in single combat. We wouldn't oblige them but formed a solid wall with our shields and armor. Behind this protection our crossbowmen and musketeers fired over our shoulders directly into the enemies' faces. No match for us at close quarters, the Maya pulled back to assail us with arrows, slings and darts thrown from sticks. I was grazed in the cheek by one of their arrows and then in the neck by a stick-thrown dart but, knowing that to fall behind meant death, I kept going. Finally we broke through to Ponchonton where we could hear the sounds of heavy fighting. Our two forces now united and drove the still fighting Maya through the tiled streets into their main plaza and out the other side.

"*Alto!*" the Caudillo shouted. The infantry and cavalry came to a ragged stop as the officers echoed Cortés' order. Cortés thrust his blood-smeared sword over his head and made a circle with its tip. The soldiers formed around him in a triumphant ring.

"I take possession of this land and all that is in it in the name of his Majesty, Carlos I."

The Caudillo strode over to a tree with an enormous trunk. He slashed the tree three times with his sword. "Anyone here" Cortés looked around with fiery eyes "who disagrees with my action is invited to challenge me—right here, right now!"

Imagine the situation. We had just fought a desperate battle and here was Cortés challenging all-comers to a duel. Incredible. Not surprisingly, nobody took Cortés up on his challenge but I heard members of the Velásquez' faction grumbling.

We counted up our casualties and found that we had, including myself, fourteen wounded and no men dead. The savages had lost heavily but had dragged most of their dead off and we found only eighteen. The next morning we discovered that Melchior had run away, leaving his Spanish clothes hanging from a tree. This was especially ominous because Melchior was aware of our tactics and weaknesses.

As bad as things were, during the night, they got even worse. As I returned from relieving myself, a naked Indio flushed from the thick vegetation next to me. Without thinking, I brought him down with a blow to the back of his head. I pushed the man into camp.

"Look what I found, gentlemen," I prodded my terrified Maya. As were most of his race, he was short with a broad chest and a Roman nose. His penis was shriveled with fear.

Cristóbal Olid strode up, "A spy. I'm sure the Caudillo will want to discuss a few things with him."

"Where is he?" I was proud of my capture and wanted to present him to Cortés, myself.

Olid ignored my question. "I'll take over from here." He seized the Indio by the back of the neck and started to lead him away. I followed.

"Stay here, de la Peña. If the Caudillo needs you he'll send for you."

I considered arguing but Olid outranked me. "Tell the Caudillo that I was the one who caught him."

Olid didn't bother to reply.

I wasn't invited to the interrogation. Days later I heard the story. The prisoner tried to remain silent but when bubbling oil was applied, he spoke volumes.

"What is the plan of your countrymen?"

"They are gathering a large force so that they might destroy you in the morning."

"Why are they so foolish?"

"The one you call Melchior hates you and hates your gods. He says you are not demons but only men who eat, drink, and defecate like all others. He says that you are weak and, if we are resolute, that each one of you shall bleed in our temples."

Cortés, having determined the truth, ordered that the Maya be made even shorter by removing his head. The other Captains present at the interrogation were sworn to secrecy.

It was well he did, because if we soldiers had known exactly was happening, we would have demanded to get back onto the ships and sail as quickly as we could back to Cuba. We all knew that something was going on, though, for suddenly the officers were shouting orders and the camp was alive with movement, just as an anthill comes alive when disturbed by mischievous children. The rest of the night was spent hoisting the horses from the ships and trying to give the stiffened animals a little exercise. Other soldiers worked on their various weapons, lubricating their crossbow pulleys and carefully cleaning their muskets as still others prayed for their deliverance.

Javier de la Concha, a tall, square-shouldered man and one of our Extremeño Captains, was barking orders and directing soldiers. I cringed as he slapped one of the men in the face. The object of the blow was Enrique Presa, a slight, red-haired fellow from Andalucia. The blow was delivered with such force that Presa was staggered. Presa straightened himself and answered Concha's blow with defiance.

"I am not taking my man into battle. He's trained to be a servant, not a fighter, and I will just not risk it."

"No, mozo?" Concha warned. "Take it from me, he is going. By the looks of him, even if he can't use a sword, he can tear the Indios apart with his bare hands."

Nearby stood a giant Negro. Concha had a point.

"He's too valuable. He's worth ten Indio slaves."

The edge in Concha's voice was dangerous. "Do you think I give a damn? I'm riding on a horse worth five lazy blacks so you can expect no sympathy from me. The Caudillo has ordered it and that's the end of the argument."

I could see that Concha was about to deliver another blow. I decided to intervene. "Can you tell me what's going on around here?" I, as had everyone else, heard the screams of the captive during his interrogation. Concha had been present and should know something.

"We're getting ready for a battle." Concha swung his boot at a slow moving soldier and left him sprawling in the dirt.

"You—you're not serious, are you?" I stuttered, "If it's bigger than the one we've had so far, we're in trouble. A lot of us are wounded and all of us are dead from exhaustion. The Indios will only have to mop us up."

Concha turned to face me, but I couldn't see his eyes in the dark. "Don't worry, de la Peña. The boss knows what he's doing. He wouldn't enter a battle that he thought we couldn't win."

Concha was an excellent soldier and an unswerving partisan of the Caudillo. Although he had the narrow face of an aesthetic, imagination and intelligence were not his strong traits.

I doubt that Concha could see the expression on my face but he heard it in my voice. "I know the Caudillo has calculated the risks and reckons that we can come out on top otherwise he'd be a total madman—but—have you considered that he just might be a total madman. The only good reason we stopped here, anyway, was to get a little fresh water—which we've already done. Look at this God forsaken place. It's not worth one soldier. Besides, Grijalva's men say the real gold lies to the north."

"I'll tell you what." Concha squared off to me menacingly. Even in the dark I could see that his hand was on the pommel of his sword. "I recommend that you do exactly as you are told."

"Exactly?" I also brought my hand to Bebidor's hilt, leaning forward and bending my legs.

Concha, considering his options, pivoted and strode into the darkness.

"Very, very nice." The voice was female and contemptuous. Francesca de la Barca was standing but a few feet away. "Thousands of savages to deal with but you would fight one of our own."

She was dressed in a white gown from her throat to her ankles. It was spotted with the blood from the wounded.

"*Es un cochino.*"

"Perhaps, but considering our circumstances, even pigs are useful." Her voice took on a more conversational tone. "What do you think is going on tonight? Nobody seems to know."

"There's going to be a battle."

"For what purpose, might I ask?"

"That's the same question I've been asking. Any small point that we needed to make with the indígenos has been made—it's time to get on with our expedition. Not only are we wasting time but we're risking serious trouble."

"I take it you have no faith in your Caudillo?"

"Faith?" I chuckled mirthlessly. "Faith is for the iglesia, señora, not for the battlefield. I am starting to believe that the Caudillo has too much faith for all of our good."

"Yet you wear the cross of Our Saviour." She was looking at the wooden crucifix hanging from my neck.

She must have noticed my hesitation. "A sentimental decoration."

"Then you are a pragmatist, Señor de la Peña. I am not certain that this venture is the proper" —she searched for the word— "abode...for pragmatists."

"Y tú, señora?" She flinched at my use of the familiar "tú".

She waited in silence before responding to my question. "I have invested everything I own."

Chapter 31

The Caudillo wasn't asking my opinion, however, and the next thing we knew, we were being formed up in companies because Cortés was planning to take the battle to the enemy. The date, and I remember it exactly, was March 25, 1519. Cubano Indios hauled our cannons. Cortés and twelve others were mounted on caballos armados and armed with lances. Captain Diego de Ordaz, like me, was an espada and had a reputation from the Italian wars. Ordaz was given command of all of the foot soldiers.

Ordáz recognized me. "De la Peña, take those men." He pointed at a company of about twenty-five men, including four musketeers and four crossbowmen. "You must keep them together during the march. You are to take your place between the companies commanded by Ramírez and Castro."

"Sí, Jefe." I was proud of my new responsibility but frightened of failure at the same time.

"When we encounter the enemy," Ordáz said, "things will happen quickly. I expect you and the others to react even without my direct orders."

Ordaz's helmet partly obscured a huge and disfiguring scar, the result of a battle axe having removed part of his face somewhere to the south of Taranto.

"If the enemy is in small force we will form up in straight battle line, staggered with musketeers, crossbowmen, and cannon. Should, on the other hand, we meet with the enemy in overwhelming numbers, the companies will meet each other in a circle, with our firepower inside. Otherwise the enemy may force our flanks. Understand?"

"*Absolutamente, señor.*" I knew what I must do but I wasn't sure if I could do it.

●●●

As we were organizing our force I noticed, to my dismay, that I had been assigned Presa and his slave. The Negro was a huge man with bulging muscles. His skin was as black as the inside of a cave. He was wearing a shiny helmet, cotton armor, breastplate and copper greaves for his legs. He held his shield and sword in a death-like grip and his eyes rolled in their sockets. '*Por Dios,*' I thought, 'he'll be more dangerous to us than to the enemy.'

"Presa! What's your man's name?"

"Gilberto, señor."

"I hold you personally responsible for your slave. If he runs he'll leave a hole in our line."

"I'll do my best, señor."

From the look of Presa, he was as likely to run as Gilberto. For that matter, most of my men were on the edge of panic and we hadn't even seen the enemy, yet.

"It's going to be fine, hombres," I tried to reassure them. "I've had plenty of experience fighting against the best in the world— these Maya are pitiful fare. They won't even provide us with much sport."

A couple of my men actually looked relieved and I noticed men from the other companies were listening to my speech. I went on:

"Mosqueteros y ballestas, stand behind our espadas, and shoot between their shoulders. Mosqueteros, do not shoot too early—get them into point-blank range. Espadas form a tight shield wall—un muro de escudos—and give them the points of your weapons. Ranks are to be held under all circumstances. If the enemy flees, it may be a trap. Do not pursue until I tell you to do so."

● ● ●

Ordaz ordered us to take a line of march that took us through a swamp. The footing was difficult for the soldiers and even worse for the horses. The infantry became separated from the Caudillo and his horsemen. Nevertheless, we marched steadily to the small village of Cintla near to which is an open plain. As we entered the plain the sight was almost unbelievable. After all these years I can close my eyes and see that plain again. Fear burned it into my brain.

There the enemy stood in his serried ranks, thousands by the tens of thousands. Their faces were painted black and white and still others had the faces of animals. They were clad in quilted cotton armor that extended down to their knees and was decorated with feathers, copper bells and beadwork. On their heads were tall-feathered plumes that blew like ripe wheat in the wind. The enemy was armed with their fearful two-handed swords, some studded with sharks' teeth and others with black, razor-sharp stones. Other warriors were armed with stout bows and still others with spears and shields. Also present were slingers with pouches filled with stones and balls of baked clay. Some carried wooden throwing-sticks. I do not know the Tabascan word for these but in the land of Mexico, the natives called them *atalatl*. No matter what they are called, they are dangerous. Using these instruments the Indios hurled darts with armor penetrating force.

The sounds of savage chants, whistles and drums were deafening, making it difficult to even think. For a few moments our column halted, every man transfixed by the terrifying sight. I felt my bowels loosening and had to fight to control myself. I glanced at my soldados. Every one of them—with the exception of the Negro, Gilberto—was ashen with fear. One reluctant soldado had urine running down his leg.

"*Adelante!*" shouted Captain Ordaz. We officers echoed his order down the line. We marched by column into the savanna and did a left turn to face the enemy even as our cannons were dragged up and the crossbowmen and the musketeers took their positions. "*Ave María, gratia plena....*" I heard a soldier whimper behind me.

Maya holy men entered the open ground between the two armies chanting incantations, burning copal, and making stabbing gestures towards our force with knives of shiny black stone. At the same time, our two friars walked back and forth praying and sprinkling Holy Water on our soldiers. Suddenly, naked painted warriors broke through the enemy ranks. Some cavorted, tumbling along the ground and leaping into the air turning flips and somersaults. Others, to our amazement, engaged in a game of ball. Unmindful of the pending bloodshed, they kicked a ball back and forth, bouncing it from their heads, chests and shoulders. Finally, they kicked it into their ranks where it disappeared. One tall, magnificently muscled warrior approached us with a whoop and a swagger. With incredible strength, he threw a great-feathered lance completely over the heads of our soldiers. The spear shimmered in the sky then dropped, sinking deeply into the ground behind us. The attack broke like a towering wave striking the sand.

"*Calma, hombres, calma!*"

I spoke as calmly as a terrified man can speak to his terrified troops.

"*Prepare!*"

The enemy warriors surged forward, weapons beating time on their shields.

"*Apunte!*"

The Maya had broken into a full charge, the sound of their feet like rolling thunder.

"*Espere, Señores!*" I didn't want to fire until exactly the right moment.

"*Fuego!*"

There was the heart-stopping explosion of muskets and everything was obscured by smoke. The wind whipped the smoke away to reveal that the savages had been shocked into a sudden halt only paces from our line. Crossbow bolts injured a few Indios but, from what I could see, the musket balls themselves had inflicted few casualties. The noise and the smoke had stopped the enemy.

"*Recarge!*"

It wasn't taking the enemy long to realize that little damage had been done. A few of the more courageous warriors were already throwing themselves against our line, which was now swinging to form a circle. From then on it was bloody infantry practice with our Castilians trying to defend themselves against missiles that hummed amongst us like hornets while, at the same time, we had to fend off painted spearmen and swordsmen.

"*Retene, hombres, retene!* Hold them!!"

Seventy of our men were wounded in the first attack. Most of these were obliged to fight on but the dead and more severely wounded were dragged to the center of our circle. One espada, although wounded in the arm, chanted a constant stream of *Pater Nosters* while defending himself and methodically killing enemy warriors.

In the meantime, the crossbowmen and musketeers, firing from point-blank range, were doing fearful injury to our adversaries. So thick were the masses of Maya that even if a bolt or ball missed one it was bound to hit those in his rear. Sometimes two savages dropped at the report of a single musket. Because of my command status I was to the center of and in front of my soldiers and was therefore an obvious target. Arrows and stones rattled against my shield and armor as I thrust and slashed at my nearest antagonist. Fresh warriors replaced those I injured so that, even as I was tiring, my opponents were always strong. Twice warriors, without weapons or armor, jumped forward and grabbed me bodily and tried to drag me alive into their ranks. In both cases Bebidor ended the threat. I wasn't unique, however, as I saw savages time and again give up their weapons in favor of attempting to capture a Castilian alive.

Burgos, Castilla-León

The old Bishop stopped his dictation and turned directly to Mendoza, "Padre Mendoza, during my narrative I would like to make note of those material things that I think led to the ultimate victory of our Castilian forces. There were, in fact, multiple causes, although I doubt that the sum of them could have possibly resulted in our eventual victory. Nevertheless, for the sake of clarity, I will attempt to make the logical deductions. For example, in this battle at Cintla and as well as subsequent battles, it seemed that the Indios' huge numbers were never used effectively. Anxious to achieve glory in combat the natives would press ahead regardless of tactics, and would necessarily be forced close together to confront our much shorter battle line. Crowded together they were more vulnerable. They were unable to use their weapons as effectively as they could have. This tactical weakness was compounded by the fact that their weapons and armor were inferior to ours. The only thing in which the two sides were equal was courage—imagine trying to smash a small, hard nut with a large broom. It might be possible to do, but it would surely take a lot of technique. The Indios were all broom and little technique."

Our cannons fired in salvos cutting bloody swaths through the ranks of the massed enemy, leaving torn limbs and dismembered torsos in their wake. I saw one disembodied head tumbling high into the air. By this stage of the battle both of our sides were feeling the effects of the battle. Impressed by the strength of our firepower, the Maya withdrew to a safer distance but continued to pelt us with missiles. As our guns continued to fire, the Indios endeavored to hide their losses by throwing dirt and grass in the air to try to obscure their casualties. Seeing this, I realized that the enemy was starting to suffer.

"*Rodrigo!*" One man shrieked. I recognized the man who had pissed himself. His eyes were wild and terrible and his sword was bloody up to the hilt. "Give us the word and we'll attack!"

"Señor!" screamed Presa's manservant, his sword also dripping with blood. "No prisoners. Kill them all!"

Replacing bone-numbing fear was now the ecstasy of blood. Such is the nature of courage.

Diego de Ordaz, who noticed the ardor of my soldados, rushed to my side. "Hold your men, Rodrigo! The enemy outnumbers us three hundred to one. We must press forward as a unit, no man outpacing another.

"*Columnas reforme!*" Ordaz's order was passed to the company commanders. The defensive circle unraveled into a straight line. The leaders thrust their swords in the air, so that all of their soldiers could see, and then brought them down suddenly with a slashing motion.

"*Al Ataque!*"

We advanced with an intact front and again contacted the enemy with cold steel and gunfire. At the same time Cortés and his horsemen emerged from the forest to the rear of the enemy and, not waiting to get into formation, charged. The horses, most of which had never seen combat, performed shamefully. Shocked by the howling warriors and the explosions of guns, the horses behaved as if they found serpents coiled between their legs. Some of the horses balked, some fled to the forest and others went bucking over the battlefield. Cortés, himself, was thrown over the head of his mighty steed and Concha was not only thrown, he was kicked in the ribs. Only Alvarado and Sandoval did any damage and precious little, at that.

This might have proved a calamity had not half a dozen of Cortés' war dogs burst from the forest. It was all more than the enemy could take. The Maya panicked as, screaming, they threw away their shields and weapons in an effort to escape. The terrible mastiffs, running silently and low to the ground, ran them down. The dogs didn't bother to worry their prey but seizing the Indios from behind, snapped their necks with a toss of their heads, and continued on to their next victims. Unfortunately, one mastiff attacked Presa's slave and tore his face away.

Burgos, Castilla-León

"Why would the dog attack the Negro?" Mendoza asked.

"It is because the dogs had been trained to attack Indios. The dogs did not distinguish the dark skin of a Negro from that of a

Maya."

Mendoza was afraid to ask the next question but he was too curious not to. "How did the dogs know to attack Indios?"

"In the Indies, dogs were trained on worthless or insolent slaves—the animals learned quickly enough."

"Yes, I've heard of this. Las Casas, I believe, condemned the practice. On the other hand, your statements about the horses are contrary to my sources. Many sources confirm that horses were the deciding factor in Tabasco as in other battles."

"Cortés' propaganda, Padre. Later, after careful training and experience, the horses did prove useful. At this first battle, however, the horses—as should have been predicted—were worthless other than as shock factor. Use your common sense. They had been tied down for thirty days. They were exhausted by their trek through a swamp and, suddenly, they were confronted by sights and sounds the likes of which none of them had ever encountered. We were fortunate that they didn't die of pure fright. Speaking of horses, it is here, Padre Mendoza, that you reported that the Blessed Apostles St. James and St. Peter charged into battle, slaughtering the Maya. You have also said that our victory was the work of Jesus Christ and that, with his help, we killed eight thousand Indios in this fight. Let me tell you, Padre, if all of the Indios had been bound up with cords and we had butchered them as fast as we could, we couldn't have killed eight thousand. Not only that, but I was right there and I never saw St. James, St. Peter, nor Jesus Christ. Of course" —the ancient Bishop chuckled— "they might have been on the other end of the battlefield. All I ever saw was Francisco de Morla holding on for dear life to his bucking gray horse and Hernán Cortés thrown from his chestnut mare. In all fairness, I must say I never saw Satan either but I certainly felt his presence."

"Your Grace, I was quoting Gomarra and de las Casas, two highly reputable scholars. They may very well have been speaking in symbolic terms. The Holy Saints, although not visible to sinners such as yourself," Mendoza permitted himself a smile, "may have been animating our Christian warriors. How else do you explain your miraculous victory?

"Gunpowder, Toledo steel and Santo Hernán Cortés."

The Maya fled into the forest leaving us in possession of the battlefield. We gave thanks for our victory and here we founded a town in honor of our victory and the Blessed Virgin, Santa María de la Victoria. It seemed as if the battle, as most battles, had gone on longer than it actually had. In fact it had taken place in only an hour. Remarkably, we had only two men killed outright, both by arrows. There were more than eight hundred enemy dead as well as numerous wounded scattered over the ground. Most of the dead and seriously injured had been the victims of sword thrusts, although the cannons, lancers, and crossbowmen had all done their part. In this as in many other battles, I found that the muskets inflicted few casualties on the enemy. This is because it is difficult to keep the musket fuse lit and, even when it does stay lit, the musket frequently misfires. Even when it does fire, the musket is inherently inaccurate. True, if a musket ball hits a man, it can nearly tear him in two—the problem is with hitting him. At very close range a musket is a dangerous thing but, more often than not, once the Indios felt the musket's hot breath, they withdrew far enough to render the weapon worthless.

The crossbow inflicted more injuries than the musket. The problem with the ballesta, though, is that it is still a bow and arrow. The Indios, from their constant warfare, were not particularly frightened of arrows. The mosquete was altogether a different thing. It was something totally beyond their experience. There was the flash, the explosion and the pall of foul-smelling smoke. Even though muskets may have killed few of them, it certainly terrified all of them.

Chapter 32

"How did the men in your company fare, Ramírez?" Alfonso Ramírez was a small, serious man with somber black eyes.

"Six wounded." He scanned the stricken field. "Why?"

"For that answer, you must ask the boss." I had a throbbing headache and was sick to my stomach. "I had one of my men killed outright and, of the rest, over half are wounded—two will probably die. Five darts stuck in my cotton padding. I didn't get scratched."

I took no pride in my lack of injury. I had just experienced my first battlefield command and, when I looked out over my own casualties, I felt like an abject failure.

As soldiers spread over the field killing those Maya too badly injured to run or crawl away, I did what little I could to help our own wounded. The Caudillo, however, showing no embarrassment for his ignoble dismount, was more concerned about two wounded horses.

"Anyone here with experience in treating injured horses?"

I stood up from where I had been binding a soldier with a sucking chest wound. "Yes, from Italy," I shouted back.

"Leave what you are doing and come over here," Cortés ordered. Without enthusiasm, I walked the short distance.

"Don Rodrigo," he said, pointing to two animals that were tied up nearby "These caballos have deep wounds—it's important that they be attended to promptly."

"Sí, Caudillo, after I've attended to my own wounded, I'll treat the horses."

"I don't think you understand, Rodrigo." Cortés' anger was rising. "I want the horses treated first. Each one is worth at least twenty espadas. It would be very unfortunate if one of these horses were to die and the savages discovered that they were mortal beasts like any other."

I considered disobeying the order. "Sí, Señor, but first I must prepare a cautery."

I walked over the battlefield, stepping over the dead and wounded, searching for that which I needed. Almost all of the Maya, even in contorted death, were well muscled and thin. I stopped at one body, different from the rest. I could tell by the finery of his feathered armor that he was a cacique, a man of substance. He was as fat as a well-fed hog.

"Sancho," I called to a soldier who had accompanied me, "get me a basket from the cannon-train."

I watched as Sancho jogged back over the battlefield, artfully dodging and jumping over the bodies. Then I turned back to my Maya, checking for signs of residual life. He looked to be in early middle age and he lay, face up, with his eyes nearly closed. He could have been sleeping if it were not for the fact that the fletched end of a crossbow bolt protruded from his head, just above his right eye. Even so, I touched both of his eyes with a blade of grass that I plucked, nearby. There was no blink—the man was irreversibly dead. I cut his clothing and cotton armor away and was almost finished by the time Sancho returned.

"What are you going to do?" Sancho asked as I pulled back the last of the dead man's clothing.

"Just making liniment for the horses." I took my knife and made a long slit from the dead Maya's throat to the root of his penis. The cut edges of the wound still bled.

"*Madre de Dios!*" Sancho exclaimed, drawing back, "*Esto es la obra del Diablo.*"

"*Posible, Sancho,* but sometimes even the Devil's work is necessary." Using my knife as I have used it many times before in butchering animals, I peeled the fatty skin back from the meat of the chest and belly. Despite the thick layer of fat, the underlying muscle was massive. When touched with the blade, the muscles twitched and squirmed with unnatural life. I then cut great rectangles of the fatty skin away and placed them in the basket. By this time soldiers from all over the battlefield left off with their duties to watch what I was doing.

Several of the men held their noses. An opened corpse, even when fresh, has a certain odor.

I looked around me into their wide staring eyes. "I want all of you to watch me carefully because, in the future, it may be necessary for any one of you to do what I'm doing right now."

"*Nunca lo voy a poder hacer,*" one blood-smeared soldier contradicted.

"*Mira, mozo, por favor.*" I opened the membranes of the belly to expose the liver, the still writhing guts and the bulging globs of fat adherent to these organs. I sliced all of the fat away and piled it in the basket. I pushed the guts to one side and collected the fat from around the kidneys.

"Build me a fire and get me a pot," Within minutes a large clay pot appeared and there was a blazing fire. I put the skin and fat in the pot and placed it on the fire. Soon the fat was sizzling, and an aroma, surprisingly rich, wafted to the surrounding crowd. When the cooking was finished I was left with more than a quart of thick, bubbling grease. I threw the remnant skin and fat away and ordered the soldiers to carry the pot over to the wounded horses. I left my Tabascan—no longer obese—open to the sky. Hundreds of blowflies were already gathering.

One of the injured horses was a roan with a white blaze and had a deep neck wound inflicted by a broken branch. The other animal was nearly black with zebra stripes on his hocks. He had a wound in his flank. Both wounds were bleeding profusely, the thick blood coating their hides glowing crimson in the sun.

"Separate the horses and tie them securely."

I wrapped the end of a spear with a strip of cotton padding I had taken from the fat warrior. I placed the fabric-coated spear tip into the molten oil until it was soaked. Lifting the spear, I approached one of the horses, aimed carefully and thrust the steaming fabric into his wound. The horse went wild—screaming and kicking—then calmed down. I treated the other horse's flank wound in the same fashion, with the same results.

Cortés, crazy with anger, rushed over. "*En el Nombre de Dios*, I ordered you to treat the horses, not kill them!"

"*Mira!* " I said. " The wounds are no longer bleeding. They will heal without mortification. The horses will live." I turned from Cortés without another word and proceeded to treat our wounded in the same way I had treated the horses. Presa had already staunched Gilberto's bleeding and, despite the mortification that later set in, he survived. His nose and part of his upper jaw and cheekbone were gone and, although the wounds healed, his appearance was ghastly. Presa swore to God that he would give Gilberto his freedom should the Lord see fit to save Gilberto's life. He was good to his oath and freed Gilberto. Afterwards Gilberto became one of the most respected fighters in the army. He died during La Noche Triste.

Burgos, Castilla-León

Mendoza held his open hand up. "Your Grace? I am disturbed by your dissection of the Indio. If he were truly dead, his organs would have lost all evidence of life. You've mentioned that his muscles twitched and his viscera squirmed. These facts prove that the man was not yet truly dead and that, by cutting this living man open—you committed a mortal sin."

"Padre Mendoza, do you think that I care a worn peso for my sins, mortal or otherwise?"

"No, Excelencia, I don't."

"I will try to answer your question to the best of my ability. In that we are both men of the cloth," the ancient priest's face cracked into a grin, "let me, therefore, approach this issue from a theological perspective. As you know, the body and soul, while joined in this life, have a certain independence of one another. The teachings of Mother Church hold that the soul continues to exist beyond the dissolution of the body. At the same time, although never mentioned in doctrine, the body survives a short time after the departure of the soul. The animation of certain tissues, especially during the few minutes following the departure of the soul, is merely confirmation of this obvious fact. For reasons that I don't understand, the eyes are truly the windows to the soul. If the eyes no longer blink, the soul has passed on, forever. My fat Tabascan was well and truly dead."

"Your opinions are certainly novel, Excelencia, but, no doubt, like most of your theories, verge on the heretical. Then again, as a Bishop and an unbeliever, you apparently have no more of a problem with heresy than you do with sin."

"Correct, Padre, but, if you have paid close attention to my statements, I never identified myself as an unbeliever. I have merely stated that there are certain dogmas with which I am in disagreement. Make no mistake about it, within the High Councils of Mother Church, I am not alone."

"Are you saying, then, Your Grace," Mendoza leaned forward slightly, "that you believe in the reality of the human soul?"

"Let us say, that I recognize the possibility." The Bishop held the younger priest's stare with amused interest.

"How about beasts?" Now Mendoza was setting his own trap. Only humans have souls.

"We are getting far from our discussion of the Conquest, Padre, but you pose a fascinating question. I don't know. I can tell you this, though. When an animal dies, be it an ox or a goose, he no longer blinks and, if the animal is opened up promptly, his muscles and guts continue to function. It is exactly the same as a man. From these observations, you must draw your own conclusions. Now let me ask you a question, Padre Mendoza. Where in the body is the seat of the soul?"

"It is as you know full well, Your Grace. It is as Mother Church teaches us. It is the heart."

"Hmm." The old man's eyes held Mendoza's like a snake holds the eyes of a rat it is preparing to devour. "Let me tell you of some of my observations, then, and tell me what you make of them. You see, it was my great misfortune to be close to the *Templo Mayor* when hundreds of our men were dragged to their doom."

"How is this possible?"

"Later, in proper time, I will relate how I came to be in this unfortunate situation but, in the meantime it is sufficient for you to know that I was so close that I could see the victims, see the flash of stone knives as their chests were slashed open, and hear their screams as they died."

"What does this have to do with our discussion?"

"As you know, Padre, the Mexica sacrificed their victims by cutting out their hearts."

"Yes. It's been abundantly reported."

"Did you know that many of these men called out for their mothers and wives after their hearts were removed?"

Mendoza sat in silence.

"Therefore," the ancient priest went on, "either a man can continue to speak and think minus his soul or the soul is not centered on the heart."

Chapter 33

In addition to the enemy dead and wounded, we captured five others, two of whom were caciques. Cortés, through Aguilar, interrogated these men, and found them to be reasonably intelligent. He therefore used them as messengers. Cortés spoke to them through Aguilar.

"The battle and grief is entirely upon the heads of you incredible fools. We Castilians have every right to burn you at the stake."

The prisoners, all of whom had been stripped naked, tried to stand proud but one trembled uncontrollably. Cortés went on,

"We are a benevolent people, however, and, despite the great wrong done to us, we desire peace. Tell your leaders that they must proclaim that they are also for peace; otherwise, we must ravage your country, burn your villages and kill your women and children."

The caciques, having had enough of war, responded by sending fifteen men and women. They were carrying baked fish and maize cakes as well as their large fowls. These fifteen Indios had blackened faces wore ragged cloaks and loincloths. By their attire and demeanor it was clear that they were nothing more than miserable slaves. Cortés became very angry and told these black-faced people to return to their masters. He told them he was insulted by their gesture of sending slaves to negotiate with him and he was of a mind to renew his attack immediately.

Burgos, Castilla-León

"Now I must ask you, Padre Mendoza. In your account you correctly recount the incident of the slaves and Cortés' reaction to it, but you make no comment on it."

"There's nothing to comment on—the caciques were trying to lose as little face as possible, so they sent slaves in their stead."

"Your logic is Castilian but after spending years with these Indios, I know this interpretation is incorrect."

"What's the truth of it then?" Mendoza was resigned to being corrected.

"There was no insult intended. It was traditional for the defeated party to send slaves to the victorious party."

"For what purpose?"

"So that they could be sacrificed and eaten." Mendoza winced and the old man smiled wickedly. "Let us go on."

The next day thirty richly dressed chieftains arrived, all bearing food. One of the men seemed to be their leader. He was short and squat with a huge belly and flat nose. His earlobes, nasal septum and lower lip were perforated and distended by ornaments of gold and green stone. On his head was a circlet of green feathers and he wore a tiger-skin robe. He addressed Cortés.

"My Lord, we ask permission to bury our dead."

Cortés wished them to feel the full impact of defeat. "What do I care for your dead?"

"My Lord, the dead will rot and foul the air. Carrion birds will devour them and they will be dragged into the forest by wild beasts. Their ghosts will walk the earth and torment the living."

Cortés was imperious. "Permission is granted only on the condition that Tabasco promises peace."

"We promise, My Lord."

Nearby several horses were tied to trees opposite several of our big guns. I couldn't help but notice that the Maya, even while speaking to Aguilar and Cortés, glanced nervously towards both the animals and the cannons. I stepped to the side of Cortés and, knowing that the Indios could understand not one word of our language, I spoke openly.

"Caudillo, have you noticed how fearful these people are of our horses and cannons? They act as if they are more afraid of them than they are of us."

"I have indeed noticed, Rodrigo." Cortés winked. "You know what I think—these stupid savages believe that our guns are alive and they think that the horses are intelligent beings, even our leaders. Thank you for bringing it to my attention." He stopped and thought about it a moment. "I have an amusing idea. It may be entertaining. It may even add to their fear."

"Yes, Sir, whatever you think."

"See that cannon over there, the big one—it's the biggest gun— the one we call San Pedro. Have the men load it with as much powder and shot as it can handle. Then I want you to bring up Sedeño's mare. Tie her up behind those trees right over there where the Indios can't see her. When I give you the signal I want you to fetch the big stallion that belongs to Ortiz the musician, and tie him up downwind of the mare right on that tree right there. Make sure the stallion is tied securely because, if I know that animal, when he gets a whiff of that mare he will go absolutely berserk."

During the preparations forty more nobles arrived all dressed in gold, jewelry and fine-feathered attire. They were burning fragrant copal and wafted the smoke over us. Whether this was for ritual purposes or whether it was because they didn't like our smell, I don't know.

Cortés pretended a terrible anger. Through Aguilar he told them, "We Castilians are a kind and gentle people. All we have ever wanted was peace. So, what did you do? You attacked us! What you have done is a terrible thing and you," —Cortés pointed around to all the caciques— "deserve to be put to death along with the inhabitants of all of your pueblos."

Courageously, the squat cacique absolved himself, "Father, we had nothing to do with this war. We are as peaceful as you are and desire only friendship. It was the other tribes that caused all of the trouble. We will exterminate those who are actually responsible."

"That won't be necessary," Cortés said, "for we have come to your land on a good-will mission on behalf of our Emperor, Carlos. We, the people you see here, are Castilians and vassals of the great Emperor. He has ordered us to come to these lands and to help all of those who would enter into the Emperor's Royal service. If you people will agree to be peaceful and swear fealty to the Emperor, we will have mercy on you."

Cortés hesitated as if deep in thought, "There is a problem, though. The cannoñes and our great ciervos"—for the Indios thought our horses were some kind of deer— "are very angry. I have tried to reason with them but they hate you."

At this moment Cortés gave the signal and San Pedro went off with a roar. There was a huge ball of flame with foul-smelling smoke as the ball went whistling away into the distance. The caciques were suddenly rendered pitiful, all quaking like leaves in the wind with some falling to their knees. One previously brave warrior urinated and defecated at the same time.

"Do not fear," Cortés told them. "These things"—indicating the cannons— "are my slaves. They will not harm you."

I brought the stallion up. The animal was uncontrollable, bucking, neighing, pawing the ground, rolling his eyes and fighting violently against the rope. At the same time the stallion glared crazily toward the Maya because they were between him and the hidden mare. Horrified, the Indios were too terrified to run.

Cortés made a calming gesture. "Do not panic, mis amigos. I will try to reason with this great ciervo." Cortés walked over to the animal and got into a very loud argument with it. The horse was neighing and snorting and Cortés was arguing, screaming and gesturing vehemently with his hands and arms. The animal calmed and I led the animal away.

Burgos, Castilla-León

"The horse incident gives me the opportunity to make another correction in your account of the Conquest."

"What might that be?" Mendoza asked. "I mentioned the Indio fear of the horses."

"Indeed, you did and, as far as it goes, you were correct. Initially, at least, the Indios were terrified of our horses and would sometimes break and run at the mere appearance of horsemen on the battlefield."

"Correct, " Mendoza replied. "The Indios thought that the rider and horse were one creature, some incredible monster."

"Not exactly. The Indios weren't stupid and, even if they were, they were accurate observers. They could easily see that the horse and horseman were separate beings. Besides, most had seen beasts more fearful than horses in Moctecuzoma's menagerie. More likely, in my opinion, was that the Indios were blinded by superstition, and thought that the rider, whom the Indios already suspected was a demon—once he mounted the animal—took on some of the qualities of the beast and the beast took on some of the qualities of the man. They therefore thought that the combination of man mounted on horse was supernatural and fearful."

"Not all that different from my own writings..." Mendoza argued.

The ancient man, his hands behind him, paced as he lectured: "This also tells us something about the nature of fear and defeat on the field of battle. Men, even brave men, are much more likely to break when confronted with things which are unknown, novel or unexpected. For example, I have mentioned the reaction of the Indios to our horses and firearms."

"I've never personally been exposed to battle," Mendoza said. He was thankful that he had never had to risk his life in the field. On the other hand, as a Castilian, he sometimes wondered if he had missed an important experience.

The Obispo went on as if the younger man had said nothing. "In Italy, I saw brave men, men who had faced battle with courage and determination, totally unmanned by the attack of fighting dogs."

"Like the ones..."

"Yes, just like the ones that Cortés transported to Nueva España and used against the Maya at Cintla. They are huge, slavering beasts but if a man is not craven, they are easier to defeat than is an armed soldier. Still, the mere appearance of these filthy beasts oftentimes rendered brave men cowards. I have seen heavily armed soldiers try to outrun these dogs and, the next thing you know, the animal would have the man down, biting his face and tearing out his windpipe. The Indios, even though they had small dogs themselves, had never seen such beasts and were especially vulnerable."

"You have dealt with these animals, yourself?"

"Stand your ground, and give him a thrust in the chest or the side." The ancient priest feinted and dodged as if facing a living enemy. "Once, I swung my ax and removed the beast's muzzle with a single blow. It was laughable to hear the dog howling through his shattered head. I think we were talking about Tabasco, though."

The remaining caciques begged our pardon and the pardon of our cannons and horses and solemnly swore their eternal fealty to king Carlos. They also promised to return the next morning with presents and food. Return they did with small trinkets of gold alloyed with copper.

Chapter 34

The next gifts they brought, however, were as it turned out, were of incomparably greater value. They gave us twenty women for work and for pleasure. Several of these girls were pretty in the Indio way but were otherwise unremarkable. One of the girls, however, was beyond value—although we didn't know it at the time. The Maya gave her name as Malinali although she later told us her given name was Malintzin. She was taller and slimmer than the others with nice breasts and a full bottom. Her face, though perfect, was too solemn to be actually beautiful. She was in her early twenties, light-skinned for an Indio and more quick witted than all but a few of our Castilians.

She already had a complicated history—a history that added greatly to her value. She was the daughter of the Lord Rulers of separate small cities within the Mexican empire. Of course, at the time we knew nothing of Mexico so the significance of her childhood would have been lost on all of us, including Cortés.

Poor Malinali's father had died when she was young and her mother married another lord. Together they had a son. This presented a problem. Malinali was the heir to the cities but the new husband wanted the honors of leadership for the son of his own blood. To satisfy her husband, Malinali's mother secretly—for such an act is disgraceful even to the Mexicans—sold the girl into slavery and she became the possession of the Tabascans. The Maya therefore had given us a slave who bore a bitter grudge against her own mother and, by extension, all of her mother's people—the Mexica. More importantly, she spoke not only the Tabascan tongue but also Nahuatl, the language of Mexico. Later, when we encountered the Mexicans, by using both Malinali and Aguilar as translators, we were able to converse with all of the people in the Valley of Mexico and many of those some distance away.

Burgos, Castilla-León

Mendoza stopped writing. "I must admit a certain embarrassment, Excelencia. I have never quite understood some of the tribal distinctions of the indígenos."

The Bishop screwed up his face, unhappy at having to stop his narration. "The Maya are many groups, all of who are different from those of central Mexico. The language of Cozumel is the same spoken by the people of *Yucatán* and *Campeche*, including our enemies at Champoton and Tabasco. There are, however, differences in pronunciation and dialect. Nahuatl is the language spoken by the Azteca even though they them are of different, frequently warring groups. The Mexica are one of these groups, albeit the most important. The Tenochca were specifically those Mexica who inhabited *Tenochtitlan*, the capital city of the Mexica. Therefore Malinali was more valuable than the gold we had set out to plunder. Without her, the Conquest would have been impossible. This woman quickly learned Castilian, at which time Aguilar's linguistic talents were no longer required."

"Ah then," Mendoza exclaimed, "she was the gift of the Lord."

"*Exactamente, Padre, El Señor Diablo.*"

"No, Your Grace, Our Savior and the Blessed Virgin."

Annoyed, the old man audibly passed gas. "Malinali was named for *Malinalxochitl.*"

"And who might that be, Your Grace?"

"Maguey Flower, the beautiful sister of *Huitzilopotchli*, the most powerful demon in all of Mexico-a flower with a sharp thorn-the thorn with which their unholy priests drew their own blood. Satan laughed when he gave her up to us. He knew Hernán Cortés would know how to use her.

At the time I am speaking of, she was just property—another female. Cortés ordered all of the girls baptized for, as you know, it's a sin to copulate with heathens, and apportioned them out to his Captains. My status was such that I didn't rank with the top twenty so I wasn't given a woman.

Cortés, not recognizing her worth, gave her to his closest friend, Alonso Hernández Puertocarrero and had her name changed to Marina or Doña Marina, because she was a princess of royal blood. To the Mexica, though, she was Malintzin or Malinche. Whether these were just the Mexican rendering of her name or whether it was a term of respect I don't know. I think you should know, however, that in the post-conquest days—after the Mexicans had supposedly found Christ—the word *Malinche* became a Nahuatl slur. *Malinche* became their word for traitor.

Now here I must mention another interesting thing about the interesting man that was Hernán Cortés. Like most active and powerful men, he absolutely lusted after women. During our expedition many women would fall into our hands. As gestures of submission, Indio leaders often gave us some of the most beautiful women in the land. Like this first time at Tabasco, Cortés would, after having any such women baptized, give them out to his top Captains. If there were women left over, they went to the officers and men down the line. Cortés would never take the most beautiful women for himself.

Why do you think that Cortés was so generous, Padre Mendoza? You seem to have missed this part in your books."

"My sources tell me that, unlike your testimony, Hernán Cortés was always loyal to his wife. If he found it necessary to accept women at all it was simply to avoid offending heathen leaders and to further the cause of the Cross. Therefore he had no particular use for women. Any women he might have come by were no doubt used as menials."

"A nice theory, Mendoza, but it simply doesn't accord with human nature, especially not Cortés' nature. Cortés was a sultan with the women. By the time we completed the Conquest, Cortés had a virtual harem. Cortés was wise, though. The women he kept were attractive enough but, by handing out the most beautiful to his leaders, he kept his Captains loyal. The only times he disobeyed this rule was when he tried to force Francesca de la Barca to do his bidding and when he took Doña Marina from Puertocerrero for himself. In the case of Francesca he made a foolish, even lethal mistake but, in the case of Doña Marina, he insured the Conquest of Mexico.

Puertocerrero wasn't offended, for Cortés saw to it that he got an even more beautiful woman in exchange and Doña Marina, herself, certainly never complained—her loyalty to Cortés was complete and, I do not think I go too far to say that she truly loved him. Cortés' feelings for Doña Marina, if any, were far more complex. He fully recognized her value, though, and despite his acquisition of numerous women, he was careful that few were more attractive than Doña Marina. I think it should be noted, however, that after the Conquest and despite the fact that Doña Marina bore Cortés' child, he passed her off to an hidalgo newly arrived from Spain. Doña Marina never forgave him."

Cortés gave a sermon to the Maya through Aguilar.

"We Españoles are here to testify that there is only one God and that Jesus Christ is his only son."

The Indios were pleased.

Cortés went on, "You also need to know that although Jesus

Christ is the Son of God—God and Christ are One with the Holy Spirit. This is the principle of the trinity."

Now they seemed less certain.

He didn't stop. "It is also necessary for you to pray for intercession through the Mother of God, the Virgin Mary, the Most Blessed of Women."

Now many of the caciques were standing in open-mouthed amazement.

"Later we will teach you the names of...uh... thirty patron saints. St. James, St. Paul and St. Peter are almost as important as Jesus, but some are less important. You must honor all of them but only need to pray to your favorite. We will teach you about Religious Days, Fast Days and about Holy Relics. The Pope— Papa Sagrada—is the leader of our faith and, although he may err in the matters of men, is infallible in matters of God."

Comprehension spread over the face of the squat cacique. He spoke to both Cortés and to the gathered Maya. "I was afraid that the white men came to do us harm. I can now see that we were fools, for the white men mean only good. This one" —he pointed at Aguilar, our interpreter— "speaks as if he has a mouth full of grass but, nevertheless, I understand him. Men of Tabasco, hear me: "'The Christian God was shamed by his mother Mary for having a child without a husband—he chopped her into three pieces—it is the same as we already know.' Now tell me, Father Cortés, may we keep the skull of Chancol as a Holy Relic? If we can we will all swear allegiance to your God."

Cortés smiled, "You may keep your relic. In return I give you the image of the Blessed Virgin with the infant, Jesus."

Fraile Díaz gave the Blessed Portrait to the pagano.

The squat Indio stared reverently at the image. "We will slaughter many captives in her honor."

Cortés' eyes flashed its amber fire. "There will be no more sacrifice—The Holy Father forbids it!"

Cortés then ordered the Maya to build an altar for the image and to place a cross next to it. One of our friars, I can't remember who, performed mass. The soldiers knelt with heads bowed while the Tabascans looked on in awe. ●●●

We stayed in Tabasco for five days, attending to our wounded, of whom many died of blood loss and mortification. Cortés told the Maya that if they would agree to become vassals of Emperor Carlo that we—the forces of Jesus Christ—would rush to their assistance. Believing Cortés and knowing of our might in battle, they agreed. Their agreement was duly recorded by our notario. These were the first vassals of Emperor Carlos in Nueva Espana. Years later, I learned that Melchior, our faithless interpreter, died a bloody death on the Blessed Altar of Our Lady.

Chapter 35

Burgos, Castilla-León
February 5, 1581; 8:30 A.M.

Padre Mendoza entered their dictation room, flanked by the usual two guards. Obispo de la Peña did not bother to look up. Other than motioning for Mendoza to sit down, the old man sat with an unnatural stillness.

"Padre, I must apologize for being unable to meet with you during the past fortnight but, as you know, Santo Oficio is a hard task-master. I'm sure you'll be delighted to know that I was successful in securing the release of four conversos, three Moriscos and one relapsed Lutheran. By a deft piece of investigation I was successful in getting one of our Inquisitors, Licenciado Ernesto Padilla, arrested on charges of embezzlement. I also carefully examined the statements and writings of Fraile de Serna, the Holy Inquisitor of Málaga—I detected the taint of heresy," the old man chuckled. "I obtained the good friar's conviction on the grounds that he is a secret Illuminado. He denied it, of course, but that only proves his guilt—he will burn at the next Auto de Fe."

"Yes," Mendoza said, under his breath, "you are a great hero of the True Faith."

"Quite so. Religion has its uses."

"Has the Council inquired about me?"

"Of course. I've told them that your case is complex and requires my most careful examination. The members of the Council seem satisfied but you must realize that is because in the end, they believe that they will subdivide your property."

"You promised...!"

The Bishop shrugged his bony shoulders, "As you fulfill your part of the bargain—I will fulfill my part as well. Then the members of the *Suprema* will have to accept my judgment."

"What if they don't?"

"They will. A hard bought Bishopric is a very valuable thing. I have every one of those ladrónes by their atrophied huevos and they know it. I don't fear them but they all fear me." The old man, who was clad in the full vestments of his order, stood up and stiffly walked the few paces to the hearth. He bent over and picked up a stick from the small woodpile and tossed it onto the glowing coals.

"The morning is cold—or is it just that my fires burn low."

"The room is cold, Excelencia."

The old man stared into the flames a long time. "I'm chilled to the bone..."

"The room is growing more comfortable, Your Grace."

"Do you enjoy watching a fire, Padre?"

"I've never thought of it but...yes, I do."

The ancient man never took his eyes off the fire. His scars were flickering light. "It's a strange thing but everyone enjoys watching a fire. It's one of the things that sets us apart from the beast—I don't know quite what it is—there is the warmth, of course, but it's more than that. There's the sound and the color."

"I agree. It's the warmth and the beauty of it."

The old Bishop rubbed his hands in front of the flames. "But it's also the consumption, danger and destruction. Many a time I have seen people cast wood into a fire long past the time they needed the heat." The old man threw another log onto the fire—there was an explosion of sparks. "It's almost as if the annihilation of the wood is the goal."

"You aren't going to tell me that this ties in with you concepts of human evil?"

"Not at all, Padre—but it's interesting. Shall we continue?"

After mourning and burying our dead, we boarded our ships and continued north with fair winds and under blue skies. The men who had accompanied Grijalva announced the various points of interest. After some days sailing, we came to the Isla Blanca and the nearby Isla Verde. Close inshore was the Isla de los Sacrificios, where the previous expedition had found the butchered bodies of Indios still warm and stretched out on bloody altars. On the Thursday of Passion week, three and a half days after leaving Tabasco, our fleet anchored in the lee of the island that Grijalva had named San Juan de Ulua.

The port was decent and hundreds of Indios lined the shore to look at our ships. Two canoes filled with Indios set out from the nearby mainland and paddled directly to Cortés' flagship. The crew prepared to repel boarders but the Indios were quite friendly.

They were a different race than the Tabascans and their language was not Maya so Aguilar was unable to translate. By sign language, these indigenos indicated that they wanted to speak to our chieftain. For a time the Castilians and the Indios tried to communicate by signs and gestures but these efforts were unsuccessful. Doña Marina, whom nobody had paid any attention to before, saw her opportunity. She stepped forward and, in doing so, she stepped into history.

She indicated that she could help. She didn't speak the local Totonac language but some of Totonacs spoke Nahuatl, the language of Mexico. Through Doña Marina a complex translation was obtained. Doña Marina translated Nahuatl into Tabascan and Aguilar translated the Tabascan language into Castilian. Then, of course, when Cortés wished to communicate with the Totonacs, the reverse translation occurred.

The Totonacs, who had brought presents of food, flowers and golden trinkets, were invited on board. Everyone had questions.

"Who is your ruler?" the young soldier, Bernal Díaz, asked.

"Alas, our ruler is dead—gloriously sacrificed—in *Cholula*. Our Mexica governor now cares for us."

"Who might this governor be?"

"Teuhtlile. He is a very great Lord and lives fifteen leagues from here."

Now Cortés took over the questioning. "Is he rich? Who is his master?"

"Yes, Teuhtlile is rich in slaves and cotton mantles. He is the Governor for the great Moctecuzoma who lives in *Tenochtitlan* far to the west." The Totonac, who was nearly as black as an Africano, pointed in the direction of the setting sun.

Cortés got right to the point. "Does this great lord, Moctecuzoma, have much....gold?"

"Oh, yes! Moctecuzoma has many huge temples filled with gold, silver and green chachihuitl. He has mountains of precious, beautifully woven cloaks, and huge piles of sacred quetzal feathers. His women are the most beautiful in the world and will welcome you white-skinned teoteoh with great pleasure." The speaker's lower lip was pulled downward by a clay disc. His eyes glittered like a serpent.

Cortés, who had understood the important points of the translation, beamed hugely. "It's exactly as I promised. We are all going to be as rich as Midas. But what is a chalchihuitle and a ...teule?"

Aguilar spoke rapidly to Doña Marina and then spoke to Cortés in Castilian. "A chalchihuitl is a green stone, maybe an emerald or maybe just jade. A teotl is a god or—a devil."

"Do you hear that, muchachos?" Cortés spoke loudly so that everyone around him could hear. "These savages think we are gods—this is going to be easier than I hoped."

With this Cortés gave the Totonacs food, wine and blue beads and told them that he would be altogether delighted to meet their Mexican governor.

Chapter 36

Armed with the Totonac's golden information, Cortés decided to land our force on the mainland. Unfortunately, the country at this point was a wind-swept desolation of plains and rolling sand dunes broken up by pestilential, mosquito-ridden swamps. Still we made camp as well we could and, by cutting down brush and stunted trees, we built makeshift huts. The local Indios were friendly and even helped us do the hardest work. We soldiers established a lucrative trade and were able to trade for mats and cotton carpets to make our huts more livable while, at the same time, Indios crowded in from the countryside bringing food and small trinkets of gold.

In the meantime, our big guns were sited on the tops of dunes. A watch was established because—no matter how friendly the naturales seemed—we could never be certain.

The only attack we received, however, was that of Teuhtlile who, along with his various officials, presented himself quite peacefully on Easter morning. Our initial contact was attended by the wafting of copal incense, as was their custom. We retaliated by subjecting the Indios to our Easter service, much of which was devoted to condemnation of the Mexican practices of cannibalism and sodomy. Afterwards we gave them wine and confections, which they seemed to enjoy more than the preachments of Padre Olmedo.

"Who are you?" Teuhtlile asked.

"We are visitors from distant lands," Cortés answered.

"We are, of course, pleased that you have come, but what is the reason for your visit?"

Teuhtlile was tall and slender and clad in a loincloth decorated with complex embroidery and beadwork. Over his head, pancho fashion, was a pelt of shiny green feathers that fell almost to his ankles. His hair was shiny black and rolled on top of his head and was partially hidden by green feathers. He would have been handsome if it were not for the fact that a small disc of jade pierced his nasal septum and heavy discs of gold distended his earlobes. Also, a disc of solid gold pulled down his lower lip. Saliva dribbled down the few hairs on his chin. Despite this, he held himself arrogantly as fitting for an aristocrat of his status.

Cortés, ignoring the constant drip of saliva, stared intently at the gold in Teuhtlile's ears and lip, "We are the vassals of Emperor Carlos I, conqueror of kings and nations and ruler of most of the earth." Cortés stopped for the translation. "We have been dispatched by Emperor Carlos, so that we might speak to the great Moctecuzoma, of whom our Emperor has heard many wonderful things."

Teuhtlile attempted to retain his composure but his face betrayed his emotions. "*Moctecuzoma Xocoyotzin* is the greatest lord on the earth."

"Good," Cortés grinned, "then I am sure he will be especially delighted to hear news of Emperor Carlos. When might we meet the great Moctecuzoma? Emperor Carlos has sent gifts."

Teuhtlile reached his limit. "Who are you, to demand audience with our mighty Lord, the glorious Moctecuzoma? With his little finger he could flick you away like unclean tecpintlin on his tepolli. Give me your worthless presents and I will see whether our Lord will deign to accept them. Then, if he should so desire, there may be a correspondence."

Cortés, considering whether he would lose face by surrendering his gifts, decided not to push things. "Of course, Don Teuhtlile. It would be a good idea to get these gifts to the Lord Moctecuzoma as quickly as possible. Unfortunately, we Castilians will be delayed here on the coast for some time because we have important work to do."

Teuhtlile was presented with a Spanish treasure of less value than was the gold shining from his own face. We gave him a crimson cap, and multiple collars, bracelets and jewelry of cut glass and a richly carved chair.

"This" —Cortés indicated the chair— "is for Moctecuzoma to sit in when we visit him at his capital."

Teuhtlile, pointedly ignoring Cortés' hint, spoke so that the entire company might hear him. "The great lord Moctecuzoma Xocoyotzin speaks to the god. He knows of your defeat of the treacherous Maya and compliments you on your victory. He thanks you for helping subdue these lice for him. He has also gathered up gifts in anticipation of your arrival here on this shore. Behold the generosity of the Uei Tlatloani!"

Pitiful slaves, with dirty tunics and backs bent by the weight of their burdens, stepped forward bearing ten loads of fine cotton mantles with complex feather-work and a wicker basket filled with animals and small demons in wrought gold. We soldiers gasped but Cortés only sneered.

"I thought Moctecuzoma was a great lord." Cortés picked up the basket of golden objects as if weighing its value. "This is an insult to Emperor Carlos. I have a mind to return to my country and inform my Emperor Carlos I—the Ruler of the World—of Moctecuzoma's miserliness."

Teuhtlile's face reflected the awful consequences of such a revelation to this distant mysterious Carlos.

"Do not be angry," he said. "These are but the first of Moctecuzoma's gifts. You must be patient." Suddenly, Teuhtlile, like a child distracted by an unexpected toy, faced me in blank amazement.

"What is this?" He said in whispered awe.

"What?" I didn't understand his interest in me. Cortés nodded at me so I took one step toward the Governor.

Teuhtlile recoiled in fear. "Please do not touch me, Great Lord. I can provide you with many victims."

"I think it's your scars and your helmet, Don Rodrigo. You're the only one of us wearing a helmet."

I took my helmet off and held it out to Teuhtlile. The man sank to his knees. He was trembling. "Oh thank you, *Lord Tezcatlipoca*. Do you honor my Emperor with this holy thing?"

Cortés answered, "Yes, you may have it for a little while but only if you return it filled with gold dust. You see, we Castilians are special and have a disease of the heart that can only be cured with the purest gold. I would like to see if the gold of this country is as therapeutic as is the gold of our own country."

"Great Lord." Teuhtlile was still speaking to me as if Cortés were only my mouthpiece. "I will return this to *Tenochtitlan* where it will be presented in your temple, and we will honor it there in the presence of your sacred image. Be satisfied that Moctecuzoma himself will sacrifice comely boys before it and then he will return your crown filled with the finest grains of gold."

Cortés tried to prolong the meeting but finally the Mexican ambassadors departed stating that they had to report back to Moctecuzoma. They promised that they would soon return. I couldn't help noticing that Teuhtlile and his entourage, on their departure, looked decidedly uneasy.

Burgos, Castilla-León

"Excelencia," Mendoza interrupted, "I think you overly emphasize Hernán Cortés' interest in gold."

"No, Padre. I underemphasize it. Cortés indeed had a disease curable only by gold."

"There is nothing wrong with a certain self-interest."

"Do you remember the old homily, Padre? *Auri sacra fames*—'those who are accursed hunger for gold.'"

Mendoza ignored the jest. "On another issue, however, you said that the Mexicans knew of your battle with the Maya. My sources mentioned nothing of this. As a matter of fact, they knew nothing of the Maya before the Conquest."

The Bishop shook his head. "Didn't I tell you that you needed an eye-witness—a first-hand account? Your sources were inadequate. There is no question that Moctecuzoma, with his network of spies, heard of our victory. The remarkable thing about this is that this information paved our way for our victory over the Mexica."

"How so?"

"Remember, I told you that I was opposed to our staying to fight the Maya at what became known as the Battle of Cintla."

"Yes, I do."

"Well, from a tactical perspective I was entirely correct. Still I was wrong. Logically, there was no reason for our spending more time in Tabasco. We had delivered a sharp lesson to the Maya in the previous battle—we had nothing further to gain. It therefore only made sense that we embark and sail farther up the coast."

"I hate to agree with you, Your Grace..."

"Yet Cortés elected to stay and take his chances with an entirely unnecessary battle."

"Go on."

"Nevertheless, quite unexpected results followed Cortés' foolish decision. First, we came in possession of Doña Marina, without whom the Conquest would have been impossible. Second, we gained the reputation of supernatural invulnerability. Because of this reputation, Moctecuzoma—fool that he was—refused to repel our efforts to penetrate, not only into his empire, but his capital and even his home."

"Yes, it makes sense," Mendoza said. "*E fructo arbor cognoscitur*—the tree is recognized by its fruits. Sometimes bravado has its rewards."

"Yes indeed," the old man went on, "but it was more than bravado. Cortés was under the protection of *El Enemigo Malo*, who guided him, whispered in his ear, told him what he must do and when he must do it. You see, Cortés wasn't quite the high-stakes gambler that he may have seemed. He only bet on a sure thing."

When Teuhtlile was absent, a second Mexican governor named Pitalpitoque stayed near our camp and ordered women to bring the native domestic fowls, the large pavos—known to the Indios as *gua-jalotes*—that we now see here in España and their strange ducks with warts on their faces. Although we see them less commonly in this land, their flesh is so sweet that they are known as the Royal Duck, *el pato real*. They also brought pescados—fish—and the cake from the grain we call maíz, but the Mexica called 'God's corn'— *teocentli*. This grain is soaked with lime and ground with the metate and mano to make maize cakes—tortillas. This food was adequate for the officers but the soldiers would have gone hungry if they hadn't been able to find shellfish and barter glass beads for food. Six or seven days later, new emissaries arrived from the west.

"I am *Teoctlamaczqqui, tlillancalqui of Tenochtítlan*. Moctecuzoma has ordered us to honor you." He gestured towards twenty or so chieftains behind him. "We have gifts and we have ten slaves to sacrifice at your feet."

The Tlillancalqui was an odd looking ambassador—he was a humpback with great white blotches on his leprous skin. Nevertheless, he was covered in feathers and wore a cape of almost black fur that I came to recognize as that of a black kind of tigre mexicano.

"I'd rather you not sacrifice the slaves, Señor Tetlamaki or whatever your name is," Cortés said, "but I would like to get a look at those gifts."

"Our Lord tells us that we must first dress you in your own clothing."

"Clothing?"

"Yes." The ambassador looked at Cortés as if expecting him to explode.

Cortés decided. "Get on with it."

Chieftains, in the role of attendants, stepped up to the bemused Caudillo. One put a mask on top of his head that was the flattened head from a tigre. A rich cloak of green feathers was placed around his shoulders, green serpent things for his ears, and bracelets of gold and silver for his ankles, and a necklace of green stones for his throat. On his feet were placed sandals studded with small blue-green stones.

An attendant approached me on his hands and knees—never looking at me directly. Without looking up, he gave me a circle of shiny black stone—a Mexican buckler. The man kept crawling and, once behind me, rose and tried to attach a large mirror of similar stone to my back.

I seized him and thrust him to my front—the terrified man nearly collapsed. "No one is to get behind me, if you please."

The frightened attendant then placed the mirror on the sand while other attendants, now afraid to approach either Cortés or myself, placed other objects on the ground. These things included a fan, a large tray of gold and a buckler made from the rainbow-hued shells of large caracoles del mar. They were of a kind we had never seen before. The Mexicans told us they came from a sea far to the west of Tenochtítlan. This was valuable information because, we had heard only imperfect reports of Balboa's discovery.and didn't know that his sea—*El Mar Pacifico*— stretched this far north.

The Tlillancalqui then knelt before Cortés and, while looking down, offered him a gold cup shaped like a bird. Cortés looked into it and, without warning, swatted it away, red droplets spattering against the sand.

"Who do you think I am, you incredible fool? You wish to poison me by trying to make me swallow blood." Cortés forced himself to calm down. "Don't tell me these are all your presents?" With disgust, he tore off his pagano clothing and ornaments and threw them onto the sand.

"It is all we have," the Mexican whined. "Lord Moctecuzoma thought they were...."

"Well, they are not!" Cortés' jaw jutted forward. "What I would really like is a display of Mexican prowess. From what I've been told, one Mexican fighter is worth twenty of his enemies. I propose that we have a tournament between five of your men and five of my Castilians."

The ambassador's white blotches turned purple. "Moctecuzoma will punish us."

"Nonsense. Besides, if you lose you won't have to worry about Moctecuzoma or anything else."

"We ..."

"That's the right attitude." Cortés grinned. "Pick out your champions tonight and tomorrow we'll expect to see all of you at sun-up."

The Mexica backed away from us with strange looks on their faces. They didn't show up the next day or the day after that.

●●●

Days later, Teuhtlile arrived followed by chieftains and one hundred slaves bearing heavy burdens. Also present was a chieftain who, except for the color of his skin, could have been the twin brother of the Caudillo.

"What's the meaning of this?" Cortés demanded.

"We have brought this man for you to see." Teuhtlile indicated the Cortés twin. "To do honor to you."

"...Or to rob me of my power?" Cortés knew that the reason for the presence of the look-alike was in the realm of the magic.

The Mexica performed their usual ceremony of perfuming our party with incense and bowing, touching the ground and then their foreheads with their hands. Then the Cortés-mimic spoke.

"Our *Great Lord Moctecuzoma Xocoyotzin, Uei Tlatloani* of the *Mexica* and *Anahuac*, high priest of *Huitzilopotchli, Tezcatlipoca, Quetzalcoatl, Xipe* and *Tlaloc* extends his greetings."

Amazingly, not only did this Mexican look like Cortés but he also sounded like him and used his same gestures. He wasn't finished, though. "Our Great Prince, the Ruler of *Tlatelolco* and *Tenochtitlan*, Lord of the Four Points and Brother of *Ehecatl*, the Night Wind and subject himself only to *Tezcatlipoca, Huitzilopotchli, Tonatiuh* and dread *Mictlan*, honors you most worthy teotoh. He welcomes you travelers of the Eastern Seas to your own land. Lord Moctecuzoma wants you to know that he has been expecting you. He begs that you accept these humble gifts."

The porters, one-by-one, and with obviously practiced flourishes, rolled out mats.

Everyone gasped—gold—in unimaginable quantities, glinted in the blazing sun. Here was my helmet completely filled with fine grains and nuggets of pure gold. There were ornaments of fine gold with the appearance of beasts—leones, tigres, perros monos and many others. There were also ten beautiful necklaces, some pendants, golden collars and bracelets, pearls and green stones and a golden bow with twelve golden arrows and many other items I no longer remember. Then they brought crests of gold, plumes of green feathers and golden antlered ciervos. They also brought thirty loads of beautiful cotton cloth of complex patterns, decorated delicately with feathers. Most amazing of all, though, were two large discs, each the width of a tall man and as wide as four fingers placed together. Both were intricately carved with birds, plants and animals.

One, representing the moon, was made out of silver. The other, representing the sun, was made of solid gold. Even Solomon, in his magnificence, never imagined such wealth.

Cortés, to his credit, betrayed no emotion. Instead he spoke harshly—contempt oozing from his every word.

"In the name of our Emperor Carlos, we accept this paltry tribute."

Even the dullest of our Castilians were stunned. Our force numbered scarcely five hundred soldiers and held but a tiny toehold on a savage land that may have contained thousands or even millions of warriors. Still, Cortés pretended that the treasure was no more than the tribute owed by a conquered nation to its conqueror. I looked up and could see that Francesca de la Barca, who was paying no attention to the Caudillo's words, was kneeling in front of the great wheel of gold, tracing its diabolic engravings with her index finger.

Teuhtlile, who did not understood the exact meaning of the Cortés meaning, replied, "Now that you have received these gifts, Moctecuzoma requests that you quickly return these gifts to your Emperor, Carlotl."

"We would like to return to our homes," Cortés said, "but our Emperor Carlos, who commands all things, has given us instruction that we are to proceed to your capital city where we are to meet with your Lord and tell him the good news of Our God, Jesus Christ, and that of his Blessed Mother, the Holy Virgin...."

Teuhtlile, a thoroughgoing heathen, didn't seem to grasp the concept of a Virgin Mother. He stopped Cortés with an abrupt gesture.

"Lord Moctecuzoma is concerned for the welfare of you teotoh and has decided against your visit. The road between here and *Tenochtítlan* is long and difficult and fraught with danger—ayah—the mountains are tall and freezing. Avalanches of ice and snow tumble from their heights destroying all who would attempt to pass. Terrible beasts wait in ambush and barbarians, who care not for Moctecuzoma or the gods, will slaughter and eat you."

Cortés peered into the eyes of the Mexican ambassador—the man averted his gaze. "Our Lord Carlos, loves and respects the great king Moctecuzoma. For Carlos, we have traveled for thousands of leagues over a sea far more dangerous than a few rocky hills. We have done this thing precisely because the Glorious Carlos has ordered us to meet with Moctecuzoma and personally exchange greetings. We are touched by your Lord's concern for our safety but I would like to reassure him—Castilians are immune to hardship. We are never weary and we never sleep. Moctecuzoma is not to worry for we are capable of overcoming any enemy no matter how numerous or fierce. We Castilians do not know fear!"

Cortés then, in a poor gesture to reciprocate with the Mexican king produced a few Spanish shirts, a Florentine goblet and a few cheap children's toys.

Chapter 37

The richness of Moctecuzoma's gifts was counterbalanced by his denial of our request to visit him and the fact that the food they gave us was sprinkled with blood. It didn't take too much imagination to recognize that, should we advance on Tenochtítlan without the Emperor's permission, we would soon be confronting a decidedly unfriendly Moctecuzoma backed by Mexican armies of overwhelming strength. Divisions arose in camp as to the wisest policy with which to proceed. Some of the wealthier and probably more intelligent soldiers favored the policy of returning to Cuba and organizing a truly formidable Spanish force capable of leveling the Mexican empire and taking its wealth for our own.

I had to admit that discretion was with those who wished to return to Cuba. On the other hand, my experience with the Governor of Cuba was such that I knew if he ever got his hands on Mexico, there would be nothing left for anyone except for himself and his friends.

Cortés, his loyal officers, as well as most of the men, clearly agreed with my point of view. These men argued that reporting to Cuba meant that the greedy governor would keep the lion's share of wealth for himself. It was true that a larger army might prove to be more effective, but it also meant that the spoil would have to be divided among many more soldiers. Clearly, I thought, it was better to endure danger and become wealthy than to endure lesser danger and gain nothing.

While digging for clams one day, I came on Juan de Alva kneeling on the sand, looking out to sea. He was dressed, as most of us were, in cotton armor with his breastplate strapped to his chest. His shield lay beside him and his sword was stuck deep in the sand with the cross of its hilt level with his eyes. It looked to me as if he had been praying.

"What's wrong, Juan?"

He shook his head. "God in Heaven knows that I have done my duty but sometimes I don't feel well..."

"I can tell that you've lost weight."

He went on, "I am no cobarde but last night I had a vision. I was in a deep pit and above, the Caudillo was laughing and shoveling dirt in my face." De Alva turned to look at me, his eyes dark and luminous against his pale face. "It is an omen, Rodrigo. The only chance I have is to get back to España."

Alva was right. He had a deathly glow.

"Don't worry, Juan. Word has it that the Caudillo is sending a ship back to Cuba with the sick and injured." It was a lie but a lie is the only comfort I had to give. Cortés would never send a ship back to Cuba to save a few lives. He planned to keep his discoveries from the Governor's ears as long as possible.

De Alva turned his eyes to his savage cross, "No, Rodrigo—Cortés has ordered the Governor's strongest supporters—the ones who could pilot us to Cuba—to explore the coast north of here with two ships. I'll be buried here."

I hadn't heard this. "Whom did he send?"

"Francisco de Montejo and Juan Álvarez along with the pilot, Alaminos."

I had to agree with Cortés' strategy. Montejo, in particular, had conducted a war of whispers in favor of returning to Cuba. Now opposition to our going forward would be reduced.

"Don't worry too much, Juan. They'll be back soon and, even if they aren't, we have other ships.

De Alva didn't listen as he mumbled to his cross.

Paco Migues who, against orders, was butt-naked and red as

chile, was also digging through the wet sand. He spied us up the beach. He strode over to us and displayed his catch. From an amatl sac he poured a mixture of almejas on the sand.

"I've already got twenty, including four of the big round ones. These little ones taste a lot better, though. How many do you two have?"

To this point, Migues had not taken a close look at de Alva. When he did, he grew silent.

"Problemas, Juan?"

I answered for him. "He's had a premonition—he thinks he is going to die. He had a dream that the Caudillo was burying him alive."

Migues snorted, "Before this is over Cortés will bury all of us alive, including himself. *Hijo de la Chingada!*" Migues crossed himself. "I've had premonitions myself but, right now, me and Maldinado over there are having a good time digging these almejas." He kicked at his clams. "There's no use worrying about it, hombre, it comes sooner or later, anyway. Who wants to be a doddering old fool in the back-room of the daughter-in-law's casa?"

De Alva glanced at Migues. "I'm not feeling too good, Paco, I shit buckets but I can't eat..."

De Alva slowly stood up, brushing the sand from his knees. He gritted his teeth and pulled his sword out of the sand. Before sheathing the weapon, he considered the cross and mumbled another prayer.

"Now show me how to dig clams."

●●●

Days passed on the windswept sand dunes without a plan. To occupy my time and to further our cause I, along with some of the other men, worked with our unwarlike horses. Unlike horses trained for the saddle, we encouraged these caballos to bite, kick and lash out with their front and rear hooves. This is not difficult to do for these things come naturally to most horses. More difficult is to keep the horses gentle while making them vicious on command. By the use of maize treats and the judicious use of the whip, we were able to convert most of these useless animals into something like caballos de guerra.

Cortés, Pedro de Alvarado and Cristóbal de Olid watched me as I worked with Cortés' own animal.

"Rodrigo, I trust you don't ruin our horses—they are the backbone of our army."

"They were ruined before we got to them, Caudillo. Without our efforts these nags are worthless."

"They would have impressed the enemy. I fear that my caballeros won't be able to mount these savage beasts."

"*Mira!*" I leaped onto Cortés' saddleless horse and ran it down the beach while causing it to bite and lash out at invisible enemies. I pulled the horse around and raced back towards Cortés and his Captains. I jumped off, landing at Cortés' feet.

"The horses are safe. Just be certain you give them the proper signals at the right time and that you don't approach them from the front or the rear."

I instructed Cortés and his other captains and caballeros how to manage their own horses in battle. I also told them that they could no longer take the same liberties with the horses that they had previously—the caballos were now dangerous tools and not pets. Later, during the march to Mexico, one of our caballeros, Felipe de Manza, ignored my instructions. His own horse bit him in the chest and tore out his heart and lungs. This was a terrible shame because he was a favorite of the soldiers and, somewhere back in Spain, he left a young wife and five children.

Chapter 38

At the time I am speaking, however, we were in real danger of attack for which there were only two logical courses. First we could embark and return to Cuba or, as Cortés suggested, we could found a city on these shores and fortify it in such a way as to make it too expensive for the Mexica to attack. Now that Montejo, the leader of the Velásquez faction, was gone exploring, Cortés acted decisively. He called me into his hut one day and welcomed me like a brother.

"Don Rodrigo, how nice of you to come. In honor of our Savior and the riches of this new land, I have decided to found a settlement that we shall call *Villa Rica de la Vera Cruz.* Unfortunately, there are a few of our men who may oppose this settlement. I understand that you, however, would prefer to stay here in order to increase your fortune. Is that correct?"

"Right, Caudillo. If we return now Velásquez will take everything we have earned. I'll have nothing to show for it."

"Good. I see that we are of the same mind. The problem is that my written commission from Governor Velásquez could be interpreted—only by certain ill-informed parties, you must understand—as permission for only exploration and trading, not settlement. If we are to avoid complications we must either return to Cuba or we must—arrange—things rather differently."

"Velásquez will never consent."

"No," Cortés replied smoothly. "I don't think he will, which brings me to why I asked you to meet with me. The way I see it, our soldiers are, in fact, the citizens of our new community. Like all well-run municipalities, our new pueblo will also need administrators and a governing council. I have already spoken to some of our friends and they have agreed to serve in this council. I would like to invite you to serve, also."

"I'm honored, Caudillo, but there'll need to be an election and who is to say that I, or any of the others, for that matter, will be elected?"

"Don't concern yourself on that account," Cortés replied. "My suggested nominees will be the only nominees. Money has been placed in the right hands and my nominees will be elected... Now follow what I say very carefully. Once a town council has been established, there will no longer be the necessity for a *Capitán-General de Cuba*."

"But...." I meant to argue, but Cortés stopped me with a glance from his disturbing golden eyes.

"Remember, I said listen to me carefully. The Council will have superseded my commission and I must therefore resign. After I resign, however, the Council will need to elect its various town officials. I will then—most reluctantly, you understand—accept the new position of Capitán-General of our new community."

"But what will that accomplish?"

Cortés smiled and winked at me. "It means that—neatly and entirely legally—I will have become, the leader of our new pueblo. Our new community will not be subject to the edicts of the Governor of Cuba—only to the authority of His Majesty, Emperor Carlos I. I have no doubt that the Emperor will want us to continue all of our good work right here."

"Yes, it might just work."

"But please don't misunderstand me, Rodrigo. I have every intention that the various investors in our expedition, including the Governor, will profit handsomely from our efforts. By taking our present action—even though the Governor might not see it as clearly as I do—we are simply defending his interests. By the way, it might be a good idea if you and some of our other officers spoke to some of our soldiers. Remind them of what they have to lose should we be forced back to Cuba—it's best that we have most of the men on our side."

●●●

Along with other Cortés' partisans, I spread the message that the expedition must be forced back to Cuba should Cortés obey the letter of Velásquez's instruction. Most of the soldiers agreed that the expedition must continue into Mexico. Still there were men, some loyal to Velásquez and some who valued their lives, clamoring for our return.

"Goddamn Cortés, anyway." Pablo Magdaleño had acquitted himself courageously at Cintla, suffering wounds that had almost killed him. He had a fat encomienda in Cuba and was having second thoughts about challenging an empire. If I had his wealth I would have felt the same.

"The slimy cabrón planned it this way. He's wanted to slip the Governor's chain from the very beginning. Velásquez is a ladrón but Cortés is as bad, maybe worse."

Migues interrupted, "You may be right, Pablo, but all of us know what kind of man the Governor is. He didn't even have the cajones to leave Cuba. At least Cortés is here. You saw him at Cintla. He took as many chances as anybody in the army—maybe more. He's got the brains and the balls for it—he's a leader. If anybody can pull this off, it's the Caudillo."

"You're right," agreed another soldier. "The Caudillo is no cobarde and that's the truth of it. He'll be right there in the thick of it when the last of us soldados gets it in the neck. What's wrong with our getting our asses back to Cuba and organizing an army so powerful that these Indios will bend over and like it?"

I disagreed. "The treasure that Moctecuzoma gave us is only a fraction of what we stand to gain—I say take our chances. Keep it all for ourselves."

"A dead man has no use for gold," Magdaleño argued. "Besides, use you head, look at this land." He made a broad gesture toward the west. "In comparison, Cuba is a pig sty. This land is huge—the gold is nothing—land and slaves are the real wealth."

●●●

"What are the men saying, Rodrigo?" Cortés had moved from his flagship to an office constructed of driftwood and mangrove limbs. He had just been speaking to Gonzalo de Sandoval and now it was my turn.

"Most of the men are with us—only a few want to pull out."

"*Quíenes son?*" Cortés added their names to a list that I could see already filled two pages.

His writing finished, he leaned back and drummed his fingers on his desk, "Some of these are good men, men we need to have with us. Without them we will have serious problems. You are dismissed, Señor de la Peña."

Later, Cortés ordered the entire company to stand before him on the sand. Our Castilian women and a few of our Indios were loitering on the periphery of the crowd. The Caudillo mounted a box and spoke to the soldiers.

"I understand that many of you have questions as to whether we should remain in this land. I have given careful consideration to all of the various issues and have decided that wisdom and safety decree that we should return to Cuba and report our findings to Governor Velásquez. I want all of you to hold yourselves in readiness for our return voyage."

The crowd was shocked into silence. Then there was a murmur of protest that quickly grew into a roar of anger.

"You have betrayed us!" one man shouted.

"Leave if you must, cobarde. We will elect another Captain!" screamed yet another

"Go back to your ugly whore, Córtes."

"What are you doing tonight, Caudillo? I need a place to stick it!"

As the outrage mounted, even Velásquez's supporters joined in the opposition.

Juan de Alva, who had despaired for this life, shouted louder than most. "Piss on your mother, Cortés!"

"It's treason," shrilled Pablo Magdaleño. "He's guilty of conduct disloyal to the Emperor. *Es traidor!* Get a rope!"

A shocked Cortés calmed the crowd with a gesture. "I had no idea you men felt so strongly about our staying here. I was convinced that most of you wanted to return to Cuba. I was only trying to do the right thing by all of you."

"Don't do us any favors, Cortés!"

"I don't know what to say—I'll sleep on it overnight and give you my decision in the morning."

It may have been my imagination but it looked as if the Caudillo was trying to suppress a smile as he walked away from the muttering soldiers.

Francesca de la Barca moved toward me through the mob—she had adopted the dress of a Totonac lady. She was clad in a fine cotton dress intricately embroidered in tiny feathers that shimmered red and green in the sun. She looked straight ahead, never acknowledging the presence of the rough soldiers. The crowd parted in front of her, exactly as the Red Sea parted for Moses.

"Señor de la Peña?"

"Señora de la Barca. I trust you are well," I replied formally.

"Quite well, thank you." She tossed her head in a contemptuous flaunt. "What did you think of the speech?"

"What am I supposed to think? I told him myself that most of the men wanted to continue the expedition—but—I don't know."

"He certainly isn't taking my opinion into account." Her voice was taut, controlled. "There's a fortune to be made here. I can feel it and I'm willing to take chances. From what I know of Cortés, he's not all that much different."

"Don't feel too bad, señora. He doesn't seem to care how I feel about it, either. Then again, why should he? All I am is a poor soldier." I was both drawn to and repulsed by this woman.

"Señor de la Peña. I do not know what you are." Her gaze was unnerving. "But you're not a poor anything."

Chapter 39

There was a brisk morning wind and grains of blown sand stung our skins. Cortés, standing on a box, addressed the assembly. He was the picture of contrition. "I wish to affirm that I am loyal to Governor Velásquez and to our Emperor, Carlos I, and only act in accordance with their interests. I want you to know that I would prefer that we do a little more trading and then get back to Cuba. On your behalf, I have incurred major debts and I'm more afraid of my creditors than I am of a few Mexicanos." Laughter broke out in the crowd. "On the other hand, I will reluctantly put aside my personal concerns in the interests of you soldiers and the interests of the Crown. Although I have resisted it, some of you have insisted that we establish a colony in the name of our Sovereign—I am now obliged to agree with you. I recommend we do this thing correctly and elect the officers of our new community. I'm prepared to take nominations."

I can't remember all of the nominees but Franciso Álvarez was named public spokesman. Portocarrero, Cortés' best friend and husband to Doña Marina, was named Alcalde Mayor. Montejo, whom Cortés had sent off exploring, was also named Alcalde Mayor. This gesture was meant to placate Montejo, who was the chief advocate of returning to Cuba. As Cortés calculated, Montejo—as do all good Españoles—had his price.

Pedro de Alvarado, Alonso de Grado and I were named Regidores. Alvarado, who shouldn't have been given any post whatsoever, was also named to the post of Capitán-General of Inland Incursions. Gonzalo de Sandoval became Alguacil. Other names I remember were Gonzalo de Mexía, Javier de la Concha, Pedro Ávila, Cristóbal de Olid, and Juan Escalante. Mexía was the Treasurer. All of us working as a group formed the Regimiento.

●●●

The newly formed government convened in a shack erected for that purpose. The wind howled through the chinks in the leafy walls. The chairs were bare wooden crates.

All went according to plan and Cortés was called in. He had dressed for the occasion, although inappropriately, considering our situation and location. He was wearing a fashionable purple cloak and a green cap with downy egret feathers. Andrés de Tapia and Martín Vazquez were our witnesses and the notario, Diego de Godoy, meticulously recorded our actions.

"Señor Cortés, can you produce a copy of the letter of instruction given to you by Governor Diego Velásquez in Santiago de Cuba?" asked one of our members.

"I have it right here." Cortés drew a piece of folded paper from his cloak.

"May we see it?" He turned the paper over to Pedro de Alvarado. We members of the Regimiento, of which only two were fully literate, went through the motions of reading it. I could see that Cortés had veered far from his instructions. Not only was there no permission to establish settlements, but also none of the soldiers were even to spend the night ashore. There were also amusing provisions about Indio women—not only were the men forbidden to have sex with them, they were not even permitted to tease them. Our expedition was clearly intended to be only a superficial exploration of the coastal lands, including necessary inquiries about gold—the real conquest would come later. Cortés, however, saw it otherwise.

"My interpretation of this document," I play-acted, "is that these lawful instructions of Governor Velásquez have now been superceded by the authority of our new civil government and are no longer valid. All in agreement..."

Everyone, by prior arrangement, raised his hand.

"Señor Cortés, the Regimiento would like to thank you for your services but, in that the Governor's instructions are no longer valid, you no longer have authority to act on behalf of this expedition. You may leave."

Cortés, on cue, stepped outside.

Cristóbal de Olid, who had the mind and body of a great ox, managed to recite his lines perfectly. "Our new community needs a leader. I nominate Hernán Cortés as Justicia Mayor as well as Captain of His Majesty's armies until our Sovereign should decide otherwise. All in favor." There was a chorus of "Sí's. "It's unanimous then. Would someone ask Señor Cortés to come back in."

Cortés reentered and was told the results of our foregone decision.

"I respectfully refuse these honors," Cortés announced.

For seconds there was silence.

"What? Stop writing," I said to the notario. "We've gone through this charade precisely so that you could lead this expedition without the Governor's interference. Now you refuse? Am I the Regidor of an asylum? I think you owe us an explanation, Don Hernán."

I looked around. None of the other magistrates, with the exception of Mexía, seemed in the least bit disturbed.

"Don't get upset, Rodrigo," Cortés patronized. "It's only logical that my leadership has its price. I will agree to accept the Council's nomination if it deems it appropriate that I receive a small share of our profits."

Mexía flinched. "What might that small share be?"

"After subtraction of the King's Royal Fifth, I think it only fair that I receive one-fifth of the remainder." Cortés, who was the sword and the flame in battle, was also a Salamanca-trained lawyer.

"One-fifth?" Mexía sputtered. "One-fifth is no small amount."

Cortés spoke softly, making us strain to hear. "Considering that none of you have the qualities that can carry this expedition to a successful conclusion, one-fifth is a pittance. I want to remind you, Señor Mexía, that I am also the single greatest investor in our little adventure. In addition to my fifth, I also expect to be proportionately rewarded for my investment just like our other investors."

With the exception of Mexía, all of the other Captains seemed complacent. Had they been bribed or were they just stupid?

"Caudillo," I asked, "how do we calculate the value of the men themselves?"

Cortés didn't have to stop to think. "They shall be paid—at the end of the expedition you must understand—based on their rank and their service." He looked around the room with a conspiratorial smile—I noticed that most of the others smiled right back. "I recognize valuable service when I see it and know that it should be rewarded accordingly. You gentlemen, as Captains and officials of our new community will be handsomely compensated. As an example of my gratitude, you won't be charged for expenses like food, weapons and clothing. The other men, as is only right, shall have these expenses and any others that may be incurred deducted from their final shares."

Mexía didn't mind enriching himself at the expense of the

common soldiers but, as treasurer, any dissatisfaction over money would sit directly on his shoulders and dissatisfaction could be fatal. "I think we should come up with an exact formula before our venture proceeds further."

"I don't think that will be necessary," Cortés expanded. "We are all friends here and trust one another. Besides, we are bound to suffer further losses which will alter any agreements that we might arrive at."

"Absolutely right." Javier de la Concha jumped to his feet and glared at Mexía. "I am for the Caudillo. All others in favor...."

With the exception of Mexía and myself, every man sprang to his feet shouting agreement. I stood up slowly. Mexía shook his head, then stood up, painfully.

"It's unanimous then," laughed Alvarado. "Let's toast to our enterprise and our leader— Hernan Cortés—*Victoria y Gloria!*"

Wine, red as blood, poured down our throats.

Chapter 40

I wasn't surprised to receive a request for an audience with Francesca de la Barca. I considered refusing but decided to face her. Hiding my anxiety, I climbed onto her ship and knocked at her open cabin door. Filtered light revealed her standing to meet me. She was dressed in the same clothing that I had last seen her in. The dress hung loosely from her shoulders. Her hair had been knotted into twin braids that reached to her lower back. Even in the poor light her eyes flashed fire.

"Is it true that the Council has given Cortés one-fifth of the spoil of this expedition?"

Word traveled fast. "Maybe you should talk to the Caudillo...."

"If I had wanted to talk to Cortés, I would have done so. I am talking to you and expect some answers. What kind of arrangements has your Council made with your leader?"

"He expects to be paid for his leadership. He asked for...ah... one-fifth and we gave it to him. We also agreed that, in addition, he be compensated for the full amount of his investment."

She shook her perfect head in disbelief. "To obtain your agreement, Cortés didn't make any side agreements with the members of the Council?"

She already knew the answer.

"I expected more of you, señor, but you are a fool just like these others. Even if Cortés' promises meant something—and they don't—far less than half of the potential take of our enterprise will be available to us investors, let alone the soldiers. I'm disgusted with you and I am disgusted with myself. I have invested everything that I have and now I stand to lose it all. Mark my words—Cortés will rob all of us—only he and a few of his accomplices will profit."

A man, if he had called me a fool, would have had to prove the point with his life.

"I may be a fool, señora, but I'm not a coward. I have spent years in the army and know that anything can happen in combat. No one will rob me." I wondered if I was offering more than I could deliver. "Nor will I permit anyone to rob you."

Her voice was now dangerous. "You have agreed to Cortés' looting my investment and now you will protect me from robbery. Incredible! By the looks of things, señor, your protection is as worthless as your honor."

Stunned, I regarded her in silence. I then spun on my heels and propelled myself from her presence, vowing to never speak to her again.

●●●

After twenty-two days Montejo returned and announced that he had found a fine anchorage fifteen leagues to the north. There was a nearby Totonac town but the land was more hospitable than our windswept site of San Juan de Ulua. Cortés, after informing Montejo that he had been elevated to the office of Alcalde Major and ensuring his loyalty with an additional two thousand pesos, announced that we should relocate and establish our colony of Villa Rica de Vera Cruz at the new site. The bulk of the army moved by land but the cannons, some officers, and sailors traveled by ship.

Our march took us through country which, although lush, contained several deserted villages. Also present was a small mosque with a templo on the top containing smoking copal censors. At the bottom of the cue was the body of a slaughtered woman. Her chest had been split open, side-to-side, below the ribs. Her arms and legs were sliced lengthwise and the flesh had been neatly removed. A broad swath of blood marked where the body had been thrown from the heights above. On a stone altar, within the temple, lay the cold heart of the victim.

Except for the heat and the dampness, the rest of our journey was not so unpleasant—the country was a kaleidoscope of color. The forest was dense but we walked along a well-traveled road. Climbing vines blossomed with flowers of red, yellow and violet and the air was perfumed by their scent. Everywhere there was the hum of life. Monos—monkeys—screeched their alarms and lizards skittered underfoot. All too many serpents coiled in the dust. One soldier, as I mentioned earlier, was stung by a vibora. Later, he died.

There were birds, butterflies and game of all kinds. Alvarado laughing, his golden hair dancing in the sun, rode down a fine stag and wounded it with his lanza. At least this is what he claimed, for I didn't see the strike.

On our journey about one hundred friendly Totonacs bearing turkeys, native ducks and other food for our soldiers met us. They told us that their cacique, by the name of Tlacochcalcatl, wanted to meet us on the march but he was too fat to move. They went on to tell us that he had invited us into his capital of *Cempoalla*, which was only a short distance away. Cortés gladly accepted the offer.

Our march continued through large well-kept plantations of fruit trees and aguacates mixed with fields of maíz and calabazas of many varieties. Tomates were present in great numbers along with frijoles of several kinds twined around posts and nets. There were plantations of maguey and nopal cactus. There were also plantings of green, yellow and red chiles and fields of the green leaf that we came to know as tobacco.

Before we arrived in the town of *Cempoalla*, however, some of our horsemen returned at a gallop exclaiming that they had seen the town and the houses were made of silver. This news, as you can well imagine, threw the army into a great uproar. You can therefore imagine the disappointment when we discovered that the riders' observations were but the products of overly excited imaginations. All they had seen were mud huts painted white and shining in the sun. The town itself was large, maybe of thirty thousand inhabitants, but most of the buildings were unassuming flat-roofed structures. There were also several mosques similar to ones we had seen in *Yucatán*. Even from a distance we could see that their *templos* were stained by blood.

Throngs of men and women greeted us. They were dressed in colored robes and their ears, nostrils and lower lips were perforated and through these perforations were placed discs of wood, copper or gold, depending on their wealth. Necklaces of jewelry hung about their necks. They all carried flowers and they placed wreaths about our helmets and showered us with their petals. The degree of our welcome was unexpected and, being unexpected, was suspicious. The soldiers marched closer together keeping close lookout for ambush—but the ambush never came.

Instead we were met by the cacique of *Cempoalla* who was tall and indeed very fat. He invited the army to spend the night, giving us ample quarters in a nearby plaza. This plaza was a temple of sorts and was largely closed in by small rooms, covered by thatch and decorated with the horrific images of fiends and devils. Nevertheless, the rooms were prepared with mats of stiff woven grass on which we might sleep. I slept, or tried to sleep, in a room with ten other soldiers. My dreams were filled with nightmares and, in the morning, I was covered with bites.

The food was better than the accommodations. We were served frijoles and the *maíz* cakes we now call tortillas. We were also given *pescados* and *langostas* from the sea. The indígenous also gave us a few gold ornaments and cloaks of fine cotton. Despite this warm welcome, Cortés would not permit us to relax our vigilance. He posted sentinels and forbade any man from leaving the camp under pain of death. The night passed peacefully, however.

Chapter 41

In the morning, Cortés, myself and twenty other Captains and soldiers met with the fat cacique at his house. His home was, in design, similar to the cues we had previously seen. It was built of stone and lime and perched on top of a mosque that had steps all the way around. We entered the dwelling and greeted the cacique who, in his turn, was flanked by two nobles wearing togas. The fat man was wearing a robe of fine patterned cotton but, other than that, he was a sorry specimen. His earlobes, as well as his nostrils, were perforated and contained large golden discs. His lower lip was disfigured in a similar fashion. The size and the weight of the disc in his lower lip pulled his lip downward, exposing his teeth and interfering with his speech. He seemed to be in late middle age, although age is difficult to determine age in a person as fat as was the cacique. His jowls, chest and belly were made up of huge globs of fat.

Despite his gelatinous appearance, his black eyes examined us with a calculating intelligence. I don't know what he made of us but there can be no doubt that he believed that we were useful. He wanted our help and believed, from the reports that he had heard of our great victory in Tabasco, that we might be just the people to provide it. His information, limited though it was, transformed our expedition and doomed an empire.

"We Totonacs used to be a happy people but these Mexica have made us miserable." Tears ran down the his blubbery cheeks. "After defeating us, the Mexica took all our weapons and now we can neither hunt nor defend ourselves. They tax us into poverty and their tax collectors, in their lust, rape the most beautiful girls in front of their families. They then take these girls, as well as others, to *Tenochtitlan* to sacrifice in their temples."

Cortés leaned forward, his eyes gleaming with interest. "We are Castilians from a land far away. Our great ruler, Emperor Carlos, to lead all people to our Savior, Jesus Christ and to save them from sin, has sent us here. Emperor Carlos has ordered us to liberate his friends, the Totonacs, and destroy the evil Mexica."

The fat cacique disgustingly exposed his teeth in what must have been a smile.

Cortés went on, "A single Castilian can defeat many in battle. On the other hand, we have learned that the Mexica outnumber our force by hundreds to one. Do you have ideas how we might best defeat your enemies?

The fat Indio, possibly expecting that we could brush away the Mexicans by magic, readjusted his thinking.

"Yes, it could be difficult—*Tenochtitlan* is a fortress built on water—most people believe it is impregnable. Our gods tell us that nothing lasts forever. The Mexica belief in their own invincibility may prove to be their downfall. We Totonacs are not the only people held in bondage—others hate the Mexica even more than we do. *Tlaxcala* and *Huexotzinco* will welcome you. Ixtlilxochitl, who hungers for the throne of Texcoco, will also betray Moctecuzoma. You can put together a force of over one hundred thousand allies which, under your leadership, should prove adequate to conquer Moctecuzoma and," he salivated with sheer greed, "sack *Tenochtitlan*."

None of us knew anything of these potential allies but the possibilities were overwhelming. Cortés, without betraying excitement, bid the fat cacique farewell.

●●●

The army remained for two weeks in *Cempoalla* before continuing its march north a few miles to the site recommended by Montejo, close to the Totonac town of *Quiahuiztlan*. Off shore, the ships that had been awaiting the army, swung at anchor.

The army marched into *Quiahuiztlan* and was given a tumultuous welcome. In the town's plaza Cortés met with the lord of the town. During their discussion, as bad luck would have it, the Mexican tax collectors arrived. They were wearing elegant clothes and carried colorful flowers that they sniffed as if they were women. I could well believe they were sodomites. Servants walked in front, whisking the road. These officials walked directly past our soldiers pretending to pay no attention. The Lord of *Quiahuiztlan* trembled uncontrollably.

"I must leave you and prepare our tribute," he told Cortés.

"Nonsense. You are under our protection now. Seize these swine and tie them up. I will not only protect you but, if you put them in that room over there," —Cortés indicated a small cubicle next to the plaza— "my Castilians will guard them. If the Mexicans should attempt to liberate them, we will destroy them."

The Lord didn't take much convincing. Words were spoken to Totonac guards and, more rapidly than I can tell it, the tax collectors were taken prisoner and hustled off to their cell. That night, I was told, Cortés took these captives to one of our ships.

●●●

"Why have the Totonacs taken you prisoner?" Cortés asked innocently.

"These vermin are a rebellious people," spoke the disheveled chief tax-collector, "but they are cowards. You have told them to commit this crime."

"Not us," Cortés lied. "We are ashamed that the Totonacs have done this to you for we love your Lord Moctecuzoma. This ship will sail north until we are in lands controlled by your Prince. We will then release you."

The tax collectors, who had expected death, almost collapsed with relief. "We are grateful to you Malinche. We will report to our Lord of your love and respect."

The next day the escape of the tax collectors was discovered. The Totonacs reacted with equal rage and fear.

"How could you let them escape? They will inform the Mexica and we will be annihilated. You must protect us. Let us seek allies and march on Mexico."

Cortés showed no fear. "We will protect you and, when the time is right, we will march to *Tenochtitlan* and humble the proud Moctecuzoma."

Chapter 42

Burgos, Castilla-León

The pueblo of Villa Rica de la Vera Cruz was founded on June 28, 1519. We laid out the foundations for the Plaza Mayor, the church, town hall, barracks, slaughterhouse and, of course, the prison. Cortés, himself, dug the first trench.

"Now, Padre, I want your opinion. Why do you think that our Caudillo would stoop to do manual labor? There were after all, plenty of soldados and Indios for the job."

"He probably wanted the honor of the first spade of earth for himself—a good example to the men."

"There's truth to your conclusions, Padre Mendoza, but not the whole truth. The fact is that Hernán Cortés never knew peace—he was always moving and restless. Unlike some of our prissy hidalgos, who thought manual labor beneath their dignity, Cortés had to get his hands dirty. It didn't matter if it was digging a trench, netting fish, or tearing down a wall—it was exactly the same to him. This was equally true if he was lecturing to the army, negotiating with a savage prince, or communicating with the Spanish Court. Cortés was always there. Many times I watched him in battle. He would ride, hunched over his horse's neck, charging into the enemy and spearing them one after another. He'd kill some, scatter most and then ride back to the lines and exhort the rest of us to greater effort."

"Certainly, Excelencia, he was an exceptional man. He combined energy with exceptional courage."

The old man locked his hands together. "It was a matter of personal survival that I understand Cortés as thoroughly as possible and—yes—Cortés was a highly exceptional man. He didn't need rest like other men—he rarely slept. His energy was not only legendary; it was unholy. It wasn't specific to the work at hand and he could not turn it on and off. No matter what it was, he had to be moving and doing. Do you know what I'm talking about?"

Mendoza's brow wrinkled. "I'm not sure...."

"His energy was one of excitement and his excitement was infectious. The problem was that, when he became overly excited, he made poor choices but was still able to convince others that his unwise decisions were sound. This cost us the lives of hundreds of men. Even his courage was not courage in the ordinary sense. It was the courage of high excitement and unbridled motion."

"Still it carried you on to victory."

The old man looked puzzled, "Yes it did—but—it should have destroyed us. Interestingly, there were a few times when Cortés' energy failed him utterly and, barely moving, he laid in his shelter for days. At these times others had to take up the responsibilities of command."

Mendoza put down his plumed pen and flexed his fingers. He decided to change the subject.

"Your Grace, although I am fully aware that Hernán Cortés used all means at his disposal to advance our Catholic cause, I sometimes believe that you paint him in terms that are, perhaps, too unflattering. I notice that, several times, you have emphasized Cortés' telling untruths to the Indios. Lies to the heathen, considering the importance of what you were doing, were entirely justified."

The Bishop frowned. "In matters of truth Cortés was as sinuous as an eel."

"God moves in mysterious ways, Your Grace."

"So does Satan, Padre. Do you think that Cortés' handling

of the Governor's directive was correct? He dealt with our most Catholic Governor exactly as he dealt with the heathen Indios. As it turned out he dealt with us all in exactly the same way."

Mendoza looked down at his hands. "*Jus est boni et acqui*—the law is the arbiter of justice. Later there were lawsuits which were found in favor of Cortés."

"Ah, Padre. You are an Inquisitor to your core. Morality is determined by a court of law."

"I am not about to second guess the Royal decision."

Flames from the fire flickered in the Bishop's ancient eyes. "Why not? You don't have much to lose."

Mendoza suppressed a shudder. "The Emperor knew what he was doing—Cortés conquered a new empire for the Crown. There was gratitude."

The old man nodded. "Good. I agree with you. It was never a matter of right and wrong. It was a matter of practicality and it was a matter of action. Cortés outmaneuvered the Governor. He outmaneuvered Moctecuzoma and he outmaneuvered his Conquistadores. That's all there is to it. Cortés poured a mountain of treasure into the Royal coffers and the Emperor was grateful. If he had been otherwise, he would have been churlish. Right and wrong be damned. It's success that counts.

The Lord of Quiahuiztlan informed us that the Mexican garrison town of *Tizapancingo*, a hill town twenty miles to the southwest, was being reinforced. Cortés seized the opportunity and reacted instantly. Most of our force, including sixteen caballeros, attacked. To our amazement, the much-feared Mexicans ran like frightened children. The few savages who remained within the fortress gave up without a fight. There were no casualties on either side.

During the assault, Cortés became greatly excited. He decided to make our Totonac allies learn the lesson of power. We rode directly through *Cempoalla* and up to their heathen temples. We threw down their idols and broke them into useless pieces. We broke into wooden cages, filled with slaves waiting for slaughter, but, to our amazement, the freed victims refused to leave the broken pens.

"You tempt the Lord, Hernán," spoke Fraile Olmedo.

"I serve Nuestra Señora, old woman," laughed the red-faced Caudillo. "She shows me the path we should take."

"You toy with sacrilege, Hernán. Do not sacrifice all that we have gained."

Cortés wasn't listening and drove his horse at the fat cacique who was weeping nearby. Despite his size, the Indio moved faster than I would have credited him. It's a good thing, too, for if Cortés had struck him, the fat man would have split like an over-ripe melon.

We released the sacrificial victims and, just as in Cozumel and Tabasco, we cleaned the blood-caked stones and erected shrines with the Cross and portraits of Our Lady. The stinking papas were stripped of their filthy black robes. We cut their long tangled hair and we scrubbed them clean. We forced these men to wear white tunics and ordered them to care for the Christian shrines at the price of their lives—we made them the papas of Christ. As I later learned, once the transition was made, these unholy men performed their tasks to perfection. One God is as good as another.

"Caudillo?" I asked Cortés. "It is a dangerous thing to offend the Totonacs. After all, our success depends on their good will."

"Rodrigo, you have been spending too much time with Olmedo. You have been in the Indies but a short time and do not understand the savage. Even if it were not necessary to drag these paganos to Christ, I would find an excuse and do it anyway. The savage respects power—softness invites contempt. The only thing these brutes understand is raw force and the use of it generates loyalty."

I said nothing more, for there was a certain wisdom to his philosophy. Later, however, it occurred to me that our Caudillo applied the same gentle principles to his Españoles.

Burgos, Castilla-León

"Here, Padre, I must speak of a significant problem not related in any of the histories of la Conquista. Some of our historians, including yourself, seemed to have sidestepped this rather delicate subject. In the interest of accuracy, I have no such qualms."

"I've noticed, Your Grace, that you have few qualms about anything."

"Not at my age—but what do the Latins say? *Agnosca veteris ves-*

tigia flammae—the flame may be gone but there is still a spark. The problem I am talking about first became noticeable during the early construction phase of Villa Rica. Some of the soldiers developed a fatal malady. It started with a boil on the penis and went on to a fever that resembled a tertian ague—from there, the condition worsened. The victim's skins developed rashes and great blotches. In most cases the miserable soldier died although a few completely recovered. The disease itself was not a mystery, for we have it in España and we call it the French Disease—although—the French call it the Spanish Disease. In truth, the disease was unknown until the Great Admiral returned from his first trip to the Indies. By deduction, the disease was present amongst the Indios of the islands and was transmitted to Colón's sailors. We now know that it is the product of sexual sin and we also know that, despite the Holy Father's pronouncements, conversion to Christianity does not make a woman clean."

Mendoza was impatient. "Yes, yes. It's common knowledge."

"Españoles who later traveled to the Indies contracted the disease from native women. Interestingly, the Indios don't die of the disease, although they develop many of the same symptoms. Later, there was the reverse example of *la viruela*. The disease is common in Europe but it was nonexistent in the Indies and Nueva España. Therefore, the Españoles who developed the disease in Nueva España usually lived but the indígenous usually died."

"Do you have an explanation, Your Grace?"

"Satan was thus able to punish both continents. But to go on.... in Villa Rica, this Indio disease first became a major problem because the loss of each individual soldier, given the small size of our force, was significant. It wasn't difficult to figure out what was going on—Totonac women came to Villa Rica at all times day and night. For the exchange of one or two beads, each one of these women would service multiple soldiers. Our soldiers simply believed that all Totonac women were stupid but our soldiers were the stupid ones. The Totonacs, Mexica and most other Indios are very upright and moral. *La putería*, however, is tolerated and each one of these women was a professional whore and, as such, was especially dangerous. When Cortés saw what was happening, he ordered, under penalty of death, that no man was to lay with these women. He, more than most, knew of the danger. He had barely survived the disease while in Española. Still a few of our men, in full knowledge of the dangers, continued to risk it. Surely, Padre, the penis is a hard taskmaster. Later, as we conquered large populations, most soldiers seized female slaves of which young virgins were the most popular. Then and only then did the problem with the Indio disease—the French disease—subside."

Mendoza asked, "why should it be necessary to mention this particular problem? Unfortunate things happen in all enterprises but drawing attention to them, demeans God."

"God, Padre?"

Chapter 43

"Good news, Caudillo," interrupted Aguilar, "a caravel has arrived from Cuba with reinforcements."

"Who has arrived?" Cortés feared a Don Diego attack.

"Your friend, Francisco de Saucedo, El Pulido, is their captain. He comes with sixty men and five horses."

"*Excelente!* Tell Señor Saucedo that I look forward to seeing him."

"Tell him yourself, Caudillo. He's here."

Coming from the direction of the beach were several men on horseback. The young man on a spirited bay was the leader. As befitted his nickname he was neatly attired. He wore a jaunty hat of many feathers and was dressed in a spotless blue tunic.

"So nice to see you, Francisco!" Cortés called out.

"*Hijo de perra!* I wish I could have gotten here sooner but that miserable excuse for a ship needed a lot of work. It's a damn good thing we went to the effort, though. The crossing was rough as Hell and we'd be feeding the fishes now if we hadn't done a good patch-up job."

"Well then, I'm certainly glad that you were successful."

El Pulido spoke with great animation. He worked his arms and hands dramatically and his eyes sparkled like diamonds. He was one of those people who made even ordinary events dramatic. Although in some ways rather girlish, he was also handsome and brave. By any estimation, it is a great pity that he was later carved up like a hog and cooked up with tomatoes and chiles. Now, however, he still had the wind in his sails.

"*Hombre*! I have a lot to tell you. That half-peso cabrón Don Diego would fuck his own dog if he could. He is working as hard as he can to knife you in the back."

"That comes as no particular surprise."

"*Madre del Diablo.*" El Pulido crossed himself devoutly. "He's spread one Hell of a lot of money around. He's bribed everything in sight including important men in Santo Domingo and back in Spain. He's been granted the title of Adelantado by the Council of Saragossa and has been given all rights to explore and exploit *Yucatán* and *Mexico*."

Cortés was silent for seconds. "Now that is very bad news, Francisco, but the advantage still goes to me. For, as you can see, I am here while Don Diego sits fat and comfortable back in Cuba."

●●●

Cortés called an assembly. "I've learned that Governor Velásquez is trying to steal everything that you men have earned."

A rumble erupted from the crowd.

"He has bribed the Royal Council and you men will be left with nothing. I have a proposal that will cut the Governor off at the knees."

The crowd was stilled with a gesture of Cortés' hand. "Montejo and Puertocarrero will return to Palos in my flagship the *Santa Maria de la Concepción*. There they will promote our cause to all those who will listen. We have already won a great treasure but it is as nothing compared to what we have to gain. I propose that we put our short-term interests aside and send everything that we have gained thus far to our Emperor—and, when I say everything, I mean everything. This will not only include the gifts from Moctecuzoma but the barter goods all of you have obtained from the Indios."

"But we'll have nothing!" someone protested.

"No. You'll have nothing if Don Diego has his way. To get what we want, we need to fatten our gift to the King. Does everyone agree?"

Several of the Captains, operating under the Caudillo's secret instruction, shouted their assent. The other soldiers acted more slowly but finally the entire assembly was yelling in agreement.

"Remember—no one is to hold out. We know what you have. Our Captains will collect your donations."

The entire fabulous treasure, along with the few trinkets collected by the soldiers, was collected on a sandy spit destined to become Villa Rica's Plaza Principal. Feathered headdresses and beautiful cotton fabrics were piled up as were folded books of colorful paintings showing unspeakable monsters performing murder and other obscene acts.

Friar Díaz protested, "Let us burn these things of *El Diablo!*"

Cortés turned to Olmedo. "What do you say?"

"They are, indeed, of the Devil but they are also of the hand of man. It is good that our Emperor sees these things with his own eyes."

"I agree with you, Padre. Everything goes back to the King."

Díaz made the sign against the evil eye. "Oculus satani!"

That problem settled, things of gold, silver and jewels piled up. The huge discs of gold and silver dominated the hoard but demons, beasts, gold bells, necklaces, pendants and beautifully faceted red and green jewels also sparkled in the intense tropical light. There can be no doubt that the treasure was more than ample to influence the Emperor—still something was wrong.

Francesca, who had reluctantly agreed to the shipment of treasure, questioned our unhappy treasurer, Gonzalo de Mexía. Her questions were also directed at Alonso de Ávila, who was responsible for the Royal Fifth. "Señores, I don't wish to be difficult, but, as the various objects arrived I made my own private tabulation of Moctecuzoma's gifts. Some of it is missing. Where is it?"

I noticed that Ávila retreated into Cortés' quarters.

Mexía licked his lips. "Señora, we have also made careful lists of the treasure and, to my certain knowledge—with the exception of a few paltry items that may have been pilfered by the men—it's all here."

The woman lifted her eyebrows. "Paltry pilfering? Hardly. My record shows that almost half of the treasure is missing. I think you need to recheck your records."

"We have, señora, and all is in order." Mexía had developed a tic. "Everything is accounted for."

Followed by Ávila, Cortés emerged from his hut.

"How wonderful it is to see you, Francesca." He came up silently from behind and, as he calculated, the woman jumped at the sound of his voice. "You have been closed up in your nao and have been depriving us all of your radiance. I'm delighted that you have reappeared."

"Don't be too delighted, señor." The woman recovered instantly. "It is bad enough that your creatures have systematically looted us of the few valuables that some of us collected on our own. They have even deprived me of the clothing that I purchased for my own use...."

"We wouldn't deprive a lady of her... clothing," Cortés grinned. "Perhaps some of my men were overzealous—I'll see that they are returned."

Francesca's lip curled. "It seems that someone has generously helped himself to the treasure."

Cortés stopped to gather his thoughts before coldly continuing. "The lady is observant. A certain amount has been held back. Our Procuradores have been provided with gold for their expenses and any inducements that may be necessary to secure our cause. I have also set enough aside so that Martín, my father, can address some of the expedition's expenses and oil the wheels of influence."

"And oil both himself and his son in the process, señor?"

I had never seen Cortés truly angry before but, although he never once changed his expression, his eyes flashed murder.

"That will be enough, señora," he said lowly. "I will not have you or anyone else, for that matter, threaten the unity of our enterprise."

"Theft does not threaten the unity of our enterprise, señor?"

Francesca de la Barca, who was taller than Cortés, looked down into his eyes, exchanging hatred for hatred.

"My Lady, you will return to you quarters. If you do not do so voluntarily, I will order your forcible removal."

Chapter 44

That night, the men who had heard the exchange between Cortés and Señora de la Barca grumbled in the dark.

"That woman may be a bitch but she has more machissimo than the rest of us." The speaker was Diego de Ordaz, who had led us at Cintla. "The Caudillo took the little bit that we traded for but he decided to fatten his own purse. If we don't do something about it now, there will be no end to it."

"But what can we do, Diego?" I was sympathetic but was short of alternatives. "Cortés is the Caudillo. An appeal to Velásquez would be stupid."

"That's not the way I see it, Rodrigo," Escudero whispered. Years earlier, during the woman trouble involving Cortés, Escudero had arrested Cortés on behalf of Governor Velásquez. He had good reason to fear the Caudillo. "Don Diego may look after himself but he's still a good man. Cortés will cut all of our throats for a peso."

Fraile Juan Díaz was a man of God but, after his rebuff in front of the men, he also bore a grudge against Cortés. Now, he spoke, "This afternoon, Dona Francesca stood up to the cabrón. She has her own ship and a ship might be useful. I understand you know the Lady, Rodrigo. Perhaps you would be willing to make the proper introductions?"

"And involve her in a conspiracy? I think not. If you want to talk to her, it is your own responsibility but I'll have nothing to do with it."

"You won't consider joining us should we decide to act?" Escudero's voice was dangerous.

I ignored the threat. "Act? I know nothing of any acts—I never spoke to any of you."

●●●

I wandered in the direction of the *Santo Domingo*. I didn't know what to do. Still stinging from the Lady's insult, I wanted to prove her wrong. I found a skiff on the beach and rowed it to her side. Using a rope, I pulled myself up to her deck.

Pedro Robago, the ship's master, propelled himself down the forecastle ladder. "What are you doing here? The Lady has ordered me to keep you off of her ship. Get off!" Robago's Morisco ancestry was written on his face. His nose was hooked and his hair was black and curly.

"I have an important message from the Caudillo."

That stopped him, "She is in her cabin, de la Peña. It's late but I'll ask her if she will see you." He disappeared down a hatch and reappeared in less than a minute.

"She'll see you but make it quick."

The cabin was sweltering and the Lady was seated at the edge of a bed made of boxes pushed together. She was dressed for the heat in a thin cotton nightgown. She greeted me with a questioning look but made no effort to protect herself from my eyes.

"What does Cortés want of me, now?"

Not knowing quite why I had come, I hesitated before answering. "I'm not here because of the Caudillo—I am here of my own accord."

"Presumptuous of you, señor. I think you had better leave."

"I heard something tonight—something you need to know about."

"What is it?"

"Some of the men are complaining about Cortés. Right now, it's just talk but it's talk that has an edge to it. They wanted me to come to you to enlist your help and the use of the *Santo Domingo*. I refused."

"But you came anyway, didn't you?"

"Yes, but for a different reason. They may still approach you. I just wanted to warn you."

"Warn me of what, Señor de la Peña? Do you think I am a child that needs to be protected by a man?"

"No, señora. I simply wanted to tell you...." I didn't know what I wanted to tell her.

She tilted her head as if trying to see me better. She put her hand against the bulkhead as if to steady herself. "I've been impolite. You have come to help me and have done so at some risk to yourself. I thank you."

"You're welcome, My Lady. May you sleep well." I started to back out.

"Senor, before you leave, why did you want to help me. I'm nothing to you."

"Sometimes, My Lady," I reached for the right words, "we all need help. Besides, I promised to protect you."

She picked at her gown. "I didn't ask for your protection."

"It doesn't matter, señora—I made the promise to myself."

●●●

Someone informed Juan Escalante who reported to Cortés.

Along with Pedro de Alvarado, Javier de la Concha and Gonzalo de Sandoval, I attended the examination of the informant, a soldado named Bernardino de Soría.

De Soria was a small tanned man with a black bush of a beard. He sweated in the cramped quarters of the Caudillo's office.

"What is the plan, señor?" Concha asked.

"We were to seize one of the small ships—one of the brigs—and kill its master. We would then sail and intercept the *Santa María de la Concepcion* along with your Procuradores, Montejo and Puerotocarerro. After killing them, we would take the treasure and deliver it to Governor Don Diego."

"Who are the conspirators?"

"Our fraile, Juan Díaz, along with the men of the Rock, Alfonso Peñate and his brothers. Diego Cermeño, Velásquez de León, Alonso de Escobar, Juan Escodero and Diego de Ordaz are also involved."

Cortés now took over the questioning. "Who is the ringleader?"

Nervously, De Soria picked his nose. "The Padre and de León, Caudillo."

"Were there others? Was Doña Francesca involved?" I held my breath.

"The friar approached her but she refused."

"Were there others?"

"Others knew but there were no other plotters."

"You are dismissed with my thanks, Señor de Soria. Men like you will be well rewarded for your loyalty."

De Soria, looking relieved, squinted as he left the Caudillo's office and faced the glare of the sun.

"Don Javier?" Cortés spoke to his faithful dog, de la Concha. Concha, although blessed with the physique of a warrior, was not so blessed in facial beauty. His skin was darker than most Indios and was pockmarked with the scars of la viruela. His nose was long and thin and his black eyes were too close together. Although his lips were thick and sensual, his mouth seemed too small for his face.

"Sí, Caudillo."

"Men who would betray their fellows will, when the time is right, betray me. I sense there will be battles in the future—I doubt that Señor de Soría will survive."

"I share your doubts, Caudillo."

Chapter 45

Villa Rica de la Vera Cruz was now a thoroughly civilized community, I thought, as I watched Escudero's body jerking at the end of a rope. Earlier, the Peñate brothers had received one hundred lashes apiece and de Umbria had half of his foot amputated with an axe. Juan Cermeño, the pilot, was condemned to hang. Cortés took mercy on him and commuted his sentence—instead, Cermeño's cojones were cut off. The flow of blood was stanched with a red-hot iron that seared the root of his penis. When the wound healed, it grew at a sharp angle, causing him to piss himself every time he passed water.

Given Cortés' mood I hesitated to speak to him but I wasn't able to hold my tongue. "You aren't to be trifled with, Caudillo, but what will you do with the other plotters?"

He nodded his head, "Do you remember the old proverb, Rodrigo. *Quien a uno castiga a ciento hostiga?*"

"Punish one and a hundred are punished."

"Exactly, I've made my point."

The others were imprisoned but, later, released. Some, including Diego de Ordaz and Velázquez de León, became some of Cortés' most loyal followers.

● ● ●

The Caudillo called a secret meeting of the Regimiento.

"Gentlemen, the recent rebellion has caused me to reappraise our mission. Most of our men will put up with great hardship but, as long as they sit here on the coast, they will sooner or later take council of their fears and demand that we depart this land—it is inevitable. I therefore propose two difficult but mutually compatible courses of action. First, we must remove the temptation by" —he looked around to gauge our reaction—"demolishing our ships."

Olid and Sandoval started to laugh but I knew the he wasn't joking.

"Caudillo, I respect your judgment." I didn't really respect his judgment. "But to eliminate our only path of retreat flies in the face of every known military principle. We are confronting an enemy of potentially overwhelming power and destroying our ships invites total annihilation."

"Nevertheless, Señor de la Peña," Cortés eyed me closely, "the ships will be destroyed. Second, we will leave a small garrison in Villa Rica and the rest of the army will march to Mexico. I intend to visit the great gold-plated Moctecuzoma in his great gold-plated palace. In the meantime, though," Cortés continued, "we must keep our own council. I'll order the ships to careen on the beach in order to inspect for signs of la broma, the shipworm. To our unpleasant surprise our inspectors will discover that the hulls are riddled with the worm and the ships are no longer seaworthy. To make the best of a bad situation, you understand, we must then dismantle the ships and use the wood for buildings and the fittings for whatever purpose that we can find."

"And the sailors, Caudillo?"

"They will learn to be soldiers."

Burgos, Castilla-León

"Padre Mendoza, I know that you disagree with me when I assert that Cortés was guided by *El Diablo*."

"I do."

"But then you must think that Cortés was a fool?"

"By no means. As you yourself have observed, he was an exceptionally gifted man."

"On the other hand, only a fool would deliberately place our small band of Conquistadores at the total mercy of an unknown foe."

Mendoza sat back, smiling complacently. "He was not a fool, Your Grace. He conquered a continent."

"*Reductio ad absurbum, Padre*, but you're right. Fools are seldom successful, at least not in the long run. Still the man was successful, ridiculously successful, yet his success was the product of decisions that, if taken one-by-one, were not only foolish, they were overtly stupid. His decisions were the decisions of a madman. His acts were the acts of an idiot. Yet he was foolishly, stupidly, overwhelmingly successful. What is the sense of it? He was touched by the infernal."

"He was touched by the Divine," Mendoza countered.

The ancient prelate wasn't listening. "For better or worse we obeyed the Caudillo. All of the ships ground up on the sand and, after their examination by one of the ship's masters in the pay of Cortés, all but three were declared unfit for the sea. The only exceptions were two of the brigantines to be used for exploration and another for the transport of supplies. Despite the Lady's vigorous opposition, Doña Francesca's *Santo Domingo* was marked for destruction along with the rest. Guns, sails, anchors, altars, rigging, capstans, and other equipment were removed first. Then, the soldiers and sailors, thinking that there was no alternative, tore the ships apart. Planks, keels, rudders, ribs, spikes, nails, wire and hatch covers were all torn up. Much of this became part of Villa Rica although some of this was later transported to the banks of *Lake Texcoco* to be resurrected in far more lethal forms."

"As I check my previous manuscript, Your Grace, I see that your account differs from my record. Cervantes, who is a reliable source, uses the word *quemando*—burning."

"A simple misspelling, Padre. A as you know full well, the word is *quebrando*, the word used for 'breaking things up.' Besides, I was there and promise you that, although the ships were thoroughly demolished, they were not burned. Think about it. If we had torched them we would have been deprived of the ships' materials. Besides, if all of the ships had suddenly caught fire, the men would have hanged Cortés from the same gallows where Escudero rotted. As always, Cortés preferred subterfuge. It amused him to pretend that la broma was destroying the ships. To be certain, many of the men recognized that they were being tricked but sometimes men will ignore a lie that covers up the truth, even when the lie is obvious. After all, Padre Mendoza, is not the word for shipworm—*la broma*—the same word we use for a jest? The men willingly participated in their deception and, in doing so, many participated in their own destruction."

Mendoza wasn't finished. "Also, Your Grace, my manuscript attests to the fact that Diego Velásquez indeed learned of the departure of Cortés' Procuradores in *La Santa María de la Concepción*."

The old man nodded. "That's absolutely correct, Padre—intrigue and deception was the framework upon which our little expedition was built. Cortés was not the only one capable of mendacity. Montejo and Cortés' supposed best friend, Puertocarrero, against direct orders to bypass Cuba, sailed directly to Habana. To be certain, the ship sailed again before Velásquez could seize the ship. Even so, someone did get the news to the Governor. Don Diego actually sent a ship to intercept the *Santa María* in the Bahama channel. When the interception failed the Governor immediately dispatched a fast caravel to Spain. His messengers notified his friends in the Royal Court and thus diminished the impact of the *Santa María*'s arrival."

Mendoza scratched his head and then carefully smoothed the displaced hair. "Why do you think that these orders were disobeyed, Your Grace?"

"Montejo and Puertocarrero were concerned about their plantations and women. This makes sense but, you must remember, the ship's master and his officers must have been in agreement. I reckon that the detour was not an act of outright rebellion—the ship, after all, did sail and complete her mission. More likely, Montejo and Puertocarrero as well as the ship's officers and many of the men had doubts about the ultimate command. Velásquez still had an excellent chance of taking control and hanging Cortés and his Captains. To stop off in Cuba and slip Velásquez a little friendly information was simply politic. Someone, maybe everyone, was playing, as they say, both ends against the middle. As it turned out, this minor act of treason nearly defeated our expedition and, in so doing, cost uncounted lives."

Tlaxcala

Burgos, Castilla-León
February 4, 1581 8:05 A.M.

"Did you sleep well?"

"No, Your Grace, the dankness of my apartment has caused a flare-up in my reumatismo. The pain is agonizing and prevented me from sleeping."

The old man pretended genuine concern. "Why didn't you tell me about this earlier?"

"Perhaps a physician could see me?" Mendoza hoped to pass a message.

The Bishop shook his cadaverous head. "Nonsense—they're just a bunch of quacks. With me, you have the best physician in the Peninsula."

Mendoza looked doubtful. "Where did you study?"

"I've been trained by the Great School of Life. Show me where your trouble resides."

Mendoza was less than hopeful. "It's—here—in my great toe."

The Bishop rose from his chair and walked around the table. "Take your shoe and stocking off."

As Mendoza removed his right stocking, a fetid odor filled the room. The great toe, where it meets the foot, was inflamed and swollen.

"As you can see," the younger priest explained, "I'm not malingering."

"No, Padre, you certainly aren't." The Bishop grasped the toe and gave it a twist.

"OIY!"

"Yes, beyond any doubt you are suffering from la gota. I've seen cases where the malignant crystals erode through the victim's skin. I've seen still other cases in which the victim's body was deformed and his kidneys destroyed by jagged stones—in all of these cases the victim died."

Mendoza's eyes widened. "You don't think that will happen to me?"

"*Praesente medico nihil nocet, Padre*. You're lucky to have been arrested. With me as your physician you now have a chance for a cure. Otherwise, it's quite certain that you will go on to suffer an agonizing death."

"What can you do?"

The old man scratched the scars on his forehead. "Fortunately, quite a lot—we've been much too good to you, Padre."

"Too good?"

"We have catered to your whims and not to your health. We've been feeding you altogether excessive quantities of meat and wine."

"It doesn't compare with the table my own housekeeper sets for me."

"I'm certainly not surprised, Padre. You've supped too lavishly for a very long time. Fortunately, I'm in a position to remedy this."

"What kind of remedy?"

"No more red meat and wine. Bread, turnips, a few peas and an occasional fish will be adequate—think of it as a Lenten fast."

"Truly, Your Grace, it's not all that bad. It's probably just my tight shoes."

"No. It's definitely the gout. *Bene diagnosticur, bene curatur.* I'm afraid it's an occupational hazard of the priestly vocations. The poor campesinos seldom suffer from it."

"But...."

"You needn't thank me—I'm saving you for selfish reasons. Now, where were we?"

Chapter 46

"*Mis soldatos y amigos, la suerte está echada,*" Cortés exhorted the assembled army. "Seldom has such an awesome responsibility been placed upon the shoulders of mortal men. We have come a great distance and endured many hardships but all, until now, has been but preparation for this moment. To the west lies a heathen empire, a kingdom of savagery and wealth beyond the imagination of man. God and Emperor Carlos are depending on us, and us alone, to drag the proud Moctecuzoma down and bring the true Catholic faith to this new continent. Our path will be difficult and will be paved in the harsh stones of pain, sorrow and blood but, in the end, we must win the most valuable prize the world has ever known. As we go forth, I want each man to kneel down before Our Savior and the Blessed Virgin. I want each and every one of you to dedicate himself to God, for like Rolando and the Cid, who battled the infidel Moors, we dedicate ourselves to the destruction of the heathen and to the elevation of the True Cross. Each of you must always remember that no matter how difficult or fearful our task, God will judge you all. He who acquits himself well, even if he should die, will be rewarded in Heaven." -

● ● ●

After the speech our frailes had to limit the confessions to five minutes each, for there was not a man in the army who did not feel the need to unburden himself from his sins. Even I, who had not confessed in years, was moved to repent. A weary Olmedo, who had already listened to many others, heard my confession. I didn't bother to confess of my acts in battle, for I knew there must be more death in the future. Neither did I confess for the lives of the Inquisitors I had taken, for I felt no guilt. I did, however, confess.

"Forgive me, Padre, for I have sinned."

"Yes, my son?"

"I have abandoned a girl in Italy, Padre. She was carrying my child."

The friar hesitated, knowing that restitution, given the distance and circumstances, was impossible.

"*Veinte Ave Marias y Pater Nosters.*"

I didn't bother. I knew that recitation of a few lines would only compound my guilt.

"You must have led the life of a monk." I had not seen Doña Francesca as she stole up behind me.

What did she know? "It's between me...."

"Most of the men are taking their full five minutes and more—you, my errant knight, didn't take a minute."

"Very observant of you, señora. Might I ask how much time you spent with the Padre?"

"No, you may not. Besides why should I go to Confessional now when most of the soldiers are preparing for the march?"

"You're right—you women are staying behind."

"But I did go to Confession, Rodrigo, though I did it from

habit." I'd never seen her smile before. I liked it. "I'm not at all certain that I want to be forgiven of my sins."

"An interesting perspective, My Lady, especially when the friar's time could have been put to better use by one of the soldiers."

"But I am going along with the army."

"But I thought...."

"I know what you thought. You thought Cortés would never let me go. When I told him that I was determined to keep an eye on my investments, he said I could go. He didn't even put up a fight."

I was silent for several seconds, "That doesn't sound much like the Caudillo."

"No" —her eyes twinkled— "but, if the fool does have ideas, he doesn't know who he is dealing with. Cortés doesn't trust me. He thinks it is safer to keep me with the army than to let me sit back here stewing in Villa Rica. Besides, a few of the other women are going–the Ordaz sisters are frothing at the mouth. María de la Estrada is going and José de la Garza insists on taking his mistress, Louisa Álvarez."

"The Ordaz sisters," I said, "can take care of themselves but it's stupid for de la Garza to take his woman with him. I mean no offense, My Lady" —I bowed from the hips— "but you must be mad."

"Señor de la Peña, I am not unconscious of my own safety, but what makes you think it will be safer back here in Villa Rica?"

That stopped me a moment. "Here on the coast you're farther from the Mexican army."

"What good does that do, Rodrigo? If Cortés is defeated the Mexica will swoop down on Villa Rica like wolves on a flock of sheep."

"But there are the three brigantines."

"They won't help. Those who are in Villa Rica will be dead before they can move. Not only that but those who stay here will be at more risk than those in the rest of the army. If Moctecuzoma has any sense, he'll wipe out our pueblo and cut off any chance that the army has for retreat. There's also the very real possibility that Velásquez will attack from the sea—if he does, he will treat the people here like traitors. There will be executions and the fate of the women could be worse."

I shrugged my shoulders. "It sounds like you've thought the whole thing out."

She looked pleased with herself. "I have."

I still wasn't sure I agreed but her logic was sound. The village of Villa Rica would be weakly manned and could very well be at greater risk than the main army. A Mexican attack would be unexpected and there would be no time man the brigantines. Cortés' destruction of the fleet meant that everyone would die horribly.

"You make a strong argument, My Lady."

"Of course, but that's not really why I am determined to go. The army is going to go strange places and will see things beyond imagination. I'm going to see them, too."

"So you're going, señora." I bowed again, but his time, respectfully. "*Estoy a su servicio.*"

● ● ●

Juan de Escalante, whom Cortés trusted against any persuasion by the Governor, was appointed Captain of the garrison of Villa Rica. As a military force, the garrison didn't amount to much—there were one hundred fifty men, most of whom were sailors and soldiers who were old, sick or wounded. Juan de Alva, because of his weakness, was ordered to stay behind but he wasn't taking it well.

"That cabrón, de la Concha, tells me that I must stay behind. Who in Hell does he think he is? I've got a mind to call him out."

I reckoned that de Alva was making a show of it but I humored him. "Juan, you've been sick. Don't you think it best that you stay here and take it easy until you get better? You can catch up, later."

"Take it easy?" de Alva sputtered. "Did I hear you right? Cortés has given Escalante orders to build a city during the next few months. If he has it his way it'll be bigger than the fortress at Granada with the Alhambra thrown in. I'd rather die on the march than sweating my life out in this swamp."

De Alva had a point. Escalante was the arm of the Caudillo. The sick could expect no special treatment—they'd be worked to death.

"I'd like to help you but there's really...."

"You can help. Just hide me in your company. Concha will never recognize me among the others. *Maldición!* I plan to see the sights along with the rest of you."

"I don't know, Juan...."

"Do it for a friend."

I sighed. "You'd better not die on me."

He got a far away look in his eye. "Can you imagine it, Rodrigo? There's *Tenochtitlan* and, after that, a whole continent with one golden city after another. I'm told that there are dog-headed people and people who can fly."

"I certainly hope not." I shook my head. "Regular Indios are bad enough."

The rest of the army, of about three hundred men, forty crossbowmen, twenty arquebusiers and fifteen horse was ordered to go on the march. Over one thousand Totonac fighters, and another one thousand tamanes, or porters, each of whom can carry fifty pounds, stiffened our force. Besides their usefulness as bearers, the tamanes, who were also good in bushcraft, would build our shelters, nightly. Our carpenters built wagons for transport and as carriages for our cannon. On completion many of the Totonacs marveled at the mystery of them—they had never seen such carts before. Forty Indio nobles also came along as willing hostages. They served as guides and ambassadors to the various villages we came to.

Chapter 47

The army set out on the sixteenth of August, 1519. We soldiers wore both our quilted armor as well as metal plate. We carried our own weapons but the tamanes carried everything else. I was given command of the same men I had led at Cintla plus six men we had captured from an errant ship belonging to Francisco de Garay, the Governor of Jamaica. At first they were outraged by their capture but, on hearing of the great prize in front of them, they thanked us for taking them with us. I was ordered to march in the van.

On the first day, our journey was through the sweltering lowlands of the Totonacs but, by the second day, the trail started to climb toward the far-off mountains. We passed through the village of Xalapa and then, with great volcanoes and mountains to our right and our left, the track became even steeper. The air became cool and the country changed from tropical jungle into forests of oak. We then passed through the small villages of Coatepec, Xico-chimalco, and then Ixguacan. All of the inhabitants seemed eager to curry our favor. They gave us tortillas and fowls. In turn, our priests preached the word of the Lord and set up crosses and shrines to memorialize our passage.

We entered a narrow defile that we named El Paso Nombre de Dios. Icy winds blew from the heights like fingers of death. We gritted our teeth and trudged on. The sky opened up and pelted us with hail and freezing rain. The tamanes, who labored at pushing and pulling the heavy guns up the steep grade, suffered terribly and some of our Indios from Cuba died during the night. The rest of the army struggled on, each of us bending into the bitter wind as we entered a lifeless plain.

The land was swept by the remorseless wind and—although there was a lake—it was so salty as to be undrinkable. For three days we labored forward with no food and little water to drink and, even though I was protected by my cotton armor, I was wet from the constant drizzle. Everyone was completely miserable but, focusing on my own survival, I paid little attention to the plight of others. I did notice that some of our weaker men, as well as some of the women, had huddled together for warmth on our carts. This increased the work of our tamanes but they were used to hardship and moved forward without complaint.

I saw that Francesca de la Barca, wearing warm native dress, trudged forward, never asking for help. Cortés, excited and never tiring, rode his horse from the front to the rear of the column and then back again, encouraging unhappy stragglers or, when words didn't suffice, striking them with the flat of his sword.

"Are you making it, Juan?" I was worried about de Alva. "Maybe you should hitch a ride on one of the wagons?"

"I'm fine..." he wheezed. "I'm making it just fine."

He didn't look fine. His lips were blue and his skin was blotchy. Each step was an act of determination.

"*Hola, Compadres!*" Despite the conditions, José Maldinado had left his place in the middle ranks to visit with old friends. Pablo still had a gut albeit reduced in size from Cuba. His weight, however, wasn't slowing him down.

"Hola, Pablo. What do you think?"

"I think" –motioning to the naked land– "that we must pass

through Purgatory before entering Heaven. What's wrong with him?"

"He's just a little chilled."

Maldinado laughed. "That's because he doesn't eat enough." He patted his great belly. "If you don't have a fat woman to keep you warm, you'd better be fat, yourself."

"*Tienes una gorda en Cuba?*" I asked.

"*Anda!* I've got three of them, each one fatter than the other."

"Then why are you here?"

"It's the company, hombre. Those fat girls are Hell in bed but they aren't much for high-toned conversation, just a few grunts and squeals when I hit the right spot." He slapped me on the back so hard that I almost fell down. "I'd rather be here."

●●●

We turned west, passing to the north of the salt lake. The track improved gradually. We marched through the poor villages of Altotonga, Xalacingo, Teziutlan and Tlatlauquitepec. We then traveled along a ridge and entered another high pass that we named El Paso de la Lena. On the far side of the pass, the country improved. The road passed lengthwise through a narrow valley, rich with plantations of maíz and other native crops. The track then climbed again through forests of pine before opening up to cultivated country. A large town was visible in the distance.

The place was made up of flat-roofed buildings, along with the mosques that the Aztecas call teocallis. They were similar to those that we had already seen, complete with idol houses perched on their tops. Some of our Portuguese soldiers said it reminded them of the white town of Castilblanco in their own country. This town's name was *Zautla* and was subject to the great Moctecuzoma. Its people spoke the language of Mexico and observed the Mexican custom of large-scale human sacrifice.

Close to the center of town there was a large square complete with stepped and blood-soaked teocallis. In one location there were orderly piles of festering skulls. Only a short distance away, there were great piles of leg bones. The skulls were so neatly arranged that we attempted to count them. The numbers were so great that we soon gave up the effort but the skulls numbered in the thousands. Also present were great racks of skulls and moldering heads, skewered on horizontal poles. The stench was incredible. All of these disgusting things were attended by three black painted, black-robed priests whose long hair was tangled and matted with blood. This is, or at least was, the Mexican custom. The Mexica, without pretense, worshipped the Devil and his familiars. They believed that their priests achieved Satanic sanctity through filth and blood.

From our sojourn in Cozumel, Tabasco and the land of the Totonacs we were familiar with the Indio worship of death but we had never seen anything of this fantastic scale. After seeing these sights, I heard several men grumble that the destruction of our fleet had been a stupid mistake.

"I don't like it," said an old soldier, Hector Herrera, as he pondered the skewered heads. He was a man in his fifties and walked with a slight limp, the gift from a Berber in North Africa. "The sacrifice of our little band wouldn't draw a crowd."

I tried to make light of his fears. "Look at the bright side of it, Hector. There are not enough people in this town to eat more than a hundred or so at a time. These bones are the trophies of generations."

"There is no bright side of it, Rodrigo. Many of these skulls are fresh and, before this is over, both of our heads will be grinning on a rack."

"I don't think I'll dwell on it. Besides, we saw the same on the coast. This is just on a—well—grander scale. We'd better get used to it, if—when—we get to *Tenochtitlan*, it's going to get worse."

"That's what I'm afraid of, Rodrigo. No doubt we're doing God's work but, when I see things like this, it makes me wonder if we are too proud and that we might be putting God to the test. If we are, none of us will get home alive."

"We'll make it. Not only will we make it but, from what I can tell, we'll have so many allies that we won't have to do much fighting. Mexico is a rotten fruit barely hanging from the tree—a breath of wind and it will splatter on the ground."

Herrera looked me hard in the eye. "I've been fighting since I was younger than you and I've been fighting ever since. I'm here on this expedition not because I think I'll get rich but because I have to be somewhere and this is as good a place as I know of to make my last fight. You younger men hope to reap fabulous rewards, but the only reward for many of these fools will be the honor of place on a rack of stinking skulls."

●●●

The cacique of Zautla was a man named Olintecle, a tall dark-skinned man with ritual scars on his chin and bare chest. He greeted us with cool dignity. He gave us food and let us stay in rooms that had been prepared for us. Many of us crowded around as Cortés, through his interpreters, questioned Olintecle.

"How big is this town of *Zautla?*"

"There are twenty thousand."

"You are the vassal of the Moctecuzoma?" Cortés asked.

"Is not everyone a vassal or slave of our Lord? Even now a detachment of his warriors is stationed in my city."

"How many fighters does he command?"

"Moctecuzoma commands thirty great chiefs, each of whom has one hundred thousand warriors. Each subject town has a garrison of warriors and Mexican armies are always in the field."

This piece of information stopped Cortés for a moment, "And *Tenochtitlan?* What is it like and how big is it?"

"The city is the largest in the world and is built in the waters of a great lake. It is connected to the mainland by three broad paths, each of which stretches farther than a man can see. Each of these trails is broken by wooden bridges which can be easily removed for defense."

"Then Moctecuzoma, if he should have such defensive preparations, must not be as secure as you suggest."

Olintecle stiffened. "*Tenochtitlan* is invulnerable. The land is thick with spies and the lake is patrolled by hundreds of boats. The city itself is cut by many canals and each building and house is a fortress."

"Is there much gold?"

A smile played at the corners of Olintecle's mouth. "Moctecuzoma has so much gold that you teotoh will choke on it. The wealth of the world flows into *Tenochtitlan*. To protect it, Moctecuzoma has the blessings of the gods *Huitzilopotchli* and *Tezcatlipoca*—every year twenty thousand die in their honor."

Cortés was nonplussed. "I hear what you say, Olintecle, and I have no doubt that Moctecuzoma is mighty in this land. I tell you now, we are Españoles, who have come from lands on the other side of the sea to lead Moctecuzoma and all of his people away from the sins of murder, sodomy and the eating of human flesh. I tell you this because we are the servants of the Emperor Carlos and have been commissioned in the name of Our Savior, The Lord Jesus Christ."

Now it was Olintecle's turn to be nonplussed. "I have not heard of these but Moctecuzoma will welcome them as his slaves."

"You misunderstand me, Olintecle. Moctecuzoma will shortly become a vassal of Lord Carlos. If you have any sense, you will now agree to bow down before our Monarch. It is best that you give us gold as a sign of your loyalty."

"Gold? Malinche, you ask for gold?" Olintecle's eyes glittered like a rat's. "I will give you nothing without the permission of Moctecuzoma."

●●●

The next days were spent in debate as to which was the best way to proceed. Olintecle stated that the shortest route to *Tenochtitlan* was through the Mexican tributary city of *Cholula*. Mamexi, who was the chief of our Totonacs, privately disagreed. He held that our best course was through the Republic of *Tlaxcala*, for *Tlaxcala* was a well-known enemy of the Mexica. He believed that the Tlaxcalteca would welcome the chance to become our allies.

"The men of *Cholula*," I asked through our interpreters, "are they friends of Moctecuzoma?"

"Like us, they are great friends and servants of the Lord Moctecuzoma and obey his every command."

"And the Tlaxcalteca? Are they good people?"

Olintecle raised his upper lip in a grimace meant as a sneer. The fact that his lower lip was pulled down by a golden labret only made him more grotesque. "The Tlaxcalteca are not people—they are a pestilence."

"Ah, then Moctecuzoma hasn't converted them into vassals and slaves?"

"If our great Lord wished to do so, he could do it with the flick of his little finger. It serves his purposes to keep them wild as he does the animals in his hunting reserves."

"I don't think I understand?" I was learning the politics of Mexico.

"The Tlaxcalteca are the prey on which the Mexica train their young warriors. They are the meat that Moctecuzoma serves to his Gods."

"Then, if these people are to provide a suitable challenge for the Mexica, they must be good fighters."

Olintecle hesitated. "Are cornered rabbits good fighters?"

Cortés who had been listening nearby, held up his hand. "Thank you, Rodrigo—you have cut to the heart of our problem." He turned to the other men who had been listening to the conversation. "Although he doesn't know it, our friend here has confirmed what the Totonacs have told us. The Tlaxcalans have good cause to hate the Mexicans—it's there we must go."

Chapter 48

We departed *Zautla* with some gladness. In his eagerness to see us leave, Olintecle gave us four girls, a few minor gifts and twenty of his best warriors. Before we left, however, Cortés decided to prepare the Tlaxcalteca for our visit.

Cortés dictated letters to me. These letters bore words of peace and were to be delivered by nervous Totonac messengers. Of course, the Tlaxcalteca would have no way of divining the meaning of these documents but, to Cortés, this was of no matter. By sending the letters, Cortés had conformed to Royal and Ecclesiastical law. If the Indios failed to understand their contents, that was their hard luck. Along with the letters Cortés also sent a broken crossbow, a sword and a red Flemish hat.

"Caudillo?" asked a suspicious Miguel Flores. "I don't wish to question your judgment but, rather than send these weapons of war, why not send beads and glass jewelry?"

"I want these people to understand that they are to be our allies in war against the Mexica."

"But will they understand your intent? Isn't it more likely that they'll think that your gifts are a challenge?"

"Miguel, Miguel," Cortés sighed, "despite your youth and the balls hanging between your legs, you're no better than an old woman. If these savages don't understand my peaceful intentions, then we will have to make very certain they get the—point."

Burgos, Castilla-León

"You see, Padre Mendoza, this was Cortés' strategy. He may have appeared to be impulsive but he did nothing on a whim. He wanted us soldiers and, to be sure, the Royal Court itself, to think that he desired peace. In actuality, however, he lusted for victory over *Tlaxcala*. Earlier he had spoken to the Totonac leaders as well as the chiefs of *Zautla* and he knew very well the signs that were necessary to provoke war. He was operating on the same principle that he had used on the Totonacs of *Cempoalla* when he destroyed their temples. To Cortés, a voluntary ally was less reliable than an ally who had been humbled at the point of a sword."

"But he risked disaster."

"So it would seem but, as I have told you before, things that to most men would be ridiculous gambles were to Cortés the waters of life. Cortés was not gambling; he was in the employ of Satan."

"Your Grace, you continue to jest with me. Time and again you have confirmed that your march was that of triumphant Christianity. Cortés not only set up shrines and planted crosses, he toppled graven images and preached against the iniquitous practices of idolatry and human sacrifice."

"At the time I would have agreed with you, Mendoza, but no longer—men mistake harm for evil. There can be no doubt that the Mexica did terrible harm but, in doing so, they were not necessarily evil. They were exercising the rituals of their own faith, a faith they had been born to and a faith that they never questioned. In following their tradition, no matter how horrible it was to our eyes, they did good. If they had not done so, they would have been evil."

"But good and evil are absolutes."

The ancient priest pondered the younger man's statement. "Would it surprise you if I were to tell you that I agree with you? There is such a thing as truth. The individual, however, is seldom privy to such an absolute. Each man and woman must wander in the field planted by his fathers."

Mendoza's back stiffened. "Holy Mother Church is immutable Truth."

"You make my argument, Padre. At one level it is possible to assert that Cortés was obeying the edicts of the greater good by suppressing the Mexican customs."

"I do."

"On the other hand, Cortés engaged in wholesale lies, extortion, theft and torture. Also, there were times when destruction could have been averted, but Cortés invited it. By the moral standards of our own Catholic religion, he behaved like a ravenous beast. Might may make right, Padre, but it's seldom moral. Cortés, whatever small good he might have done, was the willing agent of *El Diablo*, Himself. His piety was but a pretense and was part of the duplicity that was Hernán Cortés. At Morning Prayer or at Vespers, he was always the first to his knees and was always the one to pray most vocally. He preached more than the priests and he would have attacked each heathen temple if not held back by Fraile Olmedo. It was all an act meant to deceive his men, the Crown and later, the historians of our faith."

"No good, Your Grace. I am insightful enough to recognize that mortal men, many of whom may have erred in their piety, have furthered the cause of the Church. Cortés was an example of one of these men. His conversion of the heathen may have been bloody but it was final. He brought millions to the bosom of Christ."

The Bishop considered Mendoza's words. "Padre, we have mentioned that, before the foundations of this world, there was a great war in Heaven."

"Yes, the forces of God prevailed against those of Lucifer."

"Does not Lucifer mean the 'bearer of light'?"

"Yes. If he had followed that which is Holy, he would have been the one chosen."

"What were the issues that embroiled the Heavens in battle?"

Mendoza said nothing.

"What were the issues, Padre?"

"Lucifer had a plan by which all of mankind would be returned to God."

"That's right, Padre, but you left out an important part. Lucifer had a plan by which man would be compelled to do right. God rejected the plan."

Mendoza continued to sit in silence.

"Cortés was the agent of Lucifer. He forced Christianity exactly as Mohammad forced millions to Islam at the point of the sword. Neither Cortés nor Mohammad was that much different from—*Santo Oficio*."

From Zautla we marched over mountainous tracts, to the high Mexican fortress town of Iztaquimaxtitlan. In the distance, a great mountain poured huge plumes of smoke into the sky—I was reminded of the volcano near Naples. We waited the return of our messengers but there was no sign of them, and we proceeded on our way. As we marched we met our two messengers who, as they claimed, had narrowly escaped from the *Tlaxcalteca*. They arrived in a state of terror.

The two men bowed down before us. "Do not punish us, O Malinche. We have delivered the messages and explained that you are good and hate the Mexica."

Cortés didn't seem surprised. "Then what was the problem?"

"The men of *Tlaxcala* took your gifts and used them to wipe the filth from their backsides. They seized us and beat us with sticks."

"What did they say?"

"We are going to kill those whom you call teotoh and eat their flesh. Then we shall see whether they are as brave as you proclaim."

"Gentlemen," Cortés turned to his officers. "They have taken the bait."

Pedro de Alvarado whooped, "*Entonces, adelante y la buena suerte!*"

Exultant, the Caudillo took up the cry. "Compadres, since we are few, we must always be as ready and as much on the alert as if we were already in the presence of the enemy. When we spot the hostiles, those of you who are on horseback must hold your lanzas short and aim for their faces. To prevent them from seizing your weapons and wresting them from your hands, deal them repeated thrusts and keep your lances moving."

● ● ●

Within the next two leagues, we noticed Tlaxcalan scouts in distance. Efforts to get them to approach us failed so Cortés and his horsemen rode out to them, supposedly to convince them of our peaceful intentions. Supposedly I say, because these Indios, who had seemed peaceful enough, went wild after hearing the words of the interpreters.

Although few in numbers, they fought like cornered beasts.

Our caballeros killed five but at the cost of two horses killed and three caballeros wounded. The enemy was able to accomplish this feat because they were armed with their great two-handed wooden swords, which is called in their language, *maquahuitl*. They are studded with the same black razor-sharp stone, called *iztli*, that they use for their knives and other weapons. So cunningly are these swords made that the stones are difficult to dislodge even with great force.

We soldiers thought this small action was an end to the trouble but, out of nowhere, there appeared hundreds of feathered warriors, girded for battle. Our horsemen, who had unwisely pursued the first small party of Indios, found themselves far from the infantry and had to fight for their lives. Fortunately for themselves, these caballeros managed to cut their way back to our main force. A few of these men were wounded, one of whom died days later. We dressed the wounds of the injured men and horses with the fat of a dead warrior.

We cut up the dead horses for their meat and hides. The heads and guts were buried in deep holes. Even though the Tlaxcalteca knew that they had succeeded in wounding the animals, Cortés thought it best that we hide the fact that a horse could die, rot and molder away like any other beast. After doing these things we marched forward and were met by two suspicious-looking ambassadors bearing banners of peace.

"We are the men of *Tlaxcala*," they said, "and beg your pardon for today's fighting—it is not our fault but the fault of the Otomi barbarians who live in our country. We have not been able to reason with them but, in our shame, we would like to pay you for your beasts, because we know that you teoteoh value them highly."

Burgos, Castilla-León

"Obispo, It sounds like the *Tlaxcalans* weren't too frightened of your horses if they wanted to buy them."

"They wanted to buy them precisely because they were in awe of them and afraid of us. Much later, after I learned the language of Mexico, I discovered that our translators had made an error. They never mistook our horses for deer. Think about it—all male deer have some kind of antlers but our horses, some of which were conspicuously male, never had antlers."

"Again, Excelencia, you are indulging in revisionist history."

"Not much—the Azteca believed that our horses were another variety of savage beast—the xolotl—a creature of deep forests. I had the opportunity to see one of these monsters in Moctecuzoma's menagerie. The thing bore a superficial resemblance to a horse. It was as large and had hoof-like claws on its feet. Had it not been for its long and mobile nose and sharp teeth, it would have been a horse. I doubt it could have been saddled, though—it was ferocious and chewed the bars of its cage. The Mexica told me it was a familiar of the great god Tlaloc and prowled the night in an eternal pursuit of corpses. With such an impressive reputation, it is small wonder that the Indios feared our horses and feared us more for mounting such demons. I'm wandering off the subject, Padre. We continued our march towards Tlaxcala. That night was a hungry one as the men singed off the needle-like hairs of the red fruit of the nopal cactus in their fires. The flesh of the fruit is good and sweet but, for all that, is mostly tiny seeds. Another dish that we tried, on the advice of the *Cempoallans*, is the fleshy leaf of the nopal itself. We scraped off the spines and cooked them in pots. The nopal leaf, although it fills the stomach, is slimy and tasteless. Fortunately, however, we were able to capture a number of small fat, puppies around abandoned Tlaxcaltec huts. The flesh of these dogs, when stewed together with the nopal, produced a rich and tasty dish."

Mendoza reacted instinctively. "Dog? My references mention this, of course, but I find it difficult to believe that the meat, of these animals is anything other than revolting."

"Before I tried it myself, I might have agreed with you, but it is amazing how starvation numbs a person's revulsion. To be certain, our Indio allies, who regarded dog as a delicacy, proved to us that dog is quite edible. Even then, I was reluctant but when presented with beautiful, clean meat I literally swallowed my inhibitions."

"How does it taste?"

"Like all meats it has its own unique flavor but I would compare it to our local hare only lighter and more fat. Of course, I cannot swear to the palatability of all dogs, for the animals raised by the Indios were raised both as pets and as food. Meat is not a common commodity in Mexico and these dogs were castrated and fed vegetables along with anything else that they could scavenge, including, I am afraid, Indio filth."

Padre Mendoza screwed up his face. "Disgusting!"

"It's really no different in Portugal. Even their so-called aristocrats place their household toilets to fatten the hogs."

"But the idea of eating dog."

"The first time I doubt I could have devoured a dog that I personally killed and skinned." The old Bishop grinned at Mendoza's discomfort. "Such is the power of the mind over the stomach. *Cibi condimentum est fames.* Later, after I had eaten meat prepared by others and, when I was driven by hunger, I had no problem whatsoever in snapping their necks, peeling off their skins and broiling them until their meat sizzled."

"We met with several hundred armed Indios who announced themselves to be our Otomi enemies. Cortés then sent forward three prisoners that we had captured in the previous day's fighting, but the Otomi wouldn't listen. Cortés then called up our Escribano, Diego de Godoy, and through our interpreters Aguilar and Doña Marina, the Requerimiento was read, for Cortés insisted that all violence must be legal. Our demands, which were totally incomprehensible to the Otomis, were greeted with jeers followed by a shower of stones and arrows. We responded with crossbow and musket fire. '*Santiago y cierra España!*' We charged against the Otomi line. I killed one warrior before he knew I was on him. The Otomi broke and ran into a narrow arroyo through which a small stream flowed. We pursued them but—like Jason sewing the dragons' teeth—thousands of screeching Indios literally rose from the ground. The enemy army was spread over the slopes and plain in terrifying splendor—pagan banners snapping in the wind. Their legions were resplendent in the red and white shields and banners of their general, Xicotencatl the Younger. Most of the hideously painted warriors were naked except for their breach clouts and weapons. Chiefs and noble warriors were better protected. Some were covered, from their ankles to their necks, in protective armor of woven maguey, decorated by many colored feathers. The faces of snarling beasts surmounted the heads of some of our enemies. Still others wore quilted tunics with kilts of fur and feathers and elaborate headdresses of black, green and blue feathers. A few of the wealthy warriors wore chest armor of thin metal that looked like gold but was, as we learned to our disgust, only copper. In addition to their quilted armor, cloaks of feathers covered the wealthiest fighters and those of the highest ranks wore ridiculous devices that were attached to their backs and rose above their heads. From everywhere was the glint of iztli and yellow metal. The shields and weapons of the Otomi were similar to those of the Tabascans, except better made. They carried light targets of wood bound with sinew or rawhide. The faces and edges of these shields were decorated with feathers or animal tails intricately worked to look like animals or demons. There were whole ranks of slingers and archers and there were still others bearing short wooden at-latls. With these sticks the Indios could, at short range, hurl light feathered spears with enough force to penetrate plate armor. Other Otomi wielded long spears tipped with leaf-shaped heads embed-ded with itzli fragments. Other spears were shorter and armed with flint or sometimes copper. Some of these spearmen were able, with a twitch of their wrists, to recover their weapons by means of cords attached to their weapons. Still others carried battle-axes or clubs of copper or stone. The highest ranking and most powerful warriors carried the lethal *maquahuitl*. When fear dries your mouth and loos-ens your bowels, the numbers of enemy are greater than the grains of sand in the sea. The numbers you give in your *Histories*, Padre, are excessive."

"One hundred thousand? Those are the figures of Cortés him-self."

"Cortés never minimized his accomplishments and had reasons to exaggerate. I must admit, though, that at the time, I wouldn't have argued with ten times that number. More realistically, the number must have been closer to thirty thousand or smaller—maybe a lot smaller. It hardly matters, though. We were still outnumbered by many times."

●●●

The Otomi had lured us into a trap although they did not at-tack at once. Dramatically, the Otomi ranks stood motionless even as their war drums pounded, trumpets blared and flutes trilled. Then their ranks surged forward and for a brief desperate time, it was every man for himself. The air hummed with missiles of all kinds that clattered against our shields and armor. We Castilians were forced into a defensive ring even as our horsemen tried to force a path into our ranks for our cannons. Our allies did great service as they threw themselves into the heart of the melee. It was spear against spear and maquahuitl against maquahuitl as the Indio enemies engaged in combat as ancient as the land around us.

The Otomi seemed especially anxious to engage the men of *Zautla*, which gave us time to form up and even time to watch the Indio manner of combat. The foemen spent more time in swagger, challenge and insult than in direct conflict. When fighting did occur it was one-on-one or two-on-two with fighters of similar rank challenging one another—then the fighting got serious. The warriors would charge towards one another with great leaps while slashing at one another with their swords or spears and defending themselves with their shields. The outcome was always in question until one warrior suddenly went down. At this point the losing warrior ceased all resistance—the victor would chant a rhyme as, from the rear ranks, slaves would appear to drag the unresisting loser off to his fate.

The ritual fighting reduced the fury of the Otomi onslaught but, even so, we almost gave way. The Otomi threw themselves against our shields even as our pikes skewered them and our swordsmen cut them down as if scything bloody wheat. Crossbow bolts thudded, penetrating shields, sinking deeply into the flesh of their owners. Musket balls blasted through living flesh, rarely missing the packed masses of warriors at point-blank ranges. The leaden balls penetrated bodies, shattered limbs and exploded heads. The only thing that slowed the killing was the loading of the weapons. The mosqueteros increased their rate of fire by estimating the powder charge and using undersized balls so that they did not have to stop and use their ramrods. This decreased what little accuracy a musket had, but given the situation, accuracy was unimportant.

The weight of the defense rested on the sword, the shield, plate armor and the helmet. Without these, we would have been annihilated. Even with these defenses it was a near thing, for a Mexican club can stun a man wearing a helmet. Missiles and spears can wound an unprotected face and penetrate cotton armor. A maquahuitl, although usually a wounding weapon, if wielded with enough force, can sever an arm or a leg and even slash through chest armor.

I saw that my men were tiring. "Keep together. Shields up and don't let them get between you!"

Missiles banging against my shield and armor, I screamed a confidence I didn't feel. "*Buen obra, hombres.* We've almost got them now."

One warrior dived in under my shield seizing me by the legs. I placed Bebidor's point over the point of his spine where the body meets the neck. I leaned into it and felt the separation. I rolled him over with my foot. His eyes blinked up at me but he no longer moved his limbs.

Two others attacked me as a coordinated team. One was using a maquahuitl and one a throwing spear. They hit me at the same time but the spearman staggered back with a crossbow bolt in his face. The maquahuitl man was good and, for a time, we were even. His shield deflected my sword towards the ground but I surprised him with the reverse blow that caught him directly between the legs and struck solid bone. He dropped both his sword and shield and his eyes widened in horror. Blood spurted into the soil.

For de Alva's safety, I kept him on my right side. Despite his weakness, he fought intelligently, never wasting motion. Rather than hack and slash at his opponents, he permitted them to waste themselves against his shield. Then, when they exposed themselves, he pierced them with a quick in-and-out.

"*Buen hecho, Juan!*" Two Otomi lay at de Alva's feet and a third staggered back with a wound under the chin.

He didn't waste his time with words but concentrated on his next opponent, an exquisitely muscled youth. De Alva's sword entered his chest.

Three warriors, sensing de Alva's increasing weakness, crowded against him. I got one, my musketeer killed the second and de Alva wounded the third.

We held but the Otomi, with their courage and huge numbers, should have defeated us—all they really had to do was to attack us in unceasing waves. They would have taken their casualties, to be sure, but if they had done so, they would have eventually worn us down to nothing. Instead they attacked us en masse. They crowded together, one fighter impeding another, with the rear would-be heroes crowding and pushing the forward men onto our swords and spears. Even their numerous dead tripped them and their wounded clutched at unwounded fighters.

Burgos, Castilla-León

The ancient priest stopped as if to consider the events of long ago. "It was in this battle, Padre Mendoza, that I first noticed the Indio tactic that, in my opinion, most contributed to their defeat."

"Yes, you have already mentioned the impact of horsemen."

"The horses were important, to be certain, but, even our horses would have been useless had not our enemies consistently blundered."

"How so?"

"I had previously noticed the Indio mistake while we were fighting against the Maya but had simply attributed it to over-zealousness on the part of a few of their warriors. In our fights against the Otomi and Tlaxcalteca and later against the Mexica, I saw it time and again."

"Ah...you are trying to keep me in suspense."

The old man would not be denied, however. "Occasionally warriors would throw down their weapons and try to take a live Castilian captive. Usually this led to the extinction of the unarmed warrior—rarely, however, it succeeded. If Indio warriors actually succeeded in pulling a man out of the battle line, unarmed slaves would run out of their ranks, bind their victim hand and foot and drag him away.

"Yes, I'm aware of this. They preferred warrior victims for their pagan orgies."

"Correct, but, in your works you failed to give this tactic the importance it deserved—it was the single factor most important in the Mexican defeat. As the numbers of our enemies less overwhelmed me, I was sometimes able to study the people I was killing. The indígenos honored personal courage above even military victory. To perform deeds of daring before a living, fighting enemy was the epitome of valor. I saw warriors strike armed Castilians across the face with a light stick, or even their bare, open hand, and then retreat without trying to strike a wounding blow. For, you see, it is more valorous to walk away from a standing enemy than it is to walk away from a dead one. Therefore, the Indios almost never tried to kill us and those of us who did die in battle were usually the victims of multiple superficial wounds. At most, they tried to wound and cripple. From their point of view, a dead enemy was worthless whereas a living captive was food for the gods and a glory to his captor. These things are connected to their heathen religion and their concept of honor. Their tactics were, no doubt, adequate when confronting enemies with similar codes of conduct. In the case of Castilian enemies, however, such tactics were usually fatal—as Christians we had no reluctance to kill. My question to you, Padre Mendoza, is why do you think that, once the Indios learned of our lethality, they didn't shift their tactics to match our own?"

"I was of the understanding that they did."

"Only marginally. For the most part, they never learned to match our tactics. They always fought to obtain captives, even when their empire was being pulled down around their heads."

"Then it must be common stupidity."

"Or uncommon stupidity, but there were other factors as well. The truth is that, given the Indio weapons, and the strength of our armor, it was difficult to kill a Castilian outright. In some cases bodily seizure of one of our men may have been more effective than an attempt to kill him on the spot. Mostly, though, I'm inclined to think it has to do with the nature of their society. To them religion and war were not only connected. They were, if you can possibly imagine, exactly the same thing. Children were carefully trained in the moral codes and the mysteries of their religion. The training of boys in the arts of war was but one aspect of this instruction. This training was so very effective that it burned into their minds an unwavering method of combat. They were incapable of adapting even when confronted by a foe using alien tactics. Also, you must remember, their war against us was, even for them, a war of faith. For them to have altered their tactics would have been unthinkable—it would have made their resistance pointless. Nevertheless, their inability to adjust and their adherence to custom defeated them even more certainly than did Spanish steel."

Mendoza was silent for several seconds and then leaned back in his chair contemplating what he had been told. "In the long run, Your Grace, would it have made any real difference?"

The old Bishop looked into the younger man's eyes, for once impressed by his victim's insight.

"No, it wouldn't. Even if the Mexica had made no mistakes; even if they had fought us on the beach or ambushed us in the passes and fought until we were totally exterminated, it would have made no difference. Yes, they might have gained a few years and maybe, just maybe, they would have learned something from our tactics and weapons. They would have lost any niggling doubts about our supernatural natures and they might have made military alliances not easily subverted by Spanish lies. They would have lost most of their fear of the horse and they would have inflicted thousands of Castilian casualties but eventually, painfully they would have lost everything. Larger, better-equipped and even more ruthless armies would have arrived. Wars might have dragged on for many years but eventually, just as day follows night, the Mexica would have tasted total, bitter defeat. There is, from my point of view, one major difference though— Cortés had failed. No matter what eventually happened, I would have been slain and devoured."

Chapter 49

The battle that was later called *Tehuacacingo* was still a very near thing. Fortunately our gunners were able to unlimber their cannon and ruin the enemy. Cannon balls plowed through their ranks killing and wounding dozens with every shot. Even so, the Otomi were valiant and attacked not only our espadas but also our caballeros. At one point, their most powerful warriors decided to capture one of our horses. Singing their battle hymn, they attacked and laid hands on the mare owned by Juan Sedeño. I knew this horse well—I had trained it for combat on the beach of San Juan de Ulua. Despite all my pampering, the horse's luck ran out.

Sedeño was incapacitated by three wounds he had received in fighting the previous day. He therefore lent his animal to Pedro de Morón, the best and most courageous horseman in the army. Morón, along with three other caballeros, charged into the enemy masses with inadequate support. Howling Otomi attacked from the flanks and, seizing Morón's lance, dragged it from his hands. Still other savages slashed and grasped at Morón, toppling him from his saddle. Morón's companions attempted to protect him from the enemy but were forced back by their numbers. I saw what was happening and decided to save both the man and his horse. "Keep together!" I pointed towards our fallen man. "*Morón!*"

I was at the point of a phalanx driving into the enemy. Surprised, the savages parted in front of us and were killed before they could turn to confront us. Some of my men gave aid to the fallen Morón as I tried to recover his wild-eyed mare. Slashing to my right and left I forced my way to her side. I dropped my shield and clawed my way to the kicking horse's back, seized the halter, and tried to guide the animal back to our lines.

An Otomi reached up and grabbed my leg. A short distance away another warrior, putting all of his strength behind his atalatl, drove a dart through my plate armor. Another warrior swung a great blow with his maquahuitl, nearly decapitating the mare. The animal dropped from under me and rolled, trapping my leg. I should have been a dead man but the Otomis tried to jerk me free. Bebidor saved my life. I slashed at both the enemy as well as the leather girths. My foot came loose with the saddle. Defended by my companions, I recovered my shield. We dragged Morón back to our line but, to our disgrace, the Otomi gained the carcass of the mare and dragged it into their lines. Later, the dead horse was sacrificed to their gods along with the red Flemish hat and letters that Cortés sent to the Tlaxcalteca. Cortés was appalled when he learned that the horse had been cut into pieces and sent to *Tlaxcala*. If the Otomi and people of *Tlaxcala* had ever believed that our horses were magic, they believed it no longer.

From the place in my chest where I had been struck, blood flowed from under my armor and soaked the underlying padding. I was in pain but could still swing a sword. Gradually, we forced the flagging enemy back. Finally they quit altogether, marching in orderly ranks towards their city, carrying their dead and wounded with them.

"Rodrigo," Cortés reproached me, "you jeopardized our force by pulling your men out of line."

"It won't happen again."

"If it does, I'll strip you of your rank."

"I'll make you proud, Caudillo."

Francesca de la Barca appeared out of nowhere and, in doing so, she started the sequence of events that would alienate me from Cortés, put me in the enemy camp and almost get me killed. Come to think of it, though, the trouble might have started the first time I saw her in Cuba.

Turning her back to Cortés, Francesca addressed me as if he were not even present. The Caudillo, not receiving his usual recognition, started to speak but clenched his jaw and strode away.

"Let me help you with your armor." She, along with most of the other women, had been noncombatants but would have paid the full price had we been defeated.

"Thank you, señora, but I'm sure I can manage by myself." I tried to raise my hand to my leather strap but was stopped by the pain. Without a word, she started to loosen my armor—her hands were crusted with blood.

"Are you wounded?"

"No. I've been binding the wounded—you are one of the wounded." Her face showed no emotion as she pulled the armor away from my chest. The underlying padding was soaked with dark blood. "Look at your armor—the spear point...."

I looked reluctantly. The defect in the armor was completely plugged by a shiny black stone. The stone had been broken clean at the surface of the armor plate but, on the inside, a half finger-length of razor sharp stone intruded. Using my knife, the woman cut away my blood-caked material. The cotton showed multiple tears caused by my arm and chest moving against the rigid point—the underlying flesh was slashed.

"You're lucky, Rodrigo—the wound's superficial." She cut away some of my unbloodied cotton armor, folded it, and applied it to my wound. She wiggled the itzli point from my armor, scratching her thumb in the process. She replaced my metal plate armor, binding my dressing tightly.

"Your armor should hold your dressing in place but I'll want to check your wound daily—we can't afford to lose any more of you soldiers. Here is your souvenir," She handed me my itzli point. "I saw you trying to save Sedeño's horse—*estupido*." Without another word, she turned to aid the other wounded.

Hector Herrera, who was standing nearby, had the wasted look of a man who had been in a very hard place. Even so, he looked better than most of the other soldiers.

"That is one Hell of a woman." Herrera indicated the hardworking Francesca with his white whiskered chin. "I have had the foul misfortune to know many women so I know what I'm talking about. *Ella es mucha mujer.*"

"You like her then, Hector?" Despite my discomfort, I was curious.

He looked up at me and shook his head. "She's beautiful but... there's something about her. *Tenga cuidado, Rodrigo.*"

"Me? You heard her. As far as she's concerned all I am is another wounded soldier, somebody to protect her investment."

"My dear Rodrigo, you are a fine fighting man but you are no judge of women, especially that kind of woman. She wants you so bad she's sick with it."

I rolled his words around in my mind and then shook my head. "Ridiculous. I'm just one of four hundred. *Hay muchos mas de donde elegir.* Didn't you see her? She showed not the slightest concern for me as a person—she was as cold as a fish. Even her hands were cold."

Herrera smiled happily. "Of course her hands are cold. She's scared to death for you."

"It doesn't make sense."

"It never makes sense—she hasn't admitted it even to herself. The greater her desire, the greater her fear. The greater her fear, the greater her distance."

"I'm not following you?"

"She thinks you'll be killed—and—she's probably right. Why should she give her heart" —Herrera pinched my cheek— "to a corpse?"

"I respect your white hair, Hector, but I don't see it. Besides, I don't even care for the woman—she is as soft as," I tossed my itzli point into the air, catching it in my fist, "this piece of stone."

"Do you think so, Rodrigo?" Herrera cocked his head as if trying to look behind my eyes. "Know yourself, Rodrigo. It may save you grief in the future. *Cuidado.*"

Chapter 50

We spent that night and the next fourteen on the hill called Tzompachtepetl. Freezing winds blew off of the mountains and we didn't have adequate clothing to warm us. For all intents and purposes we were under siege and had to keep constant watch. We even slept in our armor. Everyone was hungry, for the only food we had was scoured from the adjacent countryside. For water, we collected the rain. Even Cortés was questioning his malign star—time and again he sent captives to *Tlaxcala*. Now, he was sincerely begging for peace.

"What does Xicotencatl say?" Cortés asked of the returned hostage. "Will he make peace?"

"With your pardon, Malinche, I will tell you what he says. He says he will make peace with you when your flesh is grilled with green chiles."

I was still in too much pain to fight but Cortés struck into the countryside and ordered our Totonacs to round up as many civilians as possible. He then ordered that they be mutilated by cutting off their noses, ears, arms, feet and testicles. *Teopixquia*, for that is the Azteca name for papas or priests, were thrown to their deaths from the tops of their teocallis. Years later, Cortés testified that these things were the doings of our allies, but my informant, who was Valente Solís, heard the Caudillo give the order to Aguilar and Doña Marina. They, in turn, transmitted the order to the Totonacs who carried out the orders with much rejoicing.

Cortés' methods bore fruit. The next day, enemy tamanes arrived with three hundred fowls and two hundred baskets of tortillas. As events revealed, however, such gifts were meant to lull us into complacency. Shortly afterward a mixed Tlaxcaltec and Otomi army—greater in numbers than that seen in our previous desperate battle—assembled on the plain. They were ordered in the colors of their various regiments. The enemy's army marched with a blaring of trumpets and conches, the shrill music of flutes and the deep chants of warriors.

Their religion was different from that of Mexico and their papas were clad in Dominican white. These pranced in front of their army, accompanied by the deep, rhythmic boom of drums. Every one of us, including the most severely wounded, prepared ourselves for the impact.

"*Los soldados de la España Santísima,*" cried Cortés as his horse pranced in front of our exhausted men, "the enemy is legion but God is our shield. Even so we cannot afford to let the heathen get close this time. Caballeros, hold your lanzas short and strike at their heads. Keep moving and do not stop to spear a downed warrior. Musketeers and crossbowmen, aim well and make each shot count. Espadas, strike them low and in the bowels. Kick your blade loose if you must. Above all else, keep your formation tight—do not let them break into you." To impress the men with the gravity of the moment, Cortés broke into his favorite Latin phrase: "*Alea iacta est.*"

The rest I barely remember. There were clouds of smoke penetrated by crossbow bolts, stones, and darts. There were shouted orders, yells of triumph, screams of the wounded and the rattle of death accompanied by the sucking sounds of swords and spears pulled from living flesh.

A mass of elite warriors clad in the skins of beasts surged against my part of the line. Our line held, bent dangerously and then buckled. We tried to hold them but, without warning, our line burst asunder. Instantly, the enemy was among us, wounding six of my men. I defended myself against five bronze-skinned bravos. As usual, they aimed for my legs and arms, and two tried to take me alive. Bebidor pierced the chest of one and the abdomen of another and slashed the leg of a third. The others withdrew as I hacked at Indios unwise enough to have penetrated our line.

A short distance away, savages surrounded the two Ordaz sisters. They were armed as espadas and were fighting back-to-back. They used their swords and shields with brutal skill as they defended themselves, chopping down warrior after warrior until the ground under their feet was muddy with blood. I tried to fight my way to their sides but was prevented from doing so by the masses of the enemy. From nowhere, their brother, Diego de Ordaz himself, appeared in the midst of the enemy. He was mounted on his black and white warhorse and he was screaming like an animal.

He anchored his lance, spurred his horse and bent low in the saddle. The enemies' backs were exposed to Diego as they concentrated on capturing the Ordaz women. Many died before they knew they were dead. Ordaz was following orders. He aimed his lance high and pumped the weapon back-and-forth and even side-to-side. Heads clattered and disappeared abruptly when impacted by his spear. The Ordaz sisters, given breathing space, became even more ferocious. They shouted in triumph and butchered any warrior foolish enough to challenge them. I, along with my men, was able to fight my way to their sides and, together, we formed the nucleus on which our battle line reestablished itself.

Disaster was but a heartbeat away and, if the enemy had maintained their assault, we would have been finished. Just then I noticed that one group of Indios, identifiable by their green and black feathers, were retreating. Given this reprieve, we were able to close our line and assaulted our now unsupported enemy. They panicked and ran. Later we were to learn that our salvation was the gift of tribal jealousy. Chichimecatecle, the deputy of Xicotencatl the Younger, pulled his warriors out of the line. Chichimecatecle, who was an altogether inferior man, did this out of jealousy. Otherwise, we all would have died and Cortés would have gone down in history as another common fool.

Many were wounded. The injured were treated with the oil of dead men just as I had instructed at Tobasco. With interest, I saw that Francesca de la Barca in her role as camp physician was collecting and trying out Indio fat which she later used, when hot, to cauterize bleeding wounds, and, when cool, to sooth superficial wounds. As I watched her, I realized that I wasn't feeling well. I recognized the early symptoms of tertian fever.

"Let me see how your chest is doing, Señor de la Peña," Francesca ordered.

"*No se preocupa de me. Mira!* I can move my arm freely. Today's fighting loosened it up."

"I'm sure it did. Now don't waste my time. Remove your armor."

I didn't argue and pulled off my breastplate. I winced as she pulled at my dressing. An odor of pestilence rose from my dressing.

"Mortification," she whispered. "Give me your knife."

I handed her my knife, which I had not had time to clean properly. She wiped it clean on her dress. "Lay back."

I did as I was told. She knelt beside me with the knife poised above my chest. "This is going to hurt."

Both of us gritted our teeth as she carefully brought the knife down to my chest. Knowing what was coming, I did what I always did when I knew I must face an unavoidable ordeal—I pretended that my body belonged to someone else. The pain grew and blossomed into a crescendo of fire...but...the pain, as terrible as it was, belonged to a stranger. I breathed more easily as hot liquid flowed down my armpit. Francesca pushed on my wounds with her fist, forcing out the last drops of corruption. She then used cotton padding, soaked in oil, to clean out any remaining pus. The pain almost penetrated my defenses—she never noticed.

"Here's the problem." She picked at the thick, bloody fluid. "I wish I'd noticed it when you were first wounded—some of the padding was stuck in your wound." She showed me fibers matted with red-yellow pus.

"You're right." I was still trying to distance myself "I don't know why it is that a wound rarely heals if foreign material gets into a wound. It's especially true of musket wounds. I remember once in Ita...."

"I think I'll leave your wound open to the air. That way it has a better chance of staying open and clean."

"But the Caudillo has ordered us to stay in arm...."

"Your case is an exception. Besides dead men make terrible soldiers. Just ask Morón— he's lying just over there, all stiff and cold." Francesca, whose face had been neutral during the surgery, now turned savage. "Cortés ordered him to fight—a man like that—he collapsed before he could even get into the line. You are not, under any circumstances, to go into battle without my approval. *Entiende?* I will not have another preventable death on my conscience, even if it yours, Rodrigo de la Peña."

The woman had no rest for, after our more recent battle, we had sixty more wounded as well as another soldier killed. All of our horses were also wounded. Our situation— considering the fact that we were besieged—had grown worse.

Burgos, Castilla-León

Mendoza's forehead wrinkled. "There's something I have never quite understood. From my studies and, now by your testimony, there was almost always a great disproportion in wounded to those killed. In this case, for example, the ratio was sixty to one."

"You're quite right, Padre. There was, in fact, almost always a disproportion and that disproportion was to our advantage. Even the wounds that we suffered were predominantly minor."

"As you mentioned, your enemies were not fighting to kill."

"Good, Padre! You're actually listening to what I have been saying. In European battles the ratio of wounded to killed is usually two or three to one. The Azteca, unlike most European soldiers, didn't fight to kill, only to wound and capture. Also, their weapons, which were made almost exclusively of wood and stone, were deflected by our shields and armor. Our wounds were mostly to our arms and legs and, even then, they were usually minor. The reason for this was their choice of weapons. The maquahuitl, for instance, although heavy and embedded with sharp itzli stones, was designed to slice, producing a large but superficial wound. Many of their long lances and spears showed a similar complex design. Some of their spearheads were of solids tone and copper but most of them were of wood carved in the shape of a leaf with multiple fragments of itzli embedded along the edges. These weapons were not designed for deep penetration but for shallow slices."

Mendoza questioned further. "Yet even a superficial wound, if it becomes corrupted, may be fatal. Was this common?"

"Mortification is more of a danger in low, tropical places. For example, many of the soldiers wounded at Tabasco had wounds that became corrupt and most of these men died. Our wars against the Tlaxcalteca and later the Mexica were waged in the mountains or in the high valley that the Mexica called *Anahuac*. The weather was usually cool and dry, which favors the healing of wounds. Certainly wounds did mortify but when they were drained and properly cleaned, they usually healed.

We found, however, that itzli barbed weapons had their own special evil. Even though they were easily shattered by Toledo steel, if they did find their way into the flesh, they oftentimes broke into pieces. All of these fragments had to be located and removed if the soldier was to expect a full recovery. Otherwise the soldier sickened as his healed-over wound reddened and swelled. Sometimes, the swelling would burst, discharging foul pus along with shards of the hidden itzli and any threads of clothing or filth that may have been forced into the wound by the initial blow. The best policy, however, was to wait until the right moment, pierce and drain the wound and scrape away any corruption and foreign material from the wound."

The old Bishop went on, remembering his treatment of wounds long ago. "It is important, however, to know that right time to cut. If done too early, and the pocket of pus has not yet formed, the surgeon can actually spread the corruption with fatal consequences. If done too late, the wound may not burst spontaneously, and the soldier not only sickens, he dies."

"Judging by results of your expedition, your physician—Pedro López—must have been adequate to his job."

"López?" the Bishop snorted. "He was as useless as teats on a fish. Early on we learned that the Mexica had a cerveza that they made from the maguey cactus—it is called octli or pulque. Wisely, Cortés ordered that no one was to drink this brew. López insisted however, that we keep a supply to ease the pain of the wounded. Cortés acquiesced with the result that López, who was known to have been a useless sot in Cuba, became even more useless in Mexico.

Later, while we were in *Tenochtitlan*, López built a secret distillery. From the octli he made an evil brew that has, as I have since learned, become popular amongst the Indios and even some of the Españoles." The old man shook his white head. "López' gift to the world—it has ruined more men than *la viruela*. Other than that, López was a man totally without quality. He was not even much good at cutting hair. The medical treatment that we received was mostly from the women. Having learned surgical techniques in far-off Italia, I taught Francesca as well as some of the interested soldiers some of my skills. I'd like to think that my knowledge saved the lives of many of our men—it may have even saved our expedition."

Mendoza smiled. "A curious boast, Your Grace, in that you believe that the Conquest was a thing of the Devil."

The ancient priest smiled right back. "*Homo sum, humani nihil a me alienum est*—all of us labor for Satan. Even when we do things that most men think are good, evil often triumphs."

"Assuming for a moment that you are right, Your Grace, how might a person know that the good things he does promotes the ultimate good?"

"He can't."

"Come now, Your Grace. There are surely a few things that have no potential for evil. A parent, for example, who devotes himself to a sick child."

The ancient priest studied his hands. "If the child should die, you may be right. The parents' efforts, although they may have been futile, produced nothing of evil. If the child should live, however—the rare child will mature into a monster. The parents' attempt to do good will then have ultimately produced evil. We veer from our topic. Shall we go on?

The two dead soldiers were buried deep and secretly, for Cortés did not want the enemy to know that Castilians could die. That night I grew feverish as I lay on the cold soil in lee of a great stone. Francesca, who had been checking the wounded well into the night, found me lying huddled for warmth. I was shivering and covered with sweat.

She knelt beside me and, although the dark was relieved only by the light of campfires, I could see that her face was care-worn.

"Rodrigo, how long have you been like this? You should have called me."

My teeth were chattering so violently that I could barely get out the words. "B...d...don't worry. It's not the wound—I know the signs—it's the fever. I got it in Cuba and now I pay its price whenever I get down in condition. I'll be all right. Don't worry. I'll be all right."

She didn't argue and disappeared into the dark but appeared, minutes later, with four tamanes. "We need to get you out of the wind. They'll carry you to my shelter."

I didn't protest. My shaking chill had turned into burning heat as I tried to strip off the few clothes that I wore. Someone restrained my hands and I remember nothing else.

Chapter 51

Later, after I recovered from my confusion, I learned what had happened. Ambassadors arrived from *Tenochtitlan* professing friendship and distributing gifts. They warned us of the treachery of the Tlaxcalans and warned us that we should withdraw from this country. They also told Cortés that he should return to the coast, citing the usual hazards of travel to *Anahuac*. Afterwards, we also received fifty Tlaxcalteca who were a little too friendly. The Totonacs, however, noticing their suspicious behavior, told Cortés that the men were spies. He seized some and put them to the torture. They informed the Caudillo that Xicotencatl planned a night attack. Cortés then grabbed all of these would-be ambassadors, tied their arms behind their backs and cut off hands, thumbs, ears and noses and strung them around their necks like pendants.

The mutilated Indios huddled in front of our leader. "Tell them, Doña Marina," Cortés said, "that they must warn their masters that we Castilians never sleep and can divine their every trick."

Marina, cool and aloof in her white doeskin dress, translated every word.

"Now tell them, My Lady," -Cortés looked at his woman fondly- "any spies that attempt to enter our camp again will be burned alive."

● ● ●

That night, Cortés, active as usual, prepared for the expected attack. He gathered all of his men together including the sick and wounded. I learned later that the Caudillo, accompanied by Javier de la Concha, came up to her shelter and demanded that I accompany the attack. I remember nothing of it. I was told that I tried to get up but Francesca lost her temper and I returned to my bed.

"I'm afraid I must insist, my dear," Cortés lisped. "We will need every man."

"Look at him—he can't even stand. You can't have him."

"The cowardly cabrón," Concha snarled, "hiding behind a woman's skirt." He removed his sword from its sheath. "I'll bet he stands up fast enough when I shove this up his ass."

Francesca blocked the entrance of her shelter with her body.

She made her appeal to the Caudillo, knowing that talking to Concha was pointless. "Examine him yourself. If he leaves this hut he's a corpse. He's of no use to you now but, as you know, when he is fit he is one of your best fighters."

"What you don't seem to realize, Señora," Cortés argued gently, "is that our situation is truly desperate. If we don't prevail tonight, Rodrigo's future services, no matter how meritorious, will be pointless. We need him tonight. Even if he can't fight, his mere presence in the line may dissuade a few of our foes. I want him."

"No!"

Cortés paused to consider. "I see that you are adamant, señora. Still my need is no less than your own. As they say, *no solo de pan vive el hombre*—a man lives not by bread alone. It seems that we have some grounds for negotiation."

"Negotiation?"

"The man's life is valuable to you, is it not?"

Francesca thought quickly, "All of our people are valuable."

"Of course but knowing the plight of this particular soldier, perhaps you might be willing to...well...to favor your Caudillo with your company. My needs, after all, go beyond the mere military."

She shrugged. "*Porque no, Caudillo*? What's it to me. One man is as good as another,"

Cortés frowned at the implication. "Rodrigo may stay where he is. I will call later."

"I can hardly wait, my Caudillo."

Concha spoke before he was out of earshot of Francesca. He wanted her to hear his words. "I envy you, Caudillo. That one's a real wildcat. I'd be willing to wager that she'll leave a few marks on your back."

Cortés laughed, "I'll leave my marks on her as well. You can depend on it."

●●●

The battle was not quite as desperate as predicted. The Tlaxcaltec forces, after a few gunshots and charges, evaporated into the night. During the next several days I was still weak but I started to regain the use of my mind. Francesca sensed my recovery but still thought I was out of my wits. At night she would wrap herself around me as if trying to warm a small child. Once, I felt her lips on my throat.

It aroused me.

Startled, she jumped up—she hadn't realized that I had regained my senses.

"You're feeling better, Rodrigo. I'm so pleased. Soon you may return to your own quarters."

That night, I felt better. Francesca fed me a stew prepared from the flesh of captured fowls. Several men arrived at her hut.

"Can Rodrigo talk? We'd like to speak with the two of you." The speaker was Alonso de Grado, my fellow Regidor. He was one of the older men in the army and owned a rich encomienda in Cuba.

"Yes. We both can speak. What is it?"

De Grado looked uncomfortable. "We know that both of you have had some trouble with the Caudillo and we thought that you might want to listen to what we have to say."

I was unaware of trouble with Cortés. I'd been senseless during his visit.

"Go on," Francesca said.

"The expedition is doomed," he said. "Since we left Cuba we've lost fifty-five men dead. Most of the rest of us have been wounded, some of us more than once. We aren't mutineers but we reckon that if we can get enough like-minded people on our side, we can convince the Caudillo to return to the coast, rebuild a couple of ships and get us back to Cuba while still a few of us are left alive."

"But I'll lose my investment," Francesca argued.

De Grado nodded. "Your investment will not seem very important to you as these dirty savages are taking their pleasure with you just before they butcher and devour you. Can't you see what's happened? We came here because we believed the Totonacs when they claimed that the Tlaxcalans would be eager to be our allies. Instead we're about to be annihilated by these same people. If, by some miracle, we should survive them, how do we stand any chance against the Mexicans who are many times more powerful?"

I thought on de Grado's words. "It has been tough but a retreat may be more hazardous than an advance. I can't lend you my complete support but I will support your putting the question to the Caudillo himself."

"And you, señora?" de Grado asked.

"I feel the same."

"Good, but Don Rodrigo I know that you have been out of your senses for days. I feel duty bound to inform you that Javier de la Concha has called you *un hombre fuera de honor*—a coward."

"*Qué!*" I raised myself on my elbow, hot blood flushing my face.

"And, my pardon to the Señora," he went on, "the Caudillo is boasting to all who will listen that Señora de la Barca is to warm his bed. He tricked her into the promise by threatening to use you in battle when you were too ill to defend yourself."

I fell back. My teeth clenched in fury.

Francesca's voice was ice. "You didn't need to mention this, señor—I know how to deal with pigs," she said.

"Before we meet with the Caudillo, I thought it would be a good idea if Don Rodrigo learned the truth about Cortés and Concha."

"Thank you, Señor de Grado," I said. "I truly appreciate the information." My mind was on fire. "I ask for only one other thing. Wait three days before confronting the Caudillo. I must regain some of my strength."

"What are you thinking of, Rodrigo?" Francesca interrupted. "It will be a week or more before you are strong. Besides, he has too many friends."

"Three days will be enough. Will you give them to me, Señor de Grado?"

Chapter 52

I spent the next two days in Francesca's hut. But, now that I was fully alert, she slept away from me. In the corner—I remember her closeness and the warmth of her body. I recovered my strength quickly and, by the end of the second day I was nearly normal.

"So good to see you, Rodrigo." Cortés shook my hand like a long lost friend. "For a time I was afraid we might lose you."

Francesca, de Grado, José Magdaleno, Paco Migues and thirty other men were gathered on the ground in front of Cortés. All of the Captains, including de Concha, stood behind the Caudillo.

"Now tell me what this is all about," Cortés said.

De Grado was the spokesman and spoke as bluntly as he dared, "Many of us think it was a mistake to have scuttled the ships—not even Alexander or Caesar tried anything like this. Most of us were never consulted about it and now we've learned the whole thing was a farce. We tempt God. Considering our losses and considering that most, if not all, of us can look forward to a brutal death in these lands, we ask that you to reassess our situation. We believe that the wisest policy would be to return to the coast, rebuild two or three ships and return to Cuba for reinforcements."

Alvarado lifted his lip in a sneering reply but Cortés stopped him with a look. "Well spoken, Alonso. You bring up good points, all of which I have carefully considered. You are quite right about Caesar and Alexander. As great as they were they were never as bold as we are. Because of this, our names will go down in history and will, if I am an accurate judge, be written larger than those of all previous conquerors. I know our enemies seem insurmountable but I also know that God and his angels are fighting at our side. Every night they whisper the old proverb in my ear. 'Los mas los Moros, los mas los botines—the more the Moors, the greater the spoil.' Our riches will be great, señor, both in this world and in the next."

"Besides," Cortés went on flawlessly, "if we were to retreat the very stones will rise up against us. Those of our allies, who have been our friends, must declare war against us. We will never have time to build additional ships. We will only have time to die. Better to bear up manfully and trust to our faith in God. Then, Providence willing, we will advance and conquer the heathen and deliver all of this land to Christ and Our Lady."

De Grado replied with less confidence, "My name in a history book, no matter how large, will be thin consolation to my widow and children. Perhaps if we moved quickly to the coast before the Indios expect us. What do you think, Don Rodrigo?"

I couldn't help but notice that Concha gave me a hungry look—or maybe the look was for Francesca. I stood up slowly and for seconds stared directly at Concha. He grinned right back at me.

"Well, Rodrigo?" Cortés asked.

"I agree with you, Caudillo. It's too late to return. We may all leave our bones here but now we have no choice." Cortés looked relieved. "That's not why I came here, though."

Now he didn't look quite so comfortable.

"Everyone here knows about it, including you, Señor Cortés. Your trusted Captain, Javier de la Concha, is a very brave man."

Cortés was dumbfounded. "Yes, Rodrigo, we are all aware of Señor de la Concha's courage but, then again, we're all brave—Don Javier hardly needs you to sing his praises."

"I disagree, Caudillo. I would like to compliment Javier on his great courage—it takes a courageous man to call me a coward when I'm flat on my back."

There was a stunned silence. Even Cortés was caught flat-footed. Francesca started to stand up and Concha jerked his sword halfway from its scabbard. Cortés looked me hard in the eye. "There will be no dueling in my army!"

"Do you call me a cobarde, Javier?" —I pulled my sword from its sheath— "Do you have the testicles to call me a coward to my face?"

"That will be quite enough, Señor de la Peña," hissed Cortés.

"Come now, Javier. Let me hear you say it. If you cannot say it then, with all in attendance, you publicly confess your own cowardice."

Cortés tried to override my words by shouting. "Say nothing, Javier! Señor de la Concha is a loyal soldier and will not be taunted into a duel. His honor remains unblemished."

"Unblemished? I want all of you to look at him."–I took one step forward–"He fears me—look at him tremble. *El es la definición de la cobardía!*"

Cortés got up, his face flushed with anger. "This assembly is dismissed. Everyone with the exception of my—Regidor—Don Rodrigo."

The assembly dispersed although de la Concha backed away but slowly, never taking his eyes off me.

"You incredible fool!" Cortés shouted, "You risk the unity of my... our... expedition to settle personal feuds."

I peered into Cortés' amber eyes. "I risk nothing. To permit your Captain to insult me in your presence and the presence of others, risks our enterprise. It is behavior unbecoming of a commandante."

"You dare question me."

"Yes, I dare question you, my shining Caudillo. You've managed to surround yourself with ignorant boot-lickers. It's no wonder that your decisions are weak."

"Your statements are mutinous, señor. I will not tolerate this kind of ..."

"For example," —I interrupted—"your rather unfortunate decision to put pressure on the Señora de la Barca..."

Cortés face, which had been red, now blanched with pure hatred. "You arrogant little..."

"Of course the Lady means nothing to me but the success of our mission does. Doña Marina, however, is absolutely essential to the furtherance of our cause....if she were to become..."

"Keep Doña Marina out of it!"

"Of course, Caudillo, but have you noticed how the Indios have their own pet name for her—they call her *Malinche*. Not only that—but they also refer to you by the same name. It is almost as if they do not distinguish between the two of you. If Doña Marina should grow unhappy with you, who knows what she's capable of? Who knows what will happen?"

"You think you can threaten me? You don't know who you are dealing with!"

I bent over so that my face was close to that of the Caudillo. "I know exactly who I am dealing with. Keep Concha away from me. You may enjoy his company but I can't stand the stink of him."

Burgos, Castilla-León

"Excelencia, I can understand your unhappiness with Cortés but, considering your circumstances, wasn't it foolish, even stupid, to deal with him so bluntly?"

"Perhaps, Padre, but I calculated my chances and knew that I was taking no additional risk by baiting this particular lion in his lair."

"You don't think so? He'd already hanged Escudero, another man he thought of as an enemy."

"True but, as soon as Cortés became fixed upon Francesca de la Barca, my fate was certain. Have you never heard of Uriah?"

"But Uriah, the Hittite, was Bathsheba's husband. You were only Doña Francesca's patient."

"Once I entered her hut, sick though I was, Cortés assumed

that I was her lover. Previously he thought that he had time to seduce Francesca but once I came into her hut Cortés moved—as was his nature—decisively. He planned his assault almost as carefully as he planned his assault on *Tenochtitlan*. The only difference was that, in the case of *Tenochtitlan*, only a weakling stood in his path. Francesca, however, was not Moctecuzoma. I had no doubt that Cortés would arrange my death, in which case his problem would have been cut in half."

"But your open opposition to Cortés put you at even more risk."

"No. By confronting him openly, I protected myself from any of his orders that would have been clear-cut homicide. He was dangerous, but he didn't have enough power over our ranks to have committed obvious murder—such an act would have been more effective at destroying his leadership than if he had lost a major battle. I still had to fear assassination but, then again, I would have had this worry in any event."

"What can I say?" Mendoza looked at the frail old man as if seeing him for the first time. "You're still alive."

"And Cortés is not. He has been quite dead these many years."

Padre Mendoza fell silent.

The ancient priest, his eyes gleaming with its cold blue light, went on. "You see, Cortés and I are, in all too many ways, the same person. He never forgave and—neither do I. Cortés owed a debt to all of the Españoles and even the Indios whose blood soaked the ground of Mexico. It took a very long time but I would like to believe that my shadow blighted Cortés' last years."

"But he died of old age."

"Indeed." The ancient priest's faint smile was the rizor sardonicus of a corpse.

Felipe Galindo, who was a one-time musician approached me. "Rodrigo? Have you heard the news? There's a party of cacique's headed this way and it looks like they want to talk peace."

"How many are there?"

"Forty or fifty, with several chiefs, and they're not carrying weapons. I think the Caudillo has pulled it off. *Es un milagro de Dios.*"

"Don't get too excited, Felipe—these Indios are slippery."

The ambassadors soon arrived in the camp and I could see by their dress that four were indeed great nobles. Cortés greeted them in front of his hut. The Tlaxcalteca bowed their heads, which is their sign for peace. They then approached Cortés, touching the ground with one hand, kissing the earth, prostrating themselves three times on the ground and burning copal. A tall man strode forward.

"I am Xicotencatl, the son of Xicotencatl the Elder." Despite his rank, the general was clad only in a simple loincloth made of coarse fiber. He was broad shouldered and aged about thirty-five. He bore himself proudly but his face was scarred and his black eyes were lifeless. "We have come to make peace with you. Our sorcerers told us that you were in the employ of the Mexica, our mortal enemies. These sorcerers lied and we have sacrificed them to *Matlalcueyeh*—the Green Woman. We wish to beg your pardon because we now know that you are mighty warriors and teotoh who spit on the Mexican dogs. We desire to make an alliance with you against *Cholula* and *Tenochtitlan*."

Cortés made a pretense of anger. "We entered your country desiring only peace, yet your armies attacked us three times. We grieve for all of your people that we have been forced to kill but the blame of it rests entirely on your head. For these offenses you deserve nothing better than the destruction of all of *Tlaxcala*."

Xicotencatl didn't react.

Cortés went on, "We Castilians are a kind people and are prepared to forgive you. We thank you for the food that you now bring us. I ask that you return and bring your leaders and elders to our camp. I will then negotiate an eternal bond of peace and friendship between our two peoples."

The nobles departed with the usual green beads. They left us guajolotes and other food as well as four women to grind our maíz and some men to chop wood.

Chapter 53

Burgos, Castilla-León
February 16, 1581 6:45 A.M.

Mendoza entered the dictation room accompanied by his glowering guards. The Bishop was already seated, facing the fire. He didn't turn around for a full ten minutes and, when he did, he barely glanced at the younger man.

"You look quite well this morning, Padre, better, I think, than I've seen you before."

"Thank you, Your Grace. It has been some time since we met... ten days. Based on my present starvation diet, I've probably lost weight."

"And you're better off for it. I must apologize for my delay, however. I would myself like to see our work proceed rapidly but *Santa Iglesia* will not be denied. My personal interests are entirely secondary to those of the Holy Office."

Mendoza shook his head and then sat down.

The old man went on, "I hope you understand that, although your present service may seem onerous at times—you are serving God."

"What?"

"Is not God distinguished from Satan by Truth and, by serving me, are you not serving the Truth?"

Mendoza leapt back to his feet. "To even speak to me of the truth is an abomination. Your heresies are those of the infernal pit."

The old man's face cracked into a grin. "Yes...yes....yes. Shall we go on?"

"The great Moctecuzoma now wishes to become a vassal of your Emperor Carlos. He will give Emperor Carlos an annual tribute of gold, silver, chalchihuitl, fine cotton cloth and whatever goods that he may desire." The speaker was a tall, very dark Mexican clad in a brightly patterned cloak. The Mexicans were worried about a Castilian peace with *Tlaxcala*.

"Does this mean that Moctecuzoma will now welcome us into *Tenochtitlan?*" Cortés asked innocently.

"Our Lord would like to meet you but he has not been well. The road, moreover, is tedious and dangerous. It is best that you return to your village."

Cortés frowned. "I thank your Lord, for his presents and especially for his offer of vassalage. I'm so pleased that I would like a few of you, the representatives of Moctecuzoma, to stay with us as we conclude our peace with *Tlaxcala.*"

The ambassadors looked nervously at one another as Cortés went on. "The Tlaxcalans will not dare to harm you as long as you are under our protection. I think it would be good for you to see how we Castilians conclude a real peace. We'll prepare shelters for you."

Within a short time, Xicotencatl arrived with fifty of his greatest nobles. They were arrayed in red and white finery, which are the colors of Xicotencatl's people. Seeing the Mexican ambassadors, Xicotencatl's nostrils flared.

"Don't be alarmed, Don Xicotencatl. The presence of these Mexicans does not diminish my love for your people. Peace is a good policy for everyone."

"Not between the Tlaxcalteca and these tlalatl." Xicotencatl turned to speak directly to the Mexica, for they both spoke the same language. "For us, there can never be peace. I will not rest until the last Mexica man, woman and child suffers on the stone of the Green Woman."

Xicotencatl turned to address Cortés again, "The Mexica and the men of Cholula have fought against us for more years than can be remembered. Not only do they commit the sacrilege of worshiping false gods, they have forced us into poverty. We used to be rich but we now have no gold, cotton or even salt for our meals. The greatest offense that these tzcintli have committed against us is their claim that *Tlaxcala* survives as a nation merely for the sake of flowery wars to collect warrior victims for their gods. This is a lie! We survive because the Mexica despite their numbers, do not have the manhood to defeat us."

Xicotencatl continued, "Our elders have held a council and have concluded that you Castilians, against whom we have been unable to prevail, must be teotoh who will protect our women and children from the ravages of these unclean Mexica."

"For many years," Cortés replied, "I have known of the goodness of *Tlaxcala*. It was with deep surprise when your forces so unjustly attacked us. Nevertheless, I gladly forgive you and will seal our friendship with the gift of these precious gems." Cortés gave Xicotencatl a fistful of green and blue beads.

Xicotencatl along with his other chieftains left us with heads bowed in peace.

For minutes, the Mexican ambassador stood in silent arrogance. "I trust you teoteoh are not such fools as to believe these lies."

Cortés raised his eyebrows and said, "Lies?"

"The Tlaxcalteca are famous for their treachery. They could not defeat you fairly on the field of battle, so they trick you with this sham peace. I warn you now—their city is a trap—enter it and you must bleed to their false god."

Cortés threw back his head and forced a great laugh. "We are not in the least bit worried. If they try to ambush us it will please us to kill their people and level their city to the ground. We are therefore not fearful of entering *Tlaxcala* and testing their sincerity."

●●●

For the next days we were treated to the spectacle of both Mexican and Tlaxcalan delegations vying for our favor. The Tlaxcalteca wanted us to proceed immediately to their capital, with the Mexica warning us of our peril should we do so. The Mexica reinforced their warnings with gifts of gold, feathers and jewels but the Tlaxcalteca, who were indeed poor, could compete only with shipments of food.

Cortés, seemingly forgetting his disagreements with me, spoke to me as if to a friend. If the truth be known, he knew his other Captains were fools. He may have hated me, but he valued my opinion and was too clever to express his true feelings.

"What do you think, Rodrigo? These Mexicans are clearly liars themselves but they have a point. The Tlaxcalans would have destroyed us if they could, so why should we trust them now? Is it wise to enter their city?"

"Caudillo, you plan to enter Tenochtitlan, which, if we can trust our informants, is a far more dangerous place than is *Tlaxcala*. If you really want my opinion, I tell you that your scheme to take over Mexico from its capital is madness. A better plan would be to attack *Tenochtitlan* from the shores of its lake. Now that *Tlaxcala* has been defeated, rumors of our invincibility will spread over this land like a mist. All the people who hate the Mexica will flock to us—all they need is Castilian edge and leadership. Let them topple Moctecuzoma and we'll pick up the pieces."

Cortés disagreed. "My plan has the advantage of leaving *Tenochtitlan* and its people intact. You get more milk from a cow that is living than from one that is dead."

"True, but that is assuming that we can milk the cow. From everything that we have heard of the Mexica, I doubt that they'll stand still for it."

Cortés stroked his beard. "Your opinion is noted but you have still not told me what you think about entering *Tlaxcala*."

"I heard their ambassadors. We've convinced them that we can't be defeated. As long as we maintain an impression of strength we have little to fear from them. In the meantime, though, we are under no pressure to move. Both the Mexica and Tlaxcalteca are increasingly worried by our immobility, which works to our advantage—let them twist in the wind."

Cortés nodded and said, "You may be right. For the time being, at least, both of the cows give milk."

●●●

A party of elders arrived in the camp. They were dressed handsomely but, on close inspection, their clothing was made of coarse fiber. I found out later that this fiber is pulled from the great leaves of the maguey cactus, which the Indios grow on dry ground. This clothing was proof that the Mexica were successful in preventing the Tlaxcalteca from trading for either raw cotton or prepared cotton cloth. Nevertheless, the clothing was beautifully made, dyed with bright colors and decorated with the feathers of colorful birds. One wizened, stooped-over viejo who identified himself as the elder Xicotencatl, was the spokesman. He was blind and had to be led to Cortés.

"Malinche, Malinche, we beg your pardon again. If we had known how good you and your teoteoh are, we would have swept the dust from under your feet. You must not believe the Mexica lies. Our people will rejoice when you visit our city."

Cortés grinned and slapped his thigh. "Señor, we thank you

heartily for your invitation and all of the food you have been sending to our camp. We have only delayed our journey to your city because we don't have enough tamanes to push our great metal gods."

Even though the ancient man could not see the nearby cannon, he had clearly heard about them. Cortés led the old man to one of them. The viejo touched the sun-heated metal as if it were holy.

"Why have you not mentioned this before?" The old man spoke solemnly, as befitted the presence of these iron deities. "I'll order help, immediately."

Five hundred warriors and slaves arrived within the hour. The next morning our little army, arrayed defensively, moved slowly toward *Tlaxcala*. Later, Cortés reported that *Tlaxcala* was a city larger than Granada. This may be true but, except for its numerous teocallis, its buildings were unimpressive. Nevertheless, the rooftops and streets were crowded with friendly appearing Indios some of whom offered us bouquets of sweet scented flowers. In this pleasant but suspect environment we were to spend the next twenty-four days.

Our newfound friends led us to great courts completely surrounded by buildings and teocallis. The rooms for our troops had already been prepared. Some rooms were merely sheds, covered by thatch but others were halls decorated with monsters and scenes of bloody sacrifice softened by fresh flowers that perfumed the air. Always the bedding was the same—a mat of maguey fiber with blankets of animal skins.

Our Indio allies, they were quartered nearby—the disgusted Zautlanos returned to their own land. The people of the city were adorned in the dress of their particular tribe, of which there were four. All of their clothing was brightly colored and decorated. Some of the people wore cloaks like Roman togas that were worn over the maxtlatl, or loincloths, that all men wear. Still others wore garments that looked like pantalones. The women wore short white skirts covered by a tunic although poorer women dispensed with the tunic and, much to the delight of our soldiers, went bare-breasted.

Burgos, Castilla-León

"Your Grace, there are many reasons why I developed an early fascination with the Conquest. In part, I'm sure, this is because even though there are many answers, there are still many questions. Here is a case in point. Days earlier, you had waged war on these indígenos, killing many thousands. Each dead warrior inevitably left grieving family and friends. How is it possible that when you entered their city you were greeted with anything other than hatred?"

"A good question, Padre, and, although I was there, I'm not certain that I have the answer. First, however, most of their losses were Otomi who lived in a different part of their realm. Second, because the Indios dragged off their dead and wounded it is likely that we overestimated their losses. Thirdly, and I think most importantly, we were dealing with people who lived in a veritable garden of war. Losses, although they must have caused grief as profound as anywhere else, were simply accepted. In our case, their losses had been sustained over a period of days. In their wars with the Mexica there were losses over generations. Hatred for the Mexica was therefore ingrained in their souls and, when they started to realize that we could help them discharge their rage, they accepted us fully and without reservation. Their welcome for us was not because they had suddenly come to love us. It was because they so loathed their Mexican enemies."

Some of our benefactors were not quite as welcome to us, however. Teopixquia arrived, clad in white cloaks with hoods. Despite the purity of the color, these priests were as filthy and as blood-caked as all the others that we had encountered. Their fingernails were long and curled with black blood clotted beneath them. Their earlobes dripped with blood, for their faith demands that they sacrifice their own blood to their gods. These filthy, ill-smelling men carried braziers of live coals and burned copal in our honor. In response, the next morning, the previous rebel, Fraile Juan Díaz, said mass for the army. Padre Olmedo, who we all preferred, was sick with the fever. Xicotencatl the Elder and another old pilli, for this is the Azteca word for cacique, watched our ritual in approval.

"We have prepared a gift for you, Malinche."

Mats were spread over the tiles and a few poor items of gold and maguey cloth were laid upon them.

"We do not have the wealth of that thief, Moctecuzoma, but we pray that you accept our humble offering."

Cortés, by now realizing that the value of the Tlaxcalteca was far greater than a little gold, replied with all the charm he could muster, "I value these gifts from friends more highly than I would value a room full of Mexican treasure. I accept these things gladly."

"Then," Xicotencatl went on, "we will give you that which is more valuable even than gold, salt and chalchihuitl. We, the nobles of the house of *Tlaxcala*, give you our daughters so that they might bear your children and bind us in eternal friendship. Even I, who am the most respected in this land, offer you my own daughter. She is a beautiful virgin who I trust you will use with pleasure, Malinche." With this Xicotencatl gestured that he would like to touch Cortés, for he couldn't see him. Cortés, with some hesitation, let the old man explore his head, face and body with his hands.

"You are well made, Malinche, and have the bristles on your face of a mighty teotl."

Dozens of women were given to us, some of whom were slaves. Among them were five lovely girls of high birth, one of who was Xicotencatl's daughter.

"We honor your daughters, Xicotencatl," Cortés preached, "but our god, the great Jesus Christ, will not permit us to have sexual intercourse with nonbelievers."

"Ay! Your God must be powerful indeed to keep your tepollin soft when tempted by such women."

"No, viejo, you are mistaken—Castilians are always hard."

"Ee-ya-ya! Our daughters will be happy!"

Cortés went on to give his standard speech about the evils of devils, Hell, sodomy and human sacrifice. He preached of the glories of the Lord, Jesus Christ and his mother, Mary, who was a virgin before, during, and after Christ's birth. He went on to tell them that they must, for the sakes of their souls, forsake their old gods. When Cortés was finished, Fraile Juan Díaz, who had agreed to add his voice to that of Cortés, spoke, "We have seen these cages where you keep your captives. We have seen how you feed and fatten them for your Devils. In the name of the Lord, Jesus Christ, I order that you break these cages and release your victims."

"We hear you, Malinche," the old man said, ignoring Díaz. "Give my people time. You must remember we have worshiped our gods for many generations and they have protected us from disaster. If your gods are as good and as powerful as what you say, my people will finally accept them—in the meantime let us go easy."

Padre Olmedo had dragged himself from his sickbed, fearful that Cortés and Díaz would bring disaster to us all. "The old man is wise, Hernán, and knows his people. Don't force the issue as you did in *Cempoalla*. Take what you can and leave the rest to God."

Cortés' face registered annoyance but he shrugged his shoulders, "And the girls, Xicotencatl?"

"They belong to you, Malinche, and must therefore accept your faith."

The confused girls were promptly baptized and parceled out to the happy soldiers. The five princesses were given to Cortés' favorite Captains. Xicotencatl's daughter, who had clearly been intended for Cortés himself, was handed over to Pedro de Alvarado. Cortés may have thought that he could deceive Doña Marina by dealing with Francesca in person but, in that Doña Marina was his interpreter, Cortés' acceptance of a highborn woman was out of the question. He consented, however, to accept several lower-class girls as naborias, servants. Girls of lower rank did not threaten Doña Marina even if they did share her Caudillo's bed.

"Don Rodrigo, my friend," Cortés said expansively, "I would like to present you with a an especially lovely present." Earlier Cortés had chosen a particular girl and kept her to one side, much to Doña Marina's obvious displeasure.

I looked at the girl up and down. Most of the girls were only thirteen or fourteen but this one was closer to twenty. She refused to look at me directly and would only look at the ground. She was not one of the princesses but she was, by far, the most beautiful of the group. She was tiny and clad in a velvet-soft doeskin and her shiny black hair was tied back in a single long braid that hung below her waist. Her skin was light for a Tlaxcalteca and her eyes, which were large and luminous, brimmed with tears. Unlike most of the other girls, her face wasn't broad and her features were perfect. I couldn't see her body, of course, but her exquisite feet were exposed in open sandals.

"She's quite a prize, Caudillo."

"I thought you'd like her, Rodrigo. Padre Olmedo has christened her Doña Amelía. After all that you've done for us, you deserve a little relaxation."

Relaxation, indeed, I thought. A distance away I could see Francesca de la Barca. Her face was blank.

"I can't accept her."

"Nonsense, Rodrigo. I know she's not one of the princesses but she is, nevertheless, a highborn girl and a virgin. Old Mamaxatzin tells me that she was specially groomed to be the bride of one of their filthy gods—you're saving the girl's life. Somehow the old coot has got it into his head that you're the same god and he insists that you impregnate the girl as soon as possible. You wouldn't want to offend him, would you?"

"You gave Xicotencatl's daughter to Alvarado."

"That's different. I told him that I've sworn to the Lord, Jesus Christ that I will not touch a woman until I have defeated the Mexica. Besides, he knows that Alvarado is my chief lieutenant, so there is no insult—I'm afraid that you must accept the woman. I've already arranged separate quarters for the two of you."

What could I do? "*Sí, Caudillo.*"

● ● ●

The girl was placed in the small room reserved for us but I delayed my visit as long as possible. Grumbling in the dark, some of the womanless soldiers loitered around the plaza.

"Why are you not with your gift?" I hadn't heard Francesca's approach.

Surprised and embarrassed, I didn't know what to say. I wasn't sure why, myself. I held out my hands. "...Cortés."

"I thought so...because of me?"

I looked up at her.

She shook her head and breathed deeply. "Rodrigo, my friend, I don't know you well but I already know you better than you know yourself."

"You think so?"

"You're a man who makes war against himself." She looked away. "Take the girl—you'll be saving her life and maybe your own."

"I am my own man." My bitterness went deeper than my friendship with Francesca. "No one, not even God Almighty, can tell me how I must live or what I must do."

She peered at me closely almost as if she could compel understanding. "I've seen some things during my life, Rodrigo, and I've learned there are certain things that must be accepted as they are." She shook her head sadly. "You are a man and have a man's needs."

I tried to understand. "You've wanted someone to talk to?"

She stared into the shadows and paused before answering. "A woman alone among these...creatures—oh yes, Rodrigo." She hesitated, considering her words. "If you haven't noticed, I am a woman and I have needs, too." She turned on her heels and walked into the darkness.

Chapter 54

Moonlight streamed through the open window and I could see that the girl was standing in the corner of the room. I took no notice and sat down on my mat. The room, whether by the order of Cortés or the instigation of the Tlaxcalteca, had been carefully prepared for our love-making. The blankets were made of lush furs and the skins had been tanned to supple perfection. Flower petals covered the tiles. Portraits on the walls depicted a monster with an enormous phallus assaulting both men and women.

For a long time there was silence except for nearby shrieks as the brides were introduced to the art of Castilian lovemaking. I wondered if the men bothered to remove their armor before attempting copulation. Knowing some of the men, I doubted it.

I heard a soft sound and could see that the girl had taken several steps towards me. Even though the light was not strong I could see that she was trembling. "It's all right, little one, I won't touch you. Go to sleep."

The girl, of course, understood nothing. Instead she started to chant a monotonous tune as she swung her shoulders and shuffled her feet in a practiced cadence. Even so, her eyes were wide in horror and followed my slightest move. Still, she missed not a word nor did her feet miss a beat as she waited for me to claim her. I was perplexed. The girl was inexperienced, true, and was about to be subjected to the vile passions of a pale-skinned teotl even as the other girls shrieked all around her. Still it didn't make much sense. Why the dance and the song?

Burgos, Castilla-León

"What do you make of it, Padre Mendoza?"

Mendoza shrugged. "She was the chosen one of their filthy gods. As far as she was concerned, you were that god. Given her heathen frame of mind, she had every reason to be frightened."

"Yes, but there is even more to it than that. This particular girl had been chosen precisely because of her beauty. As I found out later this girl, as a very small child, was dedicated to the most terrible of their gods. She was petted and pampered and given every privilege. Her skin was anointed with expensive oil and she was adorned with the best clothing—nothing was too good for the bride of the god. She knew exactly what she was supposed to do and she knew exactly what her fate was to be. She knew that, on the last day of her life, exactly what songs she must sing, each gesture she must make, and every step she must take. She knew that, on that day, in the attendance of the brightly feathered nobility and of the chanting, dancing priests, she must break her musical instruments and then she would be stripped naked. She would be beaten, degraded and humiliated before the assembled crowd. She must mount the steps of the templo where, before her consort, the terrible flayed god, *Xipe Totec*, she would be raped by the high priest. She would then be skinned alive, her screams muted by the great throbbing of drums. The papa would then put on her skin like a bloody garment and dance in front of the god."

"Very nice, Excelencia."

"She knew this was to be her fate and, to the extent that anyone can accept such a fate, she accepted it. When old Xicotencatl turned her over to me, however, it changed everything."

"For the better."

"I'd like to think so but, for the girl, it must have seemed worse. Rather than become the consort of a graven image, she was now the property of the white-scarred god himself—who knows what enormities such a god is capable of? All of her teaching and training would have been for exactly nothing. Think of the girl's situation that night. She waited alone in the room anticipating the appearance of her carnivorous lord. He takes his time but she can hear him before he arrives. There are the footsteps, the clank of his armor and the hand on the door. Then he appears in person all clad in metal with his face covered by hair and terrible scars."

"You have quite an imagination, Your Grace."

"Nothing in her life has ever prepared her for such a fate. All she can think to do is to sing the song and dance the dance that would have been her last dance. Somehow, during her performance, I realized something of her predicament. I also knew that I had a problem."

"Problem, Excellency?"

"Given her belief, anything I did was bound to be a mistake. If I attempted to be kind to her, I was only perpetuating the treatment that she had received in preparation to her sacrifice. I would have been prolonging the agony. If I ignored her, she would have interpreted that as heavenly rejection, which would have been devastating. If I seized her, she may have learned that I was interested in something other than her death but I do have my honor—given the circumstances, my body would not have permitted it."

"What did you do?"

"For a time I just watched her as she went through her ritual. She obviously expected me to do something. Having no clue as to what a being such as myself wanted, she pulled her tunic over her head and stood naked before me. By Tlaxcaltec ritual, her disrobement would have preceded her humiliation and death. I can remember that my breath caught in my throat at the sight of her bare body—to think that the Tlaxcaleca would have destroyed such beauty. Nevertheless, I understood the logic for, if you think about it, the logic is also that of the Christians. God must be honored and deserves the very best. God rejected Cain because he offered mere sheaves of grain. Abel's sacrifice was accepted because it was a perfect lamb. The gods require the best. Jesus, God-Man that he was, died on the cross for mankind. All other sacrifices are therefore inferior and unnecessary. The Indios in their ignorance knew nothing of this and continued to sacrifice their very best. This girl was the best that the paganos had to offer and they gave her without a qualm."

I didn't know quite what to do. I neither wanted to terrorize nor reject her so I stepped forward and put my hand on her shoulder—she almost swooned. I put my face close to hers and spoke to her gently even though I knew that she couldn't understand my words. "Relax, my little beauty, I'll do you no harm. You are safe with me and I won't touch you."

I stepped back and sat down on my mat. "Have you ever heard the story of Helen, the most beautiful woman in the world? I thought not. I think you will find it interesting so I'll tell you everything I know."

The girl stopped her chanting but her look of horror only increased.

"Paris, who was a good looking boy, seduced her and carried her off to his home in Holy Ilios. He shouldn't have done such a thing but, then again, how could he help himself for Aphrodite, the Goddess of Love, had tricked him. Unfortunately, Helen was the wife of Menelaus, king of Sparta....."

For the next two hours I told the girl the story of Agamemnon, Achilles and Hector and then went on to tell of the Cid and the great hero, Rolando. At first the girl stood rigidly but then, her strength failing her, she sank to the floor. As my stories droned on, her look of fear subsided and was finally replaced by that of exhaustion. Her eyelids grew heavy. She settled herself on her side and then, as I launched myself into the story of *Amadis de Gaula*, she actually fell asleep. I waited until she was breathing heavily and covered her with her own tunic.

I woke before sunrise and discovered that the girl was sleeping close to me, her head on my leg. She roused when I started to get up and, realizing how near she was to me, she jerked back almost as if I had struck her. Her eyes, which had been fearful, now looked confused.

I reached out and touched her cheek with my fingers. She didn't move. I smiled as pleasant a smile as I could and told her what a wonderful person she was.

"I don't reject you, little one. Your god finds you beautiful, indeed." I leaned forward, brushing her cheek with my lips while stroking her hair with my hand. "This will be enough for now because I don't want you to be frightened of me." I took her hand and brought it up to my eyes, nose, ears and beard. I breathed on the palm of her hand so that she could feel the warmth of my breath, "See. I'm just a man." I held my own hand out in front of her and traced its vessels with my fingertip. Then I took her hand and traced the vessels. "Nearly the same, little one. We are nearly the same."

The look on her face changed as she cautiously marked the angle of my jaw with her fingertip. "Wonderful. You're starting to understand." I kissed her cheek again and smiled at her. Her look was questioning but she was no longer afraid. She looked down at her exposed body and suddenly seemed embarrassed. She reached down, picked up her tunic and quickly slipped it back on.

"You're a bright little thing and to think they would have turned you into garbage. I am at your disposal, My Lady, I look forward to seeing you later."

●●●

Ricardo Fuentes was talking to two of the other men. "How did it go for you, Rodrigo? *Hombre*! I didn't know how bad I needed it but I'll tell you it was quite a relief. A hand is no substitute for a woman."

"I didn't know that Cortés gave you a woman."

Fuentes laughed, "He didn't but he did give one to Martínez here. Unlike some of you, Martínez isn't selfish. He shared his woman with half a dozen of us."

"Martínez must be a very generous fellow."

"Well—he is—but we did give him a couple of pesos."

Chapter 55

That day we met in council with Xicotencatl, old Maximaxtzin and some of the other elders. He told us of Mexico and he told us of *Tenochtitlan*—the city was huge and was mostly built on the water. He told of the causeways that could be cut by the removal of wooden bridges. He told us that most of the houses were inaccessible except by boat. He told us that fresh water was piped into *Chapultepec*, put into canoes and sold in the city."

"Where is this *Chapultepec* and why must the Mexicans use this water? Is not their city built on water?"

"*Chapultepec* is on the nearby mainland. It is to here that the Mexica bring their water by means of a great cave. The Tenochca must use this water because the water of the lake is not good to drink. There is too much salt."

Cortés was interested. "It is totally undrinkable?"

"I am not certain but I think those who drink it become sick. I do know that the water from the mountains is better."

"Fascinating."

"Let me tell you a funny story, Malinche. Years ago, when the Mexica first opened their big pipe they did not know what they were doing. They filled up the lake and flooded their city."

Cortés laughed out loud. "That's very good. Do you think it might be possible for us to do the same thing?"

"I do not know, Malinche, but it is an amusing idea. If it were possible to do so, the riches of *Tenochtitlan* might be lost to the lake."

"Hmm."

"Let me tell you another interesting thing. Many years ago *Tlaxcala* was inhabited by giants. They were evil people so our ancestors rose against them and killed them all—here is the proof of it." Several slaves brought in a huge bone. "This is the leg bone of one of these people. See the size of it."

The bone was the one that extends between the hip and the knee. It was rotten and had a foul odor but, even so, it was enormous. It was longer than I am tall.

"Malinche, there is an itzli point embedded in this bone." One of the slaves pointed to a projecting black stone. "Indeed, there must have been a great war to destroy these giants."

Cortés ran his hands over the enormous bone. "If you will let me have this thing, Xicotencatl, I will send it back to our Emperor Carlos. He will be amazed."

Burgos, Castilla-León

"What did you make of this great bone, Your Grace? The Philistines produced Goliath but the possessor of this bone must have been even larger."

"I don't think it belonged to a man. The bone is that of some enormous animal. Perhaps, as our Conquistadores explore all of the recesses of the Nueva España, they will find this mighty beast. I certainly hope so, for it must be larger than the greatest elephant that ever existed."

"But where was the bone found?"

"The Indios said that they dug it from deep in the ground."

"Then, Excelencia, both you and the Indios must be mistaken. The bone is from some giant mole."

"Malinche, I know that you and the rest of your teotoh will march on our enemies in *Tenochtitlan*. I believe you should march by way of our friends in *Huexotxinco*, otherwise you must travel to *Cholula*."

"Why should this be a problem?"

The Cholulans are the ancient allies of the Mexica and are, if possible, even more treacherous. They are numerous and warlike and have attacked us many times. If it were not for the fact that they were so stupid and let us know of their plans well in advance, there would be nothing left of us."

Cortés stroked his beard. "If we bypass *Cholula*, we will leave a powerful enemy in our rear. Is this wise?"

For a moment the old man was caught without words. Apparently strategic considerations were a minor component of Mexican wars. "No matter what your decision, *Tlaxcala* will support you with many warriors. Now that you have taken our daughters to be the mothers of our children, we are of one blood. Your defeat is our defeat. Your victory is our victory.

I want you to wait before you march. The gods of the great mountain, *Popocatapetl*, are angry and spew their smoke and flame into the heavens. It is a bad omen," he said.

"Yes, Xicotencatl, we have seen the fire on the mountain but this is a bad omen for the Mexica, not for us." —Cortés thought carefully before going on— "I will send a few of our teules to the mountain to prove that it is not offended by us."

"Diego!" Cortés pointed at Diego de Ordaz. "I want you and old Hector Herrera to climb up the volcano." Cortés thought a moment. "Take de la Peña with you. I'll ask the Tlaxcalteca to send guides with you. If I know these superstitious cabrónes they'll refuse to go far. All you have to do is to climb until the guides are out of sight, wait a while, and then return. That should be good enough."

●●●

We were accompanied by two chieftains from *Huexotzinco*, which lies closer to the mountain than does *Tlaxcala*. Even before leaving the city, they warned us that it would not be possible to climb higher than half-way for the tremors and flame were more than a person could bear. Even so, we climbed the mountain, picking our way between huge stones that had been discharged during previous eruptions. Halfway up, there were several small cues that had been built when the mountain was silent. All of these structures were stained with dried blood for the Indio answer to all things that they did not understand was human victims.

Our guides refused to go further and indicated by signs that we all should turn back. We called them cowards and continued on to the summit, despite the fact that ash was drifting through the air and small, very light stones were pelting around us. We protected ourselves by placing our shields over our heads.

The roar of the inferno, along with its smoke and rain of stones, grew so intolerable that we considered retreating.

Ordaz spoke manfully, "Just think of this as another battle, señores. God will protect us and we shall prevail."

Even so, we took cover and waited for an hour before the eruption abated. Struggling forward, sometimes even crawling, we managed to reach the summit. The wind was stiff and blew most of the smoke and ash away from us. There was a great crater, half a league wide, and, within the center, the stones glowed a dull red as ash and stones shot into the sky with the sound of hundreds of iron cannons. We couldn't hear to think.

In the other direction the sky was clear as we looked, for the first time, into *Anahuac*, the great Valley of Mexico. A great lake reflected the blue of the sky and filled much of the Valley. On the shores of this lake there were glistening, white cities and pueblos. Close to the center of the lake was the largest city of all. Even from this distance, which was many miles, we could see the three causeways that connected to the mainland.

We looked on with awe until the wind shifted and the shower of stone and ash increased—the air grew foul and it was difficult to breath. We retreated as fast as we could. Soon breathing became easier and the ash abated.

"Look here." I pointed to a boulder that was covered with a dusting of yellow powder. I touched it with my hand. It stuck to my skin. I carefully sniffed at it. "If I didn't know better, I'd say this stuff is el azufre."

Herrera bent down and scrapped some into the palm of his hand. "They use sulfur in gunpowder, Rodrigo. If we were to ever get low...."

"All yellow powders aren't sulfur." I scrapped some of the powder into my pouch. "When we get back we'll show it to our gunners. They'll know."

We made our way back to *Tlaxcala* where the natives greeted us with open-mouthed awe. Diego de Ordaz reported to Cortés but I looked for Franciso de Orozco, the Captain of our cannoneers. I didn't know him well but I knew that he was one of our veterans from Italy. He looked older than he must have been for his face was wrinkled and weather-beaten and covered by a full white beard. Along with several of the other men, he was rolling dice in the shadow of one of the temples. Orozco was losing.

"*Qué pasa, Francisco?*"

"*Malo.* I have lost my woman and even the little gold I held back from the Caudillo. If this keeps up, I'll have to cover my bets with my ass."

"I have something to show you that may improve your mood."

Orozco looked up questioningly. "Just one more throw, Rodrigo. My luck is bound to change."

It didn't.

"What do you have to show me?"

I opened my pouch. "I found this on the volcano. It looks like sulfur."

The game was instantly forgotten as Orozco's eyes grew wide. He felt the powder between his fingers. "You might just be right but I know how to prove it. Somebody get me some fire!"

One of the players got up from the game and teased a live coal from a nearby brazier. Orozco poured the powder onto the tiles, making a small pile. Orozco rolled the red coal into the yellow pile.

The powder started to melt and emitted evil fumes that smelled like something long dead. It suddenly flared and burned with a pale blue flame.

Orozco stood up, grabbed me by both ears and kissed me hard on the mouth. "Muchas gracias, Rodrigo! You've saved our lives. I was worried about our gunpowder but now that we have a source of azufre, I think our worries are over."

"Won't you need things other than sulfur?"

"Yes, but we can make charcoal and saltpeter. We can't make sulfur. Is there much of it?"

"Not much on the way up but I think there's plenty in the crater."

"Then, if we can't outfight the Mexica, we'll blow them *al Infierno*."

● ● ●

Francesca had been awaiting our return. "So you're back, Rodrigo. Must you volunteer for every mission? Now that you have a woman you have incurred responsibilities."

"I didn't volunteer for this one. Cortés ordered me to go. What could I do?"

"Nothing," she shrugged. "Your sense of honor is going to get you killed, Rodrigo."

"I saw *Tenochtitlan*, Francesca. I saw it at the top of the mountain." I looked at her quietly. "I think you should know the truth. We are like a mouse armed with a sewing-needle trying to slay a lion."

She actually laughed, "Maybe so, but I doubt that you want to give your Caudillo the satisfaction of being eaten, first." The amused expression on her face didn't change but her eyes became serious. "When the time comes, I won't be able to do it myself and I won't let anyone else do it." She touched my arm and came closer to me. "I do not want to be taken prisoner."

Herrera had judged this woman well. Without saying a word, I bowed, turned on my heels and walked away.

I returned to my quarters to find Doña Amelía crouched in the corner. I could tell by the look on her face that all of her fears had returned. Probably she heard of our exploits on the mountain. Such things are the work of gods.

"This is ridiculous, little one," I spoke softly but I was determined. "I'm not dangerous. As long as I live, you're safe." I tried to think of something I could do to prove my point. I couldn't think of anything I hadn't tried already. "Come with me." I took her arm but she was so terrified she could scarcely walk. Nevertheless I dragged her across the plaza to where Aguilar was quartered. He was sitting in the sun.

"Can you tell her that I don't intend to tear her apart?"

Aguilar grinned, "I'm only starting to learn their language but I'll try." Haltingly, he spoke to the girl. Her terror subsided as she tried to understand Aguilar's words.

"Tell her I'm not a god and that I will protect her."

"I don't know all of the words but I'll get as close as I can. If you want her to really understand, we'll need to get Doña Marina." Aguilar winked. "She and Cortés are taking their siesta."

"Give it a try then, Jerónimo. I think she's intelligent and once she gets the general idea it will probably go better. Otherwise, I'll have Doña Marina talk to her."

Aguilar spoke again, sometimes hesitating as he searched for the right words. I could see by the girl's look of incomprehension that all of Aguilar's words were not correct.

"Tell her that I am just un hombre—a man."

He spoke to her and in order to emphasize the point I pulled at the skin on my arm and let it spring back. Comprehension started to creep into her face. She spoke back rapidly to Aguilar.

"What does she say?"

"I don't know. She's talking too fast... something about fire and blood and priest. I think it's getting through to her that you are not a god but maybe she thinks you're a priest."

Aguilar spoke again, pointing at me.

"What did you say?"

"I told her 'no' to fire, blood and priest and 'yes' to you and to life. It's about as good as I can do."

"Thank you, Jerónimo. You're a friend."

I walked back across the plaza. This time, however, I didn't take her arm. I merely gestured that she was to follow. She hesitated, but then she came.

"I'm hungry and I'll bet you are too." Some of the men were roasting fat turkeys and the whole corn cobs—known to the Indios as elotl—over a brazier. They were squatting, eating their meat with grease running into their beards.

"Here we go." I sliced off a wing and handed it to her. "I know that the company here is a little rough but we can't always choose our companions." I cut off a leg for myself. "See that man, there. He is ugly as a toad and hasn't bathed for a month."

"Who are you kidding, Rodrigo? That little chica can't understand a word you're saying. Besides, you haven't taken a bath, either."

I laughed, "You're right, Homero, but judging by the size of the lake I saw from that mountain, the Mexica are going to give us a bath that will clean us up real good. And as for this muchacha, amigo, I'm trying to teach her how to conduct herself in polite company."

Amused, Francesca stood a short distance away, listening to our exchange. I motioned to her. "I would like you to meet Amelía, señora. I plan to roast her here on this fire and serve her up to all of my friends. Maybe you would like some ribs?"

"You're frightening her, Rodrigo."

"No, I'm not. I'm trying to help her."

"You certainly have a way with women." She turned to the Indio girl. "I would like to introduce myself. My name is Francesca." Francesca pointed at her chest and slowly spoke her name several times, "Francesca. Fran-ces-ca." Then she pointed at the girl's chest, "Amelía. A-mel-ía."

The girl seemed perplexed but pointed at her own chest, "Amlan?"

Francesca beamed, "Amelía, Amelía."

"Amelan." The girl pointed at Francesca. "Fanca."

"Bueno, Rodrigo. This girl is intelligent. Be careful what you say around her. She'll be speaking Spanish within weeks." Francesca pointed at me. "Rod-ri-go."

"Rog..."

"Rod-ri-go."

The girl pointed to me without fear, "Rogotli..." She pointed back to herself, "Amelan."

"I like her," Francesca said. "Give her to me during the days and when you are gone. I think I can make something of her."

"And I can't?"

"I doubt it," she smiled sweetly.

Hector Herrera, who was sitting a few paces away, motioned to me. As Francesca continued with her language instruction, I went to him.

"What did I tell you about that Italian woman, Rodrigo? Was I right?"

I shook my head. "It looks like I might have two women."

Hector laughed, "No, Rodrigo. Two women have you. Now you must really learn to dance."

What could I say?

"I'm an uneducated man but it doesn't take much schooling to know what is going on. As long as the Italian woman has control, you can enjoy the Indio girl to your heart's delight. If, however, she thinks that she has no say, then God help you."

"I'm not sleeping with either one of them."

Hector raised his eyebrows in disbelief. "So much the worse for you. You'll have all of the blame and none of the pleasure. You're the man in the middle. Cortés has got you where he wants you."

"Any suggestions?"

Hector winked at me. "Both of them."

"That would be dishonorable."

"Unlike you, Rodrigo, I'm but an ignorant campesino. *Buenas Suerte.*"

That night Amelía seemed more comfortable. Her look of terror had been replaced by one of simple suspicion. She no longer thought of me as a god but, as a man, she had her doubts.

"Go to sleep, Amelía," I said wearily. "I'm tired and I must get up early to stand watch. Buenas noches."

●●●

I have always been able to wake myself up at the time when I desired and woke before my time for the watch. The moonlight through the window illuminated the girl curled in the corner. I got up without disturbing her, thinking how complex my life had become and all because of an Indio girl who couldn't pronounce my name and believed things I couldn't imagine.

The moonlight played its magic over the silver courtyard and temples. I sat on the steps of the largest teocalli watching for movement or stray sounds. Except for the high-pitched yips of Indio dogs, the night was quiet. A few of the more nervous men, no longer able to sleep within the confinement of four walls, huddled for warmth close to charcoal burning braziers. A stray evil thought passed through my mind. 'What would happen if I were to shout the alarm?' The mere thought of it almost made me laugh. I discarded the idea and thought of more practical matters. 'When the time comes will I be in a place where I can... kill Francesca? Could I even go through with it? What would it feel like to have the heart cut from my body? How about Cortés?' I looked toward his room and could see a man pacing back and forth. 'How does he do it? He never sleeps. He'll be a hard man to kill.'

In the east, there was but the slightest hint of yellow. I shivered—dawn was approaching. I wrapped my hand around the hilt of Bebidor, comforted by its touch. The hardness was that of a cold but faithful woman. I tried to remember Angela back in Italy, but I couldn't remember her face. I tried to remember her lips and the softness of her body but that was even more hopeless. How old would our child be? I breathed deeply, enjoying the strange smells of this alien city. I tried to remember the rich smells of the Spanish countryside, the smell of loam, green wheat and cattle. I tried to remember the smell of the sea. Perhaps I would never see it again. I found the thought distressing. I wondered what it would feel like to die, to no longer breathe or smell or feel. Would it be like the opening of a door into a heavenly truth or would it be the slamming of the door—nothing, nonexistence. Would it really matter?

A hundred generations ago men and women had lived and died, and they were dust two thousand years ago. A hundred generations in the future people will live, breathe, love, die and molder away to nothing. The past, present and future are all the same. I am one with the dead. I always have been....'

I stopped myself. Too much of this kind of thinking wasn't good. A man needs to discipline his mind. On the other hand, these Indios.... why didn't they just brush us away? Perhaps it was because our worlds were so totally different. We Españoles had the experience with many peoples of many beliefs and religions. We had fought most of them and bested many of them. We were shocked by the Indio practices but we weren't paralyzed. The Indios, however, were stunned. 'Victory is mine, sayeth the Lord.' A misquote but where did it come from?

The sun had risen over the flat rooftops and its golden light illuminated the plaza. Banners flapped in the morning breeze and men stirred, looking for food. My replacement was a kid named Miguel de la Torre. He had bright red hair and the top of his head only came up to my shoulders. His limbs were bony. His sheathed sword dragged on the ground. The fact that he had survived the recent battles was proof of Indio incompetence.

"*Buenos días, Miguel*. It's nice to see you."

"*Y usted, mi capitán*," he replied with a happy smile. "Did you see anything interesting?" The boy was always smiling. I suspected there was something wrong with him.

"Only Pablo Encanto...he was too lazy to use the latrine."

The boy smiled even wider. "Where did he go? I don't want to step in it."

Chapter 56

"This is the problem, señores." Cortés had gathered all of his Captains and some of his soldiers around him. "I'm determined to march on Tenochtitlan. To do so we must necessarily march through a pass between the volcanoes *Ixtaccihuatl* to the north and *Popocatepetl* to the south. If we take the northern road we will pass through the city of *Huexotzinco* which is an ally of *Tlaxcala* and should be well disposed toward us. If we go to the south, we will pass through *Cholula*, which is an ally of the Mexica.

There are both military and political considerations. The Tlaxcalans still don't trust us, and badly want us to go by way of *Huexotzinco*. They want to be able to influence us as long as possible. They are fearful that once we come into Cholulan or Mexican territory that we will turn against them. At the same time, our Mexican ambassadors are pestering me. They want to get us out of Tlaxcaltecan hands as quickly as possible. It seems that our acceptance of the princesses really alarmed them and they want us to march to *Cholula*. They are so desperate to get us out of here that Moctecuzoma has now changed his mind about our visiting his city. He wants us to visit him in Tenochtitlan where he will" –and Cortés laughed– "share his treasure with us."

"*Es una trampa!*" Andres de Ávila snapped.

"*De acuerdo,*" Cortés agreed. "But it's necessary that we let the Mexica think that we are too stupid to divine their plans. At the same time, it is imperative that we stay on the best possible terms with the Tlaxcalans. Their hatred of the Mexicans is so great that Xicotencatl the Elder has requested that we kill every last creature in Mexico. With this kind of passion they should make excellent allies."

Francisco de Lugo spoke, "We have a narrow needle to thread, Caudillo."

"This is why I am seeking your opinions."

"Perhaps we can have it both ways," I said.

"By all means, but I don't know if that will be possible."

"March to *Cholula* but with an army of Tlaxcalteca."

Cortés looked at me strangely. "Maxixcatzin has offered to supply us with warriors but what makes you think that Cholulans would accept such a force?"

"Tell them that you come as a great peace-maker. The Lord, Jesus Christ has empowered us to make peace between all the warring peoples of Mexico."

"Don Rodrigo, you are certainly learning. With such a concept we could batter down the gates of ...Hell."

●●●

Cholula is a two-day march from *Tlaxcala*. We marched forth accompanied by a force of Totonacs and several thousand Tlaxcalteca and Otomi warriors. Rumors, which were reportedly the product of bedroom talk between Alvarado and his new mistress, spread through the lines that the Cholulans were working with Tlaxcalan traitors to destroy us. Reportedly the streets of Cholula were already choked with barricades and the flat roofs of their houses were stockpiled with stones with which they would bombard us.

Cholulan envoys met us on the way to their city. Unlike the Tlaxcalteca, their ponchos were made of colorful cotton with tassels, fringes and animal tails. Their plaited hair was decorated with great plumes of egrets and herons.

Cortés didn't waste time with niceties. "We know that you are preparing to ambush us in your city."

Their spokesman, who was tall for an Indio, stared over Cortés' head without looking at him. "We have been told that you teo-teoh know our very thoughts. If this is true you will know that we mean you only good will."

This stopped Cortés for a moment. "You must swear fealty to the Emperor Carlos."

"We acknowledge him as our Lord," their spokesman said without emotion. "We also welcome you teotoh into our city but you must send these Tlaxcalec vermin home. If you will not do this we ask that you leave them outside our walls."

Santo Hernán began to preach, "Our great Lord, Jesus Christ has told us that we must lead all of you people of Mexico to an eternal peace. I understand, however, that old enmities cannot be erased in a moment. I will therefore order the men of *Tlaxcala* to camp outside of *Cholula*. Our Totonac friends, who bear our baggage and cannon, must attend us while we are in your city."

"You are wise, Malinche."

The Tlaxcalteca set up their huts outside of the great walls of Cholula— a plain verdant with farms and plantations. Maíz, maguey, chiles and tomatoes grew in abundance. The city contained, as it turned out, more templos and teocallis than the great *Tenochtitlan*, for Cholula was a city especially sacred to the Mexica and all of the Azteca. Its most important teocalli was the tallest in all of the land and was dedicated to the god *Quetzalcoatl*.

Our army, as in Tlaxcala, was quartered in one of their great plazas and was bounded by a wall that could be entered by a great gate. Disturbingly, however, food was not abundant and, by the second day, had dwindled to almost nothing. Citizens were few in number, almost as if the city had been evacuated. Those few Cholulans, who we did see, were reserved or even mocking. Nevertheless, with little to do except for guard duty, I became better acquainted with both Amelía and Francesca de la Barca, but in two very different ways.

In Francesca's case, we engaged in long discussions and, by speaking to her, I learned a great deal. She had been many places and seen many things and was afraid of nothing. She told me of her travels to the lands of the Turk and the Isles of Greece. She told me of accompanying her husband to the deserts of Africa where he died of some miserable disease.

"What were his symptoms?" I asked.

Her voice was a whisper. "At first, he told me that he had some pains in his chest. Then he grew hot and his body quaked."

"It sounds like a tertian fever."

"No. His fingers, toes and the tip of his nose grew black. Then he died."

"Just like that?"

"No, not just like that, but he died." She was silent for a while. "Tell me a happy story, Rodrigo. Tell me of your lovers."

I flinched.

"That bad, Rodrigo?"

"Worse."

"No, Rodrigo, I doubt it. Unlike most—you are a man with a conscience. Be careful, my friend. In this enterprise, a conscience is a dangerous commodity." She stroked her breast. "Do you want to talk about it?"

"No."

She sat silently for a time. "I don't judge you, Rodrigo. How could I? But as a friend I must tell you this—secrets can corrode the soul."

●●●

With Amelia things were very different because we could not speak each other's language although we often practiced together. To make things easier for her I would occasionally kiss her or touch her although I was careful not to frighten her and I was careful to control my passions.

Not surprisingly, perhaps, as I became more familiar with her, I felt my self-control slipping. Sometimes I wondered if my lust was actually for two women, one attainable and one distant. I felt carnal and ignoble, all at the same time. Knowing that my resistance was weakening, I took things as carefully as possible.

I made a point of covering Amelía with a shawl as she lay down to sleep. I also made a point of sleeping close to her without actually touching her. Sometimes I would touch her face, her arm or her hand or would brush her cheek with my lips. At first she was suspicious but then she seemed to relax. One morning, I woke to find Amelía in my arms. I embraced her closely and kissed her ear. At first she seemed to enjoy the experience but then her body tensed. I stopped and got up.

"Buenos días, little one." I bowed. "Thank you for your very warm presence."

She looked back at me questioningly, with huge black eyes.

I strapped on Bebidor and stepped out to greet the day.

That night I told her stories, little of which she could grasp. We sat very close with one of her little hands enclosed in my two hands. She leaned her head against my shoulder and, with her other hand, she stroked my leg.

I kissed her lips. This is not the Indio custom but she kissed me back. Overwhelmed by desire, I laid her down and covered her lips and throat with kisses. I stroked her bare skin with my fingertips.

She came alive with passion. She thrust herself against me and kissed me so hard that I thought that our lips must be bruised. I couldn't help myself but I still took time to caress and stroke her body. Then—well it took a while—because she was a virgin and I didn't want to hurt her. It was she, however, who couldn't be restrained.

It was oblivion. How else can I put it—magnificent oblivion. Later after we became more used to being together, she tried some things that she must have learned as she studied to be the bride of the god. I wouldn't let her, though. No trick could have possibly have been as wonderful and satisfying as was Amelia herself.

Burgos, Castilla-León

Mendoza stopped the narrative. "What do you mean by tricks, Your Grace?"

"Acts other than copulation."

"Such as fellatio, Your Grace?"

"That's but one example."

"I was led to believe—having no personal experience, of course—that fellatio can be most stimulating."

"I suppose that if I man is dealing with an uninteresting woman or if a man commits sin with another man, that your statement could be correct."

"You don't think..."

"No, I don't. Given a nubile woman and a lustful man, there is absolutely nothing that substitutes for ..."

"Not even fellatio?"

The old man grinned. "Padre, you seem to have a strong interest in this particular act. Are there others you would like to discuss?"

"I assure you, Obispo, that my interest is purely academic."

"Fellatio," the old man continued, "is an act that one man can perform on another, as are other sins that abnormal men perform on one another. Perhaps you feel a need to discuss them with me, Padre? Confession is good for the soul."

"I never...."

"Then I suggest we get back to our work, Padre."

Chapter 57

"I have questioned some of the Cholulan leaders," Cortés lectured, "and they have confirmed my worst fears. They—along with their Mexican garrison—are planning a sneak attack. The question is, señores, what shall we do? Shall we march back to *Tlaxcala* or *Huexotzinco* and bypass *Cholula* or shall we teach these Cholulans a hard lesson?" By the glint in his eyes, I had no doubt about Cortés' preference.

Pedro de Alvarado broke into a smile. He unsheathed his sword and reversed it in his hand, displaying the cross of its hilt for all to see. "For the sake of Jesus, we must never retreat. Destroy the Cholulans."

Diego de Ordaz stood up. "I'm all for honoring God but I don't think that he needs to be sated with the blood of these pagan Devils. I am for going to *Huetxinco*, or whatever they call it. If we move fast and choose a different route to *Tenochtitlan* we can avoid Mexican ambushes."

"I think we should review the facts again," I interjected. "We know that the Cholulans have prepared their streets and rooftops for defense but we also know did the same thing before we entered their city—such preparations could be reasonable Tlaxcalteca precautions."

"And the Mexican plan to ambush us?"

"We don't really know that is true, do we?"

Cortés held me in his gaze. "The Cholulan priests attested to it."

"So you tell us, Caudillo, but where are they now?"

"They died during the interrogation."

"Convenient," I said, "dead men make unimpeachable witnesses."

Cortés, not expecting opposition, started to pace back-and-forth, emphasizing his points with his hands. "I didn't tell you that Doña Marina has been approached by an old woman whose husband is a captain in their army—she says that our army is doomed. The woman offered to hide her until the killing is over. I have taken this woman into custody and—with a little persuasion, mind you—she confirms everything."

I'd been squatting but now stood up. "I find your action most interesting, Caudillo. By taking the woman prisoner you've now informed the Cholulans that we know of their plan—that is assuming of course, that the Cholulans actually have a plan."

Gonzalo de Sandoval spoke up, "You don't take the Caudillo at his word, Rodrigo? Disloyalty is a dangerous path."

"I am loyal to the expedition and do not wish to see it jeopardized by rash action."

Cortés pretended to weigh the options. "The Cholulans have sent their women and children from the city. I have also learned from the Tlaxcalans that, only last night, the Cholulans sacrificed seven men and women to their war god, *Huitzilopotchli*. They mean to kill us, gentlemen."

The story was plausible. During the previous night I had been unable to sleep because of the throb of a great drum emanating from deep in the city.

I still wasn't certain. "Perhaps, Caudillo, but I don't understand why the Cholulans would attack us inside of their city with a Mexican force on the opposite side of *Cholula*—it doesn't make sense—somebody isn't telling the truth."

Cortés suppressed his irritation. "There may be some discrepancies but the basic problem exists. We will be attacked." Not getting an immediate reaction, he went on— "I will tell you what I think. The Cholulan treachery gives us an excellent opportunity to teach Moctecuzoma a valuable lesson. Before the Cholulans can move we'll strike. Moctecuzoma will then see that his gods are worthless and his cause is lost."

"How do you propose that we teach this lesson?" Ordaz looked unhappy.

"We will lure their chieftains into our compound and crush them."

"Caudillo," I responded. "You made this decision before you called us here. Why did you bother to consult with us?"

Cortés smiled faintly. "It's always good to know who is with me and who is not."

Chapter 58

Immediately, I went to Francesca. She had a small room of her own to the back of a larger one that fronted the plaza. The rooms were lighted by slits in the wall that served as windows. By night, torches were used because the Indios had no candles. Francesca was in the patio talking to one of the soldiers.

"Francesca. I'd like to speak to you alone for a moment."

"Do you know Raul Vara?" She indicated the man she was talking to.

He was a hatchet-faced man in his thirties. His hair was long and tangled and he was even more filthy than most of the men. Several of his teeth had been reduced to rotten stubs and his breath was fetid. I noticed that Francesca was careful to keep a safe distance between the two of them.

"Yes, I know him. *Mucho gusto, Raul.* Do you mind if I speak to the Lady?"

Raul looked at me as if I were trying to rob him. "...not if you don't keep her too long," he said.

"Thank you, Raul." I led Francesca out of earshot.

"Francesca, the men will hear soon enough but I wanted to tell you alone. Some of us have just had a meeting with the Caudillo. He says there is a plot that he intends to quash—he intends to kill off the nobility of *Cholula* and he plans to do it right here in this plaza."

"When?"

"Soon. He's made a plan to lure them here and slaughter them like so many pigs. It will not be a battle. It will be murder."

"Is this necessary?"

"I doubt that it's tactically necessary to finish off *Cholula*. Cortés, however, knows the value of terror and intends to pile it to the sky. Once he has finished with the Cholulans fear will blow through the land like a gale. Given our weakness, fear may be our strongest weapon."

Her expression was bleak. "Will you do it? Will you participate in it?"

I ignored her question. "It's going to be more ugly than anything you have seen. When the pipiltin gather here, I want you to take Amelía and stay back in your rooms until it is all over. You don't need to see it and you definitely don't want to get mixed up in it. *Esconde!*"

● ● ●

Cortés gave instructions to our men. At the same time he sent messengers ordering the Cholulan chieftains to gather in the plaza at a given time. He, of course, insisted that these chieftains—to show their good-will—arrive unarmed. Clad in their ceremonial regalia, hundreds of pipiltin crowded into the plaza. After it became clear that no more chieftains would arrive, our troops moved into the plaza's only entrance. I remember Cortés sitting there erect on his horse, his helmet low on his forehead and armed with an iron-tipped lance. For a time he was completely silent, as if savoring the moment. A hush settled over the restless audience. Cortés then spoke, his voice harsh and cold as ice.

"We have learned that you, the leaders of *Cholula*, have been plotting to destroy us. Do you have any explanation?"

For the moment, there was no response except for a ripple of disquiet that spread through the assembly. One of the greatest pipiltin of *Cholula* stepped forward and gave the expected excuse. "We are the vassals of Moctecuzoma."

"That may be true," said Cortés triumphantly, knowing that his trap was in place. "But you must pay his price—*el pecado se paga con la muerte*. By the authority of the Emperor Carlos I, you are all ordered to die!"

An arquebus exploded and suddenly all was confusion. There were gunshots, shouts, screams and the sound of iron striking flesh. I drew Bebidor—I could feel its lust—I denied it. It didn't matter, Cortés and his mounted Captains made up for my absence. They charged into the midst of the terrified Indios, striking to the right and left with their spears. Horsemen and infantrymen killed and killed again as the plaza tiles grew slippery with blood. Chieftains, who would have been worthy adversaries in battle, died like frightened children. Some huddled, clutching at one another, as if the touch of fellow victims could protect them. Other men ran shrieking as Castilians pursued them with drawn knives and swords. I saw one ancient man kneeling in front of Javier de la Concha, his hands held in front of him in surrender. Concha put his weapon down, almost as if he would take him alive, but then, laughing, he seized the viejo by the throat and strangled him slowly.

I saw my friend, José Maldinado, methodically chopping his way through clumps of terrified Indios, a gleeful look on his face. Paco Migues was backing him, killing all that Maldinado wounded.

In my mind, I was transported back to Extremadura. There was a corral full of forty sheep. By the tracks I could see what had happened. During the night, a cur had dug under the fence and attacked the defenseless animals. All of the sheep were dead or dying. Some were hamstrung, others had their throats torn out, and still others were dragging their guts—the dog had eaten nothing—he had killed for the sheer joy of it. How similar, I thought, are men to dogs. It was good that I had put the women safely in hiding. When men are in a killing frenzy, anything is possible.

The killing was almost finished when, two hours later, Tlaxcaltec warriors joined us. They had been alerted by the sound of our gunfire and had broken into the city, taking captive all those Cholulans they encountered. Our allies looked on the blood-smeared plaza with contempt. So many lives wasted that could have been better used to honor their gods. The teoteoh knew nothing of war.

Cholula, the ancient enemy of Tlaxcala, now lay naked before raging Tlaxcalteca. The warriors who had accompanied us sent fast runner back to Tlaxcala, rousing their entire army. Indios and Castilians banded together in an orgy of destruction. Templos and teocallis were put to the torch. Women who had been unwise enough to remain in the city were searched out and raped. Riches of the city were stripped. Except for the gold and silver—which Cortés managed to save for himself—all other goods were carried back to Tlaxcala. Painted Otomi and Tlaxcalteca, the same ones that we had faced on the plain of Tzompatchlepetl, joined with Españoles and stalked through the smoking buildings, killing or capturing all Cholulans they encountered. The captives were tied and marched to *Tlaxcala* where they were sacrificed in a glorious triumph that lasted for weeks.

Burgos, Castilla-León

Mendoza looked up. "Even though I have defended Cortés, I am aware that he had his faults. I'm also aware that the slaughter at *Cholula* was, according to Las Casas, one of the more questionable of his deeds during the Conquest."

"I think that most of his deeds were questionable but Cholula was exceptional."

Mendoza agreed. "Las Casas writes that there was no Cholulan plot and that Cortés simply manufactured it to justify his subjugation of Cholula. Other writers, however, dispute this and claim that the danger was real. What is your opinion, Your Grace?"

"My opinions are several, Padre. Much of Cortés' evidence was less than powerful. The first we heard of trouble was the supposed talk between Alvarado and his Tlaxcaltec princess. The problem is that Alvarado and the girl couldn't speak a word of each other's language. As I have related, Cortés then told us that the Cholulan chieftains, who were privy to the plot, admitted to it for reasons no stronger than appeals to their honor. This doesn't make sense. If Cortés lied to us about this, it is possible that everything was a lie."

"Then you don't believe that there was a plot."

"I didn't say that. I said that Cortés lied to us. There was evidence that they were preparing for something, although their preparations may have been precautionary. Later, Moctecuzoma said that there was a Cholulan plot, but he had nothing to do with it. In my opinion, Moctecuzoma was always plotting but given his indecision and cowardice, little ever came of it.

If there had been a plot that involved many Cholulan chieftains, they wouldn't have responded to Cortés' request for them to assemble before us—these men died in ignorance of their supposed complicity. The killing was cold-blooded murder.

Don't get me wrong, though, even murder can be strategic. Cortés never hesitated to use the sword but his motives were not those of blood lust. He was driven by strategy and he was driven by greed."

"Nevertheless, Your Grace, I'm of the understanding, that he tried to restrain the Tlaxcalteca."

"Think about it, Padre, he wanted to paralyze all of Mexico. Cholula was his opportunity to do so and the *Tlaxcans* were his willing tools. For generations Tlaxcala barely survived in the face of Cholulan aggression. Suddenly, *Cholula* was laid at their feet and, let me confirm to you, *Tlaxcala* extracted every last drop of revenge. Cortés knew this was bound to happen but he made no effort to stop it for a full two days. Do you know how much revenge thousands of savages can exact in two days?"

"But the captives? Cortés arranged for their release."

"That's what he told the world. Despite all of his preachments, he let the paganos enjoy themselves which is, by the way, additional proof that they were still heathen. Have you ever hunted the fox with dogs, Padre."

Mendoza adopted a superior look. "Of course not."

"Too bad—it's entertaining—when the fox is caught it is best to let the dogs savage the animal."

"Nauseating."

"Nauseating, Padre? I find that your sensitivities are misplaced. You condemn men and women to the stake."

"I take no pleasure in it. I do it to save their immortal souls and to protect Mother Church."

The ancient Bishop shook his head in incomprehension. "We were talking about dogs. If they do not have their reward, they won't hunt. Cortés knew this. He was careful to reward his dogs with human victims."

"I don't believe it. He preached against human sacrifice."

"You forget, Cortés was the embodiment of evil. Nothing stood in the way of his ambition, certainly not a few lives. His words were only that, words. His actions tell his story.

● ● ●

After the slaughter, Cortés went to the Mexican ambassadors who had been unwilling witnesses to the killing.

His face was a mask of murder. "Moctecuzoma plotted with the Cholulans and now you too must die."

The Mexican ambassador quailed. "It is not true, we knew

nothing of it. The great Moctecuzoma loves Malinche. If you had failed to do so, he would have punished the traitors himself."

Cortés sneered. "He told us that we were welcome to enter *Tenochtitlan* but now he has reversed himself, which confirms his hostility."

The ambassador's eyes darted back-and-forth, as if looking for a place to escape. "Our Lord is pulled in two directions by our gods. One day the priests tell him that he must make you stay far from *Tenochtitlan*, the next they say he is to receive you as a fellow prince. Moctecuzoma loves you but he is a pious man and cannot go against his gods."

Cortés was implacable. "Then send him a message that, in order to prove that he loves us and had nothing to do with the Cholulan plot, he must send any of his warriors that may be near here far away and he must admit us into his presence. If Moctecuzoma does not do these things, not only shall you die, but I will destroy every one of the cities and pueblos that are on the shores of your great lake—and—I will slaughter their inhabitants."

● ● ●

Moctecuzoma's reply came in six days. His messengers brought two thousand pesos worth of gold plate, food and cotton cloaks. His messengers, of course, informed us that Moctecuzoma had no responsibility for the Cholulan plot. He even suggested that we punish the Cholulans even more severely than we had done already. He offered to pay the King of Castile an annual tribute but only if we stayed away from his Capital. On the other hand, if we insisted, Moctecuzoma would be delighted to see us, although he didn't have enough food to give us.

Cortés insisted that we push on. The leaders of *Cholula* were dead so he appointed others in their stead and ordered all those Cholulans hiding in the hills, to return. With nowhere else to go the terrified refugees started to repopulate the city, even as their ancient enemies gloated over their helplessness. In order to prevent the complete extermination of *Cholula*, Cortés ordered that *Tlaxcala* and *Cholula* make peace. Their fear of us was greater than their hatred for one another, so peace of sorts was achieved.

Chapter 59

We left Cholula on the first of November with one thousand Indio allies—the Totonacs, however, refused to go farther—they said that we would all be trapped in *Tenochtitlan* and destroyed.

We kept our usual strict formation, with our mounted scouts and most active foot soldiers prospecting the country ahead. We decided to take the narrow path on the north flank of *Popocatapetl*, itself. The pueblo of Calpan, which is an ally of Tlaxcala, sent us messengers who warned us that, at the top of the pass, there were two roads. One road was clear but the other was blocked by boulders and felled timbers. They recommended that we take the blocked road because Moctecuzoma was preparing an ambush on the cleared road. We climbed the steep path while the Tlaxcalteca labored with our cannons. At the top of the pass, there were two wide roads, one of which had been blocked.

"Which road shall we take?" Cortés asked the Mexican ambassadors.

"The cleared road is the best for it is the road that leads most directly to *Anahuac*. It also passes through the large town of *Chalco* which will receive you warmly."

"Why has this other road been blocked? You can see by the cuts that the trees have only recently been felled."

The Mexica had the look of trapped rats. "This road is a bad one with wash-outs and avalanches. Moctecuzoma ordered it closed for your safety."

"Nevertheless," Cortés scratched the scar on his lip and said, "we will take the blocked road."

Working together, Spaniards and Tlaxcalans removed these obstacles. Fearful of ambush, we moved cautiously forward. It started to snow at the top of the pass. We found some wooden huts used by the traveling merchants or pocheca, as the Mexica call them. Also present was an enormous cache of food. After posting a heavy guard, we spent the night in the shelters.

"It's as cold as a nun's ass," commented José Maldinado with a mouthful of frijoles and chiles, "but this food really warms me up."

Juan de Alva eyed a stack of dried tortillas with distaste. "Why do you think there is so much food up here, anyway?" he asked.

"I don't know and couldn't care less. Pass me some of that carne seco."

I was as hungry as everyone else. Using my knife, I cut a small piece of dried meat from a larger chunk and passed it to Francesca de la Barca, who had joined us. I cut a piece for myself and chewed it thoroughly before washing it down with cold water.

Francesca swallowed her piece of meat before speaking. "How do we know that this meat isn't from one of their sacrifices?"

José spat out the piece of meat he was chewing, washed his mouth out with water and spat again. "God, woman, you could have warned me!"

Migues wasn't as easily deterred. Smiling, he crushed some of the dried meat with the hilt of his knife and mixed it with dried chiles and slices of an overly ripe tomato. He placed the whole mess on a tortilla and happily ate it.

"It tastes just fine to me."

De Alva, not to be outdone, showed off his education. "*De gustibus non est disputadum*," he said as he chewed on a piece of tough meat.

I put tortillas in a water-filled basin to soften them up. "Judging by the amount of the food stored here, I'd say it is the cache for a large army."

"How large?" Francesca asked.

"It's difficult to estimate because we don't know whether such a force would bivouac here for one night or several. My guess, though, is that this cache could feed ten thousand men for four or five days."

"*Andale!*" Paco exclaimed.

Local Indios came to look at us. They were ordered away and we told them that if they were to return, they'd be killed. Three or four, I don't know whether they were spies or just common fools, openly returned. We gave them to the delighted Tlaxcalteca who entertained themselves for hours with their unfortunate victims.

The next morning our army moved out again. We crested the divide in the cordillera and started our descent. Low-lying clouds obscured our view of the country below. As we labored downward, the clouds thinned out and, although we couldn't see the valley floor, we could see the smoke of thousands of fires mounting into the heavens and hanging over the valley in a pall. The amount of smoke could mean only one thing. The valley below must have a population of thousands, maybe millions.

"*Bienvenidos a mi casa...*" quipped Maldinado.

Pablo Migues completed the jest, "*...dice la arana a la mosca.*"

We were now confronted with reality and the reality of it was frightening. It is one thing to contemplate the conquest off an empire. It is entirely another thing when the empire is laid out in front of you.

Juan de Alva was not amused by Maldinado's and Migues' attempts at humor. "That's defeatist talk, hombres. If their spider thinks he can eat our fly, he'll find that it has a sting."

"I couldn't agree with you more, Juan." I was working to keep everyone's mood up. "We've already seen that the savages' numbers work in our favor. The more of them there are, the more they trip on each other."

"Perhaps we should turn back." Francesca, seeing us talking, had joined our group. Like most of us, she was wearing cotton armor but, unlike us, it was covered by a blue shift that hung to her sandal-clad feet. She wore a straw hat to protect her face from the sun and, she had grown thin.

Migues responded to her, "It's too late to turn back. From now on, My Lady, we have no choice but to continue our expedition to its conclusion. I just hope it doesn't lead to the top of one of their mosques."

Francesca forced a smile. "God and your honor will prevent you from failing. Otherwise, what will happen to us poor womenfolk? You must fight to defend our chastity," she said.

Still joking, Migues knelt before her in a poor imitation of knightly chivalry. "I dedicate my service to thee, My Lady. The sodomizing Mexicans don't stand a chance."

From the heights above, a great wind howled downward and into the valley. As if by magic, the fog and the mist cleared. A great lake, blue-green in the early light, suddenly appeared in the Valley. On its banks were hundreds of pueblos and a dozen large cities. On an island to the west was the largest city of all, perhaps the largest in the world. It glittered like a white diamond—*Tenochtitlan.*

Despite the shouts of the Captains, the entire army clanked to a halt. Every man and woman viewed the Valley with unspoken awe as the wind—the icy wind—moaned and shrieked down the canyon.

...Like Carthage, Troy, Babylon and many other great civilizations of the past, Tenochtitlan and the Mexican Empire are doomed. In the next novel, *Hummingbird God*, Rodrigo relates the full horror of the methodical destruction of an ancient people.

To order copies of *Skull Rack* as well as other titles from
Harbor House, visit our Web site:

www.harborhousebooks.com

ABOUT THE AUTHOR

Ron Braithwaite is the retired Chief of Pathology at Our Lady of Lourdes Hospital in Lafayette, Louisiana. He presently resides on a ranch in South Texas directly on the Rio Grande where he enjoys studying the Spanish Conquest of Mexico and making exploratory trips into Mexico. *Skull Rack* is his first novel; the story of Rodrigo de la Peña and Enrique Mendoza is to be continued in his sequel *Hummingbird God*, which will be published by Harbor House in 2008.